The Moving Picture Boys

ALSO BY *Max Wilk*

Don't Raise the Bridge, Lower the River
Rich Is Better
Help! Help! Help! Or, Atrocity Stories from All Over
The Beard
One of Our Brains Is Draining
The Yellow Submarine
A Dirty Mind Never Sleeps
My Masterpiece
The Wit and Wisdom of Hollywood
They're Playing Our Song
Memory Lane
Eliminate the Middleman
Every Day's a Matinee
The Kissinger Noodles . . . or Westward, Mr. Ho.
The Golden Age of Television

The Moving Picture Boys

by Max Wilk

W · W · NORTON & COMPANY · INC · NEW YORK

Published simultaneously in Canada
by George J. McLeod Limited, Toronto.
Printed in the United States of America.

Library of Congress Cataloging in Publication Data

Wilk, Max.
The moving picture boys.

I. Title.
PZ4.W683Mo [PS3545.I365] 813'.5'4 78–2484

ISBN 0 393 08814 6

3 4 5 6 7 8 9 0

This one is for Dawn.

★ Part One ★

chapter 1

—Well, Number Eight Seven Six Two, your time is about up. You're going out those gates a free man. Anything you want to tell me, son?
—Nossir.
—You still maintain that you were innocent? That you were framed?
—Yessir.
—Son, I sure hope you're not going out there with hate in your heart. You've paid society your debt. Why not turn over a new leaf? Make a clean start. Isn't there somebody out there waiting for you?
—Warden, you always did treat me square, and I just want you to know, no matter what happens after I get out, I appreciate it.

DOOR SLAMS SHUT. HOLD IN CLOSE UP: THE WARDEN'S FACE. SLOWLY HE SHAKES HIS HEAD, PUZZLED AND DISMAYED.

FADE

EXCEPT for the wiry black man pushing his carpet sweeper up and down between the tables and the woman polishing glasses behind the bar, the dimly lit Cornhusker Bar was empty.

The door which led out to the street was pushed open, and a man appeared, a suitcase in his hand. In his early fifties, he wore a double-breasted blue suit; he stood hesitantly, his eyes behind their glasses adjusting to the darkness. Behind him came a second man, also carrying a cheap suitcase. Much taller than the first, his shoulders seemed too broad for the nondescript gray suit he was wearing. His face was pinkish, his eyes bland and imperturbable.

"This here is a bar," he said softly.

"Sure is," said the first man. He carried his suitcase over to the bar, set it down, and climbed up onto a stool. ''We can wait in here, LeRoy.''

''I guess so,'' said LeRoy, and joined him on the next stool. His hand free of the suitcase at his feet, he reached into his pocket to pull out a small, gleaming steel hand-exerciser, began to work it rhythmically back and forth in his large fist.

The barmaid, whose apricot-tinted hairdo exploded over her plain face like smoke from a chimney, moved without enthusiasm to take their order. Pinned to her ample uniformed bosom there was a large button which read ''I'M GLADYS. ASK ME.''

The first man squinted carefully through his glasses at her announcement.

''Don't take that long to read it, does it?'' asked Gladys.

''I'm a slow reader, Gladys,'' he said.

''Well, just so long's you don't use Braille,'' said Gladys, and did not bother to chuckle at her own witticism. ''What'll it be?''

''An ice-cold Bud,'' said the first man. ''You, LeRoy?''

''Just some Coke, Al,'' said LeRoy. ''Beer builds you a gut.''

''Yeah, and Coke's full of sugar,'' said Al.

Gladys reached behind her into the refrigerator for a bottle, flipped off its cap, placed a clean glass on top of the bottle, then deftly turned them both over to allow the beer to flow in, never spilling a drop in the process.

''Very handy, Gladys,'' said Al.

She served him his beer, then placed a bottle of Coca-Cola and a glass in front of LeRoy. ''Beer for you, sugar for you,'' she said. ''That'll be one ninety-two, with the damn tax.''

Al whistled softly.

''I'll pay, LeRoy,'' he said, and reached into his inside pocket, produced a small envelope containing bills, and took from it two singles. Gladys rang them up in the register.

He stared at the glass of beer before him, then picked it up, holding it delicately, savoring the feel of the cold glass, obviously anticipating the taste. Then he slowly raised it to his mouth and drank half of it down with one gulp.

LeRoy put down his hand exerciser and took a sip of his Coke.

Gladys grinned. "Taste good?"

Al nodded.

"How long were you boys in for?" she asked.

"In where?" asked Al softly.

"In them suits, with them cases you got? I seen a lot like you," she said. "In where I think you was."

Al stared at her.

"We was in long enough to see beer go from thirty cents a bottle to a buck and a quarter in a crappy joint like this," he said.

"Mmmph!" said Gladys.

"Sure must be tough being cooped up like that," she said.

"Get lots of time to think," said Al.

Gladys eyed LeRoy's large hand, which was back, fingers rhythmically working at his steel device. "Would you maybe mind if a person was to ask what you was in for?"

"Yeah, I'd mind, but so what?" said Al. "Armed robbery."

"Both of you?" asked Gladys, her eyes flicking back and forth between her two customers.

Al nodded.

"D'I read about it?"

"Most likely," said Al.

". . . *Say*." said Gladys, impressed. "How about that? Was there maybe a big hunk of loot?"

Al smiled thinly. "The word *was* is right," he said. He drained his glass. "There ain't no more *is*."

Gladys took a dish full of salted peanuts from below the bar and pushed them across to LeRoy. LeRoy continued to sip his Coke.

"Your friend don't say much, does he?" asked Gladys.

"Nope," said Al. "He ain't like some people."

"Meaning yours truly, is that it?" asked Gladys. "Hell, I was just making polite conversation—you don't have to go getting pissed off about it, friend—"

"I ain't pissed off," said Al. "I'm just not much on sociability, you know?"

"Okay," said Gladys. "Another brew?"

Al glanced up at the clock above the bar, which was outlined in red-and-orange neon, then he nodded. Gladys mechanically repeated her deft performance with the second beer bottle and glass, which she placed before him, before she turned to LeRoy.

LeRoy shook his head.

Al picked out two more dollar bills from his envelope and handed them to her. Gladys rang up his payment and placed his change upon the bar.

"So where you headed now? West, maybe?"

Al took a sip of his beer.

"Jee-sus," said Gladys, aggrieved. "I wasn't handing you no third degree."

"Lemme tell you something, Gladys," said Al softly. "Where we been all this time, you don't ask a person too many questions. So we're kinda in the habit of not answering. To nobody."

"Okay," said Gladys. "I got it. Like in the movies, you ain't talking."

"Just like in the movies," said Al.

LeRoy got down off his stool. "We better go, Al," he said.

"You could stay awhile," said Gladys, eying the large man. Then she smiled. "Like the fella says, there's always another bus."

"Thanks for the invite," said LeRoy.

"It could beat playing with that gadget in your hand," said Gladys.

LeRoy did not reply. Al placed a quarter on the bar.

Gladys pushed the quarter back at him. "Shee-it," she said. "You need this a helluva lot more'n I do."

Al shrugged and put the quarter back in his pocket. "Could be," he said. "Thanks."

Carrying their suitcases, the two men moved slowly through the barroom and out the door. Gladys went to the door and peered through the glass, watching them as they made their way across the street to the bus station.

"Armed robbery. Mm-*hm*!" she said. "What're you thinking, Ed? They're gonna go off somewhere to pick up the loot they got stashed away, maybe?"

The black man looked up from his carpet sweeper. "I wouldn't know," he said. "Them's not the kind I'd fool with. *No* way."

Gladys returned to the bar. "Shee-it," she said. "They didn't scare me none. The guns they was carryin' ain't loaded with bullets!"

Sloshing dirty glasses in the sink, she snickered, happily at her own joke. "That big one," she said. "He might've stayed—but that other one leads him around by the nose. I guess they get kinda weird over there in the slammer . . . y'know?"

* * *

chapter 2

—Ah, *buena sera,* Signor Webster, welcome-a to Papa Piccolino's restaurant! I have-a your table here. Who is this most charming lady you-a bring to my place?
—Luigi, I'd like you to meet Maggie Tyler—
—Ah, Signorina, I kiss-a your hand. Now, what wonders can-a Papa Piccolino make for two beautiful people who are so much in-a love?
—Love? Who said we were in love?
—Ah, you must-a not try to fool Papa Piccolino! Old Papa Piccolino—he knows-a true love when he's-a see it!

PERCE lounged in the armchair, the air-conditioning unit humming, not quite drowning out the *thumpthumpthump* of the bass which came through the thin wall next door whenever his neighbor turned up the decibel level of his hi-fi, which was often.

His eye was on the screen of the small TV on which was an early-evening quiz show, idiots jumping up and down, excitedly bidding for merchandise treasures locked away in large white boxes. Next to his hand was the glass in which was his third well-watered bourbon; the Old Forester bottle itself stood on the breakfast bar by the tiny kitchen where Vera was doing her thing at the two-burner stove, putting together their dinner.

Vera didn't like him to drink so much, she insisted on making his drinks, drowning the good green-seal bourbon with soda, as if he didn't catch on to her little game to keep him from taking on his nightly load.

. . . Well, what the hell, Vera was a good kid, she had his best interests at heart, it was all for his own good, that's what she was always telling him, right?

Loud laughter intruded from the downstairs pool area.

. . . Sometimes this place was like a railroad station.

La Casita was a modern southern California two-story apartment complex, built from standard plans, thrown up in weeks. Perce's apartment, a "BACHELOR SINGLE, FURN," was what he'd always lived in, a machine for eating, sleeping, living, the sort he'd had ever since he'd first come to L.A.

Over the years, all his places had been much the same, varying only in the neighborhood. His first was in downtown Hollywood; then, when he began to earn decent money, he'd moved to a better neighborhood, over near Olympic. Even when he'd made his big score, the original story that had gotten him his first long-term contract at Paramount, a grand a week, forty weeks firm, and he'd moved to a building on South Roxbury, more substantial and opulent, it was still the same bachelor setup.

This joint, where he'd been for the last—Jesus, could it be four years already?—was on a side street between Sunset and Hollywood, down from Fairfax, nothing special, the kind of an apartment complex full of the usual quota of people on the make, a couple of quiet fags downstairs, an actor or two jobbing TV shows, one blonde who had to be a high-priced hooker, the rest coming and going like lettuce-pickers. His bathroom window opened out on a view of the back alley, with cars parked in either direction, bounded by garbage cans, the drapes were beginning to fade, the walls so thin that you could hear arguments all over the place, and, like tonight, that damn music, whether you wanted it or not.

Fairly new now, but in a few more seasons, these instant plaster-gunned walls would begin to open up cracks, the plywood flooring beneath the nylon shag would show bulges, the sliding aluminum doors would warp and stick in their frames, and down below, in the courtyard, those chromed stairs leading into the tiny swimming-pool would begin to develop blotches of rust. Maybe the pool itself would spring a leak . . . No one would care much, the building's ownership would probably change, transient tenants would move in and out like yo-yos, probably so would he, on to some newer similar complex, built by other fast-buck real-estate syndicators on cheaper property in another neighborhood where they'd forced through zoning changes.

. . . He'd done that before, packing up his clothes, his few books and scripts, and his TV, stowed them into his car, and moved on, staying loose. In all these years, nothing much changed—except the monthly rent, which went only one way—up.

The yelling and screaming from the quiz show was getting on his nerves, so Perce leaned forward and flipped the tuner to another channel.

. . . On the screen flashed a long shot of horsemen, riding, hell for leather, across a vast Western plain, in hot pursuit of a fast-moving stagecoach. On went the chase, and then disappeared, to be abruptly replaced by close-ups, two faces, one old man with a white beard, the other a tweedy younger man, also bearded, who said, "That was a fine scene from one of your best action films, Mr. Musette, it still has such dynamic *force,* and *energy,* it truly leaves the viewer breathless."

"Yeah, I guess it does," said Musette, who was sucking on a large panatela. "Nice to see it again, after all these years."

"—Sonofabitch, Vera!" said Perce. "It's Val Musette!"

"Val *who*?" asked Vera.

"Do you believe this?" said Perce. "The old phony is being interviewed on TV!"

". . . While I was on location," Musette was telling the eager young interviewer, "I always made a habit of getting up very early in the morning, so I could watch the sun come up with my cameraman—that way, we could plan the absolutely right lighting for those action scenes—"

"Shit, the cameraman did most of your direction!" said Perce. "You never even knew which end of the camera had the lens attached to it!"

Vera peered across the room at the set. '"Shh—I want to *hear*."

". . . As we show a scene from one of your later epics," said the interviewer, "one in which you were fortunate enough to direct a bright young actress from the East—in her first film role—Laura Carruth."

"Oh, yes, indeed," grinned Val Musette, lovingly tonguing the end of his cigar. "The first time I laid eyes on that girl, I knew she was star material. She had that special inner light—"

"—That's not all you laid on her, you slob," said Perce as the TV screen filled with a full-head close-up of a much younger Laura Carruth, her long blonde hair fluttering in the wind-machine breeze, her large eyes filling with tears, carefully dropped in by the make-up man. Then the camera cut away to a long shot of a troop of mounted cavalry, riding fearlessly off beneath a U.S. Army standard into a Western sunset.

". . . Beautiful," said the interviewer. "Sheer film poetry."

"Well, I guess we tried harder in those days," said Val Musette modestly.

"Tried?" said Perce as the interview continued. "You played gin with Mort Denler every night, and you lost so much money to him that he had to put you on a show so you could draw enough salary to pay off what you owed him!"

"Oh, come *on,* Perce," said Vera. "I mean—the man did make a lot of pictures—"

"Sure—during the war," said Perce, "when all the decent directors were off in the army, or out at F.M.P.U. in Culver City. Val had flat feet or something, so he *oot*zed himself into directing—"

". . . You did get an extraordinary sense of forward motion into your outdoor sequences," the interviewer was saying. "Is there any secret to how that was accomplished?"

". . . Mmm, just a combination of talent *and* luck," replied Musette. "Plus, I always had great crews—and the actors I worked with were usually willing to give me that little something extra."

"Yeah," commented Perce. "Usually in the dressing-room, before you gave the broads that extra close-up! This bastard—he could never keep his hands off anybody. You know, the mailroom girls came in one day to the supervisor and said they refused to deliver mail to his office any more—Val would rape a snake!"

Vera brought over a steaming dish and placed it on the end table beside him. "Here, eat while you watch," she said. "It's ragout."

"I'm not hungry," said Perce as another action sequence flashed across the screen. "This guy has ruined my appetite." He gulped down the rest of his drink.

"Food's better for your stomach, Perce," she said.

". . . But Val Musette isn't," said Perce.

Vera had switched months ago to California white wine, and like all reformed drinkers, she could be a pain in the ass about anyone who hadn't.

"Well, *I*'m going to eat," she said. "I'm starved."

She sat down at the counter and began to go at the food.

Perce was silent.

". . . Why get yourself so upset?" she asked. "They interview everybody these days. I could get you on one of those shows—"

"Who needs it?" said Perce.

"It would get you exposure," said Vera.

". . . Ahhh, it's all bullshit," said Perce. "L.A. the world's capital of bullshit. Everybody scrambling around, taking bows."

"Move to San Francisco," said Vera.

Across the small screen, faces were passing now. The first was that of Randy Buck, an old character actor, then came the young interviewer, and the camera panned on to reveal the round moon-face of Harry Elbert.

Perce sat up. "Jesus! *Harry!* What in Christ's name is *he* doing there?"

"Shhh!" said Vera as the moderator said, ". . . and you, Mr. Elbert, you came into contact with Val Musette, the subject of tonight's retrospective, rather early on in your long career, isn't that so?"

Harry Elbert cleared his throat. "Yes, as a matter of fact, Val was a large influence on my formative thinking as a filmmaker. One of my early assignments was on a Western called *Phantom Gold,* and I must say, Val was an education. When I brought in the script, that first day we met, after he'd read it, he handed it back to me with red lines alongside my dialogue, and he said 'Son, you gave me a lot of extra words. Now is it okay with you if I give you pictures for every red line?' Well, I went home and read what he'd done and you know, he'd actually improved every sequence? That's what *I* call film sense."

"Fascinating," said the interviewer, "and so you, Mr. Buck—"

Perce reached over to snap off the set.

"You turned it *off!*" said Vera reproachfully.

"I don't have to sit here and listen to Harry Elbert," said Perce. "Not while I'm eating."

". . . What have you got against *him?*" sighed Vera.

"Listen," said Perce, swallowing down the knot of anger that had risen in his throat. "I *know* about *Phantom Gold.* Harry and I had been teamed on a picture, we'd turned it in, took a week's layoff for a vacation. It was Harry's idea we take a break, see? So I went to Caliente with some broad—" He saw Vera wince. ". . . Ah, nobody that meant anything, honey," he added. "What I didn't know was that Harry never left town. I'm in Caliente, and he's *oot*zing his way into Mort Denler's office, where he'd heard they were rushing a script into production—something two other schmucks had worked on for ten, twelve weeks—it needed a quick rewrite for a star—Denler was under the gun with a commitment—pay or play, see? So Harry offers to work nights—the week I'm in Caliente! He works one week, he grabs off a co-credit—and by the time I'm back from Caliente, he's already off and running on another assignment." Perce's stomach churned at the recollection. " 'Jesus, Perce,' he tells me, 'it all happened so fast—I didn't even have time to call you—and I knew you were probably shacked up, and didn't want to be interrupted, right?' So do me a favor, will you, Vera, don't sit there complaining because I don't want to sit and listen to any more of Harry Elbert's bullshit!"

"You don't have to yell," said Vera. "So Harry's got his own production company and you don't. Tell the truth—wouldn't you have done the same thing to him?"

"That is what I love about you, Vera," said Perce. "We know each other a couple of months and you're an authority on me."

. . . Which wasn't absolutely true. He'd known Vera around the club far longer than that, since the days when she'd been married to a TV comedy writer, Hal George, a wiry little man with a loud, braying laugh, which he used to punch up his own one-liners. How long had it been since Hal had dumped Vera in favor of that twenty-year-old dancer he'd met out at NBC, in Burbank, moved in with her, and died of a heart attack thereafter? "Screwed his brain out," said one of the boys in the club locker room, sniggering. ". . . But what a way to go. Short in the saddle."

"So I don't know you at all," said Vera quietly. "I do know you haven't touched the ragout."

"Ahh, I could've settled for a hamburger," said Perce, pouring more bourbon into his glass. "You didn't have to strain yourself at the stove."

"Charming," said Vera. "Perse Barnes, the Beverly Hills sportsman, bon vivant, man about town—always good for the right turn of phrase for any given situation. Knows just how to make a lady feel wanted!" She drained the wine from her glass and set it down with an angry click on the formica top. "Who needs to come here and cook for *you?* I've had better offers, believe me."

"Sorry," said Perce.

He placed a hand on her shoulder, which was tense, unmoving. "That show got me upset." He ran his hand across her brightly printed blouse to find the outline of her breast, cupping it.

". . . I suggested you *eat,*" she said.

He let go. "Okay—so I'm a bore—go out and get yourself one of those hot-shots who's working the bar at the Saloon—they've all got a full head of steam—big futures—"

"God, how I hate it when you start feeling sorry for yourself," said Vera. "What *is* it about writers? You all carry around depression like you had a tank of it on your back! What the hell, you're still in one piece, you've got all your marbles—why, you could sit down tomorrow and start working on a script, a story—a something—"

"Or my memoirs," said Perce. "Why not write them? Save the guys in the trade papers any research for my obituary."

He sat down, picked up his fork and took a mouthful of the cooling ragout. It was quite tasty; Vera was a good cook . . . Too bad he had no appetite. Conscious that she was watching him, he forced down a couple more bites. "Very good," he told her.

Mollified, she nodded. Then she glanced at her watch. "There's a nine-o'clock screening at the private room on Sunset. One of our clients, that young Frenchman with his art film. He's after us to do a campaign so it'll be eligible for an Academy Award—want to come?"

Since her divorce, Vera had been working in a small but highly successful PR outfit, Daniels/Marcus, with offices in a high-rise at the far end of the Strip. ''Why not?'' she'd once said when he asked her why she'd decided to work in that puff factory. ''I'm handy with a typewriter, and it's a hell of a lot more interesting than selling real estate.''

''. . . No thanks,'' he told her. Tomorrow he had an 8:30 A.M. lesson scheduled, and after that, a full morning on the one court which the club permitted him to use on weekdays. ''Sorry, but this old crock has to get his shut-eye. Tomorrow is strictly an earning day.''

Vera got up from the bar and began cleaning up, rinsing, and stacking. Perce brought over his half-filled plate. ''I'll have the rest of this for breakfast,'' he said, and tucked it into the tiny refrigerator.

He ran one hand across her shapely rear. Beneath the taut fabric of her slacks, the flank was firm; Vera had to be well into her early forties by now, but she took very good care of herself. And of him, too.

. . . What was that old Larry Hart line? ''. . . You mustn't kick it around.''

''You don't have to go to that screening,'' he murmured.

''Mm. That's my work,'' said Vera. ''And tomorrow's a work day for *me,* too. Although I wouldn't mind staying,'' she admitted with a smile.

He patted her. ''Vera, the Visiting Nurse,'' he said. ''What do you see in an old derelict like me?''

''Not a hell of a lot,'' she said.

''That's what I figured,'' said Perce.

''What are you looking for, a reference?'' She turned, the towel in her hands, wiping off the pot. ''Listen, you're still pretty fair in the sack—when you're not depressed . . . you're good company, and you're relaxed—not like all those *pishers* I deal with every day. Christ, I get so tired of all those twenty-four-year-old hot-shots . . .''

''They run the world, sweetie,'' said Perce. His lips brushed her cheek.

She put down the pot, kissed him back without passion, then

picked up her topcoat, checked her make-up, and went over to the door. When she slid it open, the sudden dampness of the night air billowed into the room. She put on her coat. "Good night, Gramps. Stop brooding," she said. "Ugh . . . chilly out."

She closed the door behind her, and he heard her footsteps clicking down the concrete stairs.

". . . Chilly in, too," he said to the empty room. And poured himself one more for a nightcap.

He showered, then pulled the covers off the studio bed, switched off the bedside lamp, climbed in, and tried to go to sleep.

Long day tomorrow . . . chilly tonight, that meant early morning fog tomorrow. His eight-thirty session would be out in the cold and raw morning. Good old sunny L.A. The only town where you wake up in the morning and hear the birds coughing in the trees.

He chuckled.

. . . That was a Joe Frisco line . . . Good old Joe—you could always find him hanging around the Derby, or at Mike Lyman's . . . or over at Musso's, somewhere on Hollywood Boulevard, in those days when the street wasn't full of hippies and pimps, weirdos and hustlers—sure, the Boulevard was nothing, they took in the sidewalks after 9:00 P.M., a small-town main drag, sure, but you could still walk over to the newsstand without worrying whether or not somebody would yank you into an alley—

. . . Tennis at 8:30 A.M. . . . what a pain in the ass when you get to be my age, he thought . . .

Don't knock the tennis, Perce. It's the only tangible asset you have that keeps you solvent, pal. Sure, every once in a while a check drops out of the mail from the Guild, a residual on some TV show, something you worked on in the days when your friends were still in a position to throw assignments your way, not like now when everybody who's hiring is under thirty . . . but it's the tennis keeps you solvent, and when you get too old to give those lessons, it's hurry on down to Unemployment for you, Perce, don't you ever forget it . . .

. . . Yeah, but it's not the same. I used to play and *win*. I didn't stand there like some tired old oaf, batting the balls back, gently, gently, never placing the shots so my opponent goes helplessly scrambling for them, looking like an idiot—no, I'm always holding back, looking like an amiable loser, no competition, so the suckers on the other side of the net will feel good. They're taking lessons from an old champ, now they can beat the old champ . . .

Lose to keep the suckers happy . . .

. . . Winning used to make the game more fun. But even then, you had to be careful not to win too much, especially when your game was with somebody who could do you some good . . .

. . . Old Sol Torina, the head talent scout at Warners, twenty years, every Sunday morning, Jack Warner's personal tennis date up on Angelo Drive, 10:00 A.M., Sol would show up and play his three sets, somehow Jack always won, beating Sol, who'd been a champion at college and then played some pro tennis . . . *Man, J. L. you're looking mighty good out there, don't know how you do it* . . . Then Sol would go back to his office Monday, picking up his check year in, year out. Then one Sunday morning, something happened, J. L. must've needled him once too often with those rotten jokes. Hey Sol, you know the sound spaghetti makes when it hits the plate? No, J. L. Well, I'll tell you, it's *wop!* Heh heh, J. L. *you're one terrific kidder*. That morning he finally got under Sol's tough skin, so Sol forgot himself, seven or eight of J. L.'s guests looking on, Sol beat J. L. three straight sets . . .

. . . Pink slip on Sol's desk Monday morning . . .

Thumpthumpthump . . . damn music still coming from next door.

. . . But when the Greaser and I started the club, God, how long ago is it? we played to win. It was our club, why the hell not—we didn't have to kiss ass with anybody.

. . . All changed now

. . . The Greaser is still around, picking up bits in Spain, playing villains in spaghetti Westerns in Italy, still banging rich broads who remember him when he was a leading man, his arms full of Dolores Del Rio . . . amazing old swordsman.

He's got his cock, you've still got your forehand. To each his own, right? Hang on, Greaser, so will I. Your cock, my arm . . . supporting us both in our old age. God bless you, Greaser, keep it up . . . it's better than Social Security . . .

. . . Any damn day . . .

Perce chuckled. Slept.

chapter 3

—Driver, throw down that Wells Fargo strong box—and I'm warning you, don't go for your six-gun—or you'll never see another sunrise!
—Jumping Jee-hosephat, it's the Pecos Kid! Don't shoot, Kid—I ain't plannin' to be no hero!
—Right. Now you just whip up that team of horses and head for town, and don't look back!

WHEN he let himself back into his apartment, fatigue was lapping at his legs. Even though he'd carefully husbanded his energy, it was that damned little Mrs. Burton who'd finally drained it out of him. Up till her hour, from twelve to one, he'd coasted, but when she showed up, she'd insisted on concentrating on her backhand. ". . . Come on, come *on,* Perce, don't just stand there, please, give me something to send back to you!" she'd cried, damned little bitch, he'd had to extend himself to return her shots, a hell of a lot she cared he'd been out there on the court since 8:30, all she wanted was her money's worth . . .

So, smiling like a damned fool for his twenty-five bucks, he'd finally given it to her.

. . . And all the while, the last quarter hour, that skinny snot-nose Becker kid, back from his eastern college with his three pals, staring at him through the wire screen, glancing at his watch, insisting that he give up the court promptly at one, making a big deal out of it.

Sure, he'd like to have belted the kid right in the ass, but he knew better—Becker's father Leon was on the House Rules Committee, and all Perce had to do was to talk back one time, step one inch out of line, and the old man would be on his back, hell, the committee was just looking for an excuse to get him off that one court anyway. So he'd grinned, and left, walked out and started home, feeling the ache mounting up his calves, and now what he needed most was a couple of hours' sleep on the bed, because tomorrow it would be the same strain, all over again . . .

The phone rang, breaking through his semidoze. Rang again, and again.

Damn! He'd forgotten to tell his service to pick it up—

Answer—it might be a customer.

"Mr. Barnes?" The voice on the other end was unfamiliar.

"Yeah, what is it?"

"You don't know me, Mr. Barnes, my name is Chester. Al Chester?"

A low-pitched voice, almost a whisper.

"You're right, I don't know you. What do you want?"

"I'm from out of town. A friend of yours suggested I get in touch."

"Which friend?" asked Perce.

"Spud Olsen?"

. . . Spud Olsen. Spud Olsen? His mind grappled with the name. He knew it, but from where? What sort of a guessing game was this? Olsen—wait a minute, it was coming clear, he'd known him first up at Del Mar, then hadn't Spud moved out to Vegas, yes, sure, he'd been somehow hooked up with one of those stock players at Universal, the tall broad. But Spud? He hadn't seen nor heard from genial Spud—*wait—Spud was dead*. Somewhere he'd read that.

"Don't bullshit me," Perce said. "I haven't heard about him in years, so how could he tell you to call me?"

What kind of a bunco was this?

"That's a long story," said the voice. "Spud died in the prison hospital a couple years back. Was in for a phony securities rap, had himself a heart attack. That's where I knew him. He talked about you a lot, Mr. Barnes."

Okay, so he did know Spud Olsen, and they were cons together. What did that add up to? Some sort of a hustle, sure. "Okay, he talked about me a lot, and?"

"Told us you were a pretty good movie writer, Mr. Barnes. Said you know all the tricks."

"Once," said Perce. "Yeah, I guess I did."

"Spud always said you were an okay guy," said Al Chester.

"If this is a touch, forget it," said Perce.

"No. We'd just like to talk a little with you."

". . . Who's we?" asked Perce, coming awake. What the hell was this?

"Me and my brother LeRoy, is all."

"You're going to put the arm on me for something?"

"Oh, hell, no," said Al Chester. "That's not it at all. We've got us a little business proposition we'd like to discuss with you, is that all right?"

"Like I told you, friend," said Perce, "I'm tapped out."

". . . Well, now," said Al Chester, "maybe we could do something about that, what do you say? Couldn't hurt to spend a little time talking to us, could it? Spud always said you were a guy who knows all the ropes—that's exactly the kind of partner we're looking for—"

"—Thanks," said Perce. "But I don't need any partnership where I could get my ass in a sling, so if—"

"—Hey, my friend, neither are *we,*" said Chester. "We just came out after seventeen years in that same slammer, that's including time off for good behavior, and we sure don't look to go back in, nohow."

Seventeen years . . . the man had a point. So okay, what kind of proposition could a couple of ex-cons have that didn't involve some kind of under-the-table—

". . . Could we talk?" the man was asking.

Before Perce could reply, he heard the voice of the operator as it broke into the conversation, requesting more money for the pay phone. Then he heard Chester, speaking to somebody nearby, asking for more coins.

Oh, boy. Some red-hot deal this would be—with two ex-cons who were operating out of a pay phone. Hang up, he told himself. Take your phone off the hook, get yourself some sleep, let old Spud's prison pals go elsewhere—what did he owe Spud that he needed this?—too late, he heard the coin ring—

Then Chester was back. "Sorry, we don't exactly have our own phone, this is a pay booth," he said. "We just got into town, we're in a place called the Dunstan Arms, maybe you want to write down the address?''

''Listen, friend, I'd like to help you—'' said Perce.

''—It's downtown, but if you want, we could come over to you,'' persisted Chester. ''We got your number out of the book, but if we could get us a bus, or something, maybe that would be easier for you?''

Despite his initial hostility, he had to feel sorry for these two clowns, trying to set up a hustle on this penny-ante basis. How to poor mouth them?

''Listen, I'm tired, and I'm going to be tied up for a while,'' said Perce. ''Why don't you call me, like—tomorrow sometime—''

''Oh. Yeah,'' said Chester softly. ''Well, I wouldn't blame you, giving us the brush. I mean, who the hell are we? You don't know us, so you're backing off, right?''

Good. He'd gotten the message.

''But this is strictly an up-and-up deal,'' said Chester. ''All we got is a story we want to sell to the movies, see?''

Christ! Not that.

''So does everybody else I ever met, friend,'' said Perce.

''Maybe,'' said Chester, ''but would you maybe let us tell you about it?''

''Didn't I already tell you I'm out of that business?'' said Perce.

Chester was silent, and Perce began to regret his abruptness. Poor slob, with dreams of glory he'd probably nurtured all those years in the cooler—''Okay, then,'' Chester said. ''Maybe you could take ten minutes to steer us to the right parties? See, we don't even know where to start. Hell, that much you could do for us, seeing as how we all knew Spud.''

Yeah, sure. He could do that.

''. . . All right. Listen,'' said Perce, ''give me your address, we'll try to make a meet tomorrow, it's Saturday, and I'm not too busy.'' He didn't want them coming all the way up to Beverly. ''You stick around there, and I'll call you—'' Hell, they had no phone! That meant he'd have to go all the way downtown. What a pain in the ass this was turning out to be.

''Say, that'd be fine, but we have no phone, so I'd better give you our address,'' said Chester. ''We really do appreciate this, friend. Got a pencil?''

Perce took his pencil and jotted the address down, and from the sound of it, it would take at least half an hour, even on the damned freeway, which he hated. ''All right, tomorrow,'' he said, and hung up, furious with himself.

Schmuck! he scolded himself. You let them get to you. Where do you come off making points by doing favors for Spud, who's long gone under the ground? If there was ever a no-win situation, this is it.

chapter 4

—Look over yonder, Marthy. What do you see?
—A might purty valley, I'd say, Buck.
—Yep, and some day, on that valley, they's gonna be a town rising up, with stores, and banks, and horses and buggies in the streets, and buildings maybe three stories high—and when they's done building, they're a-gonna call that town . . . *Waco!*

SATURDAY morning was hot and dry, no fog, the distant hills suddenly revealed, shimmering through remarkably clear air swept free overnight of smog. He and Vera had a half-assed date to go for Chinese food at her favorite place, out on Fairfax, the Café de Chine, and then on to another of her endless press screenings afterward, but until late afternoon, his day was his own.

This afternoon, he could sit by the tiny pool downstairs and relax in the sun; meanwhile, he might as well go downtown to see the Chesters. He got out his old Caddy convertible, took it around to the carwash, filled the tank, and then headed it toward the freeway. The sooner he got this meet over with, the better.

The freeway off-ramp dropped him in a nondescript landscape, completely unfamiliar. Squat, old apartment houses from the late twenties and thirties, jammed together with small mission-style bungalows, the paint peeling from their walls, gaudy, endless blockfronts of cheap neighborhood store fronts, cheek by jowl with used-car lots and Chicano bars, all of it baking in the sun, naked and ugly. If this had once been a prosperous middle-class neighborhood, it had long since been abandoned to the bottom-liners, those scratchers and misfits and losers who idly slopped down its streets, glancing curiously at his car whenever he stopped for the light at an intersection.

Still farther downtown, he came to an area obviously sentenced to redevelopment. The Dunstan Arms was the only building left to stand defiantly in its block; the bulldozers had already razed everything else, leaving a flat field of rubble bounded by weary and ancient palm trees. Soon, an office tower would rise from these ashes, part of some vast and brutal corporate redevelopment plan, used by day, empty at night. Meanwhile, the plate-glass window of the doomed Dunstan still bore a painted challenge: ''WELCOME TRAVELERS—TRANSIENT RMS $6 NITELY—WITH BATH.''

He parked the car, locked it, went into the dark, dusty lobby, which was furnished with ancient black-leather armchairs sagging with age. The desk clerk, who was thin and sported a startlingly black hairpiece above his gray parchment-skinned cheeks, was picking his nose and studying the racing form. When Perce asked which room Al Chester occupied, the clerk removed his finger long enough to point it across the lobby. ''Over there,'' he said. ''He's expecting you.''

Perce crossed the lobby. Al Chester rose from one of the chairs. ''I'm your man,'' he said, extending his hand.

Perce shook it, surprised at the softness of the grip. In the warmth of the day, Chester wore a shabby woolen suit. Under his arm was cradled a thick manila envelope.

''That your story?'' he asked.

''How'd you guess?'' grinned Chester.

''I've got ESP,'' said Perce dryly. Behind Al Chester, from a second chair, had risen a taller man, also in a suit, his face pinkish, his shoulders as broad as a fullback's. ''This here's LeRoy,'' said Chester. ''We're the famous Chester brothers.''

Perce allowed his hand to be enfolded in LeRoy's.

Okay, he thought, a vaudeville act they aren't. They obviously expect the billing, but why does he figure me to know how they earned it?

''It's all in there,'' said Al, tapping the envelope as if in answer to Perce's unspoken question.

''Then this is *your* story?'' he asked.

Al nodded. ''From the beginning to the end,'' he said. ''You probably want to read it, don't you? That way you'll be able to tell us what to do with it, the right people to see—''

''Why don't you just give me some idea what it's about,'' said

Perce. The seedy lobby was beginning to depress him, reminding him of places he'd been to in the past, cheap and dirty places that always exuded the odor of disinfectant, stale food, and losers. A smell he'd been running from all his life.

"Well, we could go and have us a cup of coffee," said Al. "They've got a little lunch counter in back there, it's not much—"

"I'll bet it's not," said Perce. "How'd you find this place?"

"Me and LeRoy came here years back," said Al. "It was classier then." He smiled. "But then, so was we. Right now, we don't exactly have us a roll to spend from, y'know?"

Oh, Christ, thought Perce. They're counting on this story. Which means they're counting on *me*. Damn. I wish I hadn't come. Now he was hooked. The next move was to get unhooked, as soon as possible.

"I guess I could use some coffee," he said, anxious to be out of the Dunstan Arms. "Let's get in my car and go find us a place where we can talk."

"That would be fine," said Al.

"If you don't mind," said LeRoy, "I'd rather have me some tea."

Perce led the way out of the lobby.

"Say," said Al at the curb. "A Caddy. Look at them fins. Sixty-eight, right?"

"Right," said Perce, unlocking the doors. "Runs fine. Another fifteen years, and she'll be a classic."

"Good pickup, too," said Al, sliding inside. "Oh, I see you got that Hydra-Matic thing. But I guess that's standard on all of 'em. Too bad. Slows you down some."

"Makes it easier in traffic," said Perce as he steered away into traffic.

"Not so good for your getaway," said Al. "For that, we always counted on stick shift."

"I don't have any problem with my getaway," said Perce.

Al chuckled. "Yeah, but I bet you never done one with a dozen state cops on your ass, now did you?"

"No, I can't say that I have," admitted Perce.

. . . And wondered, why the hell should he feel apologetic about that?

He faced the two brothers in the bright sunlight, over an open-air table at the tacky little Orange Julius stand he'd located, a few blocks away. Al chewed on his soggy breakfast pastry with obvious relish; LeRoy sipped at his iced tea. Perce sipped his grayish coffee and waited to see which of the two would start the pitch. It has to be Al, he thought. LeRoy's the muscle, Al must be the mouth.

"That stuff is rotten for your gut," LeRoy chided his brother.

"Sure is," admitted Al. "But I'm still getting used to ordering what *I* want for breakfast, see?"

From his pocket, LeRoy produced a ball of string, and began to fashion a cat's cradle, his fingers moving deftly, the movements done without thought, by rote, from endless repetition.

"You mind giving me a rundown on this story of yours?" asked Perce, trying to keep the impatience out of his voice.

"Sure thing," said Al, wiping his lips with a paper napkin. He pulled a folded piece of lined paper from his pocket, opened it, and began to read aloud. "*Bullitt,* Warner Brothers. Nineteen million dollars. *Butch Cassidy and the Sundance Kid,* Twentieth Century Fox. Forty-five million eight hundred thirty thousand dollars. *Born Losers,* AIP, twelve million dollars. *Bonnie and Clyde,* Warner Brothers, twenty-two million seven hundred thousand dollars. *Dillinger,* AIP, four million dollars—"

"Okay, grosses," said Perce. "What're you reading *me* that list for?"

"Why, these here are All Time B. O. Champs," said Al. "This came from *Variety,* that paper about the business. Now here, *Dirty Mary, Crazy Larry,* Twentieth Century Fox, fourteen million seven hundred thousand dollars—"

"Fine," said Perce. "Hit pictures, big worldwide grosses. What's the point?"

"Well, there's lots more here," said Al, holding out the paper. "Copied 'em out. All made in the last ten years or so, all B. O. Champs, and they's all crime pictures. See what I'm getting at?"

An old woman, her feet sneakered, wearing a raincoat and carrying two shopping bags full of clothing, wandered past the table, mumbling curses to herself.

"Anybody can make a list of hits," said Perce. "Doesn't mean anything. One guy makes a crime picture, it scores, three others get made right afterward—those you don't read about. Flops they don't list. You can't sell anybody a story based on a cycle—you have to have a *hook.*"

"Hook?" asked Al.

"A handle. A grabber," said Perce.

Al blinked. "I don't get you, friend," he said.

"Something up front that gets the audience interested, and holds them. Like right now, all they want is supernatural. But it has to be something wild, see—like a nine-year-old kid who can cast spells, or a horse that's possessed. *That's* a grabber. You got something like that?"

Neither Chester replied. LeRoy's fingers moved up and down, in and out, constructing endless stringed variations.

". . . Okay, what's on your pages, then?" said Perce . . . what the hell, no sense being so rough on these two, just out of the slammer, carrying around their envelope, reading him off a list of box-office grosses from *Variety*—bringing it all to him and dumping it in his lap, they were expecting some sort of a miracle, and he wasn't going to be able to perform it for them, but he couldn't just put them down, they were friends of old Spud's. "Give me an idea of what you're peddling," he said.

". . . It's about *us,*" said Al. "How me and LeRoy was part of a bunch—well, to tell the truth, we was the ones who started it. Papers called us the Tri-State Mob. We done us a pretty good job of work on some banks, and such, and then we got together and pulled off a big mail-truck job in Nebraska."

Half an hour on "Highway Patrol," thought Perce.

"Okay, armed robbery," he said. "Big score?"

"Well, on that last job, more than six hundred G's," said Al mildly.

Three kids screeched noisily by on skateboards, narrowly missing their table.

"Not bad," conceded Perce. "If you hung on to it."

"Yeah, if," said Al. "And if we had, we wouldn't be eating in this pigsty, now would we?"

"I don't know," said Perce. "You could be playing it cozy, and have it all stashed away somewhere, couldn't you?" He grinned. "*That* would be a grabber."

Up and down, in and out, went LeRoy's fingers.

"We're playing straight with you," said Al softly. The smile never left his face, but his eyes were sharp behind the spectacles. "We're flat."

"Yeah, I guess so," said Perce dryly. "Nobody would stay in that hotel if they didn't have to. So what happened to the money?"

Al shrugged. "What happened was three of the boys got gunned down afterward, and LeRoy and me got picked up by some smartass Feds, that was in 1959. We been inside ever since."

It's not even "Highway Patrol," thought Perce. It's maybe enough for one of those old Metro two-reelers, the ones they used to call "Crime Does Not Pay." "You *and* the money," he said. "Tough."

"Lesson Number One," said Al. "If and when you pull off a big score, *don't spend*. That's the first way they find you—as soon as you start flashing your money."

". . . And that was you?" asked Perce.

Al grimaced. "Nope," he said disgustedly. "It was Buster Newhouse. Not a bad kid, pretty reliable most of the time, but I guess he'd never really gotten his paws on a lot of cash before. I told him it's better to lock it up somewhere, put it away, forget about it. Not Buster. He was pussy crazy. Shacked up with some cheap broad, she must've had something special down there, she got him to take her down to Florida, next thing she had him tossing dough around the tracks. That was all they needed."

The weak-minded country kid, thought Perce. Farley Granger . . . or Richard Jaeckel. ". . . How'd they find the rest of you boys?" he asked.

"Well, him and the other two wasn't so lucky. Knocked off while resisting arrest. Us they picked up while we was sleeping, so we're still around." He nudged LeRoy. "You always did like your beauty sleep, didn't you?" he grinned.

LeRoy nodded, and continued to construct his own tiny stringed world.

Perce finished his coffee, which was cold. "Let me tell you, fellas," he said. "Caper stories aren't very hot right now—especially this one, that happened so long ago—"

"Maybe so," said Al, "but how come crime pictures always

make money? Look at Cagney, and Bogart, and all those others—nowadays it's Clint Eastwood and that Charles Bronson, or Rod Steiger—only he's been out of it for a while—"

"You mind my asking how you got to be such an authority on what sells tickets?" asked Perce.

"Well, inside there, a man has a lot of time to read and think," said Al, ignoring the sarcasm. "I also took me a writing course by mail. Some place in Connecticut called the Famous Writers School. My instructor told me I showed some real talent."

"Why don't you take the story and show it to him?" asked Perce.

"Hell, no," said Al. "They got enough out of me already. If I cut anybody in, it's you. You're our man." He passed the manila envelope across the table to Perce. "Will you take it and read what's in there, and tell us what to do next?"

Oh, sure. And what the hell would he tell them when he'd read Al Chester's true-to-life masterpiece that he'd learned to write by mail? How could he explain to these pathetic characters that everybody in this goddamned world who ran a machine or drove a truck, pumped gas or punched a cash register—hell, even that fat idiot behind the counter here who fried hot dogs and spooned out watery chili—all of them had the feeling that his own personal life story was a God-given gift to show business? That all it took was some "professional" writer, who'd put it down on paper, and then it would be contract time, and then off to the bank with the check? Fantasy time—that producers all over this town were just slobbering with anticipation, waiting for the saga of Al and LeRoy Chester!

So here they sat, having a momentous top-level conference at this crummy Orange Julius stand on the absolute wrong end of town, and these two winners, who'd had their stash picked up, were now waiting for him to give them the Word. Staring at him like two patient dogs at feeding time.

If it weren't so pathetic, he'd have laughed.

Three young girls elbowed past their table, carrying cardboard trays, which one of them narrowly missed spilling onto his shoulder.

". . . Listen," he said. "I'll read this stuff, and I'll try to figure out if it'll work as a movie or not. But I have to tell you up front—

I'm only one guy. If I don't like it, I'll level with you, but that's not the end of the damn line—you could always take your story to someone else, right?''

''No,'' said Al. ''Nobody else but you.''

''Damn it!'' said Perce, annoyed. ''I don't care how many copies of *Variety* you've studied, they won't make you rich. This is a tough racket. I don't want you guys getting pissed off at me if I tell you the truth.''

''Fair enough,'' said Al. ''Right, LeRoy?''

LeRoy dropped his elaborate stringed design onto the table, reached across, and grasped Perce's hand in his own, closed it.

''Right, partner,'' he said.

Perce felt the blood leave his fingers. ''Enough!'' he said, pulling his hand free. ''I earn my living with that hand!''

''Don't know my own strength,'' said LeRoy. ''Sorry.''

''Watch it there,'' Al chided his brother. ''That's our partner's typing hand, remember?''

Now I'm their partner, thought Perce, flexing his hand. Christ, what a setup. Look who wants to be partners with me—two ex-cons, one a correspondence-school graduate, the other a health nut—there's a winning combination for you! We're a shoo-in for the goddamned Academy Award.

He dropped them off at the Dunstan Arms. ''Thanks for the breakfast,'' said Al. ''We'll see you soon?''

''Sure thing,'' said Perce. ''Get yourself some sun. I'll be in touch. I can always reach you here, can't I?''

''Maybe it's better we call you,'' said Al.

''Yeah, you do that,'' said Perce easily. He turned the Caddy away from the curb and drove away, headed toward the freeway.

He wanted very much to get out of this crummy neighborhood and back to his own pad, where they could only reach him by phone, through his answering service. He'd read their story, write them a note, put it in the mail back to them . . . and that, hopefully, would be the end of that. Whatever he owed Spud from the old days, he'd have paid it off.

. . . Meanwhile, that lousy coffee had given him heartburn.

* * *

chapter 5

"HOW WE GOT STARTED ON OUR CAREER OF CRIME"

So now we are up to about 1953, and by now most of the family had died off, and there was just the two of us, my brother LeRoy and me, the last of the Chesters around Portlesville, where the family had been for three generations.

My brother LeRoy had a job working on the town roads in the summer, but in the winter that sort of "dried up" and all he could get was snowplowing and other odd jobs, low pay, and tough work. As for me, there was not much future in the job I had as "manager" down at Spritzer's Service Spa. Old man Spritzer was known all over town as tight. He would not give away "air" on a hot day. I could see him every morning when he would add up last night's "receipts" and stick the cash into a canvas bag and march across the street to the Farmers Bank. He was putting $125 or more a day in there, $200 or so on week ends, and any time I would say something about maybe getting another five spot in my pay envelope, all he would say to me was, "Things are rotten all over and you ought to be darned glad you have yourself a steady job, buddy." So it did not take me long to figure out there was little to be gained by arguing with that character. Meanwhile, across the street, that bank was getting itself stuffed with money, but if you asked anybody there for a "loan" to get yourself started in some kind of a business, all they would ask you about was what kind of "security" you could show them. Ha, that was a laugh, seeing as how it was that same bank that had grabbed off my grandfather's farm in 1936 because he could not make the payments on his mortgage!

I got to thinking about all that. And one night I was lying awake, trying to figure out some way to get out of this situation, when all of a sudden it "hit me." All that money in that bank, and nine miles away, another bank in Ives, with just as much, maybe more, and six miles farther, an even bigger bank in Turkton, all of them getting fatter all the time, and nobody complaining much. Back in the old days, when the James boys, or the Clantons, or the Daltons, or any of the other "outlaws" ran around this area, they'd of found it very easy to knock off any of those little country banks, but nowadays, in the 1950s, with all that "post-war" progress, everybody was too busy making a "buck" to think about an easier way to take one. The easier way would be to catch the banks when they wouldn't be expecting anybody to hold them up. Why not? If you did it carefully, and got the hell away from there, you didn't have too many cops to worry about, and it was one sure way to get out of pumping gas and changing spark plugs for a lousy $67.50 per week.

So I went one night and talked it over with my brother LeRoy. At first he was against the idea. He did not think you could get away with it, but then I took a piece of paper and drew it all out for him, to show him how, if we were careful, we could take over the place in Ives without too much trouble.

I happened to know a girl who worked over in that bank, and she had told me a lot about what it was like in there, and how their "security" system worked. There was a cable tied in to their burglar alarm system, they switched it on every night after everybody went home, and it was hooked into the "police station" in Ives.

Now the thing about the Ives police was that they had two cruisers, one to patrol the downtown, which wasn't much, only a couple of blocks, and the other stayed around the station, to answer any and all emergencies . . .

My idea was that if we could start something a little ways out of town, such as a fire, that would get the police cruisers out of our way. Meanwhile, we could move in on the bank, where nobody would be expecting any trouble, and "knock it off." It was a simple idea, but as the fellow says, "all great ideas are simple."

The idea was to take the bank on Friday, when they had lots of cash in to cover the week end, to cover all the local people's needs, et cetera.

I talked it all over with LeRoy and after a while he was convinced we could swing it. My main point was we had nothing much to lose. It was not like robbing people, or stealing from friends. Whatever that damn bank lost, they would have it covered by insurance, and it doesn't take much to figure out what crooks run those outfits!!!

So the following week we got down to work on my plan . . .

. . . Thirty pages later, they'd knocked off their first small-town bank, and helped themselves to a few Gs, bingo! A successful hit. For the next year or so, they'd repeated their act, working up and down the state, refining their techniques. Just a couple of good old country boys, self-taught, handy with cars and guns. Al, the careful planner, LeRoy, his trustworthy muscle, very fast learners, pretty soon they'd made so many successful scores that they'd become minor-league celebrities, a pain in the ass to the authorities, but not spectacular enough yet to be considered big time.

Typical Horatio Alger story, what every small-time hood dreams of—*boys, we got to make us one big score*. Maybe we ought to try for a bank truck, one of them steel vaults on wheels that delivers the payrolls to the feed factories and stockyards and mills . . . what do you say we round us up a couple of extra guns, reliable extra hands, and go for broke?

So they'd sat down, and planned it, and done it. Got away with a big, fat six-figure heist, split up the take, retired from the business. The rest of it was exactly as Al had said—one guy began spending his share, and from then on, it was only a question of time before the Feds picked up the others. Final score, three down, two off to the pen, and the loot mostly recovered . . .

No gimmick here. No hook. No springboard . . .

It was the sort of pulp-magazine garbage you might have unloaded at Republic, or Monogram, in the old days, when Morrie and Frank King were turning out their shaky-A crime stories. A couple of fair minor-star names, lots of gunplay, shoot-'em-up chases on deserted streets in downtown L.A., the whole show made for peanuts on a nine- or ten-day schedule—all those pictures you still see at 1:00 A.M. on the cheap channels, broken into every seven or eight minutes by used-car commercials featuring some clown on his open lot on Washington Boulevard.

But not in 1977 . . . there certainly wasn't anything on these pages of Al's that would start a producer drooling, nothing to attract Charles Bronson. Not in a business run by accountants and bright young hot-shots with slide rules, where what you had to start with was the whole screenplay, done on spec, all proved out for them to see (and then to have rewritten) from Scene One, right down to the final Fade, you had to put every word of it down on paper, between binders, lay it on the desk (next to all those other unsold screenplays, stacked in mute piles) before anybody would even talk to you . . . and even then, what kind of guarantee did you have that somebody bankable, a Steve McQueen, or a Redford, this new kid George Segal, would take a fancy to it? And then you went through the same megillah with a bankable director, one of maybe the golden five or six that were acceptable, all of them with commitments for pictures up ahead of your project.

. . . No thanks, brother Chester, go deal with somebody else, maybe one of those eager pushy kids fresh out of UCLA Film School, or one of the long-haired geniuses up at the American Film Institute, let *him* sit down and sweat over a screenplay, and then take it and run with it.

Not for Perce Barnes.

(He could hear them already. "Perce *who?* What're his credits? . . . Hell, didn't I see that picture when I was a kid in high school?")

. . . And who needed that?

"This is very interesting. Where'd you get it?" asked Vera.

. . . He came awake, blinked, sat up, saw her sitting in the chair across the room, wearing his shirt and nothing else, the reading light on, Al Chester's manuscript in her lap.

She must have gotten out of bed some time ago, but he hadn't heard her leave.

Briefly, he told her about the Chesters and Spud.

"What are you planning to do with it?" she asked.

The bedside clock said 6:45.

"What do you suggest?" he said, yawning.

"This stuff is fascinating," she said. "It has a wonderful . . . naïve feeling, you know? Sort of *cinéma vérité*."

"Yeah, sure. It's been done a million times," he said. He got out of bed, padded across to the kitchenette to find himself some cold juice.

"You know what this could be?" she asked. "It's the kind of material that a European director would go nuts for. Somebody like Forman, or Bo Widerberg, those guys who come here and shoot a typically American story with their own particular eye—soft focus, shoot it in the Middle West—and then all the critics go crazy and rave about what an original vision they have . . . you know what I mean?"

"Okay, fine, why don't you waltz the Chester brothers over to Europe and find them a genius of their own?" said Perce. Draped in nothing but his shirt, she was suddenly very desirable. He leaned over to run his lips over her shoulder, enjoying the warmth of her. ". . . And meanwhile, let's go back to bed," he suggested, running his fingers down to her ample breasts.

"On the other hand," Vera mused, "it could be something for Aldrich, or Bob Altman. They love the crime scene, and this is almost like history, and if it were handled properly, shot on the actual locations—"

"You're a smart lady, go handle it," he suggested. "I'll give you the Chesters' address, it's a fascinating *cinéma vérité* dump downtown, you could make a meeting with them and start building a package deal—"

"You mean, you're not at all interested?" she asked.

"Not a hell of a lot," he said.

"Why not?"

"Because I'm out of the business," he said, his hand still exploring her.

"Oh, since when did you retire?" she persisted. "They must have brought it to you because you could do something with it—"

". . . Come on, honey, it's too early in the morning for this." he murmured. His mouth on hers, he urged her from the chair toward his rumpled bed. The manuscript fell to the floor, pages spreading out. He was hot for her, almost as if he were a youngster, and she began to respond.

This is one business I haven't retired from, he thought, as they locked together.

. . . In the early morning he was always stronger. Was that a sign of old age?

"Good?" he asked.

"Nice," she said.

". . . Some like it in the springtime, some like it in the fall, but I like it in the morning, that's the best time of all . . ." he sang, and chuckled.

They dozed.

. . . So she liked the Chester story? Okay, fine. But it didn't improve his opinion of its commercial chances.

Maybe, in the old days, something could have happened with it. If you had somebody to hustle it. Somebody like Danny Fretwell. Good old Danny, playing four, five sets of tennis at the club on weekends, stopping to take calls, closing deals on the phone that hung out there on the wall of the court. What was it old Manky had said about Danny? ". . . It must have been difficult for Mrs. Fretwell, his mother, giving birth to a baby with a telephone growing out of its ear. . ."

. . . He snickered.

"What was that for?" asked Vera.

". . . Thinking about Danny Fretwell," he said.

"The producer?" she asked.

"Before that he was an agent," said Perce, and repeated Manky's famous line.

"Funny," said Vera.

"He was a dynamite guy," said Perce. "I ever tell you about the weekend Danny pulled off my biggest score?"

"mmm," said Vera.

". . . Oh, he knew them all—all the big boys," he said fondly remembering. "They never scared him for a minute, Cohn, L. B., even Goldwyn, every one of them screamed at him—'you sonofabitch, Fretwell, you're a goddam robber, you're barred from my lot!" 'Why sure, L. B. that's okay, I'll just have to do business with you by phone. You know my number, don't you?' He knew he had them by the balls—he had a Tiffany list, sold 'em for Tiffany prices, greatest damned salesman I ever saw at work, swinging from deal to deal, had the guts of a burglar. . ."

"Mmm-ph . . ." said Vera.

". . . I remember that time when I brought him the thing about the Harvard guy who ended up on the riverboats, the thing I found in a magazine. Did a couple of pages on it, all I had to do was to tell it to Danny, between sets, he grinned and said 'Cary Grant—we put him together with Bette Davis, she's the rich broad who loses her plantation—Jack Warner's going to drool for it!' "

. . . But we didn't go to Warner, oh, no, he was too smart to do that. He gets on the phone and mentions it to Bill Dozier, who's got his own unit over at Universal, who's looking for something for Joan Fontaine, but he warns Dozier he's already got interest in it at Metro, he knows Dozier will get somebody at Metro to leak to him, sure enough, that gets them stirred up at Metro—somebody from Metro calls Danny to find out where the hell is this property U-I is hot for, Danny plays it dumb, what treatment? Now they're beginning to sniff around like beagles, the word's spreading, sure enough, old J. L. gets word from one of his spies there's this hot property Grant is hot for—Cary hadn't even seen the thing, he was on vacation somewhere, but J. L. has a commitment with him for a picture, and he needs a property, and he calls Danny and chews him out, what the hell is Danny doing not submitting the story, what sort of a private double cross is this? Danny says "Jesus, J. L., I don't even know if this is right for you, and besides, you told me yourself you weren't going to go over fifty G's for anything, business is rotten, so if I *did* make a deal for this, I'd want sixty."

"You goddamn robber, if you take this piece of crap about the riverboat gambler and sell it to anybody else, you'll be barred from my goddam lot permanently—I'll give you fifty, no trading, understood?"

"Jesus, J. L., you've got me over a barrel, Metro and U-I are hot for it, but I don't want you to get sore, we're pals, so I'll tell you what, fifty for the property, but you have to let me sell you my own writer to do the script. Not the Epsteins—it has to be my guy, okay?"

. . . One short weekend, he had the whole deal locked up by Tuesday morning, before Warner even thinks to check it with Cary Grant . . . Beautiful. Thursday morning I go to Danny's office and he hands me a check for forty-five big ones. ''Easiest five Gs I ever stole,'' he tells me, a big grin on his face. ''I wanted to see how fast I could pull off a swindle, and, by God, I broke my own record.'' Then he gets serious, ''Just between the two of us, Perce, you think there's really enough for a picture here?'' . . . He hadn't even *read* the goddamned couple of pages!

''. . . Well, that was when he put me together with John Trump, who knew all about Harvard and that Ivy League bullshit, and we got a script out of it, and Cary Grant liked it, and Warner went around happy as a king, telling everybody how he'd screwed L. B. out of the property!''

Nobody around like Danny any more. Finally he went to New York and became a producer. Before he left, he said to me, ''. . . Shit, I'm so tired of watching these klucks make mistakes with the properties I sell 'em—I figure I can't do any worse—and who knows, I might even be better!''

Vera yawned.

''You told me that story,'' she said.

''I did?'' he said, surprised. ''Funny, I don't remember—''

''You told me about Danny Fretwell, and then about the deal you got at Columbia, with Sidney Buchman, the jockey story—and the one you sold to the English producer,'' she said.

''Why didn't you stop me?'' he asked, irritated.

''I really wasn't listening,'' said Vera. ''I was thinking.''

''Sorry,'' he snapped. ''I wouldn't want to interrupt your train of thought.''

Vera turned over and stared at him. ''Tell me,'' she said, ''are you going to spend the rest of your life reminiscing?''

''What the hell does that mean?''

''Just what you think it does,'' she told him. ''You're becoming one of those guys who live on nostalgia. You waste a lot of time being a raconteur when you could be doing something now, right now.''

''Ah, screw you!'' said Perce angrily. He got up from the bed. ''If I'm such a tired, old bore, why do you come around?''

He went into his bathroom and slammed the door. Brushed his teeth, combed his hair with trembling hands, waiting for the anger to subside. He stared at himself in the small mirror. He had most of his hair, there were few lines in his face, for his age he was in pretty damned good shape. So he told a few old stories about his friends? Who the hell needed her and her smart cracks?

When he emerged from the bathroom, Vera was up and had begun to dress.

"You're sore," she said.

He did not answer.

"Good," she said. "All I meant was that you ought to take a shot at trying to make a picture script out of that manuscript." She had picked up the pages and placed them all neatly in a pile on the nearby table. "So you don't have Danny Fretwell around to make a deal for you, so what? There are plenty of other guys around town you could talk to."

Oh, sure there were. Plenty of young smartasses who didn't even know who he was, and couldn't care less. "Don't give me that," he told her. "My credits don't mean much today. What the hell makes you so sure the world is waiting for my next script? Go out there and win one for the Gipper, is that what you think it's all about?"

Vera finished buttoning her blouse, then she tucked it into the waistband of her slacks. "What do you think I am, some kid? Of course, it's tougher than that. I've been around this town almost as long as you have, and I've seen as much of the game as you have, how you have to play the angles, and kiss ass, and brown-nose the guys up above you, but somehow the good stuff gets done, doesn't it? So instead of sitting around this apartment and sopping up bourbon and feeling sorry for yourself because all your pals are dead, you could take another shot at it, couldn't you?"

"Better to light one candle than to curse the darkness, eh?" he said. "You went from Rockne to Father Flanagan in one fast jump." He began to chant, "Hello, Father, well hello, Father, it's so nice to have you back again—"

"It wasn't Flanagan, he was a Christopher, and shut up!" she told him, and slammed the bathroom door shut behind her.

When she emerged, her hair was combed and her face done. She went to pick up her purse. He had the water boiling for coffee, and handed her a cup of instant. Sundays Vera went to visit her invalid mother in a retirement home far out in the valley. Hardly a pleasure trip.

''Thanks,'' she said.

''The old bore still has a bit of class,'' he said.

''You writers,'' she sighed.

''Lady, you've got the wrong number,'' he said. ''I give tennis lessons.''

''All I meant was—if you wanted to try and do something with that material they gave you, I'd *help.''* she said. ''I do know a few angles, you know.''

''. . . And if I didn't?'' he asked.

She sighed. ''Oh, the hell with it,'' she said. ''I'd probably still come around.'' She put down the cup and embraced him.

''Even when I reminisce?'' he asked. ''Face it, Vera, the game's over. They've got other players on the field. So okay, it doesn't bother me much—''

''The hell it doesn't,'' said Vera. ''I saw you the other night. Remember when Harry Elbert came on and started running off at the mouth?''

She picked up her purse and let herself out of his apartment.

After Vera left, he set about cleaning up the place. Sundays there was no maid service. Then he went downstairs, walked to the deli two blocks away, picked up some eggs and juice, a copy of the Sunday *L.A. Times*, brought it home, and made himself some breakfast. Then he read for an hour or so.

It was almost noon when he picked up the Chester manuscript again. What the hell had she seen in it that he hadn't, anyway?

He began to read it again, from page 1.

. . . When the first notion struck him, he automatically reached for a pencil, to make a note. Damn, there wasn't even a pad around his place, it had been so long since he'd needed one.

He pulled a shirt card from one of his freshly laundered shirts and began to scribble.

NO KICKOFF
just two small-town guys, figuring out how to rob a cheapo bank.
Plot takes too long to get rolling

NO DAME!!
Are these guys faggots? Didn't either of them have a sweetheart? Find something female

SUSPENSE?
starts after the big score—will they be caught or not? Not soon enough. Maybe start at top of story in scenes where they are set up to pull off the robbery——then flashback, to how they got into this whole ballgame—
—then banktruck robbery plays off like in Asphalt Jungle, or that French picture Dassin made . . . for climax.

It was almost suppertime before he got something real to go on. Of course! It was sitting there, all the time, waiting for him to pick it up!

NEMESIS THREAT—
Old-time Fed, maybe. Tough, hard-bitten guy—by accident stumbles across the first or second bank holdup by the Chesters—while they're still small timers—he gets interested, follows their career—sort of like that French inspector, what the hell was his name, in Les Misérables—Charles Laughton played him—

—They don't know he's watching them

—He is their NEMESIS—

—Follows their career from a distance, waiting for them to try for the big time, he's sure that's what they'll do some day, and he's RIGHT!

So when it happens, he's happy, now he knows it's them, and he sets out to prove he's right—

BUT

they're smart—(Al said never spend the loot) and for a while he's wrong. None of the money surfaces—

—Nemesis feels like a schmuck—

—Boys are home free—UNTIL

the idiot down in Florida (pussy crazy) is conned into going to the track—money shows up—

And now he's right!

Sonofabitch, he said to himself, getting up and pacing the room, feeling the sense of excitement that came when you'd finally pushed the damn rock uphill—this makes it into a story! Something an actor could get his teeth into—you get yourself a guy like Kirk Douglas, or Burt Lancaster, or Karl Malden to play the old cop, the Fed, whatever he was—and then you play against him the story of these two small-time hoods developing into big timers—you use the young Bridges kid, or what the hell was his name, Carradine, old John's son—and now you've got yourself some tension going . . . There's a setup for you!

Depleted, he slumped back into the chair, coming down from the high he'd been riding.

Then he got up and made himself a drink. Sipped the bourbon, stared at the notes he'd been scribbling for the past half hour.

Okay, so there was something there, and he'd found a hook, a handle, the gimmick he'd been nagging himself about . . . In the old days, that was the easy part. After this, you were off to the races, six weeks on salary, you turned in a first draft . . .

But now, in 1977, what in hell was he supposed to do with it?

* * *

Monday he gave his morning of lessons, went home, and made some more notes. His answering service gave him the message; a Mr. Al Chester had called. He ignored it. Not yet . . .

It was Wednesday afternoon before Al called again.

''Called you Monday but you weren't in,'' he said.

''I was busy,'' said Perce. ''How're you guys doing down there?''

''Not so much,'' said Al. ''This ain't exactly the most exciting neighborhood we ever been in, but I guess after where we was, it'll do.'' He cleared his throat. ''We were wondering did you read the story.''

''Yeah, I did,'' said Perce casually. ''And I did some thinking about it.''

By now he had seven pages of notes, on his new yellow pad.

''What do you think, partner?'' asked Al.

Partner, eh? Don't rush me, thought Perce. Sweat a little. ''I'm not sure,'' he said. ''You know, your story has a lot of problems going for it.''

"Uh huh," said Al. "But that's where you're supposed to come in, isn't it?"

"Bottom line," said Perce. "All I see from my end is a lot of work. Sure, it's a true story, and that means you and your brother think a whole lot of it—what the hell, you *lived* it. But somebody else has to take and jazz it up, put it in shape . . . and that's me. So if I did anything with it, I'd have to keep any money I got for writing it."

"Uh huh," said Al. "What would that add up to for us?"

"I'll level," said Perce. "Not a hell of a lot until we sell it. *If* we sell it."

". . . Supposing we sell it, then how do we split?" asked Al.

"Like I said, I keep the money for writing, and then we cut up the money they pay for the rights," said Perce. "Say . . . fifty fifty."

There was silence from the other end. Then Al cleared his throat. "You mind my saying that doesn't sound like much of a deal?"

"Sure," said Perce. "You mind my saying you're not in much of a position to get a better one?"

Al cleared his throat again. "Three-way split," he said. "LeRoy and me, each a third. You get the other."

Okay, fine, thought Perce, what the hell is the difference? The money to buy the rights won't happen unless somebody buys the treatment I'd have to do anyway—I get the edge, I get mine up front.

. . . If I get anything, he reminded himself. The whole thing is such a wild shot, anyway . . .

"Al," he said, "you're one tough trader."

"I'm only thinking what's fair," said Al.

The operator's nasal voice broke into the call, requesting more money for the ensuing three minutes.

"Hold it," said Al. There was the tinkle of coins hitting the pay box, and then he was back on the line. Real high finance, thought Perce. "What'd you say?" Al was asking.

"I didn't," said Perce. "But I've been thinking. What the hell, Al, you're a friend of old Spud's, no sense horsing you around. I keep the script money, three-way split on the rights, if and when. Deal?''

''. . . How about a little something in front?'' asked Al.

How about that? He was supposed to underwrite these clowns, as well?

''Sorry, pal, I haven't got any bread for that, we'll just have to go on faith,'' he said. ''What's the matter, you on your ass?''

''Well, we can manage for a while,'' said Al.

. . . You just do that, thought Perce. I'm not running any benefits for you two characters.

''What do we do next?'' asked Al.

''I'm going to get us a letter drawn up,'' said Perce, ''and then the three of us sign it, all legal and proper, that'll protect us all, and then I'll start kicking your story around, see what I can make out of it. Right?''

''Sure,'' said Al. ''Then we're gonna hear from you?''

''I'll call you by the weekend,'' said Perce. Oh, hell, they couldn't be reached down there. ''No, you call me, say Monday—after lunch. Okay, partner?''

''Sure,'' said Al and hung up.

Easy, thought Perce. Too easy. Not much fun in it. If and when anybody bit for the treatment he had to write, it would be simple to juggle the numbers around, whack up the price so that the treatment got most of the money. Too bad the Chesters didn't know much about the way deals got made. The money for their rights would end up being much less than his fee . . . so he'd always have a big edge.

Why not? Where were they without him?

Smiling, he picked up the yellow pad.

In the dusty lobby of the Dunstan Arms, Al Chester emerged from the phone booth. LeRoy stood outside, waiting.

''What's he say?''

Al held up his thumb and forefinger in a circle. ''We did it!'' he said happily. ''He is hooked. Hooked nice and tight—just like I figured!''

''No shit,'' said LeRoy admiringly.

''C'mon, let's go celebrate,'' said Al, pulling his brother across the lobby toward the entrance. "I'm gonna have me a banana split. Oh, this is gonna be some beautiful score," he said as they went out the door. "It's gonna make our last one look like nothing!"

They started down the bright, sunlit street. ". . . You're sure he's not gonna chicken out on us when he finds out?" asked LeRoy.

"Nossir," said Al. "The way I figure friend Barnes—he's as hungry as we are—only he hasn't waited as long to make a score as we have. You'll see, he'll get greedy."

LeRoy shook his head. ". . . I only hope we didn't wait all this time—and end up picking us a chicken for our front man."

Al clapped his brother on the back. "Come on, now, stop fretting!" he said. "If he's a chicken in the middle, we're gonna be on both sides of him, all the way to the score." He beamed.

". . . Okay," said LeRoy. "What do we do next?"

"Now *he's* carrying the old ball," said Al. "We go get an ice cream sundae—and we wait."

". . . Ice cream is fattening," said LeRoy.

"Okay, then, I've got a better idea," said Al. "Let's us go get laid."

* * *

chapter 6

—Operator, put me through to the City Desk—this is Brick Watkins—*hurry!* Hello, City Desk? Watkins! Put a rewrite man on, quick! I'm down at the Governor's Mansion and I'm sitting on top of a keg of dynamite! Tear out the front page and get ready for a replate—I've got a story that'll tear this town wide open! Are you ready?

A COUPLE of nights later, Vera came by.

"Listen, I'm sorry about last week," she began carefully. "I don't know why I think I have a license to manage your life—" Then her eyes had flickered over his shoulder, she'd seen the sheaf of scribbled pages on his table, next to the typewriter at which he'd tried to begin work, the wastebasket piled with the wadded-up, discarded pages. "—Wow," she said. "You decided to take a shot at it after all. That's just great!"

"Only a treatment," he told her. "Something to try and sell the thing. That's all."

"Because of my half-time pep talk?" she smiled.

"Not exactly," he said, unwilling to concede that she had indeed gotten to him. "I started reading the thing again, and I found a handle I liked." Hesitantly, waiting for her reaction, he sketched out the notion of the old Fed spotting the Chesters early, keeping his eye on their career, developing into their unknown nemesis.

"Beautiful!" said Vera. "If it's written well, it's the kind of part you can get somebody like Matthau interested—"

"Of course," he said. "He's already heard about it, he's drooling to read it—the Morris office calls every day. Walter's been one of my fans for years—"

"You've got hold of something solid here," she mused. "The kind of a rich part you could cast—Kirk Douglas, or Glenn Ford, Lancaster? Fonda, maybe—"

"Now who's reminiscing?" he scoffed. "The Hit Parade of 1949." He went to pour himself a well-watered bourbon; he was pleased with her reaction. "Honey, none of those guys is worth a dime at the box office today—"

"You get the right package put together, you'll see, they'll want it!" said Vera. "Who were you thinking of for Al?" It was too early to talk about casting! . . . Hell, he didn't even have five readable pages yet, and already she had him going into production! "Let's talk about something else," he told her.

She shrugged, turned away.

He knew he'd put her down, now he felt contrite.

"Hey, listen, sorry," he said. "I'm nervous about this, you know? Trying to get the feel of it—I don't want to worry about what will happen to it when I'm finished—and by that time, when it bombs—which it probably will—"

"Stop that!" she said angrily. "Even you don't sit down to try and write a failure, do you?"

"What do you mean, *even* me?" he said. "If I didn't think it would work, why in hell would I try a treatment?"

". . . I don't know," she sighed. "Let's talk about dinner."

Settling the deal with the Chesters was simple enough. He'd had a letter agreement drawn up by Sy Rodman, his attorney—no need for a full contract, not at the price per hour Rodman's office charged—Sy had assigned some young kid in the office to write it, and when Al Chester called again, he was ready with the typed copies for the two brothers to sign. Saturday afternoon, he drove downtown to meet with them.

He couldn't face the Orange Julius stand again; this time he took them to a decent restaurant, a steak place at the foot of Wilshire, the Pacific Diner, he hadn't been there in years, but in the old days it was one of the best.

When the waitress brought them menus, Al glanced at it, and whistled at the prices. "Yeah, I know," said Perce, "but don't worry about it. I'll pick this tab up—it's an occasion."

He didn't want to ask about their financial status, but Al volunteered the news. "LeRoy got himself a job yesterday."

LeRoy nodded.

''That's great,'' said Perce, relieved. At least they wouldn't be on his back for the next few weeks. ''What doing?''

''Washing dishes,'' said LeRoy. ''Four to midnight.''

''Gets two sixty an hour,'' said Al.

''Minus deductions,'' said LeRoy. Perce glanced at the large man's hands, saw they were pinkish and cracked. ''They sure take a lot away,'' added LeRoy. ''All those taxes.''

''I'm out looking, too,'' said Al. ''Figured from what you said the other day, we're not about to get hog fat-rich by the end of the week.''

''What kind of a job you after?'' asked Perce when they'd ordered.

''Not too much choice, is there?'' asked Al. ''Everybody says getting on welfare is easy, but I don't want any of that. I don't mind working, but a man my age, no references, no background, he can't pick and choose. Jewish fella a couple of blocks away has a gas station, says he could use me to pump gas and work at the car wash there.''

''How about the money?''

''The magic number, two sixty,'' said Al.

Both brothers read through the typed letter, used Perce's pen to sign it, and then Al carefully folded up their two copies and tucked it into his pocket. Then the waitress brought their food, grilled chopped sirloin with side orders of hash browns, expensive, but first-rate. Al began to eat with obvious pleasure; LeRoy pushed away the hash browns.

''Costs a lot but it's good,'' said Al, between mouthfuls. ''You know, back when me and LeRoy went inside, a man could do pretty well on a hundred a week. Live on it, maybe even stick a little aside in the bank, for the future—''

''Until you two guys came along and took it out, eh?'' asked Perce.

''Shoot,'' said Al disgustedly. ''That was all small stuff. We never really hurt any bank—they just keep on growing. Look at these big ones around here, downtown—big buildings, eighteen, twenty stories high—all stuffed with mortgages, and loans, and securities—why, even if we was to try it again, which we sure ain't, we're so out of our league it ain't funny. A couple of flies, trying to take a bee hive."

"Come on," said Perce, "You're talking like an old also-ran. You're as good as you ever were."

And immediately thought, Jesus, I sound like Vera.

Al shook his head. "Prison slows you down," he said very matter-of-fact. "I'm back to where I started, pumping gas. Nothing much to show for the in-between." He smiled ruefully. "Just waiting for you to give me and LeRoy a stake for our old age. Right?"

Both brothers ate silently, obviously waiting for Perce to say something.

"Listen," he said. "I'm not about to shit you. I'm going to try and do something with this story of yours, but I want to warn you going in—you two and me, we're not exactly the hottest items around. The movie business isn't holding its breath waiting for us to show up, you know? It's an interesting story, I'm not a bad writer—"

"You got your name on some damn good pictures," said Al.

"How do you know that?" he asked.

"We looked 'em up," said Al.

"Well, then you know there hasn't been one for a few years now," said Perce.

"Listen," said LeRoy, and he reached over to grasp Perce's arm. "You got our story now. Just do the best fucking job you can with it, okay?"

"Hell, of course I will—" said Perce, feeling the strength of LeRoy's grasp like a sudden band of iron around his arm. The big man held it firm. What was this all about?

"We trust him, LeRoy," said Al. "Now let him go. Remember, that's our partner's writing arm."

"Yeah," said Perce, flexing his fingers to restore the circulation. "And I need it to write my name on this check, too. Or else we'll all end up washing dishes."

Back at his apartment, alone, he kept at it.

Some mornings, it was pure hell, getting cranked up to write at noontime after a long morning spent out on the damn tennis court at the club, talking tennis to his clients, playing the sympathetic M.D. to their faulty backhands and their rotten services, keeping them happy, giving them value for money. He'd come back to the apartment, make a sandwich, sit down, force himself back. No, no nap, that was too easy an out, no phone calls, don't pick up the paper, keep the TV switched off, ignore the noises all around you, *concentrate*. No quitting today, Perce, baby, you have to do at least two decent pages before you can have your first afternoon bourbon . . .

Goddamn treatments! He'd forgotten how much work this kind of bastard storytelling was. It wasn't prose, it wasn't a screenplay, it was a half-assed shapeless blend of both. To do it caused him to flex muscles he hadn't used in years, the old talents he'd assumed were still there . . . but like any sinew you didn't work with, proved weak and flabby.

Lonely. Damned lonely! Here he sat, day after day, trying to create incidents, patches of dialogue, something to get a buyer with some development money in hand to nip at this saga of the two small-town hoods and their Midwest crime saga. Now he didn't even have Vera to argue with at night, she'd had to go away for a week, back East to one of those phony film festivals, one of her office clients had a picture entered in it, at the last minute she'd been asked to accompany him, filling in for his regular man at the office who'd come down with the flu.

". . . I'll read it when I get back," she'd promised.

"You'll read it when I'm finished," he told her, annoyed she was leaving.

"Okay, I'll wait until after Matthau reads it," she'd replied.

The damned apartment was beginning to bug him.

In the old days he'd always written with somebody else, another face, a voice, someone to argue with. Starting with Shitheel Harry Elbert, nervous Harry, he sat at the typewriter, Perce did the pacing, ootzer Harry, nagging, come on Perce, *stop staring out the window at the broads, let's get this scene written—*

What a relief it had been to be teamed up with Johnny Trump, after Harry had screwed him, Johnny, Ivy League, polite, always in his J. Press Chipp jacket and button-down shirts, even after two years in Hollywood, soft-spoken, apologizing for the pages he'd bring in in the mornings, if you don't mind, Perce, old boy, I had a few notions last night so I wrote them out, see if you like them . . . Mind? The kid wrote like an angel. Now he was long gone, too, back East, turning out novels that won prizes, he'd been smart, he'd gotten out of this town.

. . . Today he'd even settle for that English playwright he'd worked with, what was his name, Derek something-or-other, a pompous little half-fag pain in the ass, always giving him short lectures on the correct way to pronounce words—("I spell you *s-u-c-c-i-n-c-t,* Mr. Barnes, pray pronounce it?"). As if you'd ever use the damned word in a script! And after him, that crazy gag-writer, Morey Drucker, who spent the whole day on the phone lining up broads, who dropped one-liners into the script, let's give the kid an insult joke here—"You're like an old stove—big belly and no head!" Stinks? Here's another—"You're so dumb, it takes you an hour to cook Minute Rice!" Here's another—"Baby, you got a tongue that could clip a hedge!" Here, y'want another—

No, one-line insults he didn't need.

. . . He needed to write.

Come on, Perce, get going. Stop staring out the window at the broads.

(Wouldn't it be a laugh if he could unload this project on old Harry Elbert himself?)

Not a chance. Harry hardly spoke to him at the club—barely nodded to him whenever their paths crossed. Sonofabitch, all he had to do was to nod his head yes—there'd be a deal, Harry had plenty of production money ready to spend . . .

Forget that, Perce, *go back to work.*

. . . Damn writing, damn it to hell.

Any writer who said he enjoyed doing it was either a liar or a compulsive. Oh, sure, Neil Simon claimed he got his jollies writing three-act comedy hits, maybe Sidney Sheldon got his rocks off dictating three novels at a time, that Frenchman, Simenon, he banged them out—but every other writer he'd ever talked to had admitted that deep down, he hated writing. Most of 'em would do anything to postpone sitting down at the typewriter . . .

. . . Remember that story about Dick Fletcher? He was doing a script for Fox, a big one, he had the weekend in which to finish the last eight, nine pages, it was due on Zanuck's desk on Monday, under the gun, he brought the work home, he needed absolute peace and quiet, okay, so Mrs. Fletcher pitched in to do her part, she promised she'd take the kids away from their house for the day, it was Saturday, he had to have the house to himself so he could do those pages.

She left the house at nine, took the kids to the beach at Santa Monica, keep them there till lunch, then fed them, then she took them to that crazy little playground over on La Cienega, ran them ragged, then fed them some supper, gone all day . . . by that time the kids were exhausted, so was she, but she took them off to an early movie, didn't get back to their house until eight that night, they all staggered into the house, it was for Daddy, Zanuck's favorite writer! *Was he finished?* Hell, the procrastinating s.o.b. had made all the beds, done the laundry, waxed the floors, and now the poor slob was sitting in their pantry, *polishing the silver!*

—enough, you're back in 1950 again, no more reminiscences, he told himself. You've got another two pages to go, *today*.

Today two, tomorrow two, at the end of two weeks, he'd have almost thirty pages. How the hell long should a treatment be, anyway? Forty, fifty?

One day, a guy had been talking to Lubitsch, a playwright just in from New York . . . "How long, Mr. Lubitsch, should a screenplay *be?*" Lubitsch waggled his cigar. "As long as it's *good*."

. . . and another thing, he didn't have a title for this thing. What the hell should he call it, once it was finished?

Here he was, worrying about a title, and he wasn't even halfway through.

. . . And after it was finally written (if he finished) and he took it out to some service and had it typed up, Xeroxed, put between covers, *then* what was he going to do with it?

What was that other thing about titles, what that Broadway producer had told him once, when he'd asked what it was made a good title? "You know what a good title is? *The title of a hit*."

. . . Wearily, he went back to work.

* * *

chapter 7

THREE DOWN, TWO LEFT STANDING
The story of Al and LeRoy Chester

Screen treatment by Perce Barnes

FADE IN:

It's the 1950s, the era of Eisenhower, seven-inch TV screens, crew-cuts, and rock and roll.

We open on a quiet Midwestern street. A heavy armored truck comes slowly down toward us, headed for the outskirts of town, toward a factory.

Inside the truck, stacks of neatly packaged federal literature, money, all bagged, nearly six hundred thousand dollars' worth.

The driver and his guard make this run each week.

Every time they do it, they stop at this corner, where there's a small coffee shop. There the guard will get out, go inside, call the main office to report in, and pick up morning coffee for himself and the driver.

Quick cuts, as the truck approaches. Across the street, two men in a car. A driver at the wheel.

Parked on a side street, a second car. Two men inside.

All is quiet. The men in the cars glance at their watches.

The armored truck lumbers to a stop outside the coffee shop. With a hiss, the front door opens, and the guard begins to climb out.

Moving with precision, from the parked car across the street a man dashes across, a stocking mask on his face, cradling a shotgun, followed by the second man, also masked.

One of them backs the guard against the side of the truck, the second waves the driver out. The two uniformed men are relieved of their weapons, and are forced into the second car, where they are driven away, a gun at their heads.

Seconds later, the armored car rumbles down the street, one masked man at the wheel, the second beside him, the six hundred thousand headed in an opposite direction from the factory.

The accomplice pulls off his stocking mask. Chortles with pleasure. "We done it, LeRoy!" he yells. "Our big score!"

* * *

The two *Chester* brothers, *Al* and *LeRoy,* in their finest hour.

A couple of typical American boys, small-town youths in overalls and sneakers, the kind of kids who grew up down your block, maybe you were in the same grade with them, played one old cat with them on a vacant lot, Saturday nights you chased girls with them downtown at the drive-in, Sunday mornings you were in the same Bible class.

You went on to become a lawyer, or an insurance man, or a car dealer.

. . . Al and LeRoy Chester went on to become bank robbers.

* * *

-2-

It's half an hour after the armored truck was held up.

Back in FBI headquarters, deep in one of the busy offices where the machines chatter, and the phones ring, we pick up *Bert Hughes.* Gray-haired, hard-jawed veteran of many years of crime investigation. There may be plenty of younger men coming up through the ranks, but Bert shows no signs of slowing down yet. He can hold his own with any of them.

Right now he's staring at the teletype as the news comes in—long after the fact—the driver and his guard have been released out in a deserted field—their armored truck has disappeared, the holdup efficiently carried out by an unidentified gang, which has gotten away with a rich haul, estimated at more than six hundred thousand.

"Unidentified, hell!" says Bert putting down the bulletin. "It's got to be those boys. I've been watching them a long time—now they've finally gone and done it."

"You still hipped on those two?" asks one of his younger associates. "What makes you so sure it's them?"

"I've been in this business a long time," says Bert. "I go by smell. These two guys aren't dumb—but I've got one little edge on 'em. I know them—but they don't know *me.*"

Now we dissolve through, backward in time, to a quiet, semideserted main street in the Midwest, the kind of town where the farmers come in on the weekend to do their shopping, and the biggest excitement is whether or not the high-school basketball team will win the All County championship.

Young Al Chester pumps gas at the local station, strictly a dead-end job, but at nights, he does a lot of reading. His brother LeRoy, who's a good athlete, has found a job spreading sand from the back of the town truck during the winter. Summers, he works on the town roads.

It's a quiet summer night, and the two Chesters are lounging in the town square, opposite the local bank. They'd like to go down to the Elks Club dance, but they can't spare the price.

"You know something?" Al says to his brother. "We got nowheres to go but up."

"Agreed," says LeRoy. "Question is—how do we get there?"

We cut to the inside of the small local bank. A sleepy, quiet place, one teller, a short line of people waiting to put their money in . . . A bank which probably hasn't changed its ways since it was founded, forty, fifty years back . . .

*** *** ***

-66-

. . . It's early morning. As dawn breaks, we hear only the sound of crickets and tree toads. In the distance, we are shooting down toward the old farmhouse where the Chesters are holed up. In the driveway is their getaway car. A shadowy figure tiptoes up to it, bends down, and lets the air out of the front tire.

Then, as the sun begins to come up, we begin to see a ring of gleaming police cruisers all parked strategically around the farmhouse, the cops crouched behind the cars, wearing bullet-proof vests and shields, their guns at the ready.

Bert Hughes stands behind one of the cars, a bull-horn in hand. He holds up his hand for a signal—checks his watch—then he calls "Okay, boys—we've got you surrounded! Party's over—throw your guns out and come on out—no sense our blasting you, is there?"

Cut to the inside of the farmhouse.

We see the two Chesters, caught by surprise. Al nudges LeRoy, who carefully peeks out the window.

Panning shot, from their point of view, as we see all the law-enforcement forces lined up, their guns pointed at the house.

LeRoy turns to Al. "Looks like the whole damn U.S. Army out there."

"How the hell did they find us?" muses Al.

"Doesn't matter—the question is, what do we do next? You want to give up?" asks LeRoy.

Al shrugs. "You got a better idea?"

Hold for a long pause.

Then we cut back to the exterior, where Bert Hughes is waiting.

"Let's blast 'em!" mutters his second-in-command.

"No—hold it!" cautions Bert. Camera zooms in over his shoulder, and in the distance we see the farmhouse door cautiously open, two rifles are thrown out, then a submachine gun. Then, in the distance, we see a hand raise a white handkerchief.

Close up of Bert Hughes, tired, triumphant, as he watches the Chesters emerge. The police close in on the two.

Flanked by burly cops, the two unshaven desperadoes are led toward a waiting cruiser. They pass Bert, who steps forward, grinning. "Well, now," he says, "I've been waiting to meet up with you boys for a long time."

They stare at him, unable to figure out who he is.

"Been one of your fans for a long time," says Bert. "You don't know me, but I sure do know you. You had yourselves a real good run—while it lasted—but it's all over now, eh?"

"Not for good, it ain't," says Al, and spits on the ground.

As the two Chesters are led away, camera begins to pull back in a long shot, high above the scene, so high that finally the figures of the two gunmen are merely a pair of ants on the green landscape. Drawn by the sight, a crowd of spectators is watching as the Chesters are bundled into the cruiser. It drives away.

The crowd slowly begins to break up. Closing titles are superimposed over, and then we

FADE OUT.

* * *

chapter 8

—Stranger, I don't know where you hail from, or what's yore business here, but I'm a-warnin' you. This town ain't big enough for the both of us. Clear out of Ponca City by sundown.

LYING back in the Jacuzzi, Harry Elbert was relaxed, the bubbles flickering against his muscles, the tension at the back of his neck was ebbing, for the first time in days he was feeling good.

God knows he was entitled. He'd just beaten Joe Pollock, the surgeon, a pretty good player, 6–4, 7–5, and that after almost a month off the courts . . . these last weeks, he'd been so goddamned busy getting his new picture ready for the start date. Meetings, arguments, all the constant hassles, closing the deal with Vin DeLuca, cocky bastard whose agents had held him up for a 5-per-cent hunk out of the first dollar plus one mil up front, goniffs—but what the hell, DeLuca knew he was worth it, he knew DeLuca was worth it, the kid was the hottest piece of merchandise in the business today . . .

. . . But then he'd had to convince all the International-United boys, those killers from the conglomerate which owned the studio, hard-nosed slide rulers, all they knew from pictures was if the operation didn't show a ten-per-cent increase in net, compounded over last year, out, you could look for another job, that was the way old Mike Tudor had I-U set up, open up Mike's chest, you'd find a computer—three trips he'd had to make back East to convince Mike personally that he knew what he was doing, remaking a big classic Western with DeLuca, the Boston kid who still hadn't learned to ride a horse!

Westerns *had* to be the next big trend, he would be betting seven mil of I-U's money that he was right about *Cimmaron*. Disaster pictures were played out, who in hell could think of another way to scare people, the supernatural had been worked over too often, nobody wanted to do World War II, leave that to Joe Levine and his blockbuster (which might just go on its ass) sci-fi was too chancy unless you got something wild and way-out like *Star Wars,* you couldn't make a nickel with a comedy unless you found a pre-sold property, even then, a Broadway hit could bomb out, that left you detective stories—he'd thought of maybe remaking *Maltese Falcon* but the sonsofbitches who owned the rights weren't letting it go, that left the one open field nobody was looking at today, the Western. "I don't care about your age-group surveys," he'd told Tudor. "This is action, adventure, you can tie it in with the schools, it's American history at its finest, and for the Richard Dix part, I put in a guy so hot, all we have to do is announce he's gonna *belch,* and the people start tossing in money!"

". . . Okay, Harry, *if* you're right," said Tudor.

He didn't need to discuss the alternative. Harry understood the game plan at I-U. So did anybody else who survived there.

. . . He got out, showered, then toweled himself, glancing at his body in the locker-room mirror. All of his own hair, not too much gray, he didn't need one of those phony wigs everyone wore, stomach still relatively flat, he was still fit, not bad for anyone his age. The doctor had run him through all the tests last month, pronounced him in good shape, but had cautioned him maybe to slow down a little, maybe to take himself a little rest and relaxation?

Okay, he'd be going for a little of that now.

He glanced at his Cartier watch. 4:40—that gave him half an hour to get out to Brentwood, what a laugh, getting dressed now when five minutes after he arrived there, he'd be out of his clothes again and rolling on the bed with that crazy young English broad, Fiona. Just what the doctor ordered was Fiona, she and her educated tongue would take good care of him, a sexy creature he'd met on his last flight to London, warm and understanding, she dug middle-aged men, she flew as stewardess to London once a week, she brought him back Partagas No. 2 Cubans in her empty Tampax tubes, what more could a man want?

In his doeskin slacks and silk shirt, his bench-made Italian loafers, he pulled on his cashmere jacket. Let the rest of the town wear tailored jeans and embroidered denim shirts and all that silly crap—all those hard-driving young bastards who were nipping at his heels, screw 'em, Harry Elbert was still king of the hill, first cabin all the way, a class act—his last picture had done eleven mil domestic, would do nine foreign—let them try to do as well!

Stepping jauntily out of the locker room, sunglasses protecting his eyes against the bright sunlight, Harry came downstairs, walking past the glassed-in dining room, waved to a few of the old regulars who sat inside, schmoosing and playing gin, made his way past the open-air tables flanking the courts toward the club exit gate. There he stopped by the small office. Myrna, the operator on duty, smiled up from her switchboard. "Going home, Mr. Elbert?"

"No, back to the studio," he lied. "Anybody calls, tell 'em I'll be there, late meeting, okay, honey?" He had already arranged with his secretary to field all calls, even his wife—she was to report that he was in an emergency script meeting, unavailable, with Vin DeLuca and his manager. After seven he'd leave Fiona's place, he would head home, in time for whatever dull dinner party his wife was giving tonight.

As he came out of the club, headed for his Rolls, he spied a familiar figure coming toward him, tanned, slightly stooped, that loping walk, tennis sweater, and slouch hat—Perce Barnes.

No way to avoid speaking to him, he knew Perce was still around the club, poor sonofabitch gave lessons each morning here, but he hadn't run into him in years.

Amiably he thrust out his hand. "Hiya, Perce," he said.

Perce stopped, shifted the manila envelope from one arm to the other, then shook Harry's hand. Then, shyly, he grinned.

"Hey there, *Harry,*" he said. "You look terrific."

"You don't look so rotten yourself," said Harry. Which was true enough. Perce was lean, his eyes sharp behind the sunglasses, yeah, but what the hell, he was out on the courts every morning, what else did the bum have to do but to keep fit?

"Hear you're starting another big one," said Perce. "Good luck."

"Thanks, I'll need it," said Harry. "How're they hanging, Perce?" His eye went to the manila envelope. "Still hustling?"

"Not as well as you, Harry," said Perce. "But as a matter of fact, I'm glad I ran into you." He tapped the envelope. "Got something here that just might interest you—your kind of stuff. It's a story I ran across the other day, I've been tinkering with it and it's absolutely fascinating—"

"Yeah, sure," said Harry, anxious to cut the conversation short. "But right now my head's all wrapped up in my next, y'know—"

He began to walk purposefully toward his Rolls, hoping he'd shaken Perce, but Perce was following him. "It's the damndest crime story you ever read," he was saying. ". . . Two young farm boys who come out of the Midwest, end up working a big heist on a bank truck—then they're hunted down by the Feds—and it's all true—and I think I found the angle that makes it work—"

"—Sounds terrific," said Harry briefly. Christ, what a piece of junk—something right out of a Brynie Foy B, with Paul Kelly, or Lyle Talbot—poor Perce, he was really out of it—

"You really like it?" Perce asked hopefully. "I haven't shown it to anybody yet, but I could give you a copy—"

"No—not the kind of thing I'm looking for, old buddy," said Harry. Why couldn't he shake this character? "Maybe one of the young directors around town would go for it—"

He unlocked the front door, held it open so the air would flood the interior, these damn Rolls leather seats got so hot—Perce hung on. "Yeah, sure, Harry," he was saying, "but I don't know any of those guys, and they sure don't know *me*—"

"Ah, come on," said Harry, climbing into the Rolls, putting his key into the starter, "don't give me the humble bit, Perce, you're as good as you always were, find yourself a good agent and let him do the hustling—"

"My guy's been dead two years," said Perce. "Which of the guys around town do you recommend?"

"Go see Sam Grant, he's the hottest guy around—" said Harry as the Rolls engine purred softly into life.

"—Sam Grant?" said Perce. "He wouldn't even answer my call." He leaned across the window sill. "Unless—Harry, could I use your name?"

Harry hesitated.

"Old times?" Perce said, half smiling.

"Sure, what the hell, why not," said Harry expansively. He pressed the button which ran up the window electrically, he wanted the air-conditioning on, the glass rose up, shutting Perce off from further conversation. Before it did so, he added, "Remember, pal, it's what you got between the covers that counts."

Through the tinted glass window, he saw Perce smile and wave, his mouth forming the word *thanks*.

Harry backed up the Rolls carefully, then pulled it away from the curb. Damn—if he didn't get out of Beverly right away, he'd hit all that going-home traffic from UCLA on Sunset, that would make him late for Fiona, the one thing she didn't like was to be rushed.

Through his rear-view mirror he saw Perce, his manila envelope under his arm, one hand still raised in a wave.

. . . At least he'd shaken that poor character.

Wandering around town like a ghost, peddling some phony piece of junk. Didn't he know he was through, finished, deader than vaudeville? That was the trouble with all these bums, they never knew when to throw in the towel.

. . . But Perce had been pretty good once, hadn't he? Made good money, got his name on some good pictures.

. . . It could happen to you, too, Harry, said a small, chilling voice. *Cimmaron*—even *with* Vin DeLuca above the title—could bomb out, die, and if you don't come up with another big winner fast—after that, all of Tudor's hired guns are ready to shoot you down. Couple of years from now, that could be you, wandering around town, just like old Perce, peddling some dumb project out of a manila envelope.

"Forget it!" he snarled aloud, and snapped on the radio to turn on the stereo that would drive away his thoughts.

* * *

Perce stood in the sunlight and scribbled the name "Sam Grant" on his manila envelope.

Too late to call Grant's office tonight, tomorrow he'd do it first thing. Sam Grant was a powerhouse, a real dealer, he had big clients, directors and writers, six-figure people, he picked and chose the ones he wanted to handle. Using Harry Elbert's name would get his call through . . . after that, he had to go it alone.

. . . God, how he hated Harry Elbert's guts. Cocky bastard, for years he'd seen him around, at Guild meetings, or in restaurants, here at the club, Harry had hardly spoken.

Half an hour ago, if anybody had told him Harry had offered an intro to Sam Grant . . . He had no intention of pitching the Chester project to Harry, why, just the other night, when he'd spoken to the Chésters, it had been Al who'd brought up Harry's name, he'd mentioned that he knew Perce and Harry had once written a couple of pictures together (damn, that Al must spend his nights reading old copies of the *Hollywood Reporter!*) and when Al had suggested maybe Perce could bring their story to Harry, who was still producing, he'd abruptly turned Al off, sharply, "No, *not* Harry Elbert."

And yet, this afternoon, ten minutes ago, Harry had showed up here, he'd walked right up, stuck out his hand and shook Harry's, hadn't he? Had done a complete turnaround, stood there brown-nosing Elbert, running after him like some eager puppy, pitching the story to him, with no pride at all.

Pride? Who could afford pride?

First time in years, he had a script to hustle, a damned good piece of material, when you're hungry, screw pride. Harry was power.

What was that line he remembered, the one he'd learned back in the days when he'd done a job with that young Commie writer, Leo what was the last name?—the kid who'd kept trying to get him to join the party. "Remember this, Perce, the end justifies the means."

Okay, so Harry had tried to shake him, but he'd gotten somewhere, hadn't he, a knockdown to Sam Grant, with Harry's name attached, which Harry owed him—and if Grant took on the story because Perce had spent five minutes kissing Harry's ass—then damnit, Leo—(what the hell *was* his last name?)—*and* old Karl Marx—were right!

* * *

chapter 9

—Members of the board of Hazleton, Incorporated, may I introduce your new chairman.
—Good morning, gentlemen. I know you don't especially relish the idea of a female in this seat, but let me tell you something right now. Just because I'm a woman doesn't mean I don't know how to play rough. My granddaddy taught me every trick in the book. We're going to go after Big Jim Comerford, and we're not going to quit until we've gotten rid of him!
—Hear, hear!
—And one more thing. Don't let my powder and lipstick fool you. It's not make-up—it's war paint!

HE was into his second bourbon when Vera showed up at the apartment. "How did it go?" she asked.

"Lousy," he said.

She glanced at the open bottle. "I was hoping this was a celebration," she said. "What did Grant say?"

"Never got to see Grant," he said, dropping back into his easy chair. "My meeting was with a Miss Hastings, Miss Judith Hastings, or is it Ms.? I never know any more."

"She's from England," said Vera. "She's his Number Two, supposed to be very with it. Did she like the treatment? Or what?"

. . . Her office was high up, overlooking Beverly, the walls covered with modern-art prints, no desk, a large round glass table covered with books and manuscripts, she couldn't have been more than twenty-seven, twenty-eight, another young one. Trimly turned out, blonde, very tall, large tinted glasses, terribly polite, smoking long cigarillos, she obviously wasn't going to waste any time, this was her 3:00 P.M. and her secretary had warned him Miss Hastings had a 4:00—(nobody had mentioned lunch, lunch was when you made a deal, not when you discussed material).

She was sorry she'd kept him waiting, but she had a date in the Valley and the bloody traffic had been frightful, she'd just this moment gotten back, the day was running late, and she expected he'd like to get on with it, correct?

"Is Sam Grant going to sit in?" asked Perce.

No, unfortunately he was on his way to New York, but he'd turned Perce's treatment over to her, and she was prepared to discuss it.

"Fine, let's discuss," said Perce.

"You once worked with Harry Elbert," she remarked.

"That was a long time back," said Perce.

"Has he seen this treatment?" she asked.

". . . No, we've discussed it," said Perce, "but he hasn't read it." He didn't plan to go into the length of the discussion.

"May I be completely blunt, Mr. Barnes?" she asked. "I—" Her phone buzzed. She smiled, picked up the phone. "Yes," she said. "Yes. *Yes*. No. Absolutely not, Ozzie, my luv. We simply will not go below one hundred for it, no trading, that is the bottom line. All right, poppet, you call me back. I shall be here." She hung up, and then tapped his manuscript with a pencil.

"This story," she said. "Do I have to explain to you that there is no market whatsoever for it in its present state?"

"It's a treatment," he said. "What I figure is, if somebody reads it, and is interested, then we work out a deal—"

She shook her head. "Never mind what you figured," she said. "Totally unrealistic. The simple fact is, no one will read it until and unless there is a finished screenplay."

"How about if we got a star interested?" he asked.

"Stars," said Miss Hastings, "do not read. Directors read screenplays. If they like the script, they explain it to the star. There are five bankable stars in this town, and they are having film scripts explained to them every day. You have here a true story about two bank robbers who end up robbing a money van, being captured, and sent off to prison by an old detective who follows them. I won't say it doesn't have its possibilities—"

"Thank you," he murmured, trying to keep his temper down.

"—But not in this form, not at all," she said. "Now, may I ask you a personal question?"

Her phone buzzed again, she smiled, and picked it up. "Yes? Ah, it's you, Carlo. Are you in Rome? . . . Oh, you're in London. Sam expects to see you in New York this week about that project for Irwin and Bobby, and if we can put the pieces together, we might, I stress the word might, have a deal with Danny, provided, of course, that you guarantee the overrides above six mil. Will you get in touch with Sam at the Regency the minute you get in? Good. *Ciao!*"

She hung up, made a note on her pad, and lit another cigarillo.

"Where were we?"

"You were about to ask me a personal question," said Perce.

"So I was," she said. She stared at him through the fragrant blue smoke. "Tell me, how married are you to this material?"

Her question caught him off base. "I don't get you."

"Are you prepared to spend three months doing the screenplay?" she asked.

It was the question he'd been ducking all along. Three months locked up in his apartment, or wherever, hammering away at the screenplay, it was a helluva investment in time and effort—up to now he'd been hedging his bet, hoping the treatment would get the project off the ground—

"Would you consider, pray, allowing someone else to take a crack at the screenplay?" she asked.

"You mean, with me?" he asked, confused.

"I haven't anything specific in mind yet," she told him. "But bear in mind that this office does have ties with some rather talented directors, as well as writers—and it is my thought that perhaps one of them might be interested in taking over this material, and shaping it to fit his own particular style—his own execution."

Like the blank film coming out of a Polaroid, the outlines of the picture were emerging.

"Without me," he said.

"Essentially, yes," she said. "Of course, there would certainly have to be some sort of an arrangement made, by which you and those other two—" She glanced at his title page.

"—the Chesters," he said.

"Ah, yes. The Chesters. The three of you would eventually share in whatever became of the screenplay."

The picture was much clearer now.

"You've got somebody who wants to buy the treatment?"

Miss Hastings smiled briefly. "Hold on, I'm not proposing any sale by you, here and now. Mind you, I couldn't represent you and any of my own clients, that's unethical. But should you retain your own lawyer, say, I could imagine some sort of a deal whereby, *if* one of our people liked it, we could make some arrangement for an option, up front. But that's only if one liked it."

"And one does like it, doesn't one?" Perce asked.

She ignored his sarcasm. Picked up a pen and jotted some figures down on her pad. "Let's say, one thousand dollars down on signing, a one year option, the one thousand to be applied against a split of the final sale of the package, you and your friends could share, say, twenty per cent of the final price, up to a ceiling of twenty-five thousand dollars. How does that strike you?"

"It stinks," said Perce. He was becoming so angry that his hands were shaking.

"Mr. Barnes," she replied impassively, "there are people all over this business who'd jump at the chance to deal with one of Sam Grant's clients. Be realistic."

"Lady, I'm realistic as hell," he said. "Three of us split a grand for a year's option? It wouldn't even pay the lawyer's fee for drawing up the papers—"

She glanced at the digital clock on her desk. "Mr. Barnes, you're a capable writer, I'm sure," she said, "but you haven't had a screen credit in some time now, have you? Whoever takes this material on is doing so on pure speculation. Perhaps we could get the option up to fifteen hundred dollars but that's only an educated guess on my part."

Sharks came in all sizes and shapes, but this was the first time he'd ever encountered one who spoke like Deborah Kerr.

"No deal," he told her.

She shrugged. "You're being dreadfully hasty, aren't you?"

"No—realistic," he said.

"I always say, ten per cent of something is better than a hundred per cent of nothing," said Miss Hastings.

"Sure you do," said Perce. "Listen, honey, don't try hustling a hustler. I was in this business while you were still in your goddamn diapers—and producers were pulling this kind of shit on me while you were still finger painting. This is the first place I've even showed this story to anybody—you don't think I'm going to give it away, do you?"

"Please don't get excited," said Miss Hastings.

"I'm not excited!" he said.

"Your face is quite white," she said.

"Don't worry—I'm not going to have a heart attack here in your elegant office," he said. "You'd probably charge me rent for the use of the sofa!"

"You'll have to excuse me," said Miss Hastings, rising. She reached across the table, his treatment in her hand. "I have some-one who's due in just now. Should you want to discuss this further, just give my secretary a call."

She was fully a head taller than he. "Meanwhile," she added, as she ushered him to the door, "I hope you understand what I meant about being realistic."

"I got your message loud and clear," he said. "You don't think I can write this screenplay."

"*You* said that, not I," said Miss Hastings. "Should you change your mind, do give me a tinkle. But don't wait too long, and please do not go shopping this material around elsewhere. We do not like dealing in secondhand."

Her office door closed, and he was back in the waiting room.

. . . He strode down the impersonal hall to the Muzaked elevator, dropped fourteen floors to the subbasement parking garage, wandered through the cavern searching for his Caddy, found it at last, and got into the front seat. In the glove compartment he kept a small plastic bottle of bourbon. Only after he'd had a stiff swallow did he cease trembling, felt the rage and frustration at that Limey bitch subside into a stubborn, dull ache.

"So what the hell are you depressed about?" asked Vera. "Think positive. If she liked it enough to try and steal it, then the story must be good."

"Yeah, it's ten per cent of something," said Perce. "I break my ass on it, then she scoops it up, gets some hot-shot genius of hers to write a screenplay, they make a package—and where do I end up? El Shafto!''

''Then *you* write the screenplay,'' she suggested.

. . . How could he admit to her that after all the years of staring out the window at the broads while somebody else sat at the typewriter, turning out the pages, he had no faith that he could go the distance. Treatments, anybody could knock one out . . . but 150, 160 pages of screenplay? Too chancy.

''For free?'' he demanded.

Vera glared at him. ''Oh, face it, Perce,'' she said. ''Nobody is going to drop money in your lap to underwrite this project—unless perhaps you could get to public television, or interest the Ford Foundation in the terrible plight of the ex-convict in our modern society—''

''That's it,'' he said, and poured himself another inch of bourbon. In his best imitation of Johnny Trump, he said, ''Oh, hi there, chaps, I'm Perce Barnes, remember me, I haven't had a credit in *years,* but I do have this marvelous notion here for a perfectly dandy picture—would you mind going down to the computer and punching out an amusing little check—''

''Shut up a minute,'' she said.

''And then I'll come back next week with three pounds of perfectly marvelous dialogue.''

''Shut up!'' she insisted.

''Why the hell should I?''

''Because I'm thinking!'' she snapped.

''Be my guest,'' he muttered, and downed the bourbon while she paced up and down his small room.

Next door, the idiot had his stereo on, and the thump-thump filled the air.

She came over and stood before him, and now she was smiling.

''I get a lot of money for this,'' she said, ''but for you, I'll take a deferment. If it works, you can cut me in for ten per cent. Deal?''

''Ten per cent of what?''

''Ten per cent of what you make when I finish selling your script.'' She held out her hand. ''Deal?''

He blinked at her. She was obviously serious.

"Come on," she said. "What does it cost you? Right now you're nowhere. *I* can get you somewhere. Ten per cent."

"You sound like that English cunt," he muttered. " 'Ten per cent of something is worth more than a hundred per cent of nothing, ducks.' "

"Absolutely right," she said. "You don't have to listen to me. You can sit here and slop up bourbon and get up tomorrow and give your tennis lessons, and shlep your treatment around town and get yourself put down a few more times, or you can make a deal with me to get you out of the basement, which is where you are."

"You know something?" said Perce. "Now you sound just like old Roz Russell, in the sixth reel. Don't give me that speech—we used to *write* it—"

"*I* know how to sell you," said Vera. "You and your anecdotes about the golden age of Tinseltown, and Al and LeRoy, those two losers and their saga of unsuccessful crime—you've got a pretty good idea in that treatment, but that's only the beginning. We have got to make them want it."

". . . You forgot to call me Buster," he said.

"Oh, shit," said Vera disgustedly. "One more crack like that and you can handle the whole campaign on your own. Badly." She shook her head. "What *is* it with you? Are you determined to stay a loser?"

"Could be," he admitted.

"Then why the hell did you start this in the first place?"

He shrugged. "I guess I got carried away, ma'am."

Vera picked up her purse.

"I'm going out to have some dinner," she announced. "Do you want to come along, or would you rather sit here in the silence of your lonely room and remember your halcyon days at Metro?"

"No," he said, getting up from his chair. "If you promise to stop lecturing me, I will feed you. Must I wait until the main course, or can I have a smell of your magic formula now, Madame Curie?"

"Why not?" she said. "The secret word is a common, ordinary word, used around the house. The secret word is media exposure."

"Oh, heavens," he said, "you're going to make *me* a star?"

"For ten per cent," said Vera.

He locked the apartment door.

"Will you settle for the dinner?" he asked.

"I'm serious," she said. "Tomorrow morning, I'm having a letter drawn up, and you're going to sign it."

"Did anyone ever tell you that you're beautiful when you're angry?" he asked.

"If your dialogue isn't better than that," said Vera as she went down the stairs, "we'd better quit now."

* * *

chapter 10

MOVIELAND JOTTINGS

. . . Vet film scribe Perce Barnes, lately occupied with his work on the courts (tennis, not legal), has decided to put aside his racquet temporarily to return to the typewriter. Subject had to be something special to lure back Perce, and it is; story is a true-crime epic, working title *Three Down, Two Left Standing*. Barnes describes it as a blend of *cinéma vérité* and Rififi-type material, out of the headlines of the 1950s, a hot scene in today's market.

* * *

YOUR DAILY REPORTER

. . . Burning up the long-distance cables to Rome, vet screenwriter Perce Barnes, who is readying a true-crime saga based on the exploits of Al and LeRoy Chester, Midwestern outlaws of the fifties, and will airmail script to ace Italian director Gianno Mannani, who has a yen to make a film here in the U.S., with foreign coin . . .

* * *

"Gianno Mannani?" he asked that night. "Who the hell is *he?*"

"Who knows?" said Vera. "I made him up. The story got printed, didn't it?"

* * *

LITERATI DOINGS

. . . An interesting deal is shaping up, one which has N.Y. publishers' scouts buzzing. Long-time screenwriter Perce Barnes is at work on the true-story saga of Al and LeRoy Chester, two ex-convicts who led law-and-order authorities a merry chase in the Midwest during the fifties. Barnes, who has a string of credits dating back to that same era, feels that the Chester material is particularly right for today's book market. "There's a trend away from the wave of occult, and hard-core porn, and political memoirs we've been swamped with lately,'' he told us. ''I've got film interest already, but I've got my sights set on a pre-production book deal, hard-cover and paperback, to coincide with a film release.''

Project bears the title *Three Down, Two Left Standing,* and Barnes is being understandably coy about letting his work-in-progress out until he has assembled all the elements . . .

''Coy, my ass,'' said Perce. ''If a book publisher walked in the door, I'd kiss him on both cheeks.''

''That won't happen for a while,'' said Vera. ''I think first we better get some talk-show exposure. You're pretty glib, but how about the Chesters? Can they talk?''

''You want *them?*'' he asked. ''What would they talk about?''

''. . . It would probably be about how crime does not pay.''

''Just send a crew downtown and shoot them where they're living,'' said Perce. ''They won't need to say anything.''

''This won't be a Barbara Walters visit,'' said Vera. ''I've got a client does an all-night talk show on ABC, I think I can sell them to her, but you'll have to get them lined up first. *Can* they talk?''

''I don't know about LeRoy,'' he mused. ''But his brother Al can probably spiel a good line.''

''Right, then you set it up,'' she said. ''Then I'll take it from there.''

''You're really rolling, aren't you?'' he asked.

''Just earning my ten per cent,'' she told him.

Mrs. Tabori rapped on the door. ''You got a call on the phone,'' she announced. ''Some guy named Barnes wants you.''

Al Chester roused himself from the bed. ''Thank you, ma'am,'' he called, and emerged from the furnished room, which was at the rear of the old mission-type bungalow.

The landlady, her hair in pink plastic curlers, was a plumpish female in a halter top and pedal pushers which strained against her Rubenesque shape. He smiled politely as he passed her on the way to the pay phone.

''Hi, Perce, old partner,'' he said. ''How's the deal coming? Sell it yet?''

He nodded. ''Yeah, I'm sure it takes time. Uh huh . . .''

He listened, as Perce outlined the reason for his call.

"Radio show?" he said. "Well . . . I dunno about LeRoy. He work nights, y'know, and the people might not be too pleased about him takin' off two or three hours like that . . . Me alone? Oh, with you . . . What would we be talking about?"

Perce continued to explain.

"You think if we talk about that it'll help? Uh huh . . . Mmm. Well now, is there any money in this?" asked Al. "Sure could use a little, you know? Mmm. Well," he sighed, "I guess it couldn't hurt us to try. When's it gonna be? . . . Okay, I'll wait to hear from you. Thanks for calling, partner."

He hung up.

Mrs. Tabori had remained in the hallway throughout the call.

"Did I hear right?" she asked. "You going on the radio?"

"Looks that way," said Al.

"Hmph," said Mrs. Tabori, impressed. "You never told me you was a celebrity."

Al smiled. "That's stretching it a little," he said.

"They don't interview people unless they're important," she said. "What did you do?"

"What we did was a long time back," said Al.

He walked down the hall to his room, closed the door, and stretched out on the bed again. In another hour he was due to go over to the gas station and spend eight hours at work there; that gave him half an hour in which to doze.

There was another rap on the door. Sighing, Al got up and reopened it.

"Tell the truth now," said Mrs. Tabori. "What *did* you do? I never had tenants that was on the radio before."

". . . Okay," said Al finally. "Guess you're gonna hear it on the radio, so I might as well tell you. Me and my brother LeRoy was involved in some robberies, way back when."

Mrs. Tabori's eyes widened. "You . . . you wouldn't crap me, now, would you?" she said. "I mean, you and your brother are such polite . . . clean people. I . . . I never figured you for—"

"For what?" Al asked her.

"—For—for outlaws," she gasped.

"We're inlaws now," said Al. "Been inside, paid our debt to so-ciety, if that's what's bothering you."

He returned to his bed, stretched out, watching her.

Mrs. Tabori remained by the door.

". . . How long were you and your brother . . . in?" she asked.

"Longer than I like to remember," he said.

". . . What'd you *do* all that time?" she demanded.

"Waited to get out," said Al. "Hell, what else was there to do?"

Mrs. Tabori continued to stare at him.

"Anything else you want to know?" he asked. "Go ahead and ask."

". . . Say . . . is it true what they say, about jail?" she asked. "I mean, what you read all the time?"

"What do they say?"

". . . Well, you know," said Mrs. Tabori, her eyes suddenly gleaming with interest. She eyed Al. "I mean, all that stuff about . . . men, being locked up together with . . . men."

Al shrugged.

"Sure," he told her. "That happens. What in hell else would you expect? Man stays a man—even when he's locked up like some damn animal." The barest flicker of a smile appeared on his face. "Okay?"

Finally Mrs. Tabori spoke again. ". . . You don't look like a . . ."

She stopped. "Look like a what?" he teased.

"You know. One of them . . . gays."

". . . Depends on the time and place," said Al, his grin widening. "If you mean, would I want a woman now, the answer is, I would."

He sat up.

"Don't you talk dirty to me," she warned.

"You started it," he told her, moving off the bed.

"Where are you going?" asked Mrs. Tabori, and backed away.

"Nowhere," said Al. As he went to the door, he brushed against her, and she recoiled. He closed the door, snapped the lock.

Then he moved back toward her. ''That's so we won't be interrupted.'' he told her.

Mrs. Tabori was breathing heavily now. ''. . . You're taking a hell of a lot for granted,'' she said rapidly. ''What if I was to scream rape? And you an ex-con—''

''—Okay, then,'' he said softly, and moved toward her. ''You can open that door and go right out, now. I won't stop you. But then you'll never know about me, will you?''

He put his arms around her. ''. . . I don't know as I give a damn,'' said Mrs. Tabori.

His hands were on her now, stroking her rear, clawing at the ample flesh. ''. . . The hell you don't,'' he crooned, pushing her backward toward his rumpled bed.

''. . . Pull the shade down,'' she ordered, as he fell upon her.

* * *

chapter 11

12:09 A.M.

—It's 12:09, the shank of the evening here at KIA; your all-night station, and this is your phone friend, Rita Kelsey, the show is called "Rapping with Rita," we're going into our second hour, tonight we're delighted to be chatting with Perce Barnes, Perce is an ace screenwriter who's got a list of credits as long as, well, the L.A. phone book, and next to him is Perce's good friend here, Mr. Al Chester, the former bank robber, who's just finished writing a book about his experiences in crime, and who's been telling us all how it feels to be out of jail and free as a bird, after all those long years he and his brother spent behind bars, and right after these messages from a few of our really faithful and fine sponsors, I'm going to throw open the phone lines, and we're going to take calls, you'll get to ask these men any kind of question, don't use names, please, call us at seven eight seven two nine nine one, keep trying, call in and rap with Rita . . . so start dialing now, and if you hang on, well, remember, hang *in!* This is a special message for the ladies in the audience, girls, have you got a problem with unwanted hair? Well, as of tonight, you don't need to worry about it any longer . . .

12:16 A.M.

—and don't forget, when Bert Kanter at Kanter's Fur-Arama says he's having a sale, he's not kidding. Kanter's Fur-Arama, one eight nine eight eight Pico Boulevard, and now, let's start taking those calls, okay, Perce Barnes, and Al Chester?

—Yes, sure, Rita.

—How about you, Al, you holding up okay at this late hour?

—Doing just fine, ma'am. Enjoying it.

—Oh, I love him, he's so polite. But I only have the nicest people on this show—Line One, you're on. Rapping with Rita, hello, don't use personal names, speak up—

—Hello, Rita? I've been listening to your program tonight? I just want to say, if you believe in the teachings of the Good Book—which says "thou shalt not steal"?

—What's your point, ma'am?

—Well, ah, it also says "an eye for an eye"? And I think your guest tonight, Mr. Chester? He's been demonstrating to the unbelievers in the audience that the Good Book really works, do you know what I'm saying?

—Yes, indeed, you're absolutely right, thank you for calling and keep in touch. Line Two? You're on, no personal names, speak up—

—Hello. Am I on the radio?

—Yes, indeed you are, what's your question?

—This fella Barnes there, uh, on this point he was making earlier, that this story proves that crime does not pay, well, can I ask you, what are you trying to make it do now? I mean, aren't you and this fella Chester out to make it pay?

—Perce, you want to answer that?

—Sure. Okay, Mr. Chester and his brother stand to make a certain amount of money, but I'm sure you'd agree that anybody who sold his life story to a producer should get something in return, shouldn't he?

—Yes, but, uh, what I'm saying is, if he hadn't've been a criminal, nobody would be interested in his story in the first place, would they?

—Al, you want to answer that?

—Sure, ma'am, I don't mind answering. I don't figure to get rich from this show Mr. Barnes is writing, and what we was really interested in, mainly, was to get the message across about how we wasted most of our lives trying—

—Come on, you don't expect us to believe that, do you? Movies don't have messages, they're just made to make money, and who's kidding—

—Nobody's kidding anybody, thank you for calling in, honey. Rapping with Rita, we're here to listen to you out there and to let you have a chance to express your opinions, Line One, you're on the air, no personal names, please—

—Hello?

—Speak a little louder, honey?

—Is the man who robbed that there truck still there?

—Yes, indeed, you mean Al Chester. He's waiting for your question.

—Uh, Mr. Chester, have you ever killed a man?

—No. I can't say's I have.

—Well, how would you feel about it if you had?

—Um, I don't rightly know.

—Do you condone the taking of human life?

—I don't believe I do.

—In other words, if you had killed somebody in your career of crime, say, then you'd be against the death penalty as punishment for your crime, am I right?

—But I just told you, ma'am, I never did kill nobody.

—But people were killed—I mean, you said, when the authorities tracked you all down, three of your gang were killed, and in a way, that makes you responsible for those deaths, because it was your idea to do those robberies in the first place—

—Listen, I don't see the point of this question.

—I'm not asking *you,* Mr. Barnes—I'm asking your partner in crime, Mr. Chester—

—He's not my partner in crime, he's a man whose story I'm turning into a screenplay, and I don't see what the death penalty has to do with anything Al's done!

—You won't accept the truth, will you? Just remember, what it said up there on the wall, Mene Mene Tekel, Upharsin—and it's just as valid today as it ever was!

—Yes, I'm sure it is, cool it down, folks, you're talking with Al Chester and Perce Barnes, and before we take any more calls, I'd like to pause here for a couple of messages from some of the wonderful people who make it possible for this show to go on the air from 11:00 to 4:00 A.M.—Say, when was the last time you had yourself a real lip-smacking, stick-to-your-ribs, made-like-Mom-used-to . . .

12:31 A.M.

12:39 A.M.

—and don't forget, if you do get to Mike Morris Leisure Vehicle Village, after you've made your deal with Mike, tell Mike it was Rita who sent you, and you'll get an extra one per cent off on the best deal you ever made there! We're taking calls here, Line One is open, hello, Rapping with Rita, you're on the air, no personal names please—

—Is Mr. Chester still there?

—Yessir, I'm here.

—Mr. Chester, I'd like to ask you how you feel about gun control?

—Beg your pardon, sir?

—Wouldn't you agree that it's people like you that make owning one's own gun not only necessary, but absolutely . . . vital to protect my wife and children?

—Well, now, you see, I never was out to hurt anybody—

—But you had a gun in your hand and that meant you could kill me, say, if I just happened to be there the day you robbed that truck—and now we've got all these crackpot bleeding hearts and phony liberals trying to legislate us out of our natural, God-given American right to bear arms—if they're successful, then you could kill me, couldn't you?

—No, I don't have no gun!

—This man hasn't had a gun in his hand for over twenty years, and I resent the implication!

—Oh, ho, you're another one of those Commie—

—Thanks for calling, we're Rapping with Rita, talking here tonight with Perce Barnes and Al Chester, two fine men here. You all right, Perce? You look a little upset.

—I'm all right. I guess I think some of these questions are a little off base, you know what I mean?

—Ah, come on, Perce, a bright writer like you, you know how to handle them, this is the great American audience here, letting you know where it's all at. That's why we open these lines every night, so Mr. and Mrs. America can be heard. Remember what old Harry Truman said, "If you can't stand the heat, get out of the kitchen," well, we're here in the kitchen, and we're calling in Line Two—

—Could we please stick to the movie project, then?

—Oh, no, I never censor my audience, Perce. That wouldn't be fair to them. This is their forum, come in, Line Two?

—Um, is this that dude Barnes?

—I'm here.

—Okay, ah've been listening to you and your buddy tonight and you been giving us that jive about crime don't pay, and I want to ask *you,* man—what *kind* of crime don't pay? Now we got us here in Covina this here store run by—

—Ah, ah, no personal names, please—

—Ah can't mention his name, so okay, they knows who I'm talkin' about, these people sells furniture, they call it the Easy Payment Plan and all that jive, you dig? So me and my wife, we got us there a three-piece bedroom sweet, they call it their Monster Value of the Month, and it's been here in our place lessn' two weeks, and that mother—

—Rapping with Rita, thanks for calling, we're running a little short of time, but we're here to take your calls and listen to your point of view, Line One, no personal names, please, hello.

—Hello! I'm just calling to ask you how much longer we're going to be subjected to this hypocrisy? I mean, here you are, a public radio station, licensed by the FCC, and you're giving all this absolutely free air time to a convicted desperado, who freely confesses that his only aim in life was to rob and steal from honest, hard-working citizens—

—Just a minute, I'd like to remind you that Mr. Chester has spent many years in prison, repaying his debt to society—

—And the way I see it, it's all part of a massive conspiracy to poison the minds of the American people!

—Conspiracy?

—Don't interrupt. *I'm* on now. This Mr. Barnes, who says he's going to make a motion picture glorifying these hoodlums—

—I never said I was going to glorify them!

—Don't interrupt! You're going to make them into heroes, and little children with impressionable minds will be subjected to this garbage—

—Keep your kids home from the theater, then—

—Oh, very funny, Mr. Barnes. You know I'm on to you, and

the rest of your ilk, those foreigners who came here and seized control of the means of communication, and now you're all perpetrating smut and filth, selling your trash at high prices and getting rich at the expense of the minds of Americans—

—Listen, Rita, do we have to listen to this hysterical nonsense?

—Ah, hah! You see, the man admits his guilt! Calls me a hysteric, as if that explains what he's up to! "Methinks he doth protest too much." That's Shakespeare, someone you probably never heard of, did you, Barnes? And by the way, is Barnes your *real* name?

—Thanks for calling, this is Rapping with Rita, we're on the air to find out if you're there, come in, Line Two, no personal names, please—

—I would like to ask a question.

—Shoot, which of our guests do you want to answer it?

—To the Señor Barnes. You are going to make this picture?

—I certainly hope so.

—If it was two Chicanos who had been sent to the prison, would you be interested in their story?

—Ah, I don't really know.

—I thought not. Nobody gives a damn about the Chicanos—

—Sorry, no profanity, thanks for calling, it's Rapping with Rita, Line One, and gang, please watch the language—hello?

—Hello, Rita, I've been hanging on for hours, but it was worth it, I've got a question I'd like to ask Mr. Barnes, is he still there?

—Yeah, I'm here, but I'm not sure how much longer.

—Mr. Barnes, do you expect us to believe all this?

—Believe what, ma'am?

—Well, this whole number about the two bank robbers who've had a career of crime, and now they've come out of jail, and they're pure in heart, and cleansed, and you're going to make a movie out of their story, right, and it'll probably star Paul Newman, or Dustin Hoffman, or Walter Matthau—

—All I can say is, I certainly hope you're right.

—That's exactly what I mean. Exactly! You're just getting a movie out of this, whether the story is true or not—

—Of course the story's true!

—I don't even care if it is, what I'm saying is, you could have made it all up, you're a writer, and then found these two men, and gotten them to agree to go along with it, and nobody would ever be the wiser, would they?

—Ah, come on, lady, I don't have to sit here and listen to this. If you don't believe that Al and LeRoy Chester were in jail for armed robbery, all you have to do is to go back to the federal penitentiary where they were incarcerated, all those years—

—Don't I seem to remember that when that man, what was his name, Julius, or Murray—oh, no, Irving . . .

—Irving who?

—When he was doing the book on Howard Hughes, and stealing all that money, didn't he have everybody absolutely believing he was on the up and up—

—You're accusing *me* of being a swindler?

—Oh, I never said that, all I'm asking is, uh, how do we know, for sure—

—How do you know I didn't come off a flying saucer from Mars, and that Al and LeRoy and I are really from outer space?

—Now you're not answering my question, Mr. Barnes—

—No, and I'm not going to, I don't have to sit here at one in the morning and be polite to every kook in southern California—

—Rapping with Rita, hold it a minute now, Perce, don't get so steamed up, after all, the lady's entitled to her opinion, she's one of my faithful listeners—

—You keep her, Rita!

—Heh, heh, Perce, I do love your sarcasm, but I guess that's the sort of sardonic wit that made you a great screenwriter back in the old days—

—Thanks a lot, the lady gets on the phone and calls me a swindler, now you're treating me like a fugitive from the Motion Picture Country Home—and how about Al here, he has to come here and be subjected to this crap—

—Now come on, Perce, you came here of your own free will—

—and I can leave, too! And you can take this goddamn show and—

1:14:30
1:14:48 (Dead Air)

1:14:48

—Well now, we certainly got ourselves a nice, hot little argument here, didn't we? That's why people keep on tuning in to Rapping with Rita, night after night, you know where we are, ninety-nine on your dial, KIA, where it all happens, and just before we take some more calls, here's another message. Folks, has your plumbing been giving you problems? I don't mean your old ticker or your stomach, I mean those pipes you live with. Well, your troubles are over, gang, the minute you call National Home Consultants, they'll send a radio-controlled truck over to you, the man will ride to the rescue, when he gets through, that old bathroom of yours will purr like a kitten—

1:17

—Hi, there, we're Rapping with Rita, Line Two, you're on the air, no personal names, please, go ahead—

—Rita? Can I ask that movie writer a question? Is he the same guy who wrote a picture called *Aces, Back to Back* in nineteen forty-nine, with Dan Duryea and Peggy Dow . . . ?

—I wouldn't know, friend, he isn't here any more, he and his friend have gone home.

—Shucks, I wanted to ask him what ever happened to Peggy Dow.

—Call him up, he must be in the phone book. Line One, you're on the air, no personal names please—

—Hello, Rita, I want to ask you, did that man who was just on with you say he was off a flying saucer?

—No, honey he just behaved like it, heh, heh, what else can I tell you? . . .

* * *

chapter 12

—Your Honor! I object! The prosecution is trying to make my client out to be no better than a common criminal! This girl is a fine young woman's who's been . . .
—Objection overruled!
—But your Honor . . .
—One more word out of you, Mr. Hanson, and I'll have you cited for contempt of court!

AL wolfed down his Kingburger with Trimmins with obvious pleasure. Perce sipped his tea; at this hour, he knew better than to inflict food on himself.

"I'm sorry about tonight," he said. "You didn't really need to come out and have all that shit dumped on you."

"Hell, I don't mind," said Al, dousing his French fries with catsup. "Me'n LeRoy have been through much worse in our time."

He did not elaborate further, but went on eating.

"But it was dumb, walking out on her like that," said Perce. He was angry at himself for having behaved so childishly. "I shouldn't have let that broad get on my nerves."

"She's got her own hustle, just like everybody else," said Al. "We was out to make a little noise. Maybe we did. If we did, then it was a trade-off." He wiped his lips with a napkin. "Like the guy said, it don't matter so long as they spell your name right. Tell the truth, I kind of enjoyed it."

"You're a ham at heart, right?" said Perce, picking up the check. It was the least he could do.

"Could be," grinned Al. "Gives you a funny feeling, sitting there in that ratty little place, hearing people call in from all over, finding out what they think."

"You're an optimist," said Perce. "Most of 'em don't. I used to go into meetings with producers all the time, and I got sick and tired of hearing them tell me that the average mental age of the audience is around twelve. I'd always argue with them. After tonight, I'm not so sure . . ."

"Everybody's born with the same set of brains," said Al, yawning. "It's what you do with 'em that counts. I found that out the hard way. Me, I'm using mine to pump gas."

"Not for long, I hope," said Perce.

. . . What else could he say?

He dropped Al off outside the bungalow where the two brothers were renting a room, promising to keep in touch. Which made it nearly three in the morning before he got home. He wasn't sleepy, but he needed the rest, so he took half a Valium and climbed into bed, and finally slept.

When the phone rang, waking him, it was nearly eight.

"Good morning, Mighty Mouth," said Vera.

"Oh, Christ, you heard it," he said, through a fog of sleep.

"I stayed up all the way," she said. "Right up till the memorable moment when you blew your stack."

"That was dumb," he said, "shouldn't have let that broad get to me."

"You did fine," she told him. "Listen to me. You're going to be getting some calls today—"

"Calls about what?"

"After your performance last night, you're liable to be instant news, and we can keep the pot boiling for a while. Now wake up, I want to prime you on what to say next," she said. "If we play this right, we might just make a little hay out of what happened—"

"Hay for who? That bitch who sat there, letting the world insult me—"

"She's a client who pays," said Vera pointedly.

"You get ten per cent," he said. "*I'm* the one who had to sit there and listen to all those garbage phone calls, remember?"

"You think they were so easy to arrange?" she asked. "How many people do you think I know who stay up that late?"

"Hey . . ." said Perce, sitting up in bed. "*Hey*—are you—you mean—"

"Good, you're awake," said Vera. "Pay attention, now . . ."

VARIETY

PROD-WRITER DOES WALK
BLASTS TALK SHOW

Listeners who stayed up night before last to listen to "Rapping with Rita," KIA talk show, were treated to a display of pyrotechnics on the part of guest, vet scribe Perce Barnes. He and fellow guest Al Chester, one-time bank robber now gone straight, came on show to discuss crime-does-not-pay aspects of their new project, film *Three Down, Two Left Standing,* based on crime exploits of Chester and his brother LeRoy. Late-night discussion began to heat up when various callers phoned in to cast doubts on validity of the Chester saga. After fielding a succession of such early A.M. calls, Barnes protested to hostess Rita Kelsey about verbal abuse. Eventually Chester and Barnes took a walk, leaving hostess Kelsey with no guests for rest of her four-hour stanza.

Pressed for her side of brouhaha, Miss Kelsey told *Variety* she feels entire episode is forgettable. "Some of our guests can take the flak, some can't," she said. "If a few of the callers got under Mr. Barnes' skin, it's his privilege to leave."

Barnes feels different. "My friend Al Chester has certainly paid his debt to society," he told *Variety,* "and nobody should ask him to sit all night in that studio, for free, yet, and take that kind of hate that irresponsible listeners were tossing on him. We heard from anti-Semites, right-wingers, and gun lobbyists, people urging the restoration of the death penalty, the whole works. Some of what I heard really frightened me. Okay, it's an open forum, but my question is, how far does freedom of the airwaves extend? Should it include the right to slander a man who's paid his dues to society, and who's out now, trying to keep kids from making the same mistake? That's what the Chester brothers and I want to tell the world, and maybe the world just doesn't want to give them the chance to get their anti-violence message across."

Queried as to any further radio and TV appearances to be skedded for Al and LeRoy Chester, Barnes was dubious. "After this appearance, obviously nobody else will want them to be heard. Society is very tough on the ex-con. Doesn't what happened on KIA prove that?"

Once that appeared, the phone calls began.

Afternoons, at all hours of the night, they reached him, his damn number was in the book so they could all get through, the usual run of nuts, an old man who shouted obscenities at him, a woman who wanted to meet Al, an earnest soul who wanted to arrange for Al and LeRoy to address the Golden Age Club at a retirement center in Covina, an intellectual type, a young "Communicator" from some midget FM station at a college in the valley, who wanted to run a forum with him and the Chesters, open-ended, so that they could plead the case for reformed convicts, some old lady who was certain she'd known the Chesters back in the Middle West, and who wanted to invite them to move in with her, there was a soft-voiced character who wanted them to attend a meeting of an all-male encounter group, a kook in Glendale who had a device that used psychic waves to seek out buried treasure and would assist the Chesters in unearthing whatever loot they'd stashed away in return for a small fee, and publicity, the beggars who wanted money, the bit player actors he hadn't heard from in years who were asking could they get a part in the picture, when could they come in for an audition?

Mornings, at the club, they found him there too, nagging away, until finally Myrna at the switchboard told him, "Perce, you'd better get yourself an office, it's not that I mind, but you know the House Committee, they'll come down on you . . ."

All sorts of calls, but nothing from anybody who wanted to talk about his story.

That night he went over to Vera's small house in Laurel Canyon, to get away from the incessant ringing.

"Nothing's happening," he complained, sitting in her kitchen, while she improvised some supper.

"Just keep ducking the crazies," she said, sipping her white wine. "I've got another story planted in the *Valley Times* radio and TV column this weekend, and I'm hoping to get Vernon Scott to do a human-interest interview with you, he's UPI, that gets picked up all over the country. It takes a little while, baby, but it'll happen."

Perce poured himself another drink of her vodka. He hated vodka, it didn't agree with him, but Vera did not keep bourbon around.

"By the way," she said, "there's one person I do want you to hook up with, he'll probably call you tomorrow, make a note, it's Doctor Daniel Moresby."

''Who's sick?''

''He's *Reverend* Moresby,'' she said. ''The Church of the Revival of the Faith, in Inglewood. He wants to ask you and Al and LeRoy to be guests at his Sunday morning services—he wants his church to offer them sanctuary against the slings and arrows of an unforgiving world, isn't that beautiful?''

''Who is this bum?'' he demanded. ''One of those phonies who does faith healing and then takes up a collection?''

''He's a very legitimate guy,'' said Vera. ''And, he also happens to have an hour of television time each Sunday, *now* do you get the picture?''

''You can't be serious,'' said Perce. ''What are we supposed to do, be baptized, rise up and walk again, shout 'I've seen the light!' and take the pledge and all that crap?''

''It isn't like that at all,'' she said impatiently. ''He's very dignified, he has a very large audience—''

''No thanks,'' he said.

''Look! It will give you and the Chesters complete respect, it's the perfect PR thrust, it gets them pity, they're examples of how our callous society mocks the penitent sinner . . . get it?'' she told him, extending her arms. ''It's beautiful, friends! . . . and it wasn't easy.''

''You serious?'' he asked, finishing his drink.

''Bet your ass I'm serious,'' she told him.

''Forget it,'' he told her.

She stared at him. ''Why?''

''I thought we were selling an honest story for a picture—and now you're turning it into some—goddamned medicine show!''

''Oh, really now, Mr. Pure,'' she said softly. ''So tell me now, how do *you* think you hustle a property these days?''

He sloshed some more vodka into his glass. ''I've got a better idea for you,'' he said, his stomach churning with anger. ''Why don't you get Al and LeRoy onto 'The Gong Show'—they can come out and do a duet—'If I Had the Wings of an Angel, over These Prison Walls I Would Fly,' jazzed up a little, natch—they have to be a smash, then they can go on the *Griffin* show, good old Merv can chat with them, then maybe you can book them on 'Hollywood Squares,' the two of them in one square, that's cute, oh, and then they can go on with Sonny and Cher, they'll be fixed up with some funny sketch material about being in the slammer, and they all do a medley at the end—sad songs about men separated from the women they love—''

''Stuff it,'' said Vera.

''—Then they'll hook up with some young rock musicians,'' he raved on, pacing up and down the kitchen, ''—they get a catchy name, they can call themselves Al and the Cons—no, the *Ex*cons—they all come out in striped uniforms, they set off sirens and ring alarm bells, the kids'll love it, they'll call it prison rock, no *rock* rock—''

''Oh, shut up!'' she said angrily.

''—Then they go out and tour, state fairs, down to the Bible Belt—they can do a kind of a Johnny Cash thing, a musical monologue on being truly repentant—maybe Cash will get them to play prisons with him—they're Number One on the Top Forty—they get comic books—'The Adventures of the Super Cons'—wow! And you're responsible for everything—Vera, you're the hottest PR lady in town, you'll be Mrs. Thrust Specialist, and good luck to you!''

He collapsed into a chair, his throat was dry. His glass was empty.

. . . And what the hell was he so angry about?

He got up and poured more vodka.

''I'll tell you what,'' said Vera, her voice tightly controlled. ''Why don't you just go hand your damn story over to that English lady agent? Or maybe, go and get into a tennis game with the ghost of Louis B. Mayer, and the ghost of that demon agent of yours can sell him the story between sets—and then you won't have to worry about how I'm corrupting you and those poor innocent Chesters.''

He did not answer. What the hell was there to say to that?

''. . . Let's get it straight,'' she told him. ''Do you want to sell this story for a picture or don't you?''

''Dumb question,'' he muttered.

''All right then,'' she said. ''Call the Chesters, get them fixed up with clean shirts and ties, and we'll all spend an hour in church on Sunday.''

". . . Why are you so hung up on this goddamn church?" he asked, and even as he asked the question, it was answered in a sudden flash of insight. "Unless the minister is one of your clients!"

"So what if he is?" she demanded.

"Sonofabitch!" he cried, the anger exploding; he waved an accusatory finger. "I've brought you these two slobs, you've latched on to them, you're getting all kinds of space, it makes *you* look terrific, and you'll keep on with it until you've squeezed it dry, right? Lady, you are one terrific operator!"

". . . Oh, Perce," she sighed wearily. "Don't start going moral on me. It's like . . ." she grimaced, ". . . a whore yelling rape."

"Speak for yourself," he snarled.

She reached out to slap him, hard, and the force of her hand stung his cheek. On reflex, he grabbed her wrist, twisted it, wanting to hurt her in return.

"That's my writing hand," she said, "—and my phoning hand—you bastard, go ahead and sprain it, and when you do, you can handle this whole ballgame by yourself!"

He dropped her wrist.

His own hand was shaking violently. What the hell was he up to?

He reached out for her, and muttered, "I'm sorry, baby—" But she backed away.

Drained, almost nauseous, he sat down, covered his face with his hands. Jesus, he hadn't lost control like that in years. ". . . You're trying to help me, and I'm being a prick," he said.

There was no reply. He looked up at her. She stood there, rubbing her wrist, glaring at him.

"I appreciate what you've been doing, so help me, I *do,*" he insisted. Without Vera, where was he? "It was the vodka talking, you know that."

"All right," she said finally. "It was the vodka . . . *this* time. But if you want out of this, say so now. Otherwise, we play out this hustle until we get somewhere with it . . . and from now on, we neither of us complain about having to step in a few dog turds. Right?"

He nodded.

"If you're worried about what you'll say in church on Sunday," she told him, "you can start by testifying on how you gave up drinking vodka."

"Amen, sister," he said.

*   *   *

chapter 13

—My son, is there something you want to tell me?

—I—well—Father Mulcahy—you see, I . . .

—Take your time, son. My Boss can wait. He's used to waiting.

BEHIND Reverend Daniel Moresby, an invisible choir sang softly, the voices amplified in stereo so that the music filled all four corners of the church. The altar area was bathed in white-hot light, the lenses of the two TV cameras poked unobtrusively out from the steps below, to either side of the altar which was banked with a profusion of plastic flowers.

Moresby rose from his chair and strode to the altar. With one hand he turned the dial on it which lowered the taped music. ". . . And now that we have meditated," he said cheerfully, "may I remind you, my friends, that we here today have been witness to a precious moment indeed, oh, yes, has it not been *thrilling?*"

A single voice called out, "Amen!"

His cheeks glowing with slightly tinted make-up, his hair carefully brushed back, his neatly capped teeth glistening in the TV lights, Moresby turned to Al and LeRoy Chester, who sat beside the altar, in their dark blue suits and white shirts, perspiring slightly in the heat.

"These men, these good men, have testified fully as to their true repentance," said Moresby, his resonant voice echoing through the PA system. "Did you listen as LeRoy Chester told you that it was God who made him see the error of his ways?"

". . . Amen, amen!" said a voice.

"And his brother Al was no less sincere. Indeed, they have both given us the Word, they have shown us the marvelous healing power of our Savior, as He works His wondrous ways, even in the daily life of our teeming, confused, and complex technological society!'' cried Moresby, his arms stretched wide in his flowing gray robe.

''. . . Oh, yes, indeed!''

''We love you, my brothers,'' continued Moresby. ''Oh, we pour out our affection for you, and we wish you well in your crusade against the powers of evil darkness! May you and your faithful friend Mr. Barnes have nothing but success in your future endeavors, may your forthcoming motion picture spread the message of Good to the corrupt forces out there, may your story set a shining example of faith to our young and confused offspring, those misguided souls who are roaming the streets and broad boulevards of our angry cities, raping and robbing and pillaging, may you fight the good fight, and I want to say here and now that the sooner you get this picture *Three Down, Two Left Standing* completed and into every theater, where it will serve to drive out the forces of corruption, and filth, and pornography with which we have been inundated, the better it will be for all of us believers in Truth!''

''Oh, amen, amen!'' came the cries.

Behind the first TV camera, a technician pointed to his watch, tapped it significantly, made a sign with his finger as if cutting his throat. Imperceptibly, Reverend Moresby nodded.

''. . . And now my friends,'' he said, ''our precious television time is almost over, let us pray. Pray with me, and remember, we are here, all week long, at your Church of the Revival of the Faith, our work never ends, it continues seven days and seven nights, but unfortunately, we do live in a materialist society, alas, and there is desperate need for your support. We plead with you to share with us whatever tithe you can find in your hearts to carry on the good work and to fight the good fight. We will wait for you at Box eight seven seven seven, Inglewood, California, you here today have been generous, you out there must share the burden—whatever you send us, we accept with the Lord's blessing on you, you can be sure that it will be used well in the Lord's work! Bow your heads, my friends . . .''

His hand flicked the dial, and the music rose again.

''May the Savior bless you, and keep you, and may His countenance shine upon you. May He bring you His most precious gift of everlasting Peace, Heaven bless you all for being here this Sunday, we'll be back seven days from now, the Good Lord willing—let's make it a *good* week for the Lord!''

His hand turned the dial up again, and music filled the church.

They stood outside the church, in the bright sunlight, as the congregation filed out, headed toward the parking lot, Moresby flanked by Al and LeRoy, Perce and Vera a few feet away, she in a simple black dress, Perce in an old gray suit he hadn't worn in years.

Finally the last parishioner had shaken the last hand, and departed. Moresby patted his forehead with his handkerchief. ''I thought it went pretty well,'' he said.

''You were sensational,'' said Vera, ''as usual.''

''. . . I wasn't so sure about the choice of hymns,'' mused Moresby. ''We could have programmed something a little more apt, you know? 'No Walls Can Hold My Faith' would have been more catchy.''

''They loved you,'' said Vera. ''You're going to get a lot of very good feedback from this, Reverend, you'll see.''

''We can but try,'' said Moresby, and turned to Al and LeRoy, ''Go in peace, my brothers. Thank you.''

''Oh, no,'' said Al. ''Thank *you*. We was glad to be here, right, LeRoy?''

The big man nodded.

''And you too, Mr. Barnes,'' said Moresby. ''God bless you, and good luck on your project. How soon can we expect to be seeing this inspirational picture?''

''Just as soon as the Lord gets our cameras rolling,'' said Perce.

''Amen to that,'' said Moresby. ''And don't forget, when the picture is ready, we're going to expect to help you further. Maybe a première right here in the church? We have projection equipment, you know . . .''

''That's certainly something to keep in mind,'' said Perce.

Moresby glanced at his watch. ''Got to run,'' he said. ''Christening at two. Working for the Lord is a full-time occupation.'' He turned and hurried inside, waving a hand. ''Keep up the good work!''

". . . What a package," said Perce. "Looks like Ronald Reagan, preaches like George C. Scott, and I'll bet under that cassock he's dressed like Liberace."

". . . He's got a piece of a real estate agency, too," said Vera.

Perce dropped Al and LeRoy back at their rooming house. LeRoy had to be at work by one—Sunday was the busiest day at the restaurant where he was washing dishes, and Al would be getting time and a half for pumping gas on Sunday. "Supposed to be a day of rest," said Al wryly, "but not for us."

"You were terrrific, fellows," said Vera as the two men got out of Perce's Caddy. "Something ought to be happening, real soon."

"We'll be waiting, ma'am," said Al. "Thanks for the ride. You know something? I haven't been in a high-class church like that in years. Sure beats prison chapel, right, LeRoy?"

LeRoy nodded assent.

As Perce headed back on the freeway, surrounded by hordes of Sunday drivers hastening toward the beach, Vera said, "Your pal LeRoy, he could go anyway, but that Al, he digs girls."

"How do you figure that?"

"Easy," she said. "All that time before Moresby called them up to the altar, he was standing behind me in the wings, and he had his hand on my tush, beating out time to the hymns."

"No kidding," chuckled Perce.

"Talk about 'Rock of Ages,' " snorted Vera. "He carries around one of his own."

"Why didn't you slug him?" he asked.

"In church?" asked Vera.

"You're right," he said. "It would blunt Al's PR thrust."

She giggled. Things were better today; she could even accept his little joke.

"All right," he said. "We've done the religious bit, what's next on your master plan?"

"I think I'll go back to bed," said Vera. "I haven't been up this early on a Sunday for months."

He dropped his hand on her skirt, ran it gently over her flank. "Neither have I," he said. "Been up, that is."

"What's turned *you* on?" she asked. "What I told you about

Al?''

. . . Sharp, wasn't she? Sometimes too sharp.

''I merely want to do some of the Lord's work,'' he said. ''Go forth and multiply.''

''. . . Then let's get the hell home,'' she said, and her hand began to explore him. ''What are these?'' she asked, her fingers working at the buttons.

''Pre-zipper antiques,'' he said.

Perhaps it was because of the unaccustomed hour, noontime, with the shades hastily drawn in her bedroom, on her unmade bed, her clawing urgently at him, it was the excitement of taking her in her oddly demure basic black, her skirts up above her waist, the two of them like a pair of urgent high schoolers, Vera's cat staring placidly at them, whatever it was, their love making was wilder and more satisfying than it had been for a long time.

. . . In Perce's dream, the greaser was back from Europe, smiling, showing his perfect teeth, his torso oiled, he was in his old house by the pool, high up on Woodrow Wilson Drive, next to it the cabana where the Greaser held his private orgies. The Greaser would play the detective in *Three Down, Two Left Standing,* that was good casting, for Al they'd signed Joel McCrea, sure he was older, but he could still cut it, and for LeRoy, the studio wanted Burt Lancaster to fly back from Rome, a good solid cast. The Greaser was happy with Perce's script, he made Perce another drink and they toasted the picture . . . it had to be a smash with such a cast.

Then the Greaser took him into the cabana and showed him his latest toy, a tiny closed-circuit TV camera lens, mounted high on the wall. What was that for? The Greaser grinned. ''For a script conference,'' he said. The director would be up shortly. ''She's the first lady director I ever worked for,'' said the Greaser. ''I'm going to bring her in here, and jump on her bones, *amigo,* you operate the camera, we'll have a priceless piece of tape, it'll be the first time a star ever screwed his director!''

The doorbell began to ring, the Greaser had given the help the afternoon off, the bell continued to ring. "You go answer it, *amigo,*" said the Greaser, "get a look at her and see if you want to be in the picture with us, what the hell, you'll be immortalized!"

He went through the old house, the doorbell continued to ring, he opened the tiny window in the door to look outside, there was no woman there, but there were *cops,* two of them standing there, guns drawn, what did they want?

He went back to warn the Greaser, but the doorbell kept on ringing . . .

. . . And it wasn't a doorbell, it was a telephone, and then he heard Vera speaking? Blinked his eyes open. Heard her talking to Reverend Moresby?

Then she hung up, turned over and pushed him. "Okay, unbeliever," she said. "You didn't want to go to church? Well, get this. CBS called to pick up a two-minute clip of that TV service this morning—and they're dropping it into tonight's six o'clock news, which means they'll use it at eleven, too!"

"Why not?" he said. "You get what you pray for."

* * *

chapter 14

—Brad, it's our only hope! Call the navy and ask if we can borrow a squadron of their latest attack bombers!
—What good will that do?
—Don't you see? If they can fly above the Creature and drop their thermal bombs, the intense heat may penetrate that strange skin of his!
—And if it doesn't?
—We haven't got time to waste arguing, Brad. He's already destroyed most of Spokane, Washington!

AN accomplished dealer in fantasy, half truths, and wish fulfilment for the past three decades, it was only natural that Harry Elbert would embellish somewhat the factual history of how he came to involve his talents in a proposed production of *Three Down, Two Left Standing*.

Some weeks later, in response to a question from the girl assigned by the *New York Times* Sunday Arts and Leisure section, who'd interviewed him over a two-hour lunch at Le Bistro, Harry would modestly say ''Oh, sure, I'm known primarily as a producer of blockbusters, my latest is *Cimarron* with Vin DeLuca, as you well know, but I've always believed there has to be room on our screens for stories that aren't six, seven or eight million dollar epics. If we don't nurture them, the life blood, the creative side of the film business is in danger of drying up. After all, I cut my teeth on B pictures. They were a marvelous training school, believe me. Besides, I'm equipped with a kind of inner radar, and it blips when a good idea for a film shows up, can you understand that?''

(. . . He'd been lying in bed in Fiona's Brentwood pad that Sunday afternoon, dozing, he was relaxed on her pneumatic playground, Fiona was up, she'd snapped on her tiny Sony TV, the sound of its voices helped him doze.

It was keep-your-fingers-crossed time on the picture, twenty-seven days' shooting completed on a sixty-day schedule, the *Cimarron* rushes looked good, flown in from Arizona each night, he'd screened some this afternoon with his editor, who was doing a rough assembly every day, keeping it tight, they only had Vin DeLuca on an eight-week commitment, after that there was a bitch of a penalty payment if they went over, but, thank God, DeLuca was staying sober, he wasn't putting on weight, he was shacked up with his latest broad, some Swedish girl, you could tell from the rushes that she was taking good care of him in that Tucson hotel, please God she lasted a couple more weeks, DeLuca wore them out fast.

. . . Fiona came padding in from the shower, moist and fragrant, her long chestnut hair hanging down around her shoulders. She bent down to gather up some of her clothing, she was going to do her laundry, what she called "rinsing out my smalls," . . . what a crazy broad, such a gorgeous shape. In her uniform, very uptight, her hair done in a bun, wearing gloves, so formal, who would ever guess how wild she was in the sack?

He reached up to pull her back down on the bed, toppling her backward, she giggled softly as she collapsed on him, ". . . I *beg* your pardon, just what are you up to?" . . . somehow, this time their grappling took them to the foot of the bed, she beneath him, she urged him up, he found himself crouched above her pink back. ". . . Ah, there's a dear," she murmured as he entered her, and then his eyes closed, as he shut everything else out . . . Cowboy Harry, the Lone Rider, he and this beautiful thoroughbred rode down the canyon and began to head upward to the mountaintop.

". . . Oh, Harry, *look* . . ." sighed Fiona beneath him. ". . . They're . . . so . . . bloody . . . marvelous . . ."

". . . Wha?"

". . . Do . . . look . . . especially . . . that tall . . . silent. . . one," she said. ". . . Isn't . . . he . . . beaut . . . ti . . . ful?"

Harry's eyes fluttered open, and he caught a glimpse of the tiny TV screen. Two small figures . . . dark suits . . . some kind of a priest . . . in robes, his arms outstretched . . .

TV? *Now*? Who needed that?

". . . Come on . . . baby . . . con . . . cen . . . trate!" he urged, closing his eyes, returning *hiyosilverupupandaway* to the chase.)

". . . As for making my son my associate producer on this film, well, all I can tell you is, I'm willing to take a chance on him, the same way somebody took a chance on *me*, back when I was starting off. His generation is a damn sight brighter and more sophisticated than mine was; the two of us can help each other," Harry would tell the *Times* girl. "So let them cry nepotism, who cares? If Billy Elbert doesn't pull his weight, we'll cross that bridge when we come to it—if we come to it."

("He says he's coming back from New York. He and that Anita have finally broken up," said Mrs. Elbert.

It was later that night; while he'd been at Fiona's, she'd been at her Sunday seminar. Their paths rarely coincided until late at night. That gave them about twenty minutes each night to touch bases, at bedtime.

"She wasn't a bad broad, as Billy's broads go," said Harry, from his side of their double bed. He adjusted the sleep mask over his eyes. Martha would study late, all that material she brought in each week from her courses at UCLA. Sure, he could move into the guest bedroom, but with the damn community property laws in California, why should he give her any ideas about trial separation?

"Billy needs to find himself," she said.

"He needs to go to work," he said.

"Not just work," said Martha. "He's still searching for a career drive. A motivational impulse. It would be so much easier if he had a sense of his own *worth*."

That was her latest analyst talking.

". . . Work," he said.

"He's always been an overachiever," said Martha. "It's certainly not *his* fault that he can't adjust to the commercial arena."

. . . Of course it wasn't Billy's fault. Why should it be? Ever since he'd been born, his mother had seen to it that he had whatever he wanted. The kid had grown up in Beverly, where on Halloween the kids went out trick-or-treating in chauffeured limos, hell, Billy's Boy Scout troop went on their Sierra hikes by chartered helicopter! Then he'd gone back East, four years at that crazy Hampshire College, seven, eight grand a year tuition, then the trips to Europe, then the loft in the Village with a succession of girls, the meditation bit, the vegetarian diet, the commune in Maine, he'd done it all, always with the American Express card in his jeans. Then he'd gone into "communications," that meant equipment, he'd gone out and bought himself enough Japanese videotape equipment to set up his own goddamn TV station—portable minicam, closed-circuit replay, Nagra sound recorder, the works. Then he and his latest broad, Anita, had spent a year on a two-hour video documentary, the family history of her Italian ancestors—well, at least that sounded like it might be something salable, they could come up with something new on the Mafia, right? So they'd shelled out all the dough he needed, even for the months in Italy. "Roots" it wasn't. What they'd brought in was the dullest two-hour documentary ever done about a grandfather who was, for God's sake, an upholsterer! Some *padrone*!

"He did win that award at the Toledo Videotape Festival," said Martha. "Why do you insist on being so hostile about your own flesh and blood? Secretly, you've always been competitive with him, haven't you?"

"I'm not competitive, I'm not hostile, I'm tired," said Harry.

"When he gets here, you might sit down and talk with him," she said.

"I'm not avant garde enough," sighed Harry. "I'm a bourgeois commercial slob who needs to go to sleep so he can get up in the morning and earn a little more money to stuff into Billy's trust fund."

"That's exactly what I mean," said Martha. "You resent him."

Harry rolled over and covered his head with a pillow.

. . . He was almost asleep, it was a pink Fiona who pranced in his small-screen fantasies . . . when he felt Martha nudge him. "Harry," she urged. "*Look.*"

". . . Wha?"

"... on the late news. Here—these two convicts are in some church. Listen—they're testifying as to their life of crime—it's terribly valid stuff—"

"... Mmph," said Harry, and burrowed deeper into his pillow.)

"... The minute I first saw Al and LeRoy Chester on the news telling their story that night something inside me clicked," Harry would continue. "I got to brooding about how best to provide them with some platform from which their touching story could be seen and heard by the largest American audience possible."

(When he arrived at his office the following morning, Laura, his secretary, had his freshly made coffee ready, black, the beans ground five minutes earlier.

"Good weekend, Mr. E?" she'd asked.

"More of the same," he told her. "What about you?"

She spread his mail carefully out on the desk. "Did you happen to catch that thing on the news last night?" she asked. "There was a scene from a church in Inglewood, there were these two convicts who'd been asked to be guests of the congregation—it was really quite stirring."

"*Please,*" he complained, sipping the black coffee. "Not again. I don't want to hear any more about two convicts in a church. Prison pictures are over."

"You should have listened to them," she said. "It was all very inspirational—and it had a message for the young."

"You want to send a message, call Western Union," muttered Harry.

"Excuse *me*," said Laura, "but you're being flip. Those two men are trying to spread a little truth—and *I* for one, think they should be helped, not mocked."

He glanced up at her. What was going on with her, all of a sudden? The menopause? This was the first time in all the years good old Laura had been with him, good old reliable Laura, that she'd come back at him like that.

"Okay, fine," he said. After all, she was one damned good secretary . . . and she knew where quite a few of the bodies were buried as well. "I just meant that what happens in a church on Sunday doesn't necessarily matter here on Monday, okay?"

"If you don't mind my saying so, Mr. Elbert," she said, "perhaps it's time that it did.")

"You see, wherever I go," said Harry, "I make a point of trying to keep my fingers on the public pulse. That's what makes me different from other producers who don't ever get outside the Bel Air living-room circuit. And from all I've seen and heard lately, I realize that there's a very large section of that vast Middle America which will respond to an uplifting story that comes to grips with the problems of crime and punishment."

(An hour later, he'd been sitting in the john downstairs by Cutting Room 7, the black coffee had done its job, he was catching up on the trades, the booth door closed, when he heard the john door open, and then two voices, outside his booth.

"Wanna go to the Springs this weekend?"

"Love to but I can't. Got to go to New York on the red eye Thursday. Panic meeting."

. . . The second voice sounded familiar, it was one of those young TV executives. Not yet thirty, already a genius.

"What's the fire now?"

"Problems with the fall line-up. Network's got a couple holes opening up, we better find some replacements."

"So what's new?"

"Nothing. Same old shit. They don't want violence—but law and order has to triumph. So I gotta find a new cop show, with a twist. Got any ideas?"

". . . How about a cop from outer space, patrols L.A. from a flying saucer?"

". . . Hilarious."

There was the sound of water running in the sink.

"Hey, did you see those two guys on television, last night, those two ex-cons?"

''I don't need cons, I need *cops*!''

''Yeah, Buddy, but listen—''

The john door slammed.

Harry came into his office ten minutes later.

Laura was already working at her typewriter.

''You want your calls?'' she asked.

''Not yet,'' he said. ''Laura, what was the name of those two guys you were telling me about—the ex-cons in the church?''

''. . . I think it was Chester,'' she said. ''One was Al, and the other was—wait a second—let me see if I can remember—''

''See if you can locate them,'' he told her. ''I want to talk to them.''

''. . . May I ask what about?''

''I'm not sure yet,'' said Harry. ''Go find them, and let me think.''

. . . It had taken four blips, but at last Harry was paying attention to his radar.)

''. . . So we're out to try a little something different with this project,'' Harry told the *Times* lady. ''*Cimarron* will obviously be our major summer release, our blockbuster. With *Three Down, Two Left Standing,* I'm going to try to revitalize the low-budget field. But remember, it's just as much work to make a cheap picture, maybe even more. You have to substitute ingenuity for money. It ought to be interesting, don't you think?''

''Thus he leaves the Polo Lounge, hurrying back to the cutting room,'' concluded the *Times* piece, ''this sunburned survivor of three decades of film making who's so busy at his production labors that he rarely has time for interviews. There aren't many of his breed left here, these independent men who eat and sleep and breathe commercial films each day of the week. In this notoriously unsentimental town, Harry Elbert's four-star romance with movies is accepted by the most callous observer as genuine. Too young to be one of the early immigrant titans, too old to be considered a boy genius, call Elbert simply a man who loves to make a good movie."

* * *

chapter 15

—Well, Hudkins, there she is, ready for her first test flight.
—She's a beauty, boss.
—We've got a lot riding on her. You think you can handle my X-nineteen?
—Why sure, boss. They don't call me Ace for nothing. I can fly anything with wings and a tail.
—I know you can get her up—just make sure you can get her down.
—Leave it to me, boss. All right, boys, *contact!*

SOMEWHERE in Greater L.A. there was computer center with buttons, and when yours was pressed, above it a red light glowed, it meant HOT.

How everyone in town knew when yours had lit up, no one had ever figured out, but seconds after it went on, all the lemmings began to chase after you, clap you on the back, you had instant credit at Vegas, a front table at Chasen's, you were aces in everybody's book, baby, from the shoeshine boy outside Schwab's Drugstore right on up to Lew Wasserman in his black mausoleum at MCA-Universal, it was *love you*!

(Years back, there'd been a story about two writers' kids on the Beverly Hills playground, the two of them jumping rope, both chanting *My daddy's hot at Paramount, my Daddy's hot at Paramount!*)

. . . When your button went off, the red light went out, you were instant C-O-L-D, the lemmings knew that too, the shoeshine boy forgot the extra flick on your ox-blood, Lew Wasserman was out of town for the next few weeks, the hotel at Vegas was booked solid, you could run down Wilshire stark naked, commit hara-kiri on the stage of the Hollywood Bowl, nobody would bother to look.

The days following the CBS pick up of the news clip, Perce thought he felt the red light go on. It had been a long time . . . but somewhere the finger was pressing his button.

He could tell from the clients on his court. Somehow they all turned the conversation away from tennis around to his new project. Crime and the Chesters were a lot more interesting to Mrs. Berger than her backhand, or to Jean Swenson (temporarily) and her rotten serve. A couple of people even drifted over to watch him give lessons, not exactly the same gallery Jimmy Connors drew when he practiced, but they were there. In the locker room, there were smiles, even some hellos.

Myrna, at the switchboard, had become less irritable about his incoming phone calls, she even offered to monitor them, to screen out the cranks.

On Tuesday, Ziggy Harling said good morning.

Which had to be proof positive.

Ziggy, who hadn't spoken to him since they'd argued about the Kennedy-Eisenhower compaign! Ziggy, the same overweight slob who'd come around way back when and begged Perce and the Greaser to permit him to join the club, whining that he wanted to be treated just like one of the boys for Chrissakes, why did the club discriminate? Stingy schnorrer, his cheap tweed jacket stinking from the cheap Optimos he smoked, nobody wanted him around, but they'd taken pity on him.

Now he was Z. H., retired and rich, traveled to Europe six months each year, had a villa at Cap d'Antibes, and when the row started over Perce being permitted to give lessons on the court, Ziggy had been one of the noisiest to object.

"Hey, Perce, I saw you on the TV," called Ziggy, puffing on his gold-mounted Dunhill, blinking at him through his thick lenses. "You're the one's hitched up with those two ex-cons, right? So what are you guys up to, pal?"

"We're working on a picture deal," Perce told him, just as if they'd been in constant touch for the past fifteen years.

"Yeah, yeah, terrific, so who's handling it for you?" Ziggy demanded.

A good question. Perce certainly had no agent, least of all Miss Hastings.

". . . My lawyer," he said.

"So wait a minute, don't go running away," said Ziggy. "Siddown, have some coffee? Maybe you don't know this, but I'm working up a syndicate, a very select bunch, private investors, strictly the cream, all of us putting up dough to develop properties, even got some Arab money to hook up with, get it? Now, if this thing is interesting, I could put you in touch with my people, they listen to me, what the hell do Arabs know from a salable property, maybe we could drop some nice up-front money on you, hah?"

. . . Years back, Ziggy had wooed and married old B. K. Osterman's daughter, Rosalie. Old B. K. had been so tickled that anybody would seriously consider making it with that tall and toothy girl that he'd immediately set his son-in-law Ziggy up as an independent producer, releasing through B. K.'s company. After which Ziggy kept Rosalie pregnant, and sat in a big executive office puffing on his Dunhills, turning out one stinker after another . . . one night there'd been a party and Ziggy had made his customary noisy entrance, hadn't it been Billy Wilder who'd looked up and said, "That man has single-handedly set the son-in-law business back twenty years!"

Perce forced a smile. "Sure, Ziggy," he said. "Why don't we talk about it some time?"

"Nah, why don't we talk about it now?" insisted Ziggy. "When do I read your script? I can get you an answer in twenty-four hours—overnight, even. This could be your chance for a comeback, Perce, don't fuck it up—"

Tasteful. Always first cabin was Ziggy. The bastard had missed his calling. He should have gone into the diplomatic corps.

Over the club PA came Myrna's voice, announcing a call for Mr. Perce Barnes at the office.

"Excuse me, Ziggy," he said, grateful for the reason to get away.

"Don't play games, Perce," Ziggy called after him. "I been around a long time, remember? I know 'em all."

"Wouldn't have bothered you, hon," said Myrna, "but this is a friend of yours, says it's important."

It was Al Chester. "Hello, Perce? Say, that Harry Elbert is a friend of yours, isn't he?"

"Was," said Perce. "What's up?" . . . Harry Elbert?

"His secretary just called me, down here where we're staying."

How had she managed to locate Al?

"What'd she want?"

"Says he wants to talk to me and LeRoy about our career in crime," said Al. "Said he'd like to sit down and meet with us, maybe later today. What's your idea about that?"

. . . Good old swivel-hips Harry, still running around end, pulling his famous quarterback sneak.

"Did she mention me?" asked Perce.

"No," said Al . . . what the hell, wasn't it only a few days ago that he'd asked Harry for advice on how to market the story? ". . . But I did," said Al. "Told her he ought to get in touch with you. Said as how you'd written this story for the picture, and we made us a deal, and if he was interested, why, he should talk to you. Right?"

"Beautiful," said Perce. "You should've been a lawyer."

"Found that out too late," said Al. "Why'd he call us first? He's such a friend of yours from way back, what's he trying?"

"A little simple shafting," said Perce. "If I know Harry, he always figures it's worth a try. So if I set up a date for this meeting, when can you boys make it?"

"Any time after business hours," said Al.

"His, or yours?"

"Well, now," said Al, "I'm not about to quit these gas pumps till I see me some real money, you know?"

"Very bright." said Perce. "Harry has never been famous as a philanthropist."

"But he's the biggest around, isn't he?" said Al. "If he does our story, it'd be a real blockbuster."

"The magic word there is *if*, pal," said Perce.

"You'll do it," said Al. "We waited a long time for this, but you're going to make it worth the waiting."

Sure, sure. What did they think he was, Randolph Scott leading the cavalry troop into hostile territory?

After he hung up, he told Myrna he was expecting a call from Harry Elbert's office.

"Okay, hon," she said. "I'll put him right through."

"No, don't," he told her. "Say you can't locate me and I'll have to call him back."

"Playing games?" asked Myrna conspiratorially.

He nodded.

When you were hot, you didn't come running like some puppy. For a while, at least, he could enjoy having a bastard like Harry pursue him.

. . . And now, how could he duck Ziggy?

There were two messages from his service when he got home. One from Miss Hastings, the second, Mr. Elbert's secretary.

Let them both sweat.

He showered, and when he came out, the phone was ringing.

It was Mr. Elbert's secretary again, she'd been trying him all afternoon, Mr. Elbert wanted to know could Mr. Barnes possibly help her locate a copy of some material that had been written that dealt with two brothers, their name was Chester?

Oh, yes, Mr. Barnes just probably might be able to do that. (There were four Xerox copies stacked on the coffee table, two feet away.)

. . . That was just fine, then could Mr. Barnes arrange to have a copy of the material sent over to Mr. Elbert's office first thing in the morning?

No, Mr. Barnes couldn't do that, sorry.

Well, then, how would it be if Mr. Elbert's secretary arranged to have a messenger come by and pick it up, could that be easier?

No, that couldn't be arranged, either.

. . . Mr. Elbert's secretary seemed to be perplexed. Wasn't Mr.

Barnes at all interested in helping Mr. Elbert get hold of the material as soon as possible?

"Not necessarily," said Perce cheerfully.

"I don't think I understand," said the lady.

"Tell Mr. Elbert to call me, and I'll explain it to him," said Perce.

"Okay, fine, you're having fun letting him chase you, but don't get him angry," cautioned Vera. "Plenty of characters around this town who make deals, damn few who make pictures. Harry's a live one."

"Let him sweat a little," he said.

"It didn't take much to make *you* king of the castle, did it?" she commented.

"You Frankenstein, me monster," he told her.

"Assuming he wants to deal, who are we getting to handle it?" she asked. "We'll need someone with clout."

"I'll let Sy Rodman handle it," he said, carefully ignoring her use of the imperial we.

"Today I'll take the call from Harry," he told Myrna the following morning.

"Dig," she said. And winked.

The call came in at 11:30.

"*Perce*, baby," said Harry fondly, as if they'd been in constant touch for the past decade. "What about these Chester characters? I heard something about you knowing them—"

"You heard it from *me*," said Perce.

"I did?"

"A couple of weeks back, right outside the club here, remember?"

". . . Hell, so who can remember?" said Harry. "I've got a six-million-dollar *eppis* in production, my head is stuffed with it, you know what it's like. I've got some ideas I'd like to kick around with them—''

''With *us*,'' said Perce.

''—Oh, well, if you're hooked up with them, sure, why not?'' Harry conceded.

Always the artful dodger.

''Could we make a meet here in my office, say six tonight, I'll leave a pass at the front desk, we can talk?''

''About what, Harry?'' asked Perce, relishing this moment.

''Come on, nothing special, I really just want to meet them, *schmoos* a little,'' wheedled Harry.

''I'll bring my lawyer,'' said Perce.

''Why him?'' said Harry, aggrieved. ''How can anybody *schmoos* with shysters around? What'sa matter, Perce, you don't trust me? You getting paranoid, like the rest of the world?''

''Only lately,'' said Perce.

''And don't forget,'' said Harry, oblivious to the sarcasm. ''Bring along whatever you got on paper, will you?''

He was hooked, all right.

Now to reel him in. Carefully, so as not to lose the fish.

When the gray-haired guard at the front desk handed over the pass permitting them on the lot, he squinted at Perce through his glasses. ''You look familiar, Mr. Barnes,'' he said finally.

''Then you've been here a long time,'' said Perce. ''The last job I did here starred Rin Tin Tin.''

''We're neither of us *that* old,'' said the guard. ''You know how to find Mr. Elbert's bungalow? It's where Curtiz used to have his offices. Or should I send Rin Tin Tin with you?''

He pressed the buzzer, and Perce led Al and LeRoy through the door.

''Pretty easy to get inside here,'' remarked Al, as they went through the executive building, headed outside.

''Yeah, well try it sometime when they don't want you around,'' said Perce.

He led them out through the small green grass plots, past cutting rooms, down the broad studio street, with its gray-walled sound stages, the rows of cars parked in neat stalls, each one marked for the executive sufficiently privileged to park on the lot. The street was quiet . . . how many times had he walked here, headed to lunch at the Green Room, wandering back afterward toward the writers building, stopping to exchange gags with Julie and Phil, or hanging around Jerry Wald while he spouted rapid-fire ideas for hurry-up sales, gabbing with old Mark Hellinger, or looking over the latest blonde who'd been hired on a stock contract for the benefit of whichever producer spotted her first . . . All the guys he'd worked with, palled around with, had laughs with. Most of them gone. Was he the only one left standing here?

". . . Well now, LeRoy," said Al, impressed. "This is where it all happens. We finally made it."

That was how every yokel in America felt, when they got inside. Why should Al, who'd gotten here twenty years after the fact, feel any different?

"Relax, we haven't made anything *yet*," warned Perce.

Harry's office was opulent, and had been decorated in a style that made it resemble someone's country home in a *Lassie* picture. The paneled walls were covered with endless photographs of Harry, arm in arm with stars, directors, with politicians and everyone he'd met all these years. On the bookshelves were the leather-bound copies of the scripts he'd produced, there was a small grand piano on which reposed Harry's two Academy Award statuettes in a lucite box, lit from a spotlight above, and on the opposite wall hung a full-sized painting in oils of a very idealized Harry, Mrs. Elbert, and a slender young boy in a cowboy outfit. From hidden speakers, a stereo played soft music.

Harry had excused himself moments ago to answer the call of nature. His secretary finished serving the diet sodas from the bar behind the paneled walls, and then she tiptoed out.

Perce got up and wandered around the room, glancing idly at the desk on which were piles of scripts and other papers.

"Pretty nice, eh?" said Al.

Perce nodded.

There was the sound of rushing water behind the other wall, and he returned to his chair. Then Harry returned, buckling his belt.

He sat down at his desk; the chairs were arranged so that Perce, LeRoy, and Al were grouped in a semicircle, with Harry immutably the focus, the chairman of the board, in control.

"Okay, I'm a busy guy these days, so let's get to the *emmis*," Harry said. "Don't ask me why, but I get the feeling that maybe you two and your story about how you got sucked into a life of crime and then paid society the penalty—it just might work for a picture. Underline the word *might*. Something for Mr. and Mrs. Middle America, the drive-ins, the small towns, maybe even the youth market. Let's talk basics."

"Harry," said Perce, "we agreed not to talk basics." The screen treatment in its manila envelope was still unopened, in his lap. "We didn't bring an agent, or a lawyer—"

"Let the lawyers get to it after," said Harry. "Right now we're strictly exploring, get it? What I want to know is, providing I like the stuff that's written down, I'd want to option the story, the rights to your lives."

The music played softly.

"Some money up front, to bind the deal, maybe a payment when we go into screenplay, then a final hunk when and if we make the picture. Which has to be very low-budget. It might end up a two-hour job for one of the networks, I'm just spitballing. What do you think, Chester?"

Al was silent.

"Why should a big gun like you be interested in such a cheapo operation, Harry?" asked Perce.

Harry shrugged. "I didn't say it was a deal," he said. "I'm only talking how I see the way to go with this material."

"Which you haven't read," said Perce.

"Ah, come on, what can it be?" asked Harry. "Cops and robbers. The gang knocks over a bank truck, they get away with the loot, they end up in the slammer, they reform. That's it. It's been done a zillion times, what's new?"

"That's not exactly it," said Perce quietly.

"Of course not," said Harry, irritated. "After a good writer works it over, we get it in shape for today's audience—"

"I've already worked it over, Harry," said Perce.

''Yeah, sure,'' said Harry, with a wave of his hand. ''*Now* we give it a real polish.''

Al cleared his throat. ''Perce here has done a mighty fine job, Mr. Elbert,'' he said.

''Glad to hear it,'' said Harry. ''Now you can all make a few bucks, and let me see what *I* can do with it.''

He yawned.

''You're saying you don't want Perce to work on it?'' asked Al.

Harry shrugged. ''Perce is busy at the club every day, giving lessons,'' he said. ''Why should he want to quit a soft touch like that?''

Perce restrained his impulse to grab Harry by his scrawny throat, to squeeze it. That would make another true crime story, one much more satisfying.

''But he's our partner,'' said LeRoy suddenly.

''Okay, so whatever you guys split is strictly your problem,'' said Harry.

He beamed at the three of them.

Al glanced at Perce. Perce shook his head.

''I don't get you, Mr. Elbert,'' said Al. ''We made us a deal, and part of the deal is that Perce here is supposed to write the movie. I guess you don't understand that.''

''He understands it, Al,'' said Perce. ''He's not buying it. So I guess we better go, fellows.'' He got up from his chair.

''Go *where*?'' demanded Harry.

''You've got a lot on your mind, we wouldn't want to take up your valuable time, Harry,'' said Perce. ''Thanks for the Tab. The boys and I will just struggle along without you . . . baby.''

Harry watched, as Al and LeRoy rose.

''You guys do everything he tells you to?'' he demanded. ''What the hell, it's *your* life story, not his!''

''Like LeRoy said, we're partners,'' said Al.

They followed Perce out the door.

''Good night,'' Perce said to the secretary. ''We know the way to the front gate.''

The studio street was deserted now, the shadows lengthening as the hot valley sun mercifully went behind the mountains in the distance.

"That was quick," said Al. "What was he up to?"

"He was trying to shaft me, that's all," said Perce.

"But you just walked out on him? You bluffing?"

"A little," said Perce.

They walked on.

"Hey," he said, "You guys were terrific in there. You really put Harry down."

"He may be a big producer, but he don't have the right to pull that stuff on you," said Al. "I've seen guys get crippled for less."

"Sure have," said LeRoy.

"Tell me about it," said Perce. "Some other time."

They went past the cutting rooms, where the lights were on and an occasional squawk from a sound track blared through the stillness, and then out through the executive-office door where the cop had passed them inside.

A new, younger man was on duty. "You Mr. Barnes?" he asked, rising up from behind the glass window. "Mr. Elbert's office just called. He wants to see you back in his office—said I was to make sure you didn't leave the lot."

"No kidding," said Perce. "Okay, men, shall we go back?"

"Hoo-*eee,*" said Al. "I surely wouldn't want to play poker with *you,* nossir."

"Not when I'm holding the right cards," said Perce.

. . . Should he tell Al that he was an old, accomplished desk reader? That while Harry had been in the john, he'd glanced across Harry's desk, had caught a glimpse of an interoffice memo with a large CBS on it, addressed to Harry, one which said that the network program department would be interested in working out a development deal based on Harry's suggested concept . . . two ex-convicts in a story that stressed the law-and-order aspects of their lives?

No, that could wait. No use giving out all his trade secrets.

When the secretary ushered them in this time, Harry did not bother to rise, but sat behind his desk like some angry Buddha.

"You know this is a long walk," he told Harry. "None of us is getting any younger. You could've at least sent your car."

"You're trying to hold me up, I don't like that," said Harry.

"Your're trying to shit me, Harry," said Perce. "Never shit a shitter, pal."

"What does that mean?"

"It means you want to *ootz* me out of this deal," said Perce. "I'm not going to let you."

"Who the hell said we had a deal?"

"Come *on,* Harry!" Perce snapped. "You're busy making a seven-million-dollar picture, you didn't take time out to bring us over here unless you wanted *this*—" He waved the manila envelope.

"How do I know I want it unless I read it?" countered Harry.

"Okay, you can read it tonight," said Perce. "If you want to make an offer, I'll keep the door open until tomorrow morning. After that, I'll instruct my lawyer to listen to all the other people who want this property."

"Who're you? Irving Lazar?" yelled Harry. "People don't put me under the gun—I put *them!*"

"Harry," cooed Perce. "You called *us* back."

"Only to *talk!*" snarled Harry.

. . . It was a lovely moment, one he'd waited years for.

"Fine, we'll talk," he said. "If we make a deal for the rights to the Chester story, I'm the writer, with a guarantee for my services."

"Only if there's a cut-off," said Harry. "I keep the right to bring in another writer, if you bomb."

"I won't," said Perce. "I want an associate producer credit, too, plus a fee for that."

"To be negotiated," said Harry. "What else, I'm busy."

"Al and LeRoy here, they go into the package as technical advisors, on a weekly salary."

"Who needs them for that?" demanded Harry.

"I do," said Perce.

"Then *you* pay them!" said Harry.

"Only with production money," said Perce.

"Don't push me," warned Harry.

"Giving you broad outlines," said Perce.

Harry waved a finger. ''How do I know you're not going out tonight and peddle this somewhere else?''

''When we could have a Harry Elbert production?'' asked Perce.

''You been talking to everybody already, even Ziggy Harling, for God's sake,'' said Harry scornfully.

''Ziggy runs off at the mouth,'' said Perce, ''You know *that*.''

How the hell had Harry found that out?

He placed the manila envelope on Harry's desk. ''Here,'' he said. ''You can call me first thing in the morning and tell me if you want Sy Rodman to call. Eight A.M.?''

''Why so damn early?'' complained Harry.

''Because I have to spend the whole morning giving *lessons,* remember?'' Perce said, grinning.

Now the studio was dark, with the street lights on, the night air beginning to seep in, bringing with it the cool dampness.

The guard at the desk smiled and waved good night.

''Well, you were right, you were holding a pretty good hand,'' commented Al, as they walked toward Perce's car. ''Now what?''

''We wait and see if he calls tomorrow,'' said Perce.

''You think he'll go for that stuff about us being technical advisors?'' asked Al. ''I'm sure tired of pumping gas, and LeRoy here is getting dishpan hands.''

''Don't quit yet,'' said Perce.

The excitement had begun to drain away, and he was suddenly quite tired.

* * *

★ Part Two ★

chapter 16

—All right, kids, we're going to get this number right if we have to stay here and rehearse all night! No show of mine is going to open in New York until it's absolutely perfect! Hymie—take it from the top!

"IN the old days, we spent weeks making a picture," somebody had grumbled in the club locker room. "Now we spend months just making the *deal*."

Sy Rodman and Harry Elbert's business-affairs man had spent endless hours arguing over the contract, hassling out each clause, hammering out all the terms. For as long as it took, Perce continued giving lessons at the club, while Al and LeRoy held onto their jobs. After all, there was no telling if and when Harry would throw a curve, one that might break off the negotiation.

When the dust had finally settled, the deal emerged. Then it took another three, four days before the papers could be drawn up, more time while Harry's people fine-combed it for their changes, then Sy's further comments, and the final yelling over sentences, words, commas, even periods . . .

The final document was thicker than Perce's original treatment.

It had become a deal for a two-hour teleplay (Harry having conceded that he was probably going for a network deal). Fifteen grand for the rights to the Chester story, in two payments, on signing, the second due on the start of actual production. For Perce's writing services on the screenplay, no matter how long it took, there was a flat payment of another ten. Should Harry exercise an option for him to rewrite and polish the script, an additional five thousand. In return for their "technical assistance," the Chesters would each receive five hundred a week, for the period of eight weeks. Should the screenplay be used as the basis of a theatrical motion picture, to be released in the theaters first, Elbert's company would pay up an additional twenty thousand, and there were also stipulated payments for sequel rights, and (most importantly) ther were large royalties to be paid weekly should the property become the basis of a TV show.

When he and the Chesters met at Sy Rodman's office to sign their names and initial all the various clauses, Al asked, ''Is this a good deal, partner?''

''You're not going to get rich yet,'' said Perce, ''but you may get famous. You can do lecture tours, TV interviews, you can license yourself for comic books, they can even put out Al and LeRoy Chester dolls, maybe LeRoy will want to open his own gymnasium, hell they might even name a candy bar after you . . .''

''I'd still like to get a little more cash,'' sighed Al as he signed.

Harry Elbert's office sent word that they should report for a conference the following Monday. Perce had by now arranged for a substitute to take over his schedule of lessons, a young kid named Tommy Rose, a tennis whiz, home from college for the summer, who was delighted to pick up extra tuition money for the fall term.

Friday night, they celebrated the payment of the first money, Sy's office having carefully split it three ways, deducted its considerable fee up front, and delivered the checks to Perce.

He and Vera met Al and LeRoy at a Chinese restaurant in Hollywood, and over drinks, Perce passed out their money. ''I warned you you weren't going to get rich,'' he said, and raised his bourbon. ''But you're out of that damn gas station, aren't you? So let's drink.''

Al raised his beer. ''LeRoy, show 'em your hands,'' he said.

LeRoy held up his ginger ale. ''First night they been out of dishwater in months,'' he smiled.

Vera squinted at Perce's check through the restaurant's half-light. ''Ten per cent of that just about covers my phone bill for the month,'' she said ruefully.

''. . . Damn, that Al is horny,'' she said later that night. ''Remind me never to sit next to him in a booth.''

"I'm glad he goes for girls," said Perce. "Remember, I'm going to be locked up with him and his brother, for the next two months . . ."

But Monday Harry was away. He'd been called out of town, some sort of crisis on location where *Cimarron* was being shot. The picture was in its final weeks, they'd come to the major climax, the opening of the Cherokee Strip, and Harry needed to be on the scene.

As one of his concessions, Harry had agreed to provide Perce and the Chesters with some office space—(far from being cordial about it, complaining that he wasn't a goddamn landlord, he'd finally conceded the need for a place where the three men could meet).

The younger of Harry's two secretaries, a trim redhead whose name was Lister, led them down through the back hall of Harry's bungalow, out a door, and up a flight of stairs to a second-floor hallway, past some locked doors, into a small two-room suite at the end. The rooms were sparsely furnished with battered pieces that dated back to World War II; there was one broken-down air-conditioning unit in the window, a second window opened out onto a small, deserted back alley with a high wall. On an old desk was an even older L. C. Smith office typewriter.

The place exuded ancient cigar smoke, the carpet was pockmarked with burn marks, it was functional, anonymous, and grim. Years back, he'd sweated, paced, and argued in other suites such as this. Somehow, miraculously, screenplays did get written in them, probably because getting the work finished was a certain way of getting out of here.

But it was hard to believe that such a rabbit warren still existed . . . and as for that creaking old couch, who could catnap there?

"Boys, this is it," he said. "The big time."

"Well, the price is right," said Al.

Miss Lister came back with a fresh ream of paper, some yellow pads, she changed the ribbon in the typewriter, and left him a batch of newly sharpened pencils. "Make yourselves at home," she said, "if you need anything, just call."

''On what? asked Perce.

''Oh, you'll have a phone in here later in the day,'' she said cheerfully.

''I know what I'd like to call her for,'' said Al after she'd left.

The lot looked the same as it always had, but on the sound stages, most of which were now divided into two split stages, most of what was being shot was television, small units of people racing efficiently through episodes for various series.

It was the pace that was so different. Years back, a program B picture, a ''quickie,'' was shot in two, three weeks, and everybody complained about the rush-rush pace. Nowadays, two weeks would be a Cadillac schedule; these fifty-minute TV shows were being ground out on a regular, assembly-line six-day-and-that's-it-you're-finished-come-hell-or-high-water treadmill. A half-hour show was knocked out in three days, that was for the filmed ones; most of the situation comedies today were done on tape, which meant four days' rehearsal, then a long, grueling day taping in front of a live audience.

. . . No wonder it was no longer a business for the middle-aged.

At lunchtime he took Al and LeRoy to the commissary. The room was jammed with the usual crowd of actors and actresses, technical crews and production people. The Chesters ate and stared, Al's admiration for females of all shapes and sizes was obvious. If they expected him to introduce them to movie stars, they were out of luck. Perce didn't recognize anyone he knew. He spotted a couple of old character actors—my God, could they be that old?—but most of the people were wolfing their food, grabbing a break, studying their lines for this afternoon's work, the place was like a factory lunch room now.

''What do we do this afternoon, chief?'' asked Al.

''I'll walk you around, show you where they make pictures,'' said Perce. ''Then maybe we'll go home early and have a nap.''

''That's what I call stealing money,'' said Al.

"For you, it's legal," said Perce. "You made a hundred bucks today—just by showing up."

"How long has this been going on?" asked LeRoy.

"Ever since Cecil B. DeMille showed up here and started shooting *The Squaw Man,*" said Perce.

By Wednesday, Harry was still not back from his location.

Al and LeRoy were still jovial, a pair of tourists set loose in their own grown-up Disneyland. He'd taken them all over the lot, showing them the various departments, scenery, costumes, props, the machine shop, the carpenter shop, the whole works. Cutting rooms, the dubbing stage; they'd tiptoed onto sound stages to watch the crews at work, he'd hiked them over to the back lot and showed them the various standing sets. To them, it was all fascinating. For Perce, it was a waste of time.

He hadn't been sleeping well.

Ahead of him was the job of writing a full screenplay. On a flat deal, not by the week—which meant the longer the job took, the less he'd earn.

A full screenplay was a lot of hard work, a marathon race a hundred forty-odd pages long. Everybody and his brother grabbed your pages as you finished them, read them, Harry Elbert would criticize the lines, change the scenes, make suggestions, rip his work apart, the director would tell you a scene you'd written and rewritten a half dozen times was unnecessary, held up the flow of the story, *out*—the actors would complain that your words couldn't be spoken, they'd ad lib their own half-assed inventions, if it was crap (which it usually was) the critics would nail you for sloppy writing . . .

. . . But before any of that happened, you, and only you had to get the stuff down on the paper. You were out there alone, you were the only one who exposed himself.

It was a job he hadn't tackled in a long time, and now that he was stuck with it, he was secretly dreading it. Writing *Three Down, Two Left Standing* would be like picking up a game he hadn't played in a long time. Sure, his body would remember vaguely where it was supposed to go, his reflexes would hopefully come to life and react when they were called on, but the muscles were slack and flabby. The Writers Guild West was crammed with young, eager kids, all ready to pounce on his first draft and rewrite it, to give it the ''now'' feel.

. . . Maybe that bastard Harry had been right when he suggested that Perce belonged on the tennis court, giving lessons.

Screw Harry. He'd do the first draft, collect his money, and then, in the famous words of the Greaser, ''. . . let the fucking *sera que sera!*''

Thursday, Miss Lister came in with a message. Mr. Elbert would not be back until the following week, but he wished them all to make a meeting at ten tomorrow, in Mr. Elbert's office, with Mr. William Elbert. They were to understand that ''Mr. William Elbert is completely briefed on the way Mr. E wishes you to proceed.''

. . . Mr. *William* Elbert?

What rock had he crawled out from under?

''Your trouble is, you don't read the trades,'' said Vera, and passed over *Daily Variety,* in which there was a page-one item:

> Vet producer-scribe Harry Elbert, winding up location shooting on Vin DeLuca starrer, *Cimarron,* has assigned son William Elbert to serve as producer on a new project, as yet untitled, to be developed for a proposed two-hour vidfilm. Elbert fils has extensive b.g. in videotaping field, having copped First Prize for Docu-Drama in last year's Toledo Videotape Festival.

''. . . And I ran away from Ziggy Harling because he was a son-in-*law!*'' exploded Perce. 'Now he's run in his *son* on me—and look at this damn release—the bastards don't even mention my name!''

''Now you sound like one of my paying clients,'' observed Vera.

* * *

chapter 17

—Ahhh, Newton, how come *you* always get to be quarterback?
—Because we're playing on my father's field, and besides, it's *my* football!

". . . WELL, now, like my old man is up to his ass down there in that Cherokee Strip scene, see," said William Elbert, known to a few initimates as Billy, introduced this day as Mr. Elbert. ". . . So lemme clue you boys how I see this project."

He leaned back behind his father's desk, stretched out in the chair, the heels of his expensive leather boots atop the fine mahogany, his lean body draped in a loose Mexican shirt covered with embroidered flowers, and worn jeans. Beneath his wavy hair, his sharp eyes were protected by airplane-pilot-style sunglasses, and his upper lip was effectively hiden by a Zapata mustache.

"I've read the stuff on the pages," he continued, "and it's interesting, as far as it goes, but like, what I mean is, it doesn't go far enough, you know what I'm saying, Chester?"

Al Chester cleared his throat.

"Perce here's the *writer,*" he said.

"Yeah, yeah," said William, "now what I'm talking about is the overall feel of the story. I think we got to try for the Altman flavor, you know? Hard jump cuts, flat lighting, lots of local color, people you can smell, for real, heavy on character, real heavy."

No one replied. The stereo played softly.

Perce studiously examined his fingernails, awaiting the next words of wisdom, idly wondering were they native to this Marlboroman boy genius . . . or had he been briefed by his father?

William consulted a pad on his father's desk. "Note," he announced. "Big problem. We are missing a *girl*. Now. I kind of visualize somebody our two guys pick up along the way, a sort of thrill-kill crazy broad who has the hots for them because she wants to hump a gun . . . you know?'' He peered at Al.''Like Bonnie did for Clyde?''

''. . . I never did have me anybody like that,'' said Al. ''I guess old Clyde got lucky.''

''Yeah,'' said William. ''So you struck out.'' He turned to LeRoy. ''What about you? What kind of humping did you get, Al?''

''He's LeRoy,'' said Perce.

''Oh, yeah? Excuse me,'' said William unabashed. ''I just got into this, remember. How about it, LeRoy, want to clue us on your women?''

''I don't rightly know as I do,'' said LeRoy.

The large man's face was beginning to turn pink.

''Hell, you're not neuter, you did have broads,'' insisted William.

LeRoy's hand went to his pocket, removed his stainless-steel hand exerciser, his fingers began to work it back and forth. ''It's nothing I talk about much,'' he said.

''Look,'' said William, ''—this isn't a talk show, don't be shy, I'm only trying to see if like we can't find some honest, meaningful ongoing relationship that we can use to get our story across!''

''Man likes to keep those things private,'' said Al softly.

Again silence set in.

William's sunglasses panned around the room, focusing on the three men, moving from one to the other.

Perce resisted the impulse to snicker.

''You guys are not helping me,'' said William, a touch of petulance creeping into his tone.

''Let's hear your next note,'' Perce suggested.

''We haven't gotten anywhere on this one!'' said William.

William consulted his pad. ''. . . Does this story have to take place in the nineteen fifties?'' he asked. ''Everybody's been doing the fifties. They're getting sort of stale, you know? Why can't we move it up to the nineteen *sixties?''*

Al cleared his throat.

''We was in the pen during the sixties,'' he said.

"So?" asked William.

"We don't know much about what was going on outside," said Al.

"You can learn!" insisted William.

Again, there was silence.

"I get the feeling you guys are fighting me," said William, now sullen.

"Based on what?" asked Perce innocently.

William's boots dropped to the floor and he sat up straight. "I'm not a complete schmuck, you know," he said defiantly. "I get the feeling you guys resent me because I'm the new boy around here."

"Why, we don't hardly know you well enough to resent you," said Al. "Yet."

William's lips were set tightly.

Perce felt a brief flash of pity for the boy. Hell, it wasn't his fault that his father had shoved him into this spot—or was it? He checked himself—*watch it, Perce*—This was Harry's kid, and you better not deny heredity. Extend the hand of peace to him, he'd probably take it off at the elbow.

. . . No, the way to handle this *pisher* was to give his ego a massage, to let him feel included—but always to keep him at arm's length.

He got up and walked over to the desk. Bent down. "Can you and I talk privately?" he murmured.

Then he strolled toward the door. As he passed Al, he winked. William got up and followed him to the outer office.

Perce closed the door, beckoned William closer.

"Just between you and me," he told the boy, very man to man, "you've been around, so you've probably gotten the message. These guys are the real McCoy. Twenty years in the slammer. Don't let them fool you, they're still hard."

". . . Yeah?" said William. "I sensed that."

"You and me, we're civilians, chum," said Perce. "But you never discuss a con's personal life with him unless *he* opens up."

". . . *Ahh,*" said William.

"That big guy is a bundle of dynamite, so watch it," warned Perce. "Him I handle with kid gloves, get it?"

''Sure,'' agreed William.

''They'll be fine on the technical stuff, they'll give us everything we need, but when it comes to anything about women, or their personal life, who knows how they'll react? That *we'll* handle together, agreed?''

''Agreed,'' said William gratefully.

''Now let's go back, go through the treatment down to the end,'' suggested Perce. ''Make your suggestions, we'll thrash it all out, we'll make notes, then I'll go back to my office and try to flesh them out—then we meet again, just you and me—dig?''

''Dug,'' said William.

''We're going to have us one hell of a picture here,'' said Perce. ''Something that'll knock this town on its ass.''

''I've always thought so!'' said William happily.

''. . . And any time we get into a hassle about something,'' said Perce, ''you forget this nonsense about you being the new boy. Lay it on the line. Don't pull your punches about *anything*.''

''You can bet your ass I will!'' promised William enthusiastically

Perce led the way back inside.

Round one to *me,* he thought. Only fourteen more to go.

They spent a good part of the day going through the rest of his treatment. Surprisingly enough, a few of William's ''notes'' weren't dumb at all. Some of them were even constructive.

So, after sufficient argument, he accepted a couple. Enough to prove to the kid that he'd contributed.

. . . If you couldn't lick 'em, you did a little joining.

In this ball game, the producer always had the final word.

And on this job, he'd have to contend with two of them.

Around four, William excused himself, pleading an urgent prior appointment. He had to have his car tuned up at a special place in downtown Hollywood . . . but they could continue without him, couldn't they?''

On a friendlier basis now, very buddy-buddy, he insisted that they accompany him outside to see this new set of wheels, his latest toy.

It was parked in Harry's private space, a rakish, gleaming coupe whose lines were vaguely familiar.

"*Say,*" said Al. "That's a Studie. Hawk, fifty-three—right?"

"You knew!" said William, pleased.

"Darn nice car," said Al. "Good lines. Kind of underpowered."

"This one's got a Porsche engine under the hood," said William.

"A beauty," said Al.

"You ever have one?" asked William.

"Yeah," said Al. He grinned. "For a couple of hours, once."

"A couple of—" William stopped. "Oh, hey, *I* get it!" he said, impressed.

"They caught up to us," said Al. "That's how I know it's underpowered."

As they walked back to the office, Al spoke. "Partner," he said, "you did one beautiful snow job on that sprout."

"I had help," said Perce.

"What did he mean about me being neuter?" asked LeRoy.

* * *

chapter 18

—At last, I, Count Zarko, have possession of the Radium X-Ray-O-Graph! With this weapon in my hands, I can control the world!

—Not so fast, Zarko. Don't move—I have the building surrounded. Your reign of terror is at an end!

—Ah, so, Agent Carruthers? I think not. I hold the trump card in this game. *Bring out the girl.*

—Betty! Betty—it's me, Tom!

— . . . Who?

—Betty, darling—what has this monster done to you?

— . . . Huh?

—What do you say *now,* Carruthers? The tables are turned, eh?

—You'll never get away with this, Zarko!

AL Chester, in slacks and a short-sleeved sports shirt, strolled casually down the sunny studio street, his eyes behind sunglasses fixed firmly on the attractive young brunette who walked a few paces ahead, her trim figure draped in a 1920s-type costume, her skirts billowing free.

His brother LeRoy, in an open shirt and a pair of chinos, came toward him, turned, and fell into step beside Al. "Getting a little air?" he asked.

"And enjoying the view," said Al. "Man's got to relax sometime. What about them gates?"

"There's five," said LeRoy softly. "They's all manned, twenty-four hours a day. The one way down by the studio garage there is the one where most of the trucks go in and out. The rest of 'em is for cars, mostly."

"What about the walls?" asked Al.

"They's covered by an alarm system," said LeRoy. "Electronic stuff, all plugged into an office behind the garage building. Anybody tries to bust in anywhere, the walls is scanned by TV's—

that's to cover any area they can't see from the gates. That's so's they can get into their little mobile carts and hustle right over, see?"

"Makes you feel you're right back in the slammer, don't it?" grinned Al.

The brunette turned to hurry up a flight of stairs that led to a bank of make-up rooms on the second floor, alongside the sound stage. As she dashed upward, her legs flashed nicely beneath the brief costume.

"Never had anything like *that* in there," said LeRoy.

"She wouldn't've lasted long if she had been," said Al. "What's about the vaults?"

"The ones they got here they use to store the film that comes back from the lab each morning. Dailies, they call 'em. Then each day, they bring 'em to the editors for cutting up, see?"

"And it goes back to the vault when they're done each night?" asked Al.

"Yeah," said LeRoy. "But when it's all put together, what they call a workprint, then they store the negative over to the lab."

"You're really learning the movie business, aren't you?" asked Al.

"Well, a man's got to broaden himself," said LeRoy. "I found me a little lady down there—works for an editor, she's being mighty helpful."

". . . She don't know who you are, does she?" asked Al sharply.

LeRoy shook his head. "Nope," he said. "I'm an electrician, works down in the back lot, my name's Hank Jones."

"Uh *huh,*" said Al. "And what are you doing for *her,* Hank—trying to slip her a little short circuit, maybe?"

"Hell, no," said LeRoy. "She's married."

"Ah, come on," said Al. "This is Hollywood. Working out here is like being locked up in a goddamn candy factory."

The brothers turned the corner and started down the street toward the studio commissary.

"How's the script coming?" asked LeRoy.

"Oh, old Perce is doing just fine," said Al. "Says he's almost halfway through. We sure picked us the right boy, didn't we?"

"Yeah," said LeRoy. "I hope he stays a good partner all the way."

"We come this far okay, didn't we?" asked Al.

Bright, clear sunlight bathed the glistening swimming pool, set in a tiny patio, surrounded by expensive Japanese bonsai on a narrow ledge of terrace, high above Coldwater Canyon. It was Saturday morning, and the hum of the steady traffic below was counterpointed by the sound of tennis balls being whacked at nearby courts.

The sliding door to the Elbert house slid open, and William emerged, his long body in frayed denim, a cup of coffee in hand. He winced at the sudden light, then walked across to the lounge chair where Harry Elbert lay, prone, his eyes protected by sunglasses, his torso glistening with suntan oil. Save for the long cigar which protruded upward from his mouth like a periscope, occasionally emitting a puff of bluish smoke, there was no other sign of life from Elbert père.

"Hi," said William.

"Oh, you," said his father. "Out late, huh?"

"Yeah, I guess so," said William.

"*Schtupping,* I hope."

"Yeah," said William.

"You started early enough," said his father. "I looked for you yesterday afternoon on the lot and you'd already gone. Is she that good?"

"I guess so," said William, yawning.

"Bring her around," said his father.

"Did you read the pages we left for you?" asked William.

"Not yet," said Harry. "I'm up to my ass in the final cut of *Cimarron*—got to work all day. Who has time to read? Tell me about 'em."

William sat down. "I think they're damned good," he said. "Tight, you know? All that stuff leading up to the robbery—no waste words, lots of action. Tense. The story like—moves right along, you know?"

"How soon's he gonna be done?"

"A couple more weeks, I'd say. You know, Perce is doing a nice job. Of course, you have to keep an eye on him all the time, but when you stay with him, you know something, these old timers are pretty damn sharp, once you get to know how they operate.''

''He knows a few tricks,'' conceded Harry. ''After all these years, he ought to.''

William nodded. ''But he's—well, he's better than that. He's giving the script the right feel. Like a good nineteen forties melodrama. It's authentic, man.'' He finished his coffee. ''I *like* working with the guy.''

Harry shifted the cigar to the other side of his mouth. ''Don't build him up too high.''

''. . . I don't get you,'' said William.

''Don't get too thick with him,'' said his father, ''and with those two *schlub* ex-cons, either.''

''. . . Well, I'm like—working with them, aren't I?'' asked William.

''Let it stop there,'' said his father. ''Don't socialize. I see you going to lunch with them and all that crap. Be a little less easy, you know?''

''. . . Why shouldn't I be eating with them?''

''Okay, so eat with them, but don't get so buddy-buddy,'' said Harry. ''Because when Perce is done farting around with his first draft, we're going to want rewrites, remember?''

''Oh, sure,'' said William. ''But not a hell of a lot—Perce already knows that, we've discussed it—''

''Have you discussed who's going to do them?''

William blinked. *''Perce.''* he said.

''Uh uh, sonny,'' said Harry. *''You.''*

''Me?'' William grinned. *''Me?* Hell, I'm no writer.''

''Neither is anybody else until they start,'' said Harry, ''but you'll pick it up fast. And that's how you're gonna get yourself a co-credit on this script.''

''. . . You're snowing me,'' said William, after a moment.

''Nope,'' said Harry.

''. . . Wait a minute,'' his son protested. ''Hold it—what's the matter with Perce? He's done a good job so far—''

''Christ!'' said Harry. ''Do I have to draw you a fucking road map? When he's finished, we close him out, and then *you* take the script and work it over, with me telling you how to do it—then, when you've done the second draft, and the polish, you'll have stuck enough stuff into the script, changed the lines around, so when it comes to a credit arbitration, your name goes on it along with Perce!''

William, obviously confused, shook his head. ''You can do that?'' he asked at last.

Harry sat up, flipped his cigar toward a nearby ashtray. ''Every day of the week,'' he said. *''Look,* a split credit means you share in the rerun money if we go the TV route, if we do it as a feature, you cut in on foreign sales, you share in the TV payment, there's sequel rights, paperback money when we do a book—the works. So you'll go join the Guild, you'll be assigned to work on the rewrites, and when we're done, you're home free.''

''. . . And Perce is screwed,'' said William.

''Screwed my ass!'' protested Harry. ''He's getting money up front, he's getting a co-credit, more than he's had in years—he'll go out and get some other assignment, maybe—what's so terrible about that?''

''. . . It smells,'' said William.

''So hold your nose,'' said Harry. ''Believe me, he'd do exactly the same thing to me if he had the chance—remember that!''

He got up, stretched, removed his sunglasses, padded to the far end of the pool, and dove in clumsily, sending up a small geyser of water across the surrounding area. Harry proceeded to swim one lap across the pool's length, emerged from the water and began to towel himself. He put on his sunglasses and stared at his son, who sat, staring at his feet.

''What'sa matter, you look like you'd been hit with a truck. What's bugging you?''

''You,'' said his son. ''I don't believe what you just said. I mean—what a shafting—''

Harry reached over and patted his son's shoulder. ''This isn't a fucking commune, you know.'' he said gruffly. ''Don't worry, you'll learn to live with it, believe me.''

Draped in his towel, he started toward the sliding door.

''Yeah,'' said William. ''That's what I'm afraid of . . .''

* * *

chapter 19

—Take your hands off me, you big lug! What kind of girl do you think I am?

. . . ON a court, when you hit a bad ball, you knew it before it left your racquet, just as when you hit a good one, you could see the reaction on your opponent's face, before he missed it.

For Perce, writing in his drab office suite eight or nine hours each day, flying solo, was torture at first. He was strictly on his own, nobody to schmoos with, to swap jokes . . . nobody to yell "Fault!"

Since when was writing a script like entering a monastery? Locked up in this dingy box, how the hell could you tell if the script was going well?

Sure, he sensed that some of it was exciting. Al and LeRoy read his pages, nodded, and politely remarked that he seemed to be getting it all down just the way it was. On the occasional days that Billy Elbert (he'd insisted on the familiar handle from the second week) showed up to scan the work, the kid insisted that Perce was dead on target. "Heavy, man," that was Billy's accolade . . . but what the hell did he know?

. . . And most frustrating of all, silence from Harry. The pages went to him, but nothing came back. He was locked up with his crew of editors, trying to get his epic put together.

The first tangible hint that it was going well came from an unexpected source.

Redheaded Miss Lister (could Harry be knocking off some of that well-endowed figure?)—that silent lady who handled all the office housekeeping details, budget, the forms for payroll and accounting, the security passes, the parking spaces on Lot B outside the back gate (one for Perce's Caddy, one for Al and LeRoy, who'd invested in a small used Vega, purchased from the mechanic out in the valley who handled all of Billy Elbert's constant automotive problems).

Well-organized Miss Lister, from her there was little small talk. Silently, she'd assumed the task of seeing to it that Perce's script pages were retyped and Xeroxed each morning, then she would file and distribute them to Harry, to Billy, and back to Perce.

. . . But then, remarkably, in the middle of the third week, she volunteered the suggestion that he could use a new typewriter. The next day, his battered L. C. Smith was replaced with an opulent, nearly new IBM.

A couple of days later, she mentioned that he might like access to fresh coffee during the day. It seemed there was an extra Mr. Coffee in one of Harry Elbert's closets; it arrived the next morning, along with a can of coffee, Cremora, and a set of cups.

The next week she appeared in person, pushing a new typing chair, to replace the worn one he was using.

''Such luxury,'' he remarked. ''What have I done to deserve it?''

''Oh, this is a class operation all the way, Mr. Barnes,'' she said.

''It wasn't in the beginning,'' he said. ''Don't tell me Mr. Elbert likes the script.''

''I wouldn't know,'' she said. ''He's very busy.''

''Then I've passed my written exams with you?''

She permitted herself a brief smile. ''I've read worse.''

''If I promise to keep on turning in good stuff, what treats do I get next week, Miss Lister?'' he teased.

''The name's Audrey,'' she said. She glanced about the empty office. ''What have you done with Tweedledum and Tweedledee?''

''Gone fishing,'' he said, winking. He'd taken to sending them home after lunch. Some days, they didn't come in at all, and so what? Harry could afford it; he'd practically stolen their story, let them steal a little salary back. Besides, there was no point in having Al and LeRoy sitting on the office couch, reading the papers or waiting for him to stop writing so that they could pass the time talking about the Dodgers or about their Vega and its gas mileage.

Perce was working on a flat deal; the sooner he finished this damn first draft of the script and turned it in, the quicker he could get to the second part of the deal, the payment for rewrites.

She helped herself to one of his cigarettes.

"You know, sometimes those guys spook me," she said.

"They're a couple of pussycats," he said.

". . . I don't like the way they stare," she said. "Especially the big one."

"Well, it's been a long time since they had scenery like you to stare at," he said.

"Let them find someone else," she said, and perched her shapely behind onto the office sofa. Leaned back, and then, as one of the broken springs attacked her, she jumped up. "*Hey*—we better do something about *this,*" she grimaced. "A person could get stabbed."

"Nonsense, that couch is a collector's item," he grinned. "Would you believe that on those cushions Carole Landis began her climb to fame?"

". . . Carole who?"

He winced. "Lordy, I had no idea I was so old—or that you were so damned young."

"You're not old, you're in your prime," she said.

"Check me out after six hours at this typewriter."

". . . Why don't I see if I can't get you a better couch, so you can stretch out?" she suggested.

"Is that to keep the morale of the troops up?" he asked.

Her smile widened. "I thought you said you were old."

". . . Not that old," he parried.

A couple of days later, a new couch appeared at noontime, lugged in by two studio hands who removed the old one and eased the new one through the doorway, a broad Naugahyde job with overstuffed cushions, wide and comfortable.

He buzzed Audrey on the intercom. "Opulent," he said. "When are you coming down to test it out?"

"My name's Audrey, not Carole," she said. "Not today. Mr. E. is running us ragged."

"Feel free to drop in on the slave quarters whenever you need R and R, ma'am," he told her.

". . . Man, look at that," remarked Al, the following morning. "What'd we do to deserve it?"

"When you're hot, you're hot," said Perce.

Al read his paper, had coffee, and then went for his morning stroll. Le Roy wasn't coming in today; some private business to attend to.

After lunch, Al went down the hall to the lavatory, leaving his jacket on the sofa. A piece of folded yellow paper had fluttered out of the pocket and lay on the floor.

Perce picked it up.

On it, in Al's laborious hand, was neatly printed:

1. director makes cut
2. producer either accepts or rejects
3. if he redoes it, it is with editor
4. final cut; *workprint*
5. editor makes marks for opticals and titles
6. sends backgrounds to animation house for o & t—they are superimposed
7. effects man puts in doorslams, footsteps, sirens, etc.
8. lays separate track next on workprint, in *sync*
9. live score, added on another track to workprint
10. dubbing of voices—*looping* scenes until OK another track
11. MIXING—picture
effects track
music
dialogue track
(split for level)
room-tone track
loops
onto *one* track
12. foreign versions—(+ dialogue & effects track)
(+ music & effects track)
13. mixed track is transferred to optical track
14. now you cut negative to match workprint
15. add optical effects

16. cut into negative & spliced together
17. negative sent to *lab* with optical track
18. another print is struck from cut negative (which was combined with optical track) makes composite—or *answer* print
19. corrections made in timing and color
20. another print made—"air" or "theater"
21. NEGATIVE is stored in lab. Not in studio—lab is in Hollywood

". . . I think that's mine," said Al, pleasantly.

He'd returned and was standing in the doorway.

Perce handed him the yellow page.

"Looks like you're learning the picture business from the ground up, pal."

Al nodded. "Got a letter from one of my pals, inside," he said, carefully tucking the paper into his pocket. "He wanted to know how it worked—so I checked it out with some of the people down in them technical departments."

"He's planning to make his own picture in stir?" asked Perce.

". . . When you're inside long enough, you get some strange notions," said Al. "Got anything you want me to hang around for this afternoon?"

"You're on your own," said Perce, anxious to get back to work.

. . . It was late that afternoon, while he was riffling through Al's original manuscript, searching for the exact date on which the gang had decided to tackle the money truck, their biggest heist, that his eye lit on a sentence in Al's awkward narrative:

> . . . The whole "trick" to a successful job is to check everything out to the last little detail "up front." Don't worry if you spend months planning it all out—always remember, you only get one shot at the brass ring. You have to get it all right "going in." Or else.

Ironic, wasn't it? All that planning—and if it hadn't been for that pussy-crazy kid spending his money down in Florida, they'd've gotten away with it. The one human factor that thorough Al Chester had missed out on.

Now Al was researching the nuts and bolts of the movie business.

Almost as carefully as if he were planning a job *here*.

. . . For a friend in the slammer who was interested in the movie business?

Remarkable . . . Unless Al was bullshitting him.

Ah, what else could it be? Certainly Al and LeRoy Chester weren't going to heist this damned studio!

The idea amused him. Maybe there was a story in it. Two middle-aged cons decide to rip off a studio, they go for the payroll, probably—take the cashier's office on payday—no, that wouldn't work, everyone was paid by check—no, they'd go for something else, nowadays the whole bit was to take hostages, right? So Al and LeRoy would move into a sound stage, maybe kidnap a star who's in the midst of doing a series, a Telly Savalas, or Farrah Fawcett-Majors, yeah, sure, that was it—and they demand a half a mil in ransom from the network—

Hey, the idea had possibilities—

Back to work, Perce, he told himself. You are on a flat deal, remember?

It was almost after six when he finished the day's pages. He was tired. Now he could go home, open the bourbon bottle, and have the first drink of the day, which, God knows, he'd earned.

He got up and stretched, gathered the pages, and buzzed Audrey. He wanted to drop them off at her desk before he left.

"I'll come pick them up," she said.

A few minutes later she came in. Today she wore a demure blue sweater and skirt outfit that did good things for her figure.

"This is what I call service," he said, handing her the pages in a folder.

"You earned it," she replied.

"Take good care of that sequence," he said. "It's an Academy Award winner, at least."

She made no move to leave.

"Have you got anything to drink around here?" she asked. "I could use a blast."

''Just coffee,'' he said.

''Hell,'' she said, and dropped onto the sofa. Her face was drawn tight, and today there were no smiles.

''Hey, what's up?'' he asked. ''Is he piling it on, baby?''

She shook her head.

''. . . I guess I don't like this job,'' she said softly. ''I used to think it would be so exciting to work here, at a studio, right in the middle of everything . . .'' She made a face. ''Boy was I ever Norma Naïve. I've got to go home and take a shower so I can feel clean.''

He sat down beside her.

''What's bugging you, lady?'' he asked. ''Tell the old man.''

''You wouldn't be able to help,'' she said.

''Come on, try me,'' he murmured. ''I can be useful.''

She shook her head, again.

He snaked his arm around her, his hand found a shoulder that was stiff, unyielding.

''. . . Look, I didn't come down here to ball you,'' she said suddenly.

''No, of course you didn't,'' he said, inhaling the scent of her, his hand exploring the firm shape of her thigh. ''. . . But it's not such a terrible idea, is it?''

He moved to cover her mouth with his, and then they were struggling like two kids in the parlor until her mouth began to answer his, fiercely.

''. . . The door's open,'' she gasped, when she broke free.

''I can fix that,'' he promised, and got up to close it, snapping the ancient latch. Then he crossed to the window and lowered the blind. Christ—this was like the old days at Paramount, in the writers building—after five o'clock the bottles would come out of the drawers, and your secretary's came off . . . in time for the Happy Hour—that was one of the side benefits of working at Paramount.

When he turned back, the room was darker, but he could see that she'd risen, kicked off her shoes, and now she was pulling her sweater up over her head, revealing the shapely flesh, tanned and firm, her remarkable breasts straining at the bra.

"... Oh, baby," he told her, "you are something else." The excitement rose in him, it had been a long time since he was so stirred.

"I know," she said. Off came the bra, and they swung free, his targets for tonight, as he returned to her, his mouth roaming her topography, his hands working at the snaps of her skirt.

"... Now *you,*" she instructed, pulling at his clothes. When he had dropped them, she murmured, "... You're not in such bad shape yourself ..."

"... For an old man," and then there was no more small talk, it was a grappling, her hands clawing at him, a wrestling match in the half darkness, her cries in his ear as he peeled away the rest of her clothes to open her wide, to mount, to ride—

—her rhythmic thrusts answering his, her strength surprised him, on and on they rocked, then he was unable to hold back, his climax too soon for her, but she kept on, holding him locked inside of her until finally, with a hoarse cry, she peaked.

... In the dark office, the Naugahyde clinging to their moist bodies, they both dozed, spent.

He blinked open his eyes. Chuckled at the sight of the clothes strewn around them.

"What's funny?" she asked.

"... We've now launched this couch for future casting," he told her.

"Wasn't what I had in mind," she said.

"Aren't you proud you were first?"

"Sure," she said, and got up. She began to pick up her clothes. "But it's the second time you've been screwed today."

He dozed.

... Then, as the impact of her remark connected, he blinked open his eyes. "What does that mean?"

By now she had stepped into her skirt, was pulling her sweater over her startling red hair ... which he now knew was absolutely natural.

"Hey, lady," he said, sitting up. "Don't go cryptic on me."

Silently, she opened the latch, and went outside, and he heard the lavatory door slam.

What the hell had she meant?

He pulled on his clothes, waiting for her return.

When she came back she had repaired her face. Once again she was the demure and capable second in command to Harry Elbert's office staff.

"What did that last remark mean—about me getting screwed twice?"

"It means that—" She stopped. "I shouldn't tell you this," she continued, lighting a cigarette, "but damnit, you've been working your ass off here—and what you're writing is good—damned good—and we all of us know it—"

A prickle went up Perce's neck.

". . . So?" he asked.

"So you're going to get shafted!" she said, angrily. "And if you mention what I just told you, I'll deny it, because I work for the bastard, and I don't want to lose my job—not until I find a better one!"

She started toward the office door, but he was up now, grabbing her arm to keep her from leaving.

"Just give me the game plan," he said. "And don't worry, you'll stay in the clear."

"It's nothing very special," she said. "You're on page ninety-seven, and when you get to the fade out, that's what it's going to be—as far as you're concerned—the fade out!"

"Who takes over?" he asked, controlling himself.

"I have a feeling it's Billy," she said.

Billy?

She turned, suddenly came back and kissed him. "I like you," she told him. "You sure as hell don't deserve to be shafted like this."

Then she and the day's pages were gone, and he was alone.

He sat down on the new sofa.

Godamnit.

If Audrey was Norma Naïve, then what was he? Sam Schmuck—in spades!

. . . How incredibly dumb of him not to realize that after all these years Harry Elbert could have changed—and not to have been prepared for the bastard's tricks.

Sure, all along Harry had simply been using him, keeping him plugging away in this crummy suite, waiting for him to finish so that he could *ootz* his asshole kid into a co-credit.

He got up, left the office, his stomach churning, his mouth tasting of bile.

. . . All these weeks, he'd been working his ass off, like some Boy Scout who believed the world was built on merit badges, for once in his life concentrating on making this script the best he could—

—Leaving his flanks exposed to an old trick, such an old ploy he'd almost forgotten how it worked, a hit-and-run credit grab. The oldest game in town!

Okay, Perce, Harry has you by the left nut. What do you do now?

. . . He was dozing, sodden on his bed, when the phone rang.

"How's it going?" asked Vera. "I've been waiting all day to hear from you."

"Terrific," he said.

". . . You sound strange. Have you had any dinner?"

"Not hungry," he told her.

". . . *Perce,* are you on the sauce?"

"Yep," he said.

"Why?"

"Baby, I got my reasons," he said. "Just do me a favor tonight. Don't ask me why. I'm tired."

"Suit yourself," she said and hung up.

. . . He dropped the phone back on its hook, buried his face in the pillow.

Tomorrow he would damn well do something about it. Tomorrow he would figure out a way to screw Harry Elbert back.

. . . And if not tomorrow, the day after.

It was past eleven, and the small radio in the Chesters' newly rented two-room furnished apartment was softly playing country-and-western-style music from an all-night station.

In his shorts, perspiring slightly, Al sat at the tiny breakfast bar. Spread out in front of him were scribbled yellow pages, a brochure from the Excelsior U-Haul Rentals, an open L.A. telephone book (Central District), and a large street map of Greater L.A., on which he was now laboriously tracing a route with a blue pen.

A key turned in the door, and LeRoy, in sweat suit and sneakers, came in. He went to the tiny refrigerator and poured himself a glass of milk.

"How's it going?" he inquired, when he had finished it.

"Okay," said Al, still tracing the route. "You're out late."

"Gave a friend of mine a ride home from the spa," said LeRoy. "Weight lifter."

"Did she lift you?" asked Al, grinning.

"You're getting a dirty mind in your old age," said LeRoy.

"Helps pass the time," said Al. LeRoy peered over Al's shoulder at the map.

"Now we need timing," said Al. "Tomorrow, you take the car and follow the map, take the stop watch and figure it all out."

LeRoy nodded.

"Get any more scoop on Elbert's schedule?" asked Al.

"Lady figures he's about done by next weekend," said LeRoy.

"Good," said Al. He put down his pen, rubbed his eyes. "We're getting there." He yawned, stretched. "Me for the feathers." He went into their tiny bathroom and began to wash.

"When are you goin' to talk to Perce?" asked LeRoy.

". . . I think we're just about ready, don't you?" said Al, towelling himself.

LeRoy began to put on his pajamas.

"I dunno," he said, "I'm not sure."

"About the timing?"

"No, about *him,*" said LeRoy.

"Hell," said Al. "This is no time to start wondering about him."

"Yeah," said LeRoy slowly. "He's a hustler . . . sure. Okay, maybe we can trust him. But supposing something went wrong—how hard could we lean on him?"

Al finished brushing his teeth. "You're thinking he's chicken?"

"Not exactly chicken, no," said LeRoy.

"Then what?"

“. . . I guess maybe he’s not hungry enough, you get my drift?”

“No, I don’t,” said Al. “He’s as greedy as the next one. Maybe even more.”

“Sure. He likes money,” said LeRoy. “Question is, how much will he do to get a bundle?”

“Any man his age wants security for his sunset years,” said Al. “He won’t have to do too much, just go along with us.”

“Yeah,” said LeRoy, climbing into bed. “But if we need us a third—which I still don’t know’s we do—why *him?* They’s plenty others—”

“No, him,” said Al. “He’s our cover. We talked this all over, didn’t we? If he knows what’s going on, and he’s with us—then he has to cover for us. If we leave him out, how do we know he would?”

“Mmm,” said LeRoy, burrowing his head into the pillow. “All’s I wish was he was maybe a little . . . meaner, you know? He likes what he’s doing too much.”

Al snapped off the radio, switched off the lights, climbed into his own bed.

“Well,” he said in the darkness, “we come too far to stop here. Let’s stick to what we decided. I guess maybe it’s time to have that little talk with him, right soon.”

There was no answer. LeRoy was already asleep.

* * *

chapter 20

—You mean . . . ?
—Yeah. That's *exactly* what I mean.

PERCE reluctantly came awake. It had been months since he'd felt quite so rotten. Why couldn't medical science develop a way of transferring this sick head to Harry Elbert? The bastard deserved it.

The prospect of going into that depressing office to work did not appeal to him in the slightest; he made some instant coffee and washed down a couple of aspirin. Then he headed over to the club. He needed to get onto a court and work out some of the tensions.

It was early, but luckily old Danny Kanter was already there, nosing around for a game. Poor Danny, a loner who'd been through four wives and kept on browsing for the fifth, a lonely character for whom the club was a surrogate living room, home, even an office. His tennis game was close to being the worst in the entire membership, but this morning, it was the only game in town.

When they finished, Perce had beaten Danny three straight sets, and Danny threw up his hands, moaning, "Enough is enough! Thank God nobody was watching!"

Perspiring, they headed for the locker room. "What's bugging you today?" Danny demanded. "I thought you said you wanted a friendly game."

Perce patted the old man's shoulder. "Nothing personal."

"Bullshit," groaned Danny. "You make Nastase look like a pussycat. You played like you were out to kill."

"Maybe, but it wasn't you," Perce said.

. . . He had drained away some of the hostility, but he still had no taste to return to the studio.

So where?

There was still a script to complete—he was writing the climactic sequence where the Chesters, having pulled off the money-truck robbery, were making their well-planned getaway. Then, the dispersal of the gang, and finally, the inevitable trackdown by the old detective.

Damn. It was going to be a good script. Lean, sharp, no fat. As good as he'd ever done. Sure, and once he'd finish this first draft, he would be politely dumped. And once that genial, incoherent kid Billy (with the help of his father) finished making all the page after page of changes in the body of the script, adding a line here, changing a couple of speeches there, juggling the characters a bit . . . sure, he could have himself a co-credit!

So what was new about that? It happened all the time.

How often had he done it himself, to other, less knowledgeable writers?

Why was it so tough to swallow, this time?

. . . Hell, he didn't need some high-priced Beverly Hills shrink to explain his hang up.

In his old age, Perce Barnes, the original hard-nosed cynic, had become weak-minded. This time, he'd permitted himself to get involved in the script. He had begun to feel this was not only a good script, it was *his*.

Dummy, you broke one of the rules . . . who was it had laid them down for him, years back? Oh, yes, sure, it was Don Stewart, the best-paid writer in town, he who'd worked all those years at Metro, with big credits on top pictures, witty, sharp old Don, who'd been through the mill with everybody from Thalberg on down and survived them all, even old Louis B . . . one night they'd been at somebody's big party, one with the usual tent over the dance floor, the swimming pool full of drunks splashing around, girls being thrown in for laughs, and Don had given him the three rules for survival, the two of them lapping up their host's Dom Perignon out on the terrace.

"First," Don said, "you never write a script with Lana Turner in mind for the lead, because it always ends up being played by Norma Shearer. Second, old pal, you never do the first draft of a script. You wait until a half dozen poor bastards have worked their fingers to the bone on it, and then you take it over, and whatever you do to it has to be better . . .'' he'd chuckled. And finally, Don had said, his voice clear in the damp night, ''you must never let the bastards break your heart.''

Okay, so he'd broken the second rule, the one about first drafts. Was he about to let the Elberts shaft him and thereby break the third?

No. *Screw Harry Elbert.*

. . . He'd finish the script, take the money and run.

He got to his office at eleven. It was empty, but on his desk was a note, in Billy Elbert's illegible writing. ''Had to go out for a couple of hours, old buddy, but just wanted you to know it's going great. Pardner, keep on trucking!''

. . . And screw you, too, you hereditary young owl-eyed bastard!

Perce put up some coffee, put his feet up on the desk, and sipped it.

When the phone rang, it was Vera. In her best Florence Nightingale tone, she only wanted to know if he was all right.

''Peachy,'' he told her. ''Stop worrying. I got tired and had a few too many last night is all.''

''You're sure that's all?'' she asked.

''Why would I lie to you?''

''I can think of a number of reasons,'' she told him.

''Thanks,'' he said. ''Use 'em for anecdotes in my biography.''

''You must be feeling better,'' she said. ''You're back to your old bitchy self.''

He tried to work. At lunchtime he stopped. Read what he'd done and didn't like it. Walked out to the other room, to find Al Chester seated on the couch, quietly reading the paper.

''You was banging away pretty good in there,'' said Al. ''I didn't want to get in your way.''

''Thanks, but it stinks,'' snapped Perce, and tore up the pages. ''How come you're here? I thought you'd be out learning the movie business from the ground up.''

''Oh, I got a pretty good handle on it,'' said Al. ''Much as I'll ever need.''

''All you got is the nuts and bolts,'' said Perce. ''What you're missing is the good part—inside, where everybody is busy screwing everybody. That's the fun stuff."

"You sore at something?" asked Al.

"Don't ask," he said.

". . . Well, I figure folks around here aren't too much different from the rest. Eating each others' ass all day. Maybe they just go for bigger bites, is all. How about lunch? My treat," said Al. "How do you feel about some Jew food?"

Murray's Kosher-Rama delicatessen on Ventura was crowded, but he'd known Murray from the days when the place was a hole in the wall. Over the years it had expanded; so had Murray, who now weighed well over two hundred, as he ushered them to a booth.

Perce ordered lox, eggs, and onions. Al ordered a corned beef on white bread, with a glass of orange juice, causing the waitress to grimace.

Behind them a trio of young matrons were chattering gaily about their plans for the weekend, which seemed to include a trip to Vegas, and would cause extensive shopping this afternoon for proper wardrobe.

"What's LeRoy up to?" asked Perce.

"He's out doing some errands," said Al.

The food came, and Perce began to attack it. Al chewed his sandwich with obvious relish.

"I been thinking," he said. "Me and LeRoy got this idea. Sort of a plot, you could call it. Can I tell it to you?"

"What kind of a plot?"

"What would happen," Al asked, "if somebody was to lift the negative of a picture out of the lab vaults, take it away, and hold it for ransom?"

Perce shrugged. "Whoever owned it would pay off to get it back. Why?"

"Them negatives is worth a hell of a lot, especially before they made all those prints, right?" mused Al. "Fella could ask a nice chunk of change for it, couldn't he?"

"It's already been done," said Perce. "Some Italians did it, a couple of years ago, I think it was one of Fellini's pictures—they stole a couple of reels of his negative—Fellini had to reconstruct the whole thing from his workprint."

"That was wrong," said Al. "See, you'd have to take the whole negative, to make it worth doing. Not just a few reels . . ."

"Okay," said Perce. "So we've already got one plot. We don't need another."

Somebody waved to him as he left. Without recognizing who it was, Perce waved back.

"Oh, I wasn't talking a plot for a movie," smiled Al, wiping his lips with a napkin.

"Then what the hell do you have in mind? Something for 'Kojak' . . . Or maybe a situation comedy?"

"Not that," said Al. "See, what I'm talking about is for real. Like lifting a big one. The negative of Mr. Elbert's new picture. That Western."

Perce stared at him. Was Al serious?

"Any dessert, doll?" demanded the waitress.

"Sure," said Al. "I believe I'll have a couple of them macaroons? The kind that take out your fillings?"

"More coffee," said Perce.

When she'd left, Al said, "I'm a sucker for that sweet stuff." He leaned forward confidentially. "You think it would be worth a mil in cash for old Harry to get back his negative—before they make prints?"

. . . He *was* serious.

Obviously Al had been out in the valley sun too long.

"When the hell did you dream this up?" Perce asked.

"Oh, it's a thing I been figuring out for a long time," said Al.

"You need a hobby," said Perce, "to keep you occupied."

The matrons in the next booth had received their check, and were now noisily auditing out who owed what, and how much to leave for the tip.

". . . All that time I was sitting inside," said Al, his eye following the various shapes of the matrons as their well-packed slacks brushed by their booth, ''I had me plenty of time to think, see? So when we got out and made it to here, I got a chance to check out whether my idea was possible.'' He winked. ''I believe it is.''

The waitress served them; he picked up a macaroon and began to munch on it with pleasure. ''Thanks to you, old pardner, we're in the perfect spot to pull it off.''

Hobby, hell. This character needed therapy. They were in the middle of making his life story into a picture, to prove that crime did not pay—and here he was proposing a new one!

Perce had a sudden, ominous thought. ''Who's we?'' he asked.

''Why, LeRoy, me, and you,'' said Al. ''You're our pardner.''

Perce's stomach was churning, and it was only partially due to the fried onions.

Al attacked the second macaroon. ''A tasty pay-off,'' he mused. ''One million, split three ways, that's better than three hundred big ones each, after expenses. And no withholding taxes. How does that sound?''

Perce drained the rest of his coffee with a hand that shook slightly. ''Thanks for thinking of me,'' he said. ''But it's a little out of my line. Yours, too. Let's stick to what we're doing, okay?''

''Why?'' asked Al pleasantly.

''Because I'm too old to play Dillinger,'' snapped Perce, somewhat irritated now. ''And if you ever pulled such a thing, who do you think they'd come looking for first? Christ—you can't be serious!''

''We got that all worked out, pardner,'' said Al, wiping his lips with a napkin.

The waitress came and handed them their check; Al took it, counted out a good tip. ''Mighty good eats, lady.''

''Thank you and have a good day, doll,'' she said, scooping it up.

As they left the deli, Al said, ''I'd like to eat her macaroons every day.''

''Why don't you go get yourself laid this afternoon?'' asked Perce. ''Get your mind off that other stuff.''

''Oh, I would, but I got a few details to check out at the studio,'' said Al.

They got into Perce's car and began the drive back to the studio, the bright midday valley sunlight reflecting off the wide boulevards, the garish cheap motels, the used-car lots, the body shops, all the various monuments to middle-class living.

Beside him sat a middle-aged ex-con who was planning a heist, quietly picking his teeth with a toothpick. *Unreal!*

"Listen, Al," he said. "Do me a favor and let's forget we had this discussion."

"Nossir," said Al. "It's too good."

"They'll put you away and throw away the key!" Perce protested.

"Not if they don't catch us," said Al. "Which they won't."

"That's the way every con artist figures, going in!"

"I know that," said Al. "Don't you think I've had enough time and seen enough guys inside to know how it all works? That time back there, we was out in the clear, home free—excepting for that one crazy kid who blew it when he let them see the money. Well, this time, that won't happen, see?"

"Oh, sure!" snapped Perce. "Why not?"

"Because when we knock off this million, we're all gonna make sure it doesn't show up—not for a long, long time. We go about our business just like nothing happened. Elbert has to pay off, he's insured, we've got him over a goddamn barrel—we stash that money way down deep—where nobody gets to see it," said Al.

"Then what the hell's the point of having it?" Perce demanded. Jesus, it was like arguing with a religious fanatic!

"Don't you see why?" explained Al as if to a small child. "It's security for our old age. We don't have us pensions, or savings, or any of that stuff. Wouldn't you sleep a whole lot better knowing you had three hundred Gs stashed away, waiting for your golden years?"

"I'd sleep a whole lot better knowing you weren't serious about this!" vowed Perce. Now the guy was talking like some insurance salesman!

"Don't get your bowels in an uproar," said Al. "You think we'd pull something off without figuring out every little detail up front? Come on, Perce, we're *pros,*" he added, aggrieved.

They were approaching the entrance to the studio parking lot.

Perce slowed down, hesitant. To bring Al back inside now, to go back to his own office, to try and work at the script, all the while knowing that Al and LeRoy were wandering around, quietly casing the place . . . in preparation for a heist? Since when was he expected to do that?

Al sensed his indecision. "You go ahead and park," he said, his tone authoritative. "There's only the three of us knows what's going on. We ain't gonna spill, so that leaves only you. You'll stay clammed up, Perce."

"What makes you so damned sure of that?" Perce demanded, angry.

"Well, for one thing," said Al, smiling, "who the hell would believe you? Besides, you and old Harry Elbert aren't such good buddies—you wouldn't tip *him* off, would you?"

Sly sonofabitch. He had it all figured out, didn't he?

Perce parked his car.

Al got out of his side, began to stroll toward the studio gate.

Perce hurried after him, plucked at his arm.

"Al, I've got to know—are you serious about this?"

"Why sure we are," said Al. "Been working on it for weeks now. Getting all the little details pinned down."

. . . Of course—that explained those notes on yellow paper that had dropped out of his pocket—the long absences "walking around the lot"—LeRoy's disappearances to "do a few errands." Behind his back, these characters were rehearsing *Rififi!*

"Listen to me, Al," he said, staring into the other man's clear blue eyes. "You're out of your league here. The whole state of California will come down on you like a ton of bricks—it's not like nineteen fifty-seven any more—so do us all a favor. *Drop it.*"

Al's eyes stared back, and they were suddenly cold, authoritative.

Then the hardness vanished, and Al smiled. He patted Perce's arm. "Shit, Perce," he said, "do I tell you how to write a script?"

They walked through the gate, nodding to the studio cop on duty. Two middle-aged men, artisans, back from an off-the-lot lunch, ready to return to their labors, to put in an afternoon earning the rest of a day's pay in this huge fantasy factory. Undistinguishable from any of the others here.

. . . Except that Al was developing his own fantasy, one that would earn him an instant pay-off, in seven figures.

And he, Perce, was now an accessory after the fact.

Correction. Before and after!

Al waved. ''See you later,'' he said cheerfully. ''Got a few little things to check out.'' He left Perce and hurried down the studio street.

. . . Headed for where? The vaults? Cutting rooms? To check out an escape route—what?

I don't want to know! Perce told himself. What I want is to finish this damned screenplay and get the hell away, far, far away from these two characters—a couple of ex-cons who've appointed me their official accomplice.

Sure, Perce. You've always been smart, fast on your feet, able to sidestep, duck away, keep your nose clean. Harry Elbert is all set to shaft you, now you've been cast in a real-life heist. So tell me, smart-ass, how do you plan to bail out of *this?*

. . . Right now, you need more than a gimmick. You need help.

From whom?

Vera? Billy Elbert? . . . Audrey?

. . . What a miserable spot.

He kept on walking.

A block away, Harry Elbert steered his Rolls into the space outside the office, parked it, and got out. Behind him, the rented limo purred to a halt, and Ben Judge and Tony Staats emerged into the sunlight, their sober, dark blue suits and button-down shirts immediately stamping them to anyone passing by as eastern execs.

The three of them had just finished a long two-hour lunch at Le Bistro, good food, wine, the works. Usually he hated these midday bashes, but today he'd felt it was necessary—it wasn't merely laying it on for visiting firemen, he had to do something to warm up Judge, Tudor's second-in-command, and Staats, who was Tudor's head of marketing, or some other crap. They'd flown out to take the first look at the final cut of *Cimarron* and report back to Tudor.

Last night, after they'd gotten in, he'd been all set to send over a couple hookers to the Bel Air, two of the best head jobs in town, his own private stock, but Judge had begged off, thanking him politely and saying that he and Staats needed to go over some reports—(who the hell could trust a couple of guys who'd turn down a pair of $250 broads?). Cement-faced bastards, they didn't make jokes, refused to gossip, asked a lot of technical questions, all through lunch he'd tried to warm them up, maybe he should have hired Milton Berle to warm up these two icebergs!

. . . So now he'd take them into Room A, in ten minutes they'd be sitting there, he'd be running them two hours and eleven minutes' worth of all those goddamned weeks of sweat and work, and scheming . . . plus nine million worth of Tudor's corporate dollars.

The two men came alongside. Harry pulled out of his pocket a case with two of Fiona's finest Cubans inside, offered them, but Judge shook his head.

Glanced at his watch. "Let's go to the movies, Harry," he said. "We're on a tight schedule."

"Relax and enjoy," said Harry, and led them down the street toward the small alley that led to Room A.

As they turned the corner, the three of them collided with a man, head down, walking rapidly toward them.

Perce Barnes?

What the hell was he doing here?

"Jesus, pal," said Harry, irritated. "Watch where you're going!"

"Sorry, Harry," said Perce. "Excuse it. I—I was thinking."

The alley was narrow, and Judge and Staats stood waiting for Perce to get out of the way.

"This is Perce Barnes," said Harry. "He's a real old timer—working for me and Billy on another project."

Politely, Judge extended a hand.

"Out to clear your head, right?" asked Staats pleasantly.

"Guess so," said Perce.

"I read the pages you've been sending up," said Harry jovially. "Not bad, not bad at all. Who've you got writing 'em for you?"

Harry guffawed at his own crude quip.

Neither of the other two men reacted.

"See you around, Perce, get to work," added Harry. "Time is money."

He ushered the two guests past Perce, toward the nearby projection room door. They went inside, the heavy door closed, and then there was the sound of its lock clicking.

Standing alone in the alley, Perce's face hardened.

"You prick," he said. "I didn't need that. Not today."

He began to walk slowly away.

Then he said, ". . . Maybe I did."

Perce sat alone in the office, staring at the typewriter, seeing not the pages but the sneering face of Harry Elbert.

Then the outer door opened, there were footsteps, and a knock on his door.

"What?" he said.

Al peered in. "Just checking out," he said. "Going home."

Perce nodded.

". . . What's wrong, pardner?" asked Al. "You look upset. Isn't it going good?"

Perce looked up. "Al," he said softly, "what's it feel like to kill somebody?"

Al came in. "Well, now, I dunno," he said. "I never actually done it."

". . . Somebody whose guts you really hate," said Perce.

Al nodded. "You need to know for the script there? I guess maybe I could find somebody who ought to be able to tell you," he said.

"No," said Perce. "I'm talking for myself. Right now, I'd like to get my fingers around somebody's neck and press on his Adam's apple tight until his tongue pops out."

"Mm-hm," said Al. "They don't like it when you do that," said Al. "That's murder one, premeditated. You can plead temporary insanity, sure, but you need a lot of high-priced help to prove that in court. Now if it's an accident, or when a stray shot hits somebody—unless it's a cop, then they get hairy—you can usually get a better break, the lawyer can plea bargain, see? No, pardner,'' he concluded, ''the way I see it, murder isn't such a red-hot idea.''

He might have been kindly old Dr. Gillespie, advising Dr. Kildare.

''. . . Who've you got in mind?'' Al inquired softly. ''Anybody we know?''

''Yeah,'' said Perce. ''We know him. An asshole by the name of Harry Elbert.''

''Uh-*huh,*'' grinned Al. ''Him. Well, go ahead and think about it, if it makes you feel better, but believe me, doing it ain't satisfying. *Hurt* him—that's the ticket. Then you get to see him squirm. And,'' he added, ''you get a nice big pay-off for your trouble.''

Perce did not answer.

''Good night, pardner,'' Al said, and whistling softly he left the office.

* * *

chapter 21

—Folks, this has to be one of the greatest football games we've ever seen! State is leading Carlton seven to six, and Carlton's star player, Bruce Baker, hasn't been in the game as yet. There are two minutes to play, and it looks as though State has the National Championship sewed up. What's this? *Hold it folks*—I don't believe it—here comes Number Seventy-seven—*Bruce Baker is entering the game!*

". . . So okay, pardner," said Al. "I guess you want to know how it goes."

He put down his empty Coke can, opened a large street map of Greater L.A., and laid it out on the breakfast bar, moving away the clutter of unwashed dishes to make room.

. . . Gorgeous, thought Perce. Some setup. Three men, two of them in their skivvies, sitting around in a cheap, airless downtown apartment, plotting a million-dollar heist with a buck-fifty map and a pencil?

. . . Well, what was he expecting, a scene out of James Bond? If they *had* money, would Al and LeRoy be going for it?

"We start by picking up the negative, here—at the lab where she's stored," said Al, tapping at points with his pencil.

"Who's we?" asked Perce.

"Oh, that's LeRoy and me," said Al. "Then we drive it—"

"Wait a minute—you just walk in and help yourself?" demanded Perce.

"Don't you worry about that part of it," said Al. "Me and LeRoy can handle that."

LeRoy nodded.

". . . So now we take it over here—"

''In what?'' asked Perce.

''A truck. Panel job, probably,'' said Al.

''Where do you get that?''

Al pointed at LeRoy. ''His department.''

''You going to rent one?'' asked Perce.

LeRoy shook his head. ''We thought of that, but it's too risky. We'll just borrow it.''

His meaning was clear. ''What about plates? They can trace them,'' Perce persisted.

LeRoy shook his head again. ''They'll be switched,'' he said.

''. . . Now we park the van here,'' said Al, resuming his lecture, and his pencil indicated L.A. International Airport.

''Why there?'' protested Perce. ''Christ, that place is always packed!''

''Sure, but they got long-term parking,'' said Al. ''Nobody'll bother that truck for a couple of days. Now you come along, you pick us up, we get out, get to a pay phone, and we call Elbert. And—''

''Wait a minute,'' said Perce, his mind racing. ''His number's unlisted.''

''Then you get it—and you'll make sure nobody knows you did, so they can't trace it back to us,'' said Al.

. . . Through Audrey? No, he'd have to figure out some other way. Perce had another thought. ''How do you know Harry will be home? It's the weekend.''

''Somebody's got to be there to take messages,'' said Al. ''Or he's got an answering service. Big man like Harry don't stay out of touch.''

''. . . But if you call him, he'll recognize our voices,'' Perce pointed out.

''Not a chance,'' said Al. ''See, we got us a little electronic gizmo for that—it's one of the latest things, they use it for those poor slobs with Big C who can't talk.''

''Where'd you get it?'' asked Perce, grudgingly impressed. Al *was* thorough.

''That's our department,'' said Al. He tapped at the map. ''Now, we arrange with Elbert for a drop—over here. This is a vacant parking lot, not much lighting, after dark it's pretty quiet. He leaves all the money here—''

''Wait, this is a Saturday?'' asked Perce.

''Yeah, or if he stalls and plays cute, Sunday. Why?''

''You blew it,'' said Perce. ''The banks are closed all weekend. How in hell is he supposed to rustle up a million in small bills when they're shut?''

Al shook his head. ''Wrong, friend,'' he said. ''A big borrower like Harry—he's got banking connections. Bankers can always open up one, two branches in an emergency and get cash—especially for their good customers.''

The small un-air-conditioned room was stuffy; the windows were closed, and Perce was perspiring. ''I don't like that,'' he said. ''Seems to me you're taking a lot for granted.''

''Nothing,'' said Al, as if to a small child. ''Think how he reacts, Perce. We let him know his nine-million-dollar negative is sitting out there, baking in the sun. How long you think he's gonna sit still for that?''

''Yeah, I guess so,'' Perce conceded without conviction.

''Okay, so now he's made the drop,'' continued Al. ''We let him pick up the parking-lot ticket, he goes out there and collects his negative. We're long gone. Except, Monday morning, we're right back in the office, right there where everybody can see us.'' He grinned. ''Now, if you was looking for heist artists, would you think it was three guys up in the office, working on your script?''

No. The way Al laid it out it was a shrewd scheme. Good enough to be the basis of a caper picture, in fact.

The only difference was, in a movie you sat behind the camera and made everything work. If somebody blew it, you went back and reshot the scene. Then you took it down to the editor and he put it all together, the way it should go.

. . . If something went wrong with this heist, there'd be no goddamn retakes.

. . . And how long was he supposed to sit in that office, wondering whether the police had him under surveillance?

''They've got to suspect the two of you,'' he said.

''Let 'em suspect us,'' said Al. ''The most important thing is the money. Don't ever forget that. It's our cover. No matter what they think about us, if they can't find any green stuff, they've got nothing to hang on us."

"You better be right," said Perce.

"Yep, they're gonna be looking for that mil for a long, long time. But it won't show up, see? You got to treat the money like one of these certificates you buy at a bank. You know it's there, but you leave it sit, and forget it. Only this mil don't draw interest," said Al.

". . . And you don't get a free coffee pot for leaving it in, either," said LeRoy, with a sudden half smile.

Perce wiped his forehead.

"So where does it go?" he asked.

"You'll know," promised Al.

"When?"

"Later," said Al.

. . . Wait just a minute, thought Perce. What is this, the old Mexican switch? The million they heist disappears, out of sight, then maybe the Chesters go the same way—and what happens to *me?*

"You're going to keep it?" he asked.

Al nodded. "Where it's safe."

Perce cleared his throat. "How do I know that?"

"Well, now," said Al softly. "Seems to me that the three of us have to trust each other a lot. You're not going off to complain to the cops and turn us in—and we ain't about to tell anybody about you, are we?" He grinned. "That's what I call a pretty safe deposit."

Al made sense, but Perce still wasn't pleased with his explanation.

The perspiration was trickling down the back of Perce's shirt, causing it to stick to his shoulders.

". . . When do you figure to pull this off?" he asked finally.

"Before Elbert starts ordering prints from the negative," said Al. "The sooner the better. I figure maybe next Friday."

. . . Less than a week away?

"It's like having a tooth pulled," said Al. "The longer you sit and think about it, the worse you figure it'll be. We did all the groundwork and figuring, Perce, so now we do it and get it over and done with. All's you have to do is to go along.''

Both brothers sat, silently waiting for his answer.

. . . He'd come downtown here to this airless box, if he wasn't ready to go along with them on this cockamamie deal, why had he come? For the last day he'd been chewing on his bile, fighting down the anger within him, the hatred of Harry Elbert and his cheap, high-handed shafting. Two hours ago he'd called and arranged this meeting; he'd made up his mind to take Al's advice. Hurt the bastard, for fun and profit.

They were pros. Why was he hesitating?

''You really think this'll work?'' he asked.

''Listen, my friend,'' said Al. ''The last time we tried one of these, everything went fine. Then some other jerk blew it for us. You think I'm gonna let something fuck up this time? Neither of us is figuring to die inside the slammer.''

''Okay, dumb question,'' said Perce, somewhat embarrassed. ''Wipe it. I'm in.''

Al offered his hand. Perce shook it.

Then it was LeRoy's turn. So strong was the large man's grip that Perce's fingers tingled when he had his hand back.

Perce wanted fresh air. He climbed down from the stool.

''You'll get the number,'' Al said. ''Right?''

''Tell me one thing,'' said Perce. ''What would you have done if I'd turned you down tonight?''

''Why, we'd've gone ahead and pulled it off anyway,'' said Al. ''Only it would've been a fifty-fifty split.''

''You wouldn't worry about me knowing all about it?''

''Shit,'' said Al, beginning to refold his map. ''You wouldn't sing.''

''What makes you so damn sure?''

''Because you hate Harry Elbert a whole lot worse'n we do,'' grinned Al.

When Perce had left, LeRoy shook his head. ''I don't know,'' he remarked. ''The way I figure it, once a chicken, always a chicken.''

''Don't you worry,'' said his brother. ''He ain't no rooster, sure, but we won't lean too hard on him. It's gonna be us mostly doing the work, remember.''

LeRoy went to the refrigerator and poured himself a glass of milk.

''Yeah,'' he said, sipping it. ''Thank the Lord for that.''

* * *

chapter 22

—All right, men, synchronize your watches!

FOR Perce, the next week was to be a bitch.

Suddenly, he was the inside man. How in hell could anybody be expected to concentrate on this damned script, turning out pages, pretending that this coming Friday was just another end of just another work week, keeping a straight face, covering, and Al and LeRoy as they came and went, silently attending to their various chores . . . and all the time leaving Perce to go about his business like a double agent in some damned John Le Carré story?

Tuesday, the atmosphere began to change around the Elbert office. If there'd been tension all these last weeks, it had passed. Audrey Lister, who hadn't spoken to him since that episode on the office couch, was smiling. At noontime, even Harry's older secretary waved a greeting.

What was up?

That night, Vera supplied the answer. "Seems your old pal Harry has himself a money picture."

How did she come off hearing it before he had?

"*Baby,*" chided Vera, "this town is one big radar screen. I've picked up plenty of blips. Harry had some screenings over the weekend, and the money guys came out with dollar signs in their eyes."

. . . So Al, the planner, had been absolutely on the nose with his timing. Harry would shortly be ordering prints. Nowadays, nobody sat on a nine-million-dollar negative, not with interest rates on the film's cost ticking away on the clock.

"That's terrific," said Perce without thinking.

She stared at him. "Since when are you so happy for your old buddy Harry?"

He cursed himself for having made the slip. "You eat a man's bread, you dance to his music,'' he told her piously.

''. . . And thank you, Oral Roberts,'' she said.

. . . He still hadn't secured Harry's private number. He'd probably have to sneak into the office at the end of the day, check the phones, making sure nobody knew he was there.

Cat-burglar time.

If he needed any further proof that Harry had a potential hit, he got it that afternoon, when Billy Elbert came wandering into the office, puffing on a cheroot, jovial, beaming like some bemustached Cheshire cat. Was the cream he'd swallowed Perce's script?

Oh, hell, that was going along like gang-fucking-busters, Billy was absolutely dee-lighted with what Perce was doing—(as he damned well should be!)—but, more importantly, Billy had today made himself a real good deal. He was going to make a swap, his precious Studie was about to be turned in to a rare-car dealer up in Santa Barbara, who had the most beautiful set of wheels a man would ever want to lay his hands on, an almost pure, untouched, and in A-1 shape, with an honest 5,600 miles on the clock, Dual Ghia, which for three years had been sitting on blocks in some rich cat's garage, a classic, a dreamboat—

''You buying this, or screwing it?'' asked Perce.

''Save those lines for the script,'' grinned Billy. ''Man, I'm making a hell of a sweet deal.''

''Even swap?''

''Oh, no, we have to lay down a lot of bread, but she's worth every penny,'' said Billy. ''It's an investment. I caught my old man in a good mood, he's coming up with the financing.'' He winked. ''The old psychology. Hit him when he's high. Now I've got to go up tomorrow and close the deal, then get her trucked down here to my guy so he can tune her up, then maybe Sunday I'll take you and the boys out for a spin. You gonna be around this weekend?''

''Oh, sure,'' said Perce. ''Working. I don't know about the boys, I'll check with them.'' He had a sudden flash. ''By the way, Billy, if you're not going to be around, if I have some questions, can I reach you at home at night?''

''Why not?'' said Billy, preoccupied.

Perce pushed a scratch pad over. ''The phone number''

Billy scribbled it down, then added a second, which was

manned by the answering service. "If I'm out, don't ask where I am," he said. "That's a number I don't give out to *any*body."

"Private stock?" asked Perce, very man to man.

"The greatest," said Billy. "Man needs his relaxation."

Absolutely, thought Perce. You've been working so goddamned hard on this script all these weeks, you've earned yourself a little rest!

He retrieved the scratch pad. "Keep the faith," he told Billy. "You've been a tremendous help."

"God knows, I try," conceded Billy, and wandered out, a man with a mission, a worshiper at the shrine of the great god Ghia.

Pleased with himself, Perce chuckled. It had been so damned easy. Use your head a little, and anybody could qualify for CIA work!

Later that afternoon, Al surfaced, sat down, and helped himself to some coffee.

"How's everything going?" asked Perce.

Al made a thumb-and-forefinger sign. "I was out lining up a couple of uniforms."

Uniforms?

". . . Me and LeRoy might go into the acting game," grinned Al.

"This weekend?"

"When we get to the lab, we're gonna be delivery men," Al explained.

"Where'd you go to get the uniforms?" Perce asked.

"That's my department," said Al. "Yours is Harry Elbert's phone number."

Perce handed over a typed slip on which were the two Billy had supplied.

"Nice work," commented Al. "How'd you get 'em?"

"That's *my* department," said Perce. "What else have you got for me to do?"

"You go get your car tuned up, nice and sharp, before Friday," instructed Al. "Make sure you got plenty of gas, and better check the tires. Need new ones, better replace 'em now."

"Haven't you got something more important I can do?" Perce asked.

"More important?" said Al. "Last time we was out I heard a little knock in your engine. We surely don't want any damn breakdowns this weekend, do we?"

He finished his coffee and left.

If thoroughness was the key to the big payoff, then Al would lead them home free.

. . . But if it weren't, and there was a slip-up . . .

Right now, Perce did not want to think about that. He got on the phone to a garage in Beverly and made an appointment for the next day.

. . . That made one less day he'd have to sweat it out.

Wednesday morning he dropped off his car at the garage, for the full treatment, which was a pain in the ass since it meant taking a taxi to the studio, and another one back to town; Al and LeRoy were using their car.

He spent the day trying to concentrate on the script, but it was tough.

That afternoon Al called to suggest they all meet Thursday, late, at Perce's apartment, for a couple of hours to run through the final drill, a dress rehearsal.

He'd hardly put down the phone when he remembered he'd had a date with Vera, to go to dinner and then to a screening that night. Damn—he'd have to get out of it.

Which did not prove to be easy.

He called her at the office and when he bowed out of Thursday, she didn't mind, as a matter of fact, she had marvelous plans for their weekend—

—The *weekend?*

For that he had enough plans.

—One of her clients, a hot young director, had been unexpectedly sent off to a film festival in Bermuda, substituting for a young actress who was throwing a temper tantrum, the director had a marvelous beach pad, and he'd offered Vera the use of it for the weekend, didn't that sound marvelous?

". . . Marvelous," he murmured, except that—

—It would be just the two of them, alone in the place, all the way up the highway, past Trancas, Friday night they could do a steak on the grill—

How was he supposed to get out of this?

"Friday night I'm busy," he said.

"Doing what?"

"Working," he told her, improvising hastily, it was Harry Elbert who was leaving town next week, he needed the finished first draft done so he could take it with him and read it while he was gone, which put Perce under the gun—

"Then come down Saturday," she suggested. He could bring his pages down to the beach pad, work there, she'd bring a book to read, she wouldn't bother him, then when they were done, they could take a nice long hike on the sand, get brown. ". . . We'll be all alone—no phones, it'll be so good for both of us, lover," she said, and her inference was unmistakable . . .

Lord, how he wished he could.

"I can't," he said, cursing this rotten timing, what a pain in the ass!

"Oh, honey, why the hell not? You've been working so hard, you need a little relaxation. You know, the past few weeks, you've been so tense . . ."

That was the understatement of this, or any other, year.

"Look," he suggested, "you go on down, and if and when I get loose, I'll come, maybe Saturday night, late—"

". . . What good is that?" she asked finally.

Not very good, but it was the best lie he could manage right now.

"Perce," she said. "This nose-to-the-grindstone bit. It's not like you. Why don't you tell me the truth?"

. . . If I told you the truth, he thought, you would fall down on your office carpet in a dead faint.

"Ah, Vera," he said softly, "why would I lie to *you?*"

"I don't know," she said. "Lately, I don't know what's with you at all."

"You're right, I'm under tension," he told her. "Come on, Vera, you know what it's like, working for Harry Elbert. He's one tough bastard to please—and I want to make this thing work."

"I don't believe you," said Vera. "You can't duck away with me for a couple of days? This time, it's *me* who's asking . . ."

"Baby, believe me, I *know*—" he protested.

When she spoke again, her voice was flat. "What the hell. It's another broad?"

Oh, Christ. Not that. Not *now*.

"Of course it isn't!"

"Bullshit," she said. "Don't think I'm so dense, will you please? I know you and how you operate—lately, you've been so remote I don't even sometimes feel you're there . . ."

I'm here, he thought. Boy, am I ever here. And, oh boy, do I wish I weren't!

"Believe me," he pleaded. "It's not that at all—it's—"

"I don't believe you," she said, and hung up.

If it weren't so ridiculous, he'd have laughed.

Placating a woman—who wanted to spend the weekend in the sack—rather than to let you go for a million-dollar snatch.

. . . Whoever heard of such a complication in a true crime story?

—On the other hand, Perce suddenly remembered—who was it had tipped off the Feds to the whereabouts of old John Dillinger?

An angry, frustrated woman in red.

Remember her?

So if Vera ever suspected anything, could she turn out to be a threat?

It was a remote possibility, but as Al said, you had to plan for every little possibility. The stakes were too high.

He called up the Vendome in Beverly and ordered a couple of bottles of good red wine—a brand he knew Vera liked—to be delivered to her office, sent along with a card on which would be written, "Save some for me—I promise to try and make it. Love—P."

A peace offering.

. . . For God's sake, let's not refer to it as a guilt present!

. . . Harry Elbert eyed his new Vacherin and Constantin watch. 2:30. He had most of his desk cleaned off, he wanted to be out of the office by three, then to pick up Fiona at her place so they could get an early plane to Frisco. Everything had worked out nicely. His wife was off on her art tour, getting culture with a bunch from the museum, two weeks in Spain visiting museums. Billy was out tinkering with his new toy, that car he'd conned him into putting up all that loot for; so what the hell, he'd taken most of the money out of the trust account that had been set up for Billy's welfare, so it was no big deal. But the kid was grateful, as a matter of fact, it was the first time in weeks, ever since he'd told him about his plans for *Three Down, Two Left Standing,* that Billy had actually been pleasant.

Which reminded him, the network guy was yelling for a look at the first draft of that thing; he'd better put some heat on Perce's ass to get finished so they could move on it next week.

He buzzed Perce's office on the intercom.

"How're you coming down there?" he asked.

"Oh. Harry. It's *you,*" said Perce.

"Who were you expecting, some broad?" asked Harry. "What are you and the Two Stooges doing there on Friday, on my time?"

". . . Working away," said Perce.

"So how close are you to the finish?" asked Harry.

". . . A few days off," said Perce softly.

"What?" asked Harry. "Speak up, Perce!"

"I said, a few days off!" repeated Perce.

"Well, get your ass moving," said Harry. "You know how it comes out, get it finished. Cut to the chase."

"I'll do that, Harry," said Perce. "Count on it."

"I want to see it all before the end of next week," said Harry. "We got a lot to discuss about those pages you turned in—maybe some restructure, you know?" . . . might as well prepare the bastard for the showdown. Keep him nervous. "Some of it doesn't feel right to me," he added.

"Specifically what?" asked Perce.

"Listen, I haven't got time to go through it all on the phone," said Harry. "I'm going out of town for the weekend, when I get back I'll be more specific. Meanwhile, you keep at it, Monday maybe we can talk more."

"Where are you going?" asked Perce.

"What do you want to know for?" asked Harry. "That's my business. Go back to work."

He hung up.

Then, on his private line, he dialed Fiona.

"Hell*o,* poppet," she said. "When shall you be by?"

"I'm on my way," said Harry. "You packed? You don't need a lot of clothes, you know."

"Anxious, aren't we just?" she chuckled. "Can't wait for our dirty weekend."

"Yeah," said Harry, feeling a stirring in his loins. "You taken your vitamins? You're going to need your strength."

"Braggart," she said. *"We'll* see who wears out first."

In his office, Perce glanced at the small card. He'd already memorized what was printed on it, in Al's neat hand.

. . . In spy pictures, they tore up such a piece of incriminating evidence, chewed it, and swallowed it down. The way his stomach was behaving, it couldn't tolerate it.

. . . Harry going out of town for the weekend. Could he be reached? The whole damn thing could fall apart on that one point—where the hell was Harry going?

Should he call Al and tell him of this development?

Call Al *where?*

Check out the instructions one more time, and then he'd flush them down the toilet.

5:50 P.M.

Cutting Room 7. Adjoins Vault 17. Name on door—Dullaghan. Out-takes on rack. Take two pieces. Into briefcase. Leave lot.

6:45 P.M.

Eat dinner. Hamburger Hamlet, Beverly Hills, end of Strip. Order hamburger rare. Send it back/too well done. Complain. (Who in hell could eat anything, despite Al's insistence that he have an alibi for that hour?)

8:45 P.M.

L.A. Airport. Circle slowly, near Long Term parking. Keep circling until you see us, then pick us up.

How simple and clear.

. . . Where the hell was Harry going for the weekend?

He got up, took another Maalox, and flushed the instructions down the toilet.

It was almost four.

Two hours to go to the heist.

How the hell was he supposed to concentrate on a script about a hesit that had taken place twenty years ago?

Finally it was after five.

He went down the hall and washed up, dried his face with hands that trembled.

All over Los Angeles, people were moving, campers headed for the mountains, families headed for the Springs, for San Diego, for their beach places. To Knott's Berry Farm, or to Disneyland, or the San Diego zoo, to San Francisco, or to Baja, Mexico. To the airport to jump on a plane that would take them to Aspen or Vegas or perhaps (if you were rich enough) to a spread in Montana. As the exodus began, the freeways would be packed.

For those who were left behind, there was work to do.

(Would Harry be reachable this weekend?)

. . . No time to worry about that now.

He went back to his office, picked up his briefcase, and stuffed in the pages he'd tried to work on all this day. If they made any sense, it would be a miracle. He snapped off the lights and left.

This morning he'd come in here as Perce Barnes, the writer on a flat deal. Now he was leaving it as Secret Agent X-9.

What was it Al had said last night?

Stay loose, keep your cool, never run.

Blend into the landscape.

If anybody asks you about anything, deny it.

Coming out into the studio street, there was a touch of night air beginning to seep down, and yet that wasn't what was causing him to shiver.

Two blocks down, toward the end of one of the soundstages were the cutting rooms.

Room 7. Adjoins Vault 17.

The name on the door—Dullaghan.

In the dim light, he could make it out.

Here was the door. He put his hand on the knob and pushed.

Damn—it was locked!

Pushed again, harder. Desperately.

. . . It opened.

Al had done his work!

He snapped on the light. There, on the rack, hanging down like limp strands of spaghetti, were festoons of out-takes, removed from the final cut of *Cimarron*.

He snapped up two, that was all they needed, stuffed them into his briefcase.

Snapped off the light, came out of the room and closed the door.

Wiped the handle carefully with his handkerchief.

Walked away, his heart pumping a little less swiftly now.

He kept on going, not too fast, headed for the rear gate, being careful to blend in with the landscape. A tired writer, headed for home.

As he approached the gate, he thought he heard someone calling his name.

Imagination. It had to be!

He kept on walking.

''Mr. Barnes!'' said the voice. Female.

He recognized it.

Audrey Lister.

He turned, to find her hurrying toward him.

''Hi, stranger,'' she said, ''where've you been hiding lately?''

''Down in the pits,'' he said. ''What about you? You've been pretty scarce yourself.''

They walked through the gate toward the parking lot.

''Oh, Lord,'' she sighed, ''our fearless leader has been running our tails off. Thank God he's gone away for the weekend. Maybe the sea air will calm him down.''

''The beach?'' he asked, casually.

She shook her head. ''Frisco,'' she said. She glanced at his briefcase. ''Don't tell me you're taking work home?''

He nodded. ''He has me under the gun, too. I wouldn't mind a nice weekend up at the Fairmont.'' He grinned. ''In a double.''

''I don't know where he is,'' she said, ''all I know is I'm glad to be going home.''

Damn; *Frisco!* Could he be reached up there? He didn't dare ask her any more questions.

"On the other hand," she said, ". . . if you need someone to take dictation over the weekend . . ."

"You'll be the first person to know it," he promised.

"I'm in the book," she said, and hurried off to her car.

He went off to his.

. . . Now for Phase Two.

It was quite dark when the small panel truck with FOREMOST FILM STUDIOS stenciled on both sides drove into the parking lot behind the Classic Film Laboratories, a large complex of buildings on a quiet street off La Brea.

The driver backed it up to the loading dock, parked, and then got out. He was a middle-aged man in chino pants and a uniform jacket; he wore tinted glasses and sported a small mustache. As he walked past the parked delivery trucks and up the ramp toward the rear door, he whistled softly.

Then he pressed the night bell.

Inside, its sound echoed through the empty building.

There were footsteps, and then, a small black man peered out the barred window beside the door marked "Receiving." He pressed a button on the two-way microphone. "We're closed." he announced.

"Shee-it, don't I know that?" said the driver. "We had us a flat on Highland coming in." He waved a folded sheet of flimsy. "I called to tell you we'd be late picking this up, but your night line was busy. Who in hell was you talkin' to, your bookie?"

"Phone didn't ring at all," said the guard.

"Okay, I believe you," said the driver. "Let us in so's we can get this pick-up over with."

"What pick-up?" asked the guard.

" 'Pick up, negative,' " said the driver, reading from the flimsy. " 'Production three nine four one, six double reels, deliver to Foremost, charge to Mr. Harry Elbert, production account.' "

". . . But I already told you, we're *closed,*" said the guard.

"Hey, you new around here?" asked the driver. "I ain't seen you before. I'm Jerry Winters, been out at Foremost longer'n' I can remember . . ."

"I'm Davis," said the black man. "Billy Lee Davis. And I been here six weeks now."

"Yeah? I musta missed you," said the driver. "So gimme a break, Billy Lee, I wanta go home to dinner just the way you do, but you're stuck here and I ain't; we're ten minutes late, so what?"

Davis moved away from the glass, then returned. "I haven't got anything up here on the wall about this." he said.

Winters waved the flimsy. "Here's the order, probably came down late this afternoon, you know how they are around our place, rush your damn ass off. Let me and Ernie in and we'll be out of your hair in five minutes, okay?"

Davis peered at the flimsy, uncertain, through the glass. "What vault's it say there?"

"Looks like number nine to me. The name of the show is *Cimarron.*"

"Ci-mar-ron," repeated Davis.

Again he disappeared from view.

When he returned, he was shaking his head. "That's in Vault *eleven,*" he said.

"Guess I read it wrong," said Winters. "Who the hell can see in this light? I'll get the dolly out of the truck." He turned and whistled through two fingers. "Hey, Ernie, you lazy asshole, get out the dolly!" he called. Turned back, grinning, to Davis. "Sumbitch is probably asleep already," he confided.

The truck door opened and out stepped a taller man, also in uniform, whose eyes were also covered by tinted glasses. His cap was pulled down low. "Watch your damn mouth!" he called. Slowly he walked to the rear of the truck, opened its door, then pulled down a hand dolly which he slowly wheeled up the ramp to the loading dock.

"His feet hurt, too," Jerry confided to Davis, snickering. "Old fart's ready to be put out to pasture."

"I guess I know just how he feels," conceded Davis.

"Okay, le's go," said Jerry. "Sooner we get this show on the road, then we can all go home, and you can watch the Dodger game."

"Hell, I ain't no Dodger fan," said Davis scornfully. He pressed the buzzer which opened the door, then held it open as the two men entered, Ernie pushing the hand truck. ''Lost my ass bettin' on those mothers.''

''Ain't that the way?'' commiserated Jerry, as the outer door swung shut. Davis held out a clipboard with a pencil attached. ''You got to sign this first. Both of you, and put down the time, please.''

Jerry took the pencil and scribbled two names onto the form. ''He can't write,'' he explained, with a grin.

''Up yours,'' said Ernie softly.

Jerry returned the clipboard.

''Why's anybody want a goddamn negative on a Saturday I'd like to know,'' grumbled Davis.

''I only drive a truck, pal,'' he said. ''Lead the way.''

Snapping on lights, Davis led the two men inside the corridor that led to the vaults. The air conditioning hummed softly as they walked down the long hall.

''Man . . .'' murmured Jerry, ''this is what I call *co*-operation.''

Almost half an hour later, the panel truck nosed quietly into an inner alley that led through backyards lined with garbage cans, in a quiet residential area of one-story bungalows west of Pico.

The truck stopped, and the two front doors opened. Moving swiftly, each took a side of the panel, and began to peel away at the lettering which spelled out FOREMOST FILM STUDIOS.

When they had removed them, they wiped the sides of the truck with wet sponges. Then they removed their caps, removed their uniform jackets, rolled the clothing into a bundle, and dropped everything into a nearby garbage can.

Then Al peeled off his mustache and tossed it away into the darkness. ''Hate to see it go,'' he muttered. ''I kinda liked the effect.''

As he climbed back into the truck beside LeRoy, he glanced at his watch. ''We're running three minutes late,'' he said, ''but that ain't anything we can't handle. To the airport, James.''

''You're a real comedian, ain't you?'' said LeRoy mildly as he backed the truck out of the alley.

''Hell, I ought to be in pictures,'' said Al.

8:47 read his watch.

Perce nosed his Caddy carefully through the airport traffic, threading his way in and out of the waves of auto-rental buses, taxis, drivers dropping people off, drivers picking people up, nothing in this area ever stood still, it was constantly moving.

He kept an eye on the islands where weary travelers and their luggage stood waiting for the coaches that would deliver them to Hertz, or Avis, or Budget, where they would be supplied with wheels that would enable them to keep on moving.

This was his third go-round, and still no sight of either Al or LeRoy.

8:49.

He belched slightly; his stomach was an inferno. Down there that overdone hamburger he'd had to eat was sending off angry vibrations.

. . . Where the hell *were* they?

He had the car radio on, tuned to a twenty-four-hour news station, if something had gone wrong, he'd have heard it by now . . . the announcer would have broken in with a bulletin, reciting in that dull, monotonous voice . . . . "Police announce the arrest tonight of two middle-aged ex-convicts, caught in the act of attempting to steal the negative of a feature film from the downtown Hollywood laboratory where it was in storage. After questioning, the two men, Al and LeRoy Chester, were identified as being employed as technical consultants on another film, being prepared for early production at a major studio, where they are working with a well-known screenwriter named Perce Barnes . . ."

There's a good credit, he told himself. Even on the news, I get third billing!

In the half light, he saw two figures standing on the island outside TWA.

One of them was waving.

At him! He jammed on the brakes.

Behind him, an angry horn blared, then a cut-down Mustang with huge black tires cut out and passed him and he heard the driver curse him.

The Caddy door opened and Al slid inside, then LeRoy fitted himself in.

"Didn't you see us waving?" asked Al. "You went all the way around, we hadda wait for you a second time!"

"Sorry," said Perce. "You get it?"

Al held up a parking-lot ticket. "There's the little beauty," he said happily. "You got the out-takes?"

"On the back seat," said Perce.

"Fine," said Al. "Let's go—" he placed a cautionary hand on Perce's arm. "—but *don't go fast,* pal."

Stifling a giggle, Perce steered the car toward Airport Boulevard. Who was it said crime was difficult?

"Now for the easy part," said Al. ". . . Remember, *slow.* No time for us to be picked up by some damn speed cop. Get a couple of miles away from here, and then we go call friend Harry and give him the good news."

. . . Oh, Christ! thought Perce, suddenly deflated.

Now for the bad news.

"That may not be so easy," he said. "Friend Harry's gone away for the weekend."

"Oh? Where to?"

"San Francisco."

"Damn! When'd you find *that* out?" asked LeRoy.

"Just before I left the studio tonight," said Perce. He explained about Harry's afternoon call.

"Okay, so he's at a hotel," mused Al. "You find out which one?"

"I tried, but I couldn't," said Perce. "Even his girl, that Miss Lister, didn't know."

"You mean you asked her straight out?" asked LeRoy ominously.

"Not head on, *No!*" Perce said. "I hinted around, but she was no help, so I figured I'd better—"

"*Damn!*" exploded LeRoy. "You should've called us!"

"Where the Christ was I supposed to call you?" protested Perce. "Down at the lab—while you were lifting the negative—or maybe here at the airport? Maybe I should have had you paged!"

''I *told* you, Al,'' said LeRoy, obviously disgusted.

''You told him what?'' demanded Perce, his hands tightening on the steering wheel. ''Something gets fucked up, right away it's *my* fault? Harry Elbert leaves town, I'm supposed to know that's going to happen?''

''*Yeah!*'' said LeRoy. ''You were our goddamn inside man!''

''*Cool it,* both of you!'' said Al quickly. ''We ain't gettin' anywheres the two of you squabbling like old ladies!''

The Caddy moved on toward La Cienega, past a jumble of low industrial buildings. ''Now there's a phone booth,'' said Al. ''You pull in there and we make the first call—to Harry's service. I'll tell 'em it's important he gets the message, and we'll see what happens.''

''. . . And if he doesn't get it?'' asked Perce.

Al snorted.

''Then he's out one negative—and we're out one million,'' he said. ''Might be the most expensive fucking weekend he ever spent . . . fucking.''

Despite his tension, Perce laughed.

''You ought to be a comic,'' he said, pulling alongside the telephone booth.

''Yeah. I'm hilarious,'' said Al.

LeRoy got out, followed by Al, who crossed to the brightly lit phone booth, went inside, and dialed. When he spoke into the receiver, it was softly and with urgence. Then he hung up and came back to the Caddy.

''What'd she say?'' asked LeRoy.

''She gimme a hard time, but I told her it was an emergency. Trouble at the lab. She said she'd try and find him. We'll call her back in a while, from wherever we're eating.''

''Eating?''

''. . . Hell yes, I'm hungry,'' said Al. ''Done a good day's work, so let's us go tie on the feedbag, okay?''

LeRoy closed the door. ''Some place where the food ain't fried,'' he suggested.

* * *

chapter 23

—It's quiet out there.
—Yeah. Too quiet.

THE sound of the shower filtered through the opulent darkened bedroom.

. . . Fiona was inside, and Harry could hear her voice as she sang, some nut song about Mother Brown . . . *knees up Mother-Brown, kneesupMotherBrown.*

Knees up? Harry chuckled. That had to be her theme song. This was one broad who'd been born with her knees up!

. . . He reached out and found the silver cooler, poured himself another glass of champagne. Ordinarily it wasn't his drink, but Fiona dug it, so he'd had a magnum sent up chilled, what the hell, it was all being charged off to the production budget on *Three Down,* this whole weekend would be down as a location trip.

In a little while they'd get up, put on some clothes, maybe go find some little place where they could eat Chinks, but right now Harry was pooped, he wanted nothing more than to doze in this big playground of a bed. He set his glass down and dozed.

Humming to herself, Fiona came back into the bedroom

. . . He heard the clink of the bottle as she poured more of the stuff.

Then the covers were pulled back, and he felt a sudden ice cold shock between his legs as the stuff sloshed on him

"Christ!" he groaned.

Fiona giggled.

"Rise, my love," she said. "It is the shank of the evening and there will be no sleeping . . ."

Then more fluid splashed down.

At these prices, yet!

''Why're you wasting it?'' he complained.

''Oh, I have no intention of doing that, sir,'' she said, and settled in beside him.

. . . And then he felt her mouth as it began to lap at the Dom Perignon, busy lips, tongue tasting the wine, then him.

He sighed with pleasure.

Suddenly, the bedside telephone rang, the sound cutting through the darkness.

Who knew he was here in Frisco?

It rang again.

He struggled to reach out his hand.

''Ignore it,'' commanded Fiona, pushing him backward.

Desperately, compulsively, Harry found the receiver. ''Yeah?''

Long distance, for Mr. Elbert?

''Who wants him?''

''Los Angeles calling.'' Click.

And then a female voice came on, apologizing. ''I know it's late, Mr. Elbert, this is Madge at your service, am I disturbing you?''

''Yeah!'' rasped Harry.

''—But there's been a call here from somebody to say there's a problem at the lab? Some sort of trouble?''

The first prickles of a cold chill crept across Harry's neck, in counterpoint to the warmth that was suffusing his lower regions . . .

''What lab?''

''He didn't say, sir. It's a Mr. Simalin? Would that name be familiar?''

Simalin? At the lab?

''He leave a number?'' he asked, trying to concentrate, which was goddamned hard, Fiona was now in high gear, lapping away greedily, Christ where did she get the energy?

No, he hadn't left a number. What did he want Madge to do?

''. . . Get . . . a number . . . where . . .where . . . I can . . . call back!'' moaned Harry, and dropped the phone. Which dropped with a splash into the champagne cooler.

. . . On and on, she was all over him now, up up and finally away!

blast off.

Harry collapsed back on the pillows, spent.

Slept.

. . . Then there was the faint insistent sound of the phone ringing in the suite's living room.

With enormous effort, Harry came awake. Groaned. "You . . . get it," he instructed Fiona.

Moments later, she came back. "Los Angeles," she announced. "You can take it here."

"Where's the goddamn phone?" he moaned.

"Here, silly," she said, and placed the dripping receiver next to his ear.

Eyes closed, he said, "Yeah?"

It was the service calling again. "Take this number, Mr. Elbert," she said. "It's a Mr. Cimarron calling, and he wants to tell you about the emergency at the Classic Film Lab?

Cimarron?

. . . Emergency at the *lab?*

Harry sat up, suddenly trembling; fumbled for a pencil, a goddamn pencil or a pad, there was none on this damn table, cursing, he reached out to snap on the bedside light, couldn't find it, swung himself out of the bed, then his toes cracked against the leg of the fucking champagne cooler, he tripped over it, it crashed to the floor, bottle and ice splashing on the damn carpet, he howled at the pain—

"What *is* it, ducks?" asked Fiona in the dark.

". . . Is there anything wrong, Mr. Elbert?" asked Madge down in the answering service office in L.A.

"Everything!" he bellowed. "Wait till I find the fucking light—*ooh!*" he cried, tripping over a mound of melting ice.

"I'll hold," said Madge.

"*I* know where the light is," cooed Fiona, and snapped it on.

"You and your goddamn champagne!" bellowed Harry.

Five minutes later, in his robe, he was dialing the number his answering service had supplied.

Two rings, and then a voice answered. ''Hello. Is thiss Misster Ellbert?'' it asked; a strange metallic voice that sounded like one of the characters in *Star Wars*.

''Yeah,'' said Harry. ''What is all this shit about an emergency at the lab? Who *is* this?''

''Neverr minnd who thiss iss,'' said the voice. ''I wantt to knoww if you'd be innterestedd in buyingg the negative of a neww picture called *Cimmarronnn*.''

Harry began to tremble.

''You crazy?'' he bellowed.

''Oh, nno. We'd like to selll itt to you, Mr. Elllbert. You see, we have the negative.''

Despite the air conditioning, Harry was perspiring.

''If you wwant it back, it wwill cost you one millionn dollarss. Cash,'' droned the voice.

''Bullshit!—What is this, some kind of a cheap heist?''

''Not cheapp,'' said the voice. ''One millionn. Cash.''

''My negative is in the lab!'' blustered Harry.

''Oh, really?'' came the reply. ''Welll, if that'ss the case, thenn we don't nneed to ttalk any more, do we? Bbut jjust in case you decide you wwant to ttalk business to uss, you can call us bback in half an hourr. Hhere's another numberr. Write it downn,'' it instructed, and with a feeling of impending dread, Harry jotted down the number, 877–1909.

Click.

The line was very dead.

Harry dialed the hotel operator. ''Get me the lab!'' he ordered.

''. . . What lab, sir?'' she inquired politely.

''The one we store our negatives in!'' he yelled.

''I. . . I'm afraid I don't know which lab that is, sir,'' she said. ''Would you want Fotomat? I think they're probably closed—''

''Harree,'' Fiona was cooing, ''I'm absolutely *famished*.''

''It's the Classic Film Lab in Hollywood!'' he yelled.

''. . . I'll try Information, sir,'' said the operator.

''. . . When can we eat, poppet?'' nagged Fiona.

''Call Room Service!'' he told her.

". . . I hate Room Service," she complained.

"Then go out—I'm busy, can't you see that?"

"This was supposed to be a *gala* weekend," she said and left the room.

Finally the operator came back on the line. She had the number of a Classic Film Lab in Hollywood, did he wish to place a call?

"No, I collect numbers for a hobby, you dummy!" Harry bellowed. "Get them on the line, *now!*"

The number rang several times.

At last a voice came on, obviously sleepy. "We closed. Call back Monday—"

"Wait a minute! This is Harry Elbert!" Harry yelled. "Don't hang up—I want to know, is my negative in the vault?"

"I dunno," said the voice. "I'm the night man, and they closed—"

"The name of the picture is *Cimarron!*" Harry said, and spelled it. "It's in storage there, isn't it?"

Sonofabitch, *it had better be there . . .*

". . . *Cimarron* . . . oh, yeah, seems to me I remember that name," said the voice. ". . . Lemme look from where at—oh, yeah, now I remember. Everything's okay—them two guys picked it up—it's on it's way over to the studio. Ain't it there yet?"

". . . *What* two guys?" asked Harry hoarsely. The sweat on his palm made it difficult to hold the phone steady. A nine-million-dollar negative, pulled out of the vault . . . *by whom?*

"From your place, man," said the night man. "They done took it out of here a couple hours ago, you mean it ain't gotten over there yet?"

"Oh, my ass! My aching ass!" moaned Harry.

". . . I'm only the night man," said the voice on the other end. "You better check on Monday."

He hung up.

Fiona peered in from the living room. "Harry, my sweet," she announced, "I have Room Service on the line, I'm ordering up a lovely Chateaubriand, now tell me, do you want yours rare, or medium rare?"

"I'm being fucked and all you can think about is *food?"* he roared, and began dialing the studio number, he had to check with security . . . but he already knew the answer they'd give him.

"Do try to be a bit more couth," scolded Fiona cheerfully.

It was almost an hour later. Al and Perce stood beside the phone booth, on a deserted block of store fronts all closed for the weekend, far downtown on Third.

"When's he going to call?" complained Perce. "Anybody comes by and sees us hanging around here has got to wonder—"

"Relax," said Al. "It's like the army. Hurry up and wait."

"Were you in the army?" asked Perce.

"Hell, yes," said Al. "Me and LeRoy both. We defended our country in its time of trial."

. . . Incongruous, this sudden vein of patriotism. But why not? How about the convicts on Devil's Island, standing up proudly, Frenchmen ready to defend their country against the Nazis . . . hadn't somebody done a picture about that?

"Was you in the war?" asked Al.

"Yeah, I was in the air force," said Perce.

"Say, you was a fly boy?" said Al, impressed. "What'd you fly?"

"Ground personnel," said Perce, unwilling to explain to Al that thanks to the Greaser and his connections, he had spent two years as an enlisted man right here in Culver City, making training films for the air force in the old Roach studio, in an outfit that was known around town as the Flying Typers, hardly the kind of war record that would impress his partners, or even worth discussing here on this dark street, three decades later, in the midst of this improbable Friday-night venture—

The phone rang, the sound echoing down the street.

Swiftly placing the small electronic hand mike next to his throat, Al answered. ". . . Yesss? Oh, hello Misster Ellbert," he said, with a small grin of triumph. ". . . Rready to talkk businesss? Fine. You'll get your negative back afterr you dropp offf one millionnn in small billss . . ."

Up in the San Francisco hotel suite, Harry hung grimly to his phone. ''Wait a minute!'' he protested. ''How do I know you've got my negative? I don't even know who the hell you are!''

He'd called the studio, no one in security had reported anything coming in the gate, he'd checked with his cutters, none of them knew anything, okay, so the negative was missing, but who knew if this wasn't some cheap rip-off?

''Your negative is in a panel truckk,'' said the voice. ''The truckk is parked in a safe place. But tomorroww, when the sun comess outt, the inside of the truckk is going to get very hott . . . and the longer you wait to dropp off the moneyy, the hotter it's goingg to gett inside that truckkk . . .''

Harry winced. The delicately balanced emulsions of that color negative, sensitive to variations in heat, could be ruined. Smartass bastards—they obviously knew what they were up to!

''I still don't know you aren't bullshitting me,'' he said. ''No deal until I get proof you have it!''

''Okayy,'' said the voice. ''Go out to your mailbox, outside your house. You'll find an envelope inside. That willl be the prooff. Meanwhile, rememberr, tomorrow is goingg to be a very warmmm day.''

''. . . . Wait a minute!'' protested Harry. ''. . . How am I going to get back in touch with you?''

''. . . Don't calll us,'' said the voice. ''. . . We'lll calll you . . .''

Furiously Harry dropped the phone onto the hook.

''Food's here, luv,'' called Fiona from the living room.

''Eat it fast,'' he told her. ''We're going back to L.A. on the next flight!''

While he was on the phone to the airline, making the reservation, Fiona came in, bearing a plate with slices of pink steak all nicely arranged. With nothing on but her bikini briefs, she was still the thoughtful stewardess. ''Eat,'' she instructed. ''It simply cannot be *that* bad.''

"It's worse," he snapped. There was another flight at eleven, they'd have to be on it.

But now he had another call to make, one he dreaded.

He was going to have to locate Mike Tudor, and try to explain to that flint-nosed bastard that their nine-million-dollar investment was in trouble, deep trouble . . . because some jerk of a night man at the lab had sat there on his ass and allowed two characters to waltz in and waltz out with his—*their* negative!

And Mike Tudor was not the kind of guy who appreciated such a fuck-up, Tudor who fired people, chopped off their heads the way a chef sliced off the top of a carrot, oh, boy, he'd seen Mike in action, it wasn't a pretty sight to watch . . .

But how could he *not* call him? On a weekend, with the banks closed, he needed Tudor's help desperately—hell, old Mike probably had a bank of his own somewhere with the cash sitting in the vault, some little bank he owned as a hobby!

He riffled through his address book, found Tudor's private number, called the operator and told her to make it person to person.

"Do eat," said Fiona sympathetically. "It's all protein, and you're obviously going to need your strength."

Harry began to pull on his clothes. "Protein!" he moaned. "Why don't you understand the spot I'm in? They're taking my blood!"

"I *do* understand, I *do,*" she soothed, "but we British simply do not permit ourselves to get into such a flap. It's why we last so much longer . . ."

"Yeah?" asked Harry. "Whatever happened to your British film business?"

"No need to get nasty," sulked Fiona.

The phone rang; he grabbed it.

Mr. Tudor was on the line.

"Hello, Mike," he said. "It's Harry—I hate to bother you, I know it's late—"

"Calm down, you sound upset," said Tudor, far away in Manhattan, on the top floor of his thirty-eight-story corporate headquarters, with its four-way view.

"Yeah," said Harry. "We are in a lot of trouble, Mike," he

said, took a deep breath, and then launched into a summary of the events of this past two hours.

When he was done, the line hummed.

Finally, Mike spoke. "They're asking a million?"

"In small bills," said Harry. "It's a goddamned rip-off, but what can we do? I don't want to call in the cops, the publicity would stink, we look like schmucks, half the town will think we're faking it—"

"We're dealing with very small-timers," said Mike, and permitted himself a mirthless chuckle. "They took a nine-million negative which we expect should gross thirty worldwide—and all they want is one? I would've asked at least four."

. . . Yeah, sure you would, thought Harry, and you would've taken my left ball for security!

"I'm going down to L.A. right now and check it out," he said. "Tomorrow's Saturday and we have to raise the cash, so I'm going to need your help, Mike—"

"You expect *us* to pay the million?" asked Tudor.

"Hell, no, it's covered by insurance," said Harry. "But—"

"You're absolutely certain about that?" asked Tudor.

"I pay the premiums, don't I?" protested Harry. "But I have to raise the cash, and our banks are closed—"

"Ah," said Tudor. "No problem. I can get somebody to handle that. Check me first thing in the morning, I'll be here—the money can be gotten."

"Great," said Harry, relieved.

"But it's going to cost you eighteen per cent," added Tudor. "Per day."

"Eighteen?" protested Harry.

"That's all we're allowed to charge under law," said Tudor. "You can sign the paper tomorrow, I'll see that it's there, I assume you'll be in your office instead of up in Frisco, correct?"

"I was up here strictly on a location hunt!" protested Harry.

"Of course you were," said Tudor dryly. "Call me back the minute you've arranged the drop. And by the way, Harry, don't go making any trips to Costa Rica with our million cash, will you? I'd hate to have to explain that one to our stockholders."

He hung up.

Wrong again, thought Harry bitterly. He took *both* balls.

It was after ten when the Caddy slowed down and stopped on the quiet street that wound and twisted high above Coldwater Canyon. As Perce braked, LeRoy opened the door and got out, walked swiftly to the mailbox that stood beside the driveway entrance, opened it, and slid the letter inside.

Then, just as swiftly, he came back to the car and got in, removing the cotton gloves he'd been wearing.

''Go,'' said Al, as if Perce needed to be told to move.

The Caddy rolled down the street, headed in the opposite direction, toward the brightly lit main roads below.

''Okay,'' said Al. ''Now you drop me and LeRoy off at the apartment, he takes our car and heads up to the mountains, he stays there until Sunday morning, so somebody has to see him. Tomorrow you get to your club and you play tennis until 10:30, or so, then we meet, and call old Harry one more time. Get yourself a good night's sleep, pardner, tomorrow is gonna be a busy day.''

. . . Sleep? thought Perce. The man had to be kidding. This was going to be a two-Valium night.

''Yeah,'' he sighed.

''Relax,'' said Al, patting his shoulder. ''You're doing just fine, pardner. We're halfway there—and the rest is downhill all the way.''

''Out of your mouth into God's ears,'' said Perce.

''Now don't be blasphemous,'' chided LeRoy. ''He ain't involved in this.''

It was well after 1:00 A.M. when Harry Elbert's Rolls purred up the same street and stopped at the mailbox.

Yawning wearily, Harry stepped out. He was pooped from the trip, the drive in from the airport, the side excursion to drop Fiona off, what a goddamned nightmare of a night, at his age, who needed all this?

He opened the mailbox, plucked the envelope that was inside

from where it rested, with slightly trembling fingers he ripped it open and took out a neatly folded slip of paper, unfolded it to reveal a strip of motion picture film. He held it up to the glow of the Rolls' headlights.

Six neatly cropped frames of picture, he could instantly recognize what he saw, it was a full-head close-up of Vin DeLuca, his high-priced star, waving the settlers on at the opening of the Cherokee Strip, the climax of his picture!

"Bastards," he groaned.

Then he glanced at the paper. On it, in neatly spaced letters, clipped from a newspaper advertisement, pasted to the paper, was one sentence.

SAT 11 AM Will Call. NO POLICE Or SAY GOODBYE TO Cimmaron.

"*Okay,*" said Harry, climbing back into the Rolls. "You got yourselves a deal!"

. . . But right now, what he desperately needed was a night's sleep.

* * *

chapter 24

—Pedro, in another hour or so, it will be daylight. Tell me, my son, are you afraid to face death?

—No, Padre. I am ready to die. It is a just cause for which I fight. Each of us owes God a death, no?

—You are a brave man, Pedro. Perhaps braver than all the rest of us, even those of us who bear the cross.

—Why Padre, you're crying!

8:47, Saturday morning, a clear bright day. Perce had been here at the club for almost half an hour now, sipping coffee in the lounge, still looking for a game, any game. Not that he felt like playing this morning, he'd slept badly and awakened feeling worse, but this morning of all mornings he needed to find a partner, any warm body, to get out on a court and be seen with for the next hour or so, to be visible . . . then he'd shower and duck out of here to meet Al.

So far, nothing. There were no floaters in sight looking for a partner, and the courts were filling up, it was pushing nine, after that he'd be out of luck for an hour, he'd be left sitting here to read the papers and make conversation with anyone who came in, that wouldn't look right, not at all!

Cool it, Perce, *cool it,* he warned himself.

Then he heard a loud voice, a familiar one.

"Look what the tide washed in!" it bawled. "Hey, Perce—I heard you'd quit the business!"

Ziggy Harling.

Standing over him, blowing clouds of blue from his first cigar of the day. Loudmouth Ziggy. "I can do you a big favor," Ziggy was saying. "I had a date for quarter of nine, but the bum called and said his car was giving him trouble, so you want to fill in till he gets here?"

Who needed him?

He needed him.

"Okay, pal," he said, and got up. "I'll fill in."

"Just remember," warned Ziggy, "I'm going to be merciful. I know you've been working for Harry Elbert and you're weak, so I won't beat you too bad. Wanta make it fifty bucks a set?"

"Why not?" asked Perce. "Working for Harry, I could use the money."

"Too bad nobody's making comedies," said Ziggy. "You'd be in big demand with those jokes."

By ten fifty-five, Harry Elbert was on his fourth cup of black coffee, and his seventh phone call of the morning.

Since nine he'd been talking, first with Al Morris, the head of studio security, making certain that Morris kept a lid on the story, did not leak anything to the L.A. police, that would mean the press and who the hell needed those bastards nosing around?—then with the man Tudor had referred him to this morning from New York, Sheed, who in turn had referred him to a second guy out here named Ruggles, who was somebody in finance, and who was presently arranging with the bank Tudor used out here to get the cash ready, who was also going to meet him whenever he heard from the *goniffs* who had the negative, and arrange for the money to be delivered, as well as to have Harry sign a simple loan agreement, at a simple eighteen per cent, as agreed—

The phone rang again. Harry grabbed it.

Damn, it was Billy calling, from his pad. "Just checking in," he said cheerfully. "How they hanging?"

"Limp," said Harry. "What is it, I'm busy."

"Je-sus," said Billy, "don't get your back up—I just called to tell you I'm gonna take a ride up the coast and try out my new wheels today. Want to come?"

"No," said Harry.

"You could use a little fresh air," said Billy. "And maybe we could talk?"

Shit, he had no time for father-and-son stuff, not today. "Sorry, not today," he said. "Maybe next week, okay? Call when you get back."

He hung up and glanced at his watch.

11:04.

Where the hell was the call?

He started to pour himself another cup of black, when the phone rang again, and he grabbed it.

"It's the service, Mr. Elbert," said the girl. "We have a message that came in a few minutes ago, your line was busy, I'm sorry we couldn't get through, it's Saturday and there's only me here and—"

"What's the *message*?" yelled Harry.

"Oh, yes. It was a man with a strange voice, and he said to tell you to check your mailbox. Does that mean anything, Mr. Elbert?"

"Yes!" said Harry, and hung up.

In the mailbox was another cheap, plain envelope, and inside, another folded piece of paper. When he unfolded it, it read:

Have The MILLION in Small Bills, not in sequence
Will CALL at 3
No FUnNy StuFf
NO POLICE!

He called Ruggles downtown in the bank office where he was standing by, and told him to be ready with the cash.

"Small bills, eh?" mused Ruggles. "You want fives or tens?"

"That's your department," said Harry.

"Makes a very large package," warned Ruggles. "Say you have half fives—that's one hundred thousand right there, and the rest in tens, that's fifty thousand. Lots of bulk. Now, on the other hand, if you used twenties, you decrease the size considerably you could have two hundred fifty packs of a hundred twenties, and five hundred packs of tens—"

He sounded like a florist, arranging a goddamn bouquet!

". . . and I imagine they'll want the money transportable, in canvas bags, or something, don't you think?" Ruggles went on. "Have you got bags?"

"*You* get 'em!" instructed Harry.

". . . Let's see," mused Ruggles, "I'll have to put out the money myself, and put in a voucher. That's a problem."

. . . I know what the problem is! thought Harry, thinking of that hot sun pouring in through the patio doors, the same sun that was baking down on his precious negative, somewhere here in Greater L.A., imagining the first tiny bubbles beginning to form in the delicate emulsions.

"Call you back," he said, and dialed Al Morris at the studio, to bring him up to date.

". . . Three o'clock, eh?" mused Morris in his security office. "Great."

"What's great about it?" demanded Harry.

"Why, it means I have time to put a trace on the call—and be careful of that note, I want to check it for fingerprints—"

"Forget it!" said Harry. "You think they'd be calling from anywheres but a pay phone? By the time you got there, they'd be long gone—so forget it—"

"I think you'd better let *me* handle this," said Morris softly. "This is a job for a pro."

Dumb flatfoot! . . . Thirty years ago he's on the L.A. police, he solves a jewel robbery at old H. L. Baer's house, pins it on the maid, the old man takes him off the force and puts him in charge of studio security, he's got it made for life, he covers himself with glory back in '47 by turning the fire hoses on the mass picketers during that jurisdictional strike, ever since then he's been sitting on his ass, all those years it's been nothing much more than keeping an eye out for sneak thieves stealing secretaries' purses, now he's got a chance to play Kojak, he's getting out of control—

"Al," he said sharply, "I don't want any funny stuff today. If they think there's a tap, you could louse us up good. I want that negative back, all nice and clean. Afterward, you're on your own. Get me?"

". . . I want it on the record that I warned you," said Al piously. "You're not making another cops-and-robbers show, Mr. Elbert. This time you're up against real pros."

Who, at 2:59 P.M., were beside yet another phone booth, this one on a side street in Venice, in a quiet section of rundown business buildings and old bungalows gone to seed.

"This time, you do the calling," suggested Al, handing Perce the hand-mike device along with the slip of paper on which he had penciled the instructions.

"Why me?" asked Perce, his throat dry.

Al smiles. "Don't you want to tell Harry where to head in once? It'll make you feel good."

"*Yeah*," said Perce. "Why not?"

He dropped in the coin, dialed the number, held the mike to his throat.

"Don't get carried away," warned Al. "Stick to the facts."

Harry answered after the first ring. "Hello?"

"Helllo, Mr. Ellbert," said Perce, his voice echoing strangely. ". . . Iss the monney readdy?"

"Yeah, yeah," said Harry. "Small bills, fives, tens, and twenties."

"Good," said Perce. "Take nnotes. We wantt itt in two small suitcases. There'ss a Sallvationn Armmmy collection binn, next to a shoppingg centerr at Seventeenth and Balbboa. Leave it there by five, and gget outt of the neighborhood fastt."

"When do I get my negative back?" demanded Harry.

". . . Rightt afterr we pick upp the moneyy . . ." said Perce.

"Wait a minute—how do I know you're not ripping me off?" insisted Harry.

"You don'tt," said Perce, ". . . butt if *you* pulll any ffunny stuff at the dropp, you won't hear from uss again . . . and the negative is going to sit there and meltt."

"When will I hear from you?"

"Sixx o'clockk . . . provided the money has been picked upp. Be at your house."

"Take care of that negative!" bellowed Harry.

Perce hung up.

He and Al returned to the parked Caddy, got in, and drove off, headed back toward Beverly Hills.

"How did that feel?" asked Al.

"Terrific," Perce admitted.

Al glanced at his watch. "We've got us a couple of hours, let's get you back to the club, where they can see you," he instructed.

"Then we go out to Seventeenth and Balboa and sit a while."

"Why are we going to sit?" asked Perce.

"To make sure Harry and his people don't pull any funny stuff," said Al.

"You think they would?" asked Perce.

"Can't tell," said Al. "Our insurance policy is that negative. But if they nab us, they could always sweat us until they find out where it is. You're not ready to be questioned, are you, pardner?"

Perce shook his head.

"I didn't think so," grinned Al. "So what we have to do is to make sure old Harry isn't playing any games, get it?"

"Oh, yes, I've got it," vowed Perce.

4:50 P.M.

The Rolls pulled into the parking lot of the shopping center at Seventeenth and Balboa. Harry Elbert peered through the windshield; his eye spotted the dark-red storage bin at the far end, SALVATION ARMY stenciled on the steel doors. He steered his car toward it, then parked a few feet away.

He got out, opened the trunk of the Rolls, took out two canvas soft-sided suitcases, trudged across the asphalt to the bin, opened the lid above and with some effort tossed in the first, and then the second. With a clang, the lid closed shut.

"Good-by one million," Harry muttered. "Plus eighteen-percent interest, you bastards."

He climbed back into his Rolls and drove away, headed back to Beverly Hills.

Had he looked in his rear-view mirror, he would have seen an unmarked Ford sedan, carrying two men in civilian clothes, as it pulled into the parking lot and nosed quietly into a space a few hundred feet away from the SALVATION ARMY bin.

When it was parked, inside the front seat, the driver picked up a radio mike and pressed the button. Spoke. "Unit One, calling in, Unit One calling in."

. . . Back in his office at the studio, Al Morris, a mike in hand, pressed the button and spoke. "Where are you, Unit One?"

"In position," said the driver.

''Roger,'' said Morris. ''Where is Unit Two? Unit Two, come in.''

A second unmarked car pulled into the parking lot and took up a position on the far side of the bin. In its front seat, the driver, also in civilian clothes, picked up the mike.

''Unit Two, calling in. We're in place. We're in place.''

''Roger,'' said Morris. ''Now sit there and wait until those assholes show up.''

5:45

Perce's Caddy was parked down the street, a good fifty yards away from the entrance to the shopping center.

The parking lot was almost deserted now, the few shops at the far end that were still open were almost closed, the customers headed for home, the merchants ready to call it a day.

In the front seat of the Caddy, Al squinted through a pair of binoculars, trying to scan the scene. The sun was going down, the light was bad. ''Well,'' he said, ''if the money's there, the next question is, who's waiting around?''

''You going to go out and look?'' asked Perce.

''Oh, no,'' said Al cheerfully. ''If there's birds sitting there, we flush 'em out. Got some change? I'm going to go call.''

Perce fumbled in his pocket and handed over the coins he had left from the supply they'd started with. It had been a long day, and he was hot and bone-tired.

This, he told himself, is no job for a middle-aged man.

''Who're you going to call?'' he asked.

''Friend Harry,'' said Al, and got out. ''You keep on eye on the lot, and we'll see what happens.''

A moment later he was back.

''What's up?'' asked Perce.

Al sighed, reached in and picked up the hand mike, tucked it into his pocket. ''Getting sloppy,'' he admitted. ''Almost forgot this.''

He disappeared, headed toward a nearby phone booth.

Christ! thought Perce. That's all I need now—*him* getting sloppy!

6:04

Harry Elbert was pacing up and down his living room when the phone suddenly rang. He ran over and grabbed it.

The voice on the other end was that same familiar metallic tone he'd been hearing for almost twenty-four hours now. "Lissenn," it said, "we warnned you nnnot to pull any funnny stuff, didn'tt we?"

"What funny stuff!" Harry protested. "The *money's there!*"

". . . So are ssome copss," said the voice. "Ccall themm off, we knoww they're out here—you wantt your nnegative back in livingg colorr, or in blackk and white? It's up to yyou, Harreee."

The line went dead.

Sweating, even though it was a cool night, Harry dialed Al Morris's office at the studio. Jesus—what was the sonofabitch up to *now?*

"Al Morris here," said Morris. "What is it? I'm busy."

"Listen, you bastard," gritted Harry. "What the hell is going on with you? Have you got your people waiting out there?"

He could hear Morris breathing heavily.

"*Answer* me!" bellowed Harry.

"Yeah," said Morris finally. "I've got a little welcoming party for those creeps."

"Well, they know about it!" yelled Harry. "You're going to blow the whole drop—there's a nine-million negative out there —and you're playing Sam Spade on my time—now get those men out of there, I'll have your fucking head for this—now—*out!*"

"This is a job for security," said Morris. "That's *my* job—"

"*Out!*" yelled Elbert. "*That's an order!*"

". . . I want it on the record that *you* ordered my men off the scene," persisted Morris.

"I don't care if you print it on page one of *Hollywood Variety!*" Harry told him. "Get 'em out—and call me back when they're gone— I want *that* on the record too!"

He slammed the phone down, fuming.

6:10

Out in the parking lot, a pair of headlights flashed on, and a parked sedan started up, slowly pulled away from its position flanking the bin, headed for the exit.

"One," said Al, seated in the Caddy.

A moment later, a second pair of headlights went on, from a car on the opposite side, and it pulled away, headed for the street.

"Two," said Al, with satisfaction.

". . . Maybe there's a third," said Perce.

"Well, now," said Al, "that's the chance we're just gonna have to take in about five minutes, when we go get our hands on that million dollars, isn't it?"

". . . I don't like the odds," said Perce, his throat dry.

"If this was easy work," said Al, "everybody'd be doing it, wouldn't they?"

"How'd you know they were there?" asked Perce.

"Hell," said Al, "I'd've done the same thing myself."

6:15

"Now," said Al. "And leave the headlights off."

Perce started up the Caddy, pulled away from the curb and headed toward the entrance of the parking lot, squinting through the dark.

He pulled up alongside the Salvation Army bin, and Al jumped out. Working efficiently, he pulled open the two front doors, and piles of clothing began to tumble out. Throwing them to one side, he burrowed through the accumulation of plastic bags and assorted discards, until he encountered a canvas suitcase which he hefted, lifted up, then heaved it across to Perce. It was heavy. "There you go, pardner," he said. "Another one coming."

Perce grabbed the suitcase and tucked it safely behind the front seat.

Then he heard the sound of a car's engine in the distance, coming closer. Looked up to see a pair of bright headlights bearing down on them.

. . . A *third* police car?

Frozen, he stood there, hypnotized by the oncoming lights.

". . . *Here!*" called Al, tossing over the second suitcase.

It landed on Perce's chest, it's weight almost knocking him to the ground. In panic, moving swiftly, he threw it inside the car after the first. ". . . hurry up!" he pleaded.

The car came closer and then stopped, a dozen feet away, its headlights outlining Al as he slowly closed the door of the storage bin.

Okay, thought Perce. This is it. We've had it. We came all this way, but we blew it—

A female voice spoke from behind the headlights, jovially. "Hey, you boys putting it in or taking it out?"

Shielding his face with one arm, ostensibly against the glare, Al waved his other arm.

"Jest a-tuckin' her in so's she won't fall out, ma'am," he said, in a back-country drawl. "Night now . . ."

Then he was inside the Caddy, the door was shut.

"Go," he told Perce. "But *not fast.*"

His heart pounding like a demented maracas, Perce eased the Caddy away from the parking lot.

When they reached the street he turned into traffic and carefully made his way toward the on-ramp that led to the freeway.

It wasn't until they were safely on the freeway, in the midst of the streams of traffic moving swiftly toward downtown L.A. that he finally drew his first deep breath. And laughed.

"My God!" he said. "We made it!"

"Figured we would," said Al, who was turned and was crouched over the backseat, fumbling at the topmost suitcase. "Well, now, look at this," he said, and hefted it onto his lap. "Man that is a pretty sight! Pretty enough to fuck!"

Perce shot a glance across the seat, his eye catching the glimpse of the opened suitcase, crammed with neatly bound stacks of currency . . .

"All this pretty government literature!" chortled Al. "Whooee! Say hello to your retirement fund!"

"The way we've been going today, I may not make it to retirement," groanced Perce.

"Shoot!" said Al. "We're about done. Stop by our apartment, I'll take in the money, then you got yourself one more run by

Harry's mailbox, and we're about through for the night—''

''Listen,'' said Perce, as they sped on downtown, ''is all that loot going to be safe at your place?''

''Hell, now don't you worry,'' said Al. ''It won't be around there long. I call a cab, take it downtown to a storage locker, stash it away for the weekend, then next week I move it again. Then you go on down to the beach and see your lady friend, and give her a nice long hump to celebrate!''

''. . . I haven't got the strength,'' said Perce.

''When you haven't got the strength for that, pardner, you're dead,'' said Al. ''But you died rich.''

It wasn't a particularly funny joke, but Perce found himself roaring with laughter, along with Al.

7:35 P.M.

Saturday night in Beverly, everyone was out somewhere, eating, drinking, *schtupping,* but not Harry Elbert.

He slouched in a living-room chair, in his hand a large tumbler in which was three inches of twelve-year-old straight Glenlivet, which he'd been sipping for the past forty-five minutes as he sat and waited for his goddamned phone to ring.

Silence.

He hadn't heard from Al Morris, which meant that the sonofabitch had pulled off his people—so now he was waiting for those rip-off artists to call—and they hadn't—

—Christ, what a spot.

One million out the window? And a negative sitting somewhere out there, no word that they'd picked up the money—

Damn, maybe he'd been wrong to call off Morris. Maybe he should have let the idiot and his men close in on the bastards, grab them as they collected the money, beaten the shit out of them, and twisted their fucking arms until they'd coughed up the location of his precious negative—

—If he was out the million, plus interest, how in hell would he explain it to Tudor? To the insurance agency and the company that carried the policy? To the L.A. police, whom he'd kept out of the whole mess?

If the negative was gone, how could it be replaced? Even Gil Perkins, his head editor, and the whole staff, wouldn't be able to reconstruct it. Maybe a reel or two, out of the out-takes—sure—but the whole picture? Impossible—

The phone beside his whisky glass rang.

Grabbing for it, Harry knocked the glass to the floor.

"Yeah, who is it?" he asked.

"Checkk yourr mailboxx," said the familiar metallic voice. "Goodd nightt."

Click.

Gasping with relief, Harry dashed across the living room, pulled open his front door, hurried down the driveway past his Rolls to the mailbox, yanked it open, his hands finding another envelope.

When he tore it open, he found another folded piece of paper. Which, when he opened it, revealed a hand-drawn map of what looked to be a series of parking-lots. Clipped to the map was a parking-lot stub. "Lot Three, Long Term Parking, L.A. International Airport," it read. *"Slot 471"* was penciled on its back.

On the map, Lot Three was outlined in heavy pencil.

Harry ran back inside the house, grabbed the phone, dialed Gil Perkins's home number; earlier he'd called and told him to stand by tonight for some overtime work.

"This is Elbert," he said, when Gil answered. "Meet me in half an hour at Lot Three, Long Term Parking, L.A. International," he ordered.

"The airport?" asked Perkins. "What for?"

"To check a negative!" said Harry impatiently.

"What's it doing out there?"

"Why does everybody ask so goddamned many questions!" roared Harry, his own angry self again. "Get going!"

7:45 P.M.

Toweling himself, Perce stepped out of the shower, picked up the bourbon and water he'd left, sipped it. Then he sat down and dialed the number of the beach house where Vera was spending the weekend . . . not that he wanted to make that forty-mile trip, but it was important that he be there with her tonight. And tomorrow.

"Yeah?" she said, at the other hand. "Who is it?"

"Hi, it's me," he said. "What're you doing, honey?"

"Sitting here drinking your wine and watching TV," she said. "What the hell do you care?"

"I'm done," he said. "Why don't I run down there and spend the night?"

"I will be bombed before you get here," she said.

"I know how to wake you up," he said softly.

"Where've you been all day, you prick?" she asked. "Don't try to tell me you *worked.*"

"I'll be down in an hour with some more wine," he said. "Leave a light burning in the window."

". . . What did you *do* all day?" she insisted.

"I worked," said Perce.

8:31 P.M.

The night air resounded with the angry high screams of 747 jet engines as the planes prowled back and forth on the nearby runways beyond the airport buildings.

Harry's Rolls pulled into the gate of Lot Three, he took a ticket from the machine, and parked his car. Got out, as Gil Perkins drove in behind him and parked his Corvette next to the Rolls.

"Look for Slot 471," ordered Harry, and started walking into the rows of parked cars.

"What are we looking for there?" inquired Perkins, a thin, white-haired man. A veteran of thirty years in the business, he had long since learned that to survive, one rolled with the punch. Even on a Saturday night, in the middle of a parking lot, far from his accustomed weekend haunts.

"A panel truck, they said!" yelled Harry, who was drawn and haggard.

"What's in it?" asked Perkins.

"You'll see when we find it!" said Harry. And added, under his breath darkly, ". . . if we find it."

They rounded the end of a long row, and he led the way down through the next.

"That looks like 471 down there," said Perkins, peering through the eerie sodium-lit foggy gloom.

Perched quietly in a slot was a panel truck, the faded paint of the number beneath it read 471.

Suddenly panting, Harry strode up to the truck, yanked at the rear doors.

They opened.

By the faint reflected light, he could see inside. There, stacked neatly on the floor of the truck, was a pile of gleaming aluminum film cans.

At either side of the cans were small cardboard boxes in which were almost melted pieces of dry ice that had served as a makeshift air-conditioning system.

"Thank God!" said Harry. "Check it, Gil!"

"What am I checking?" asked Perkins.

"Our goddamn negative!" said Harry.

Perkins briskly spun one of the cans around to read the label that was pasted to its side. "Looks like it," he murmured. Quickly he pulled off the lid, examined the leader of the film inside, pulled it out until he came to picture, sniffed it with his nose, pulled the film up and held it to the dim light.

"How does it look?" demanded Harry.

". . . Can't tell for sure," said Perkins, ". . . but let's get it back to the studio right away, so I can really check it."

He replaced the film, carefully closed the can. Splitting the load between them, both men started away.

"Aren't you taking the truck?" asked Perkins.

"Let Al Morris have it for evidence," said Harry.

"You don't want to tell me what the hell our negative is doing out here tonight, do you?" asked Perkins, hefting the cans.

"Later, later," said Harry.

They reached his parked Rolls. He opened the trunk, and they tucked the film cans carefully inside. Perkins climbed into his Corvette, and the two cars headed for the nearby exit gate.

At the kiosk, Harry held out a ticket to the attendant.

The man squinted at it. ''That's nine dollars and uh half.''

''Nine and a half? You *goniff*—I've only been here half an hour!'' protested Harry.

''Read the ticket, man, it says you been here over twenny-four hours—''

''Damn, I gave you the wrong ticket!'' said Harry. He fumbled in his pocket, found a second ticket, and thrust it to the attendant. ''This is the right one.''

The attendant squinted at the second ticket. ''This one says—ah—one dollah.''

Harry produced a bill. ''Now gimme the other ticket back,'' he commanded.

''. . . Hold it, man,'' said the attendant, suspicious. ''You only got the one car, you give me two tickets—''

Angrily, Harry got out of his car, reached up and snatched the first ticket out of the attendant's hand. ''That's not a ticket, it's evidence!''

Then he jumped back into his Rolls, slammed the door and roared off.

Gil Perkins drove his Corvette up to the barrier.

The attendant glared at him. ''How many tickets *you* got?'' he demanded.

''One,'' said Perkins, and handed it over.

''One dollah,'' said the attendant. ''Shoot, that man just went through here in that Rolls—he's off his goddamn rocker, you know?''

''I know,'' said Perkins, holding out the dollar. ''I work for him.''

''Oh, yeah?'' said the attendant. ''Then he got one ticket, you got one ticket . . . who in the hell owns that third ticket?''

''That's what we'd all like to know,'' said Perkins, and drove away.

*　*　*

chapter 25

—All right, Constable Gibbons, are the doors securely locked?
—Yes, Inspector.
—Good. Now then, ladies and gentlemen, I've brought you all here to Crestwood Manor tonight because in one way or another, you are all connected with the mysterious murder of old Colonel Pickering. Shall we proceed?

BY noontime Sunday, Harry was able to call Mike Tudor with the good news, the negative was safe, Gil Perkins and his assistant had checked every damned foot of it, the heat had caused no damage; Al Morris and his security staff had taken over, returned it to the lab where it was now locked away, there were *two* of Al's men—not those clowns from the lab—assigned to guard it full time—

"A little bit like locking the old barn door, isn't it?" remarked Tudor.

"Yeah, all right, so they got our money—"

"—*Your* money," corrected Tudor.

"—No, the insurance company's!" insisted Harry.

"You called them yet?"

"Yeah, Al Morris and I are meeting their people at three," said Harry. "But the important thing, Mike, is they've got the money, sure, but we're back in the *Cimmaron* business, and we've got a winner—"

"—Who's *they?*" asked Mike.

". . . Oh, hell, we haven't a clue," yawned Harry. The lack of sleep was beginning to get to him. "So far, we've kept the lid on the story, the papers haven't smelled anything, we kept the cops out—"

"Inside job," said Tudor firmly.

". . . How do you figure that, Mike?" he asked.

''I smell it,'' said the old man. ''Too slick. Too easy. Inside job, mark my words.''

. . . Full-time boss of a multinational corporation, a ruthless pirate with a computer for a brain, a money-lending, usurious bastard who pissed ice water, now he was a detective too?

''That's an interesting theory,'' sighed Harry.

''Nights I read a lot of detective stories,'' said Tudor. ''After a while you get a feel for these things. You'll see—I'm right.''

''First we have to find 'em,'' said Harry.

''Start within your own little circle, check for the rotten apples in the barrel,'' instructed Tudor. ''Somebody who's got a grudge against you, Harry. Do you know your enemies, Harry?''

''Yeah,'' said Harry, and checked the impulse he had to tell the crafty old bastard where *he* stood on the list.

''. . . Keep me posted, it's interesting,'' chuckled Tudor.

''You bet I will,'' said Harry.

. . . That's all he had to do. In the middle of everything else, to see to it that Mike Tudor was entertained!

He dropped onto his office couch, his eyes closed. He dozed.

. . . Enemies?

. . . Hell, thirty years in this business, he'd made enough of them to fill the Beverly Hills phone book.

It was Sunday, and the two men from the Peerless Insurance Company had obviously been pursuing their pleasures. Mike Carew, the slim and wiry executive V.P., was in slacks and a sport shirt, that was his golfing outfit; his second in command, Herm Douglas, sported dungarees and a sweatshirt instead of sober dark blue, he'd been sailing this morning down at Newport Beach.

They sat quietly in his office as Harry, Al Morris sitting beside him, outlined the events of the past twenty-four hours. Douglas made notes as Harry related everything that had happened from Friday night up in Frisco until midnight last evening.

''Did you get a tape of those phone calls?'' asked Carew.

Harry shook his head. ''We weren't set up for that.''

''Too bad,'' said the executive. ''Can we have the hard evidence?''

Harry pushed over the various items that had accumulated—the letters from his mailbox, the piece of film, the parking-lot ticket from the airport lot, the small hand-printed map. Not much to show for a million-dollar snatch.

. . . Both men studied the artifacts.

"When you made the drop and left the money in the bin," asked Douglas, "did you have anybody on the scene for surveillance?"

"No we didn't," said Al Morris. "Not that I didn't want to, y'understand—"

Bastard, now *he* was getting into the act!

Harry glared at him. "*I* called Al off," he said. "They warned me over the phone—any funny stuff and the negative would never come back. Damnit, I was protecting a nine-million-dollar investment!"

"Of course you were," said Carew, very sympathetic. "And believe me, Harry, we can imagine how you felt . . . but it might have been a little more . . . helpful, if you'd checked this all out with us before you went ahead." He smiled. "After all, we're involved here to a very considerable degree."

"Sure, but a negative, sitting out there in the sun, in a parked truck—"

"You've checked on the truck?" asked Douglas.

"Yeah," said Al Morris. "Five'll get you ten it's stolen, and those are switched plates—that we can check out tomorrow—"

"Fingerprints?"

Al shook his head. "None. They were slick, the bastards, I'll give them that."

"The voices on the phone? Recognizable?"

"Some sort of a hand mike, a gizmo that made them sound like a recording, you know?" explained Harry.

"That's something for us to check on, Herm," said Carew. He cleared his throat. "Now. The money. One million, in small bills?"

"Out of sequence. Fives, tens, and twenties," said Harry. "In two suitcases."

"Which you got from the First Mutual, downtown?"

Harry nodded. "Through Ruggles—he's Tudor's man."

"Now, ah, don't get sore, Harry," said Carew pleasantly, "but before Peerless pays out a million on this claim, we're going to need something tangible to show to our accounting department. Ah, what sort of evidence do we have that you actually paid over the million?''

Harry pushed over the signed note he'd gotten from Ruggles yesterday, the paper that bound him to that damned 18 per cent per day interest.

Carew studied it.

''. . . But nobody saw you make the actual drop in that Salvation Army bin?'' he asked.

''Listen!'' Harry exploded. ''If I needed to borrow a million, for myself, don't you think I could get it at a better rate than that? I haven't got the goddamned money, *they* have it!''

''Sure,'' grinned Carew. *''Relax*. You make sense. But we have to ask, wouldn't you?''

When everything was Xeroxed, the material tucked carefully into a manila folder, both men prepared to leave.

''So now what?'' demanded Harry.

''Go get some sleep,'' suggested Carew. ''From here on, it's our baby. The important thing is—your picture is safe and sound, and let's make sure it's the blockbuster we're all expecting you to come up with, right?''

''It won't get out again, I'll promise you that,'' said Al Morris, grimly. ''And if it'd been up to *me,* I'd've seen to it—''

Big mouth, getting into the act again! Harry waved him silent.

''When do you think we can settle our claim?'' he asked.

Carew shrugged. ''As soon as possible,'' he equivocated. ''I won't say we'll enjoy handing all that cash over, but we've done a lot of business with you over the years, Harry, and we expect to do a lot more.''

''How soon is possible?'' persisted Harry, remembering that 18 per cent, mounting up each hour.

Carew patted him on the shoulder. ''I'll expedite it,'' he said, vaguely. ''Stop worrying and unwind. All this tension—it's not good for a man your age, Harry. Why don't you go take a little trip, relax—''

''Sure, and this time they'll probably steal my whole office!'' groaned Harry.

"Just between the four of us," mused Douglas, "is there anybody around the studio, somebody here in your own shop, say, who might have it in for you, Harry?"

"Sure," said Al Morris.

Harry turned angrily on him. "Who? *Who?*" he cried. "Name a name!"

"Just guessing," said Morris unabashed.

"Keep your guesses to yourself!" ordered Harry. He turned back to Carew and Douglas. "You think this was an inside job?"

"Who knows?" answered Carew. "All we do know is that somebody who may still be in southern California this morning has acquired a million dollars in fives, tens, and twenties."

"Of *your* money," said Harry.

He saw them out of the office.

When they had left, he turned back to Al Morris, thrust a warning finger at the portly, balding head of security. "You big mouth sonofabitch," he said. "Any more cracks out of you, and you can go find a job as a private detective, you hear?"

"I'm only doing what I'm paid to do," insisted Morris virtuously.

"Bullshit!" said Harry bitterly. "Don't you try to make your letter on my time—if this joint had decent security, there wouldn't've been anybody sneaking around grabbing out-takes from vaults—"

"You proved my point!" said Morris. "It has to be an inside job!"

The two insurance-company executives walked briskly down the studio street.

"What do you think?" Douglas asked softly.

"Oh . . . I'd guess this actually was a heist," mused Carew. "Old Harry-boy is an operator, sure, but he'd be a damn fool to pull something as bald as this. Unless he owes a million to somebody we don't know about, and this was his way of raising it . . . On the other hand, his credit rating is okay, so he could borrow. And not at any eighteen percent, either."

"Except we pay off the million," said Douglas.

''Not to him, to Tudor's bank,'' said Carew.

''You think it's such a good idea, keeping a lid on this whole thing?''

''You bet,'' said Carew. ''If this story got out, it would be rotten PR. Wouldn't help Harry's picture, not one bit, nor us, either. And give every small-time hood around here ideas . . .''

''So we pay?''

''Eventually,'' said Carew. ''And jack up his next premium to the sky.''

They reached his demure powder-blue Cadillac Seville; both men got in. Carew started the car and headed toward the main gate.

''Call Investigations this afternoon,'' he instructed. ''Tell whoever's there that we want a meeting, nine tomorrow, with Sid Fuller. He can handle it from here.''

The car paused at the gate.

The guard got out of his booth, walked around it, checking the license plates, accepted the proffered pass from Carew. Then he peered at both men. ''Double-checking, sir. Identification, please?''

''Good show,'' said Carew, holding out his wallet.

The guard glanced at it, returned it, and then waved them on.

''. . . Too bad they weren't doing this Friday night,'' said Douglas, bitterly. ''Do you want that Al Morris at the meeting tomorrow?''

Carew shook his head. ''No, let old Sid handle it, solo. We want our million back.''

''. . . Eighteen per cent per day,'' sighed Douglas. ''Don't you wish *we* could charge that on our loans?''

''Shame on you, Herm,'' said Carew with a straight face. ''Ours is a business designed solely to serve the public.''

''. . . Right,'' said Douglas. ''Twelve?''

. . . Harry came awake.

The bedside clock read 5:46. He'd been sleeping on and off for almost ten hours, not well . . . his nimble mind, which had tussled with script problems all these years, had refused to fold up, turn itself off.

It kept churning over possibilities, trying to put pieces together . . .

He lay in his bed, eyes closed, mind open. Outside the bedroom window there was the soft, regular cooing of those damn mourning doves

do you know your enemies, Harry?

somebody here in your own shop.

that meant somebody who wanted to make a score on him.

(somebody with very professional knowledge of the way the whole studio operated)

(who could manage to grab out-takes from a cutting room)

(somebody who knew enough to leave a valuable negative in the back of a panel truck with dry ice packed beside it to keep the emulsion from being ruined)

start within your own little circle, Harry

(Who knew there weren't any prints of *Cimmaron* yet, and picked this weekend, a weekend when he'd gone away, to snatch the negative before there were any prints made?)

pros pros

inside job

somebody who might have it in for you, Harry

(who'd know Al Morris well enough to figure that the fat idiot was planning to be a hero by springing a trap out at the scene of the drop?)

someone who's got a grudge against you

Mrs. Price, his secretary? Sixteen years in his office.

No. Honest. Straight as a die, hell, she didn't even drink, she had a few shares in his company, why would she pull anything on him? Gil Perkins? No way, Gil had plenty of money, got top dollar, had been making it for years, also had stock

but who could be sure?

How about Lister, the redhead? she hadn't been around long, he'd thought about humping her and that gorgeous ass but he'd never laid a hand on her, could she have teamed up with somebody else, it was something to think about

pros/inside job

grayish dawn light began seeping through the bedroom blinds and with it

spinning through the connections of his now-wide-awake brain came a crazy piece of deduction, four or five pieces all held together by conjecture

an answer to this whole thing?

sure, why not?

pros/heist artists/inside, inside the studio five days a week/working for him, a couple of dozen yards away from his own office, yet, the ones who'd have to know *everything* going on in the studio, maybe in his cutting rooms, sure—

working on a heist story, heist artists themselves from twenty years back, hell they'd even gone to the can for it, so they'd come out and worked their way out here to California, figured out a way to rip him off out of a million bucks—

working for *him* all the time, yet!

What a setup!

Damn— *it had to be them!*

he sat up in bed.

The clock said 6:21.

Too early.

Sleep another hour, then he'd get up, go to the studio, and then, soon enough, he'd damned well find out what that bastard Perce Barnes and those two cons had been up to all this weekend—

but what the hell would that prove?

. . . they were pros. They'd have alibis, of course.

. . . by now they'd have stashed away the money, wouldn't they?

Well, he was still going to find out what kind of lies they'd throw at him!

9:14 A.M.

Without warning, the outer door to the office suite was thrown open and Harry strode in.

Perce was sitting on the couch, sipping a cup of freshly made coffee and glancing at the morning's trade papers.

". . . Why, hello, Harry," he said. "You're up early. Coffee?"

"I had coffee," said Harry. ". . . I'm . . . ah . . . looking for your pages."

"Sure thing," said Perce. "I did some over the weekend." He got up and went over to his briefcase, opened it and took out a manila folder.

". . . You worked all weekend?" asked Harry.

"We-el, old friend, I will not lie to you," said Perce, with a small smile. "Saturday I played a little tennis at the club—"

"With who?" asked Harry.

Perce grimaced. "Ziggy Harling. Took him for a hundred. Then I went home and worked, and yesterday, I also played a little hooky . . ."

He handed Harry the folder.

"What's hooky?" demanded Harry.

". . . A day at the beach with Vera, we had a little fresh air and sunshine."

". . . Ah, who's this Vera?"

"A very generous lady friend," said Perce.

Harry nodded. Sat down on the couch, opened the folder and began to riffle through Perce's pages. "So okay," he said. "Where are the two ex-cons?"

"The Chesters?"

"Who else around here has a record?" said Harry, irritated.

". . . Delicately put, Harry," said Perce. "Keep your voice down. Al's in the can, and LeRoy went across the street to the health-food store to get some uncooked honey for his tea. He's very fussy about using only natural sweeteners." He indicated a small carton next to the coffee machine. "That's his tea, it's called Red Zinger, very potent stuff—"

The office door opened and Al Chester, the morning paper in his hand, walked in.

"We have a visitor, Al," said Perce.

"Why, howdy there, Mr. Elbert," said Al. "Nice to see you. You're reading Perce's pages? Sound mighty good to me, from what he tells me—''

''I'm *reading,''* said Harry, his eyes on the topmost page.

Al took a seat.

Without looking up, Harry asked, ''. . . So where did *you* guys go all weekend?''

''. . . Why, me and LeRoy went up camping,'' said Al. ''LeRoy sure loves to get out into open space and fish.'' He grinned. ''Don't know's you can blame him much, now, after all those years.''

''Camping where?'' asked Harry.

''Place up past Bakersfield,'' said Al. ''I can show it to you on a map.''

''I'll bet you can,'' muttered Harry.

''You like camping, Mr. Elbert? Maybe you'd like to come out with us some weekend?''

''. . . Sure I would,'' said Harry, continuing to glare at the top page of the material in his hands.

''Nice campgrounds,'' said Al. ''Plenty of room for hiking, and the fishing's good—''

The door opened and LeRoy came in, carrying a small brown paper bag. ''Sorry I'm late,'' he said. ''The girl didn't open at nine—'' He nodded to Harry. ''Morning, Mr. Elbert.''

''Yeah,'' said Harry sourly. ''Beautiful morning. So you had a lovely weekend up with Mother Nature, right?''

''Pine Lake,'' said LeRoy. ''Caught me a pair of speckled trout, too. One of them buggers was almost two feet long . . .''

''I'll bet it was,'' said Harry.

''Al took my picture,'' said LeRoy. He patted his shirt pocket, removed a small container of Instamatic film. ''Lunchtime I'm goin' to get these developed.'' He grinned. ''Then you can see I ain't lying about the size.''

''Very smart,'' said Harry. ''You with a fish, in the woods.''

''. . . I was just tellin' Mr. Elbert he ought to come up there with us some weekend,'' said Al.

''Yeah, Harry,'' said Perce. ''You've been going at it hot and heavy for the last few months, you could use a little time off.''

Harry looked up from the page, his face suffused with sudden anger. "You're a doctor, right?" he demanded. "A real specialist, you know what's good for me, you got only my best interests at heart, right? Bullshit!" He stood up. "Don't play games with me, Perce, I've been around, I don't need any goddamn relaxation, or fishing—you know goddamned well what I need!"

Breathing hard, he threw the pages onto the couch.

"I got calls to make!" he announced. "Going back to my office—and just because I'm over there, don't think I'm not on top of this—" He waved an angry finger. "You guys may be pros, but *I'm* a pro, too, don't forget that!"

"Harry," said Perce mildly, "you're upset—"

"Bet your ass I'm upset!" bawled Harry. "I want to see you people later!"

As he stormed out of the office, Perce followed him to the door. "Sure thing, Harry, we'll be here all day, waiting . . ."

The sound of Harry's footsteps receded down the hall.

Perce closed the door.

Stifled a laugh. As he began to speak, Al swiftly reached up and held a finger to Perce's lips.

With his other hand, Al pointed, first at the floor, then at the ceiling, then behind the couch.

Then he crossed to Perce's desk, wrote in large capital letters BUG?

Perce nodded.

Al tore the piece of paper into small shreds.

". . . Now why don't we all get to work?" he suggested.

*   *   *

chapter 26

—Who's that at the door?
—I dunno, but whoever it is, get rid of him!

No casting director, no matter how desperate, would ever have chosen Sid Fuller to play the part of a private investigator.

Middle-aged, stoop-shouldered, cheaply dressed, Sid might have passed for your burner service man, possibly the guard at your branch bank, or even that occasional loser type who rings your doorbell to try and interest you in a new vacuum cleaner. But as a detective? No way. Sid Fuller did not fit the part, could not ever be justified by some movie director's wildest impulse to go for off-beat casting. And no screenwriter, searching for an interesting new concept of a crime fighter would have gambled on a character such as Sid to become the hero, either of a film or even of an hour-long TV series, where detectives need some sort of charisma. Slightly pot-bellied, dandruff sprinkling the shoulders of his off-the-rack, narrow-lapeled, shiny blue suit, peering through his bifocals, how could one equate Sid with the laconic style of a Barnaby Jones, the vigor of a Cannon, Philip Marlowe's brutal cynicism, or even the worn-out virility of a Harry-O?

For more than a quarter century now, Sid had lived in a small Glendale bungalow, and driven to work daily in his even more modest car, which was usually badly in need of a wash job. To his next-door neighbors, he was Mr. Fuller, a quiet widower who tended his lawn, clipped his hedges, and kept very much to himself. If anyone on his block knew that he worked for the Peerless Insurance, he was more than likely to assume that Sid had something to do with actuarial statistics, and that assumption was exactly how Sid wanted it. In Sid's line of work, the less the outside world knew, the better.

Sid had a hobby, true, but nothing as flamboyant as, say, Nero Wolfe's propensity for imported beer and rare orchids. Nights when he arrived home from the Peerless office, after spending a long day coping with the caseload of phony insurance claims that constantly reached his desk on the nineteenth floor, Sid would prepare himself a modest supper, usually a TV dinner, or a can of chili (he'd eaten a substantial meal at noon in the company cafeteria where the price was right), and then he would wash the few dishes, and retire to his small study, there to spend several hours poring over his extensive collection of antique picture post cards. By now they filled two file cabinets, all neatly catalogued by locale and by subject matter, as precisely as a library index.

Sid's post cards were mostly scenes of another era, half a century and more ago, a simpler, less complicated time. Main streets of rural New England villages. World War I New York, with double-decker buses and old Checker cabs. Bustling factory towns of the Midwest, antique steam machinery. Primitive farm settlements, the single main street dotted with an occasional Model T, Western cow towns, the beaches of southern California in an earlier, unsprawled era. Family picnics, Victorian schoolyards, country roads, there were thousands of such curios in Sid's collection, but he kept on adding to it. His major pleasure in life was derived from filling out the gaps, either by swapping with other collectors around the country, or by spending his weekends haunting tag sales and flea markets.

To an analyst, Sid Fuller and his hobby would have provided a relatively open-and-shut case.

This quiet, methodical anonymous man who spent each day prowling through the streets of southern California, passing through a sunlit world populated exclusively by shyster lawyers, con artists and specialists in white-collar fraud, unraveling fake accident claims and phony arson cases, proving out swindlers who came in all shapes, ages, and sizes from elegant Santa Barbara homes down to inner-city tenements, had found his surcease, one which nightly permitted him to maintain his sanity.

For in Sid Fuller's business, nobody ever told the truth unless forced to, very few people were what they pretended to be, and every claimant whose name was typed in the reports in his Case Pending folders was always guilty until proven otherwise.

To survive, to operate from nine to five each day in such an uncertain world, was it any wonder that Sid spent his evenings communing with the reliability of eager 1916 drivers in goggles and dusters, preparing to scale Pike's Peak, or sailing on an as-yet-unpolluted Connecticut River, or with a row of beaming matrons, rocking in chairs on the porch of some long-vanished Catskill Mountains resort hotel?

By the time the meeting broke up at Carew's office on Monday morning, Sid had pretty much assembled the outline of the case.

He'd studied the evidence Carew had supplied, and he'd already had a brief telephone call with Al Morris, at the studio.

Carew beckoned to Sid to stick around, after the others had left. He closed the office door.

". . . We're going to have to pay, and soon," Carew confided. "But we want that money back."

"Don't we always?" said Sid cheerfully.

". . . Whenever they start spending it," Carew said, ". . . I don't care if you have a long white beard, you *be* there."

"You think it's a they?" asked Sid.

". . . I don't care if it's an it, or a baboon, or a pair of Siamese twins," rasped Carew. "That's Peerless's money, not theirs . . . You got any theories so far?"

". . . I don't know if I do," said Sid carefully. "All that stuff about the two brothers, the Chesters, working on a picture for Elbert, right nearby. Morris threw that at me right away, but I don't know. Kind of throws me. Almost too easy, you know?"

"It's *your* baby now, Sid," said Carew grimly, and ushered him out.

He spent the next twenty-four hours checking out all the available evidence. By the time he headed out to the studio, to talk with Harry Elbert, he had come up with damned little. Zilch.

That old panel truck, abandoned at the airport. Stolen, of course, picked up in Pasadena a week ago, already reported to the cops.

They hadn't identified it because of the switched license plates. Those had come off a car registered to a nurse in Culver City, who'd reported their loss last Saturday.

The ransom notes? Not much help. Dime-store writing paper, the letters cut out of newspapers at random, Scotch-taped to the paper. No fingerprints, no way to trace their origin.

The guard at the lab, Davis, hadn't much to provide, either. His description of the two "delivery men" was half-assed—men with mustaches and dark glasses, any age from thirty on up to fifty or so, southern accents . . . or could it be Okie?

The telephone voices? Disguised by a voice mike, a nice touch, it didn't need too much checking to figure out that it was a device manufactured by Western Electric for the help of people who'd lost their capacity to speak, a neat little item that could be bought for around fifty dollars in lots of supply houses around town, nothing much there to go on. But a cute touch. Shrewd.

Nor was there anything out at the Salvation Army bin. No witnesses who'd seen anybody taking anything out, besides, they'd operated in the darkness, that made a car hard to identify. And no trace of anyone's having been there since the weekend, the contents of the bin were still untouched. If he didn't know for sure that a million in cash had passed through there, he wouldn't have believed it.

. . . That left the only tangible clue to the whole damn shooting match.

The million in cash. Someday, somewhere, it would have to show. . . . And four suspects.

Perce Barnes, Al and LeRoy Chester. And—of course—Harry Elbert himself.

No matter how you figured this, you couldn't leave *him* out.

". . . Have you got any theories?" asked Sid. "Anything at all that would help, I'd sure appreciate hearing, Mr. Elbert."

Harry stared across the desk. ". . . I could swear it was those sonsofbitches," he said softly. "But damnit, they've all got alibis! Barnes—he played tennis at the club, shacked up with his broad down at the beach, and at the same time, he turned out *these*—"

He held up a sheaf of script pages.

"—So if he was out snatching a negative last weekend," said Harry grimly, "he'd've had to have nine legs."

"Could he have had partners?"

"Sure, except they were two, three hundred miles north of here, at some fishing place called Pine Lake!"

Sid made a note.

"No help there, either," said Harry disgustedly. "The bastard caught some fish, and his brother snapped his picture!"

"Mmm-hmm," said Sid, and made another note.

"Screwed," mused Harry. "So. How long is it going to take to settle up this claim?"

". . . That's not exactly my department," said Sid. "You'd have to speak to Mr. Carew about that. Now . . . is it okay if I come wander around here every once in a while, maybe check on a few loose ends?"

"For how long?" asked Harry, suspicious.

"Can't say," said Sid. "Things I need to button up." He permitted himself a thin smile. "My people don't relish losing so much money."

"You grab off premiums quick enough!" said Harry. "How do you think *I* feel—this whole thing is costing!" He leaned forward, confidentially. "Just between us, gimme an idea how long it's going to take—"

The intercom buzzer on his desk interrupted him.

He picked it up.

The voice of the secretary on the other end spoke urgently, and what she was reporting did not seem to be good news.

"Oh, Christ!" moaned Harry. *"When?"*

She spoke again.

Harry slumped in his chair. ". . . Is he going to be all right?" he demanded, a man suddenly old. ". . . Okay, okay, I better get right out there." He slammed down the phone. "Have to go," he muttered. "My kid's been in an automobile accident, up near Ventura—"

". . . Too bad," said Sid. "I hope it's not serious—"

"—Goddamned fast cars!" cried Harry angrily.

He went out of the office.

Sid could hear urgent voices coming from outside, as Harry conferred with his secretaries.

Sid put his note pad into his pocket, got up, casually wandered across toward Harry's desk.

The voices continued outside, and then a door slammed. Then, there was the sound of an engine as it started up, in the street.

Sid ran his eye across the papers on Harry's desk.

When he had finished reading them, he strolled out.

". . . Too bad about Mr. Elbert's kid," he said to the red-haired secretary.

". . . Oh, my God," she replied. ". . . He's so *young* . . ."

"Yeah, well, rough," said Sid. "Tell Mr. Elbert I'll be back."

He wandered out.

Perce and Al went off the lot for lunch at the deli. LeRoy stayed back in the office with his yogurt and brown sugar and God knows what else he was on these days.

". . . I know how it feels," said Al, munching on his pastrami on white bread. He winked. "This is going to be the hard part."

"What is?" asked Perce moodily. Ever since Harry had left the office this morning, he had begun to feel a strange depression.

"The waiting," said Al. "You better get used to it. See, me and LeRoy know about everything there is to waiting. We had a lot of practice at it—almost twenty years."

Perce lowered his voice. ". . . Is the stuff safe?"

"Very safe," said Al. "Buried deep."

. . . Locked away. All that cash. Untouchable. Not even a five dollar bill of it should be spent?

"So what good is it?" Perce suddenly demanded.

Al smiled. "It's there for when you retire."

"But—supposing I want to retire now, and enjoy it *now?*"

Al finished his sandwich. "Show any of it, and they'd be down on us like gangbusters, believe me."

". . . Supposing," said Perce, "I get sick, or I turn in my chips. Then what?"

"Well," mused Al, "if you was to need it that bad, we'd have to figure out a way to help you . . . but that's only if you really need it."

"What's your definition of really?" asked Perce.

"That's a bridge we have to cross when we come to it, pardner," said Al, wiping his lips. He signaled the waitress. "Got a nice rich piece of cake for dessert?"

"For you, doll, anytime," said the waitress. "You got one hell of a sweet tooth."

"That's not all I got for you," said Al, smiling.

"Any time after three," she said, and left.

"Okay," said Perce. "I'm in a box along with you two. None of us is getting any younger, are we? Supposing something happens to one of us . . ."

"Then," said Al, "it means a bigger piece of it for the other two, right?"

"I don't think I like those odds," said Perce.

The waitress placed a large slab of layer cake in front of Al.

"Beautiful," he told her. "Good eating."

"Yeah, doll, very tasty," she grinned.

"I meant you, honey," he said.

"You think I didn't know?" she said.

Al attacked the cake. "Tell you what, Perce," he said, ". . . think about it as a kind of lottery. Winner take all."

". . . And if I win," Perce asked, "how will I know how to collect?"

"You'll always know," Al promised.

. . . A third of a million, stashed away.

Hidden from sight. Useless. Untouchable, unspendable, drawing no interest, hell, if you had a Swiss bank account, at least they allowed you to visit your boodle, but this had to be the financial world's most frozen asset.

. . . Some retirement fund!

As if reading Perce's mind, Al said gently, ". . . You know what's the best way to handle it? *Forget about it.*"

"Here you are, big spender," said the waitress, and dropped their check on the table.

"We split, right?" suggested Al.

"Of course," said Perce. "No sense drawing anybody's attention."

Al held up the check. On its back was scribbled a phone number.

"Think she's trying to tell me something?" he asked.

On the way back to the studio, Perce's depression deepened.

He dropped Al off, went to the office and tried to write.

No help. He could not shake this strange emptiness.

. . . Ever since the heist had come to a halt, he'd felt let down. End of season. Closing night of a long-run show. The feeling washed over him . . . something like the malaise that set in after a good lay, that hollow sadness you felt when you rolled over to doze, spent.

. . . This was something you never got from crime stories. That you can't take bows for having pulled off a successful heist.

He picked up the pages and left the office. Maybe a drive would clear his head.

. . . Was this what it was like for some poor bastard of a ghost surgeon? that guy who comes into the operating room when the patient is safely anesthetized, he's wearing a mask, he picks up the scalpel and does the job, sews up the incision and disappears. The patient comes to, he's going to live—and he'll never have a clue whose hands it was that saved his life.

No, in a funny way, it had to be more like being one of those poor black-listed bastards during the McCarthy era, years back. Guys who worked out of their houses, over the transom would come a story, or a sick script in a plain envelope, they'd sit down to their typewriters, they'd sweat their brains out over it, do the job (for short money, of course) meet the producer in a back alley behind a restaurant, and hand it over in the dark. Then months later, the poor slob could go to a theater and sit and see his picture, raved over by the critics, coining money, and he, who'd done it, ended up with zilch. Or an anonymous pen name—something that Woody Allen could get laughs out of, twenty years later.

But at least those guys had the satisfaction of sitting with an audience, listening to them laugh at their jokes, or weep at the love scenes.

Hell, he told himself, right now I'd settle for vice versa.

So what did he expect? A credit on this heist?

Sure, call Vera and have her plant it in the trades. Or take an ad.

Getaway Car, Driven by Perce Barnes.

Not flashy enough. How about—

"Perce Barnes congratulates Al and LeRoy Chester on the successful completion of their first heist. Guys, it was a pleasure."

He could have cards printed, sure, hand them out—

Perce Barnes—Accomplice.

. . . That would look good as a bumper sticker—

No. He would simply have to settle for no billing.

Mr. Unknown.

(. . . Say, not a bad title. Catchy. Maybe he could work up a story to go with it. Maybe, *this* story.)

Well, why not? He'd be finished with the first draft soon, then Harry would close him out and stick Billy on the script, that meant Perce Barnes would be out of work and scratching again.

Which would make him one of the few writers standing in line down at the Unemployment Office, waiting to pick up his check—who had three hundred grand stashed away somewhere for his old age.

. . . Somewhere *where?*

He went to the club and found a game, this time with old Paul Axelrod, the club hypochondriac, who kept on telling him about his latest attack of kidney stones, but who served the purpose. After three sets of tennis and symptoms, he felt less tense, and even healthy.

He called Vera. She was out but her secretary said, "Oh, Mr. *Barnes*—she was trying to reach you, to find out about Mr. Elbert's son—"

Billy?

Hadn't he heard, it was on the radio, the kid had been in a car smash up, near Ventura this morning? No, he hadn't!

Quickly he called Harry's office, and when Audrey Lister got on, she said, "—Oh, *you*—he's been trying to find you all afternoon, you weren't in your office—"

"I was working at home," he lied. "How's Billy?"

"He's going to be all right, thank God, but he's got broken bones and he's in shock . . . wait a minute, I'll switch you."

"Where have *you* been?" demanded Harry, hostile.

"—Harry, I'm sorry as hell about Billy," said Perce. "Is Billy going to be all right?"

"Yeah, he's got to be in the hospital a couple of weeks at least," said Harry. "Goddamn fast car—his mother's flying in from Paris tonight—I've had a rotten day, I was up there three hours—listen, tomorrow morning, you and I have to sit down and talk—"

"Sure thing. What about?"

"The *script!*" Harry bellowed. "In the middle of everything the network is hocking me about your first draft, they want it over there next Monday—then we gotta have a meeting about rewrites—they're pushing me to get 'em done in two weeks—so cut out the damn tennis and running around, we got work ahead of us. Two weeks, can you handle it?"

"That's tight," Perce said, his mind grappling with the problem.

"Then get off your ass and work nights!"

Perce began to laugh, but checked himself. Of course! Now that poor Billy was out of action, there went Harry's plan to steal a credit for his son. Harry would have to rely on *him.*

What a switch! Who could have figured it?

". . . I'll see you tomorrow at ten sharp," Harry ordered.

"Sure thing," said Perce. "And Harry—please give Billy my best wishes. Tell him that's from me *and* Al and LeRoy."

". . . Oh, yeah, *them,*" said Harry. ". . . Sure. Thanks."

The tiny, red, glowing end of Vera's cigarette was the only light in her bedroom.

She nudged him gently. ". . . Hey," she murmured, ". . . you there?"

"Mmm."

". . . All the time we were screwing I had the feeling you were somewhere else,'' said Vera. ''. . . Is it that old gag, who were *you* thinking of?''

. . . Perceptive lady. If I could only tell you, he thought. Not a who. A *what*. Three hundred and thirty-odd thousand of whats.

He moved toward her, kissed her gently on the shoulder, ran his lips across her.

''. . . I don't need you to fake it,'' she said. ''If you're tired, you're excused.''

''. . . It's the script,'' he lied.

''Going well?''

. . . Better than that. Under the gun, he'd finished the first draft, met with Harry and absorbed Harry's notes and comments, most of which were reasonable, gone back to his office, and incorporated them into the script. Typed and bound in covers, the damn thing was on its way to the network. Ten, twelve days from now, it would be back, accompanied by pages of program-department comment. Then a week or two of rewrites, and he'd have *Three Down, Two Left Standing* out of his life. ''Almost done,'' he told her.

''You've been buried in there a long time, baby,'' she said. ''Maybe it's time we start doing a little media exposure for you.''

''No,'' he said sharply. Not now. This was a time to keep a low profile.

''. . . Don't you want another assignment?'' she asked.

''Not yet,'' he said.

''Then I have a better idea,'' she said. ''Finish up. Then I'm going to finagle a couple of weeks off, and you and I are going to take each other away. How does two weeks in Paris sound . . . mm?'' She snubbed out her cigarette, then he felt her moving down, her mouth flicking across his groin. ''C'est bon, n'est-ce-pas?'' she asked. ''Typically French . . .''

''Nice,'' he said.

. . . Paris? . . . Eighty, ninety bucks a day at the hotel, meals another hundred or so, two weeks at those prices would add up, sure, he had the money, but if he started spending like that, even using American Express . . . and somebody was watching, checking up on him.

. . . And if he left the country, what about Al and LeRoy?

Another week, and their deal as "consultants" on the project was over.

Unemployed, what would they do? Where would the loot go?

Supposing he came back from Paris, and they'd left, taking it with them?

". . . I'll have to think about it," he told her.

"Two weeks, it's not such a big deal," said Vera.

How could he tell her—it wasn't two weeks he was locked into. What he had going with Al and LeRoy Chester was an open-end commitment. That he was stuck with this duplicity—

—No, wrong word . . . *triplicity* . . . indefinitely?

(CONFIDENTIAL) PEERLESS (CONFIDENTIAL)
INTEROFFICE MEMO

8/19/76

FROM: Michael Carew, Executive V.P.
TO: S. Fuller, Investigation Dept.
Subject: Claim # 8177BL–12–009–17798

We are and have been under considerable pressure from the client, Harry Elbert, to settle this claim forthwith.

He informs me that he is leaving for New York on Monday to hold screenings at the I-U home offices of *Cimarron,* and he wants a company check before he leaves. He will be conferring with Michael Tudor at I-U, which, as you know, holds Mr. Elbert's note for the amount claimed.

I am certainly not going to be able to hold off on this matter past Friday morning. It has been almost three weeks since the actual occurrence in question took place. If you have any progress report on your office's investigation of this matter, and your findings, if any, please have it on my desk tomorrow at nine so that I can present them to the Claims Review Board which will meet with me at ten for a recommendation.

M. C.

(CONFIDENTIAL) PEERLESS (CONFIDENTIAL)
INTEROFFICE MEMO

8/19/76

FROM: S. Fuller
TO: Michael Carew, Executive V.P.
Subject: Claim # 8177BL–12–009–17798

In answer to your memo of this morning, you will find attached to this memo the following exhibits:

Personality profiles
Credit ratings
Social profiles
Statements of assets & liabilities
Persons friendly with or known by and to
Medical histories
Biographical data of the following persons:

1. Mr. Harry Elbert
2. Mrs. Harry Elbert
3. Mr. William Elbert, their son
4. Thekla Lurie, a domestic, employed in their place of residence
5. Andrea Boas, an "acquaintance" of Mr. W. Elbert
6. Mrs. Laura Price, Mr. Elbert's private secretary
7. Miss Audrey Lister, Mr. Elbert's assistant secretary
8. Mr. Donald LaVine, an "acquaintance" of Miss Lister
9. Mr. Gilbert Perkins, head editor
10. Mr. Perce Barnes, script writer and tennis pro
11. Mr. Al Chester, "technical consultant" on Mr. Elbert's current project
12. Mr. LeRoy Chester, also "technical consultant"
13. Billy Lee Davis, guard at Classic Film Laboratories (separated from his job 7/22/76)
14. Mrs. Vera George, an "acquaintance" of Mr. Barnes
15. Miss Fiona Colfaxx, employed by British Airways, also an "acquaintance" of Mr. Elbert's.

There are other specific individuals currently being investigated, but as of this moment, their dossiers are not complete.

So far, we have developed nothing substantial that would ordinarily be considered a lead.

As I have explained to you several times in the past, in a case such as this one, patience is the key factor. While I may have my suspicions, I must come up with proof. The file will stay open for as long as it takes us to find out where the money is surfacing.

Whether or not Claims Review decides to pay, you have my assurance that Investigations will be on the job.

S. F.

(Enclosures; pp. 1–96.
ALSO TO BE CLASSIFIED CONFIDENTIAL.)

Harry Elbert jabbed his intercom buzzer. "Did we get a call from Carew yet?"

"Not yet, Mr. E," said Mrs. Price.

Damn insurance company! Carew had promised payment by today—it was almost two thirty, and so far, no word, no check, Carew had been out of the office all morning . . . playing his games again, sure—

"Well, keep after him, and put him through the minute you get him," ordered Harry, "and meantime, hold everything else until I finish with Mr. Barnes here."

He blew his nose, he had a damn cold; he wanted desperately to smoke, but the post-nasal drip made even his precious Cubans taste worse than Roi-Tans.

He glared at the room. Perce Barnes, sitting with the script in his lap, tan and relaxed, sure, what did he have to worry about? . . . any time he felt like it, he could run off to the club and beat his brains out on the courts. And Al and LeRoy, those two geniuses of true crime, sitting on his sofa, staring at him, who needed *them?* He'd set up this script conference and sent for Perce, and they had nothing better to do than come along? He'd never liked either of them, not from the go, the big tall one with his pasty face, and that dumb hand exerciser he kept playing with, a strong bastard, nobody you wanted to meet in a dark alley; and his brother, crafty Al, all mealy-mouth and smiles, polite, sure, but deep down, a prick, that message came out loud and clear, and even though Harry hated to admit that Al Morris could be right about anything, when it came to his theory that it was the Chesters who had ripped off the negative, maybe you couldn't prove it, but Harry would bet that those *momsers* had done it, he'd give long odds it had been them . . .

And Perce?

No . . . he hadn't had anything to do with it. Perce was a hustler, sure, a con artist, but he would never have had the brains to figure out something so dangerous. It wasn't Perce's style. One thing he had to give the bastard, though, in his old age he was turning into a writer! This script of his was good, damned good, he hadn't believed Perce had it in him, not that he was ever going to tell him so, right away Perce would get ideas, probably hold him up for more dough—

''All right, let's get started,'' Harry said, flipping through the sheaf of pages from the network. ''We're under the gun with the network, I'm taking *Cimarron* to New York Monday—''

''I hear you have a smash, Harry,'' said Perce. ''Congratulations.''

''Who told you?'' asked Harry.

''. . . It's around,'' grinned Perce.

''Yeah, well maybe we have a shot at it,'' Harry said, and blew his nose. ''Now I got all this stuff from the clucks over at the network, so let's get started. Al, you and LeRoy don't really need to hang around, this is gonna be mostly technical stuff—''

''Oh, that's all right, Mr. Elbert,'' said Al placidly. ''Me and LeRoy is sort of interested in knowing how those TV people feel about our life story, you know?''

''Yeah, okay, well suit yourself,'' said Harry. He glanced at Audrey Lister, who sat nearby, her shorthand book open. ''A full set of notes on this, right? Here we go, from the top. Overall note. They feel the style is a little old-fashioned, Perce. It could use a general punching up, all the way.''

Perce nodded. ''What does that mean, Harry?''

''What the hell do I know?'' asked Harry. ''They get paid for being authorities over there. Go through the script and see if you can't sharpen it.'' He went back to the notes. ''Now let's get specific. The opening. Too quiet. The two brothers in the small town street—that whole business there needs punching up, what they want is a grabber, right up at the top.''

''A grabber?'' asked Al, puzzled.

''Listen, Perce, here's the kind of thing it ought to be,'' said Harry. ''Our two guys come driving down the street, they pull up to the curb and park, another guy comes by, he's a rich kid, a farmer's son, maybe, as he goes by, he clips their bumper, they get sore, they jump out, LeRoy pulls him out of the truck, right away there's a fist fight—''

''Excuse me, Mr. Elbert,'' said LeRoy.

Harry stared at him. ''What?'' he asked.

''. . . We didn't own no car,'' said LeRoy.

Oh, for Christ's sake, who needed this? ''Okay, okay, so now you own a car,'' said Harry, and turned back to Perce. ''The guy who slams into it goes running off to his father—''

''We couldn't afford a car,'' said LeRoy.

''Look, I don't care if you could—it's not important—we need the scene,'' snapped Harry. He blew his nose. ''Got that, Perce?''

''. . . Yes, I do, Harry,'' said Perce, ''but maybe instead of a brawl over a crack up, maybe . . . we could open with a kicker scene?''

''Such as?''

''. . . Well, say we open with the two young brothers knocking over their first bank—close up of each of them, they're scared—and over what we see, there's the voice, it tells us where they are, what they're planning—a series of freeze frames—we juggle the whole thing out of the second part and move it back, see, now what we have going for us is—*here's me and my brother LeRoy—we're robbing a bank, and we're scared—and how the hell did we ever get into this mess?''*

Not bad, thought Harry. As a matter of fact, damn good.

He nodded. ''Yeah, that sounds like it could work, so try it, Perce,'' he said. ''Remember, menace. We need menace. Meanwhile, don't let's drop the thing about the fight in the street, see if that can't be shoehorned in somewhere.'' He referred to the network memo. ''Now. Here's another comment. Your love interest down in the second half, after they've pulled off the heist. That girl, Marie, the one the kid picks up with in Florida, the hoor. She isn't acceptable. They all feel she's too much of a hoor—no sympathy for her—''

''She was a hoor,'' said Al. ''A cheap little two-bit broad who—''

''—I don't care what she was really like, it's what she's got to be like in our show!'' said Harry firmly. ''Perce, tone her down. Give her some sympathy.''

''Such as?'' asked Perce.

''Oh, please, do I have to think of everything?'' said Harry. ''She's a drifter, a victim of circumstances, a loser. Maybe she comes from a broken home—''

''Broken home my ass,'' said Al softly. ''She probably broke it herself.''

''Look, Al,'' said Harry ominously. ''We're trying to get some work done here. I'm running short of time, you got any comments, save 'em for later, okay?'' He turned back to Perce. ''. . . Perce, you'll take care of the hoor, right, you'll warm her up.''

Perce nodded.

''I still say, the girl was no damn good,'' persisted Al.

Perce turned to him and held up a warning finger. ''We can discuss it later,'' he said.

''No discussion! *Do it!''* ordered Harry. Damn it, what was this, a debating society? He waved the interoffice memo. ''Here, we have a real problem, also character. The two boys, in the beginning. Here's what they say. 'LeRoy. Too enigmatic. Suggestion; why doesn't he have a sweetheart? For instance, a small-town girl he went to school with, who loves him and tries to persuade him against taking on a life of crime?' ''

The office was silent.

Then LeRoy spoke. ''No,'' he said. ''I don't want that.''

''*You* don't want it?'' replied Harry ominously.

''I . . . didn't have a girl,'' said LeRoy. ''Leastwise, not one ought to be in this picture.''

''Mr. Elbert, what my brother is saying is maybe it's a bad idea,'' said Al.

''Hold it, fellas,'' said Perce urgently. ''Save this for later.''

"No, I guess not," replied Al. "I mean, LeRoy has a right to tell you whether or not he had a sweetheart, don't he?"

"Whether he had a sweetheart or not doesn't mean a damn thing *now,*" said Harry. "We are making a *picture.*"

Jesus, how much longer did he have to put up with this?

". . . But it's supposed to be a true-life story, ain't it?" asked Al.

"True life, true life! What the hell—do I have to sit here and argue out every little stinking point with you two?" Harry exclaimed. "The network says they want him to have a sweetheart, what the hell difference does it make if we put in a girl? A nice young kid, sweet-faced, jeans, open shirt, you know what I mean, Perce? The Hoosier sweetheart bit—like Jeanne Crain, maybe, in those Fox pictures? Farm type, drives a tractor, small-town girl, but really stacked. Call her . . . Laura," he commanded.

Perce nodded, made a note.

Al snickered. "Laura," he repeated.

"What's wrong with that?" Harry asked softly.

"Well, now, if there was any kind of a girl hanging around our town like that," said Al, "she wouldn't've lasted long, I'll tell you."

Harry blew his nose. "Al," he said, "I want to get this script in shape for the network. I want it done fast. You two are in here on a pass. I don't want to hear anything more out of you, understand?"

"Wait a minute, Harry," said Perce. "You can't blame the boys for trying to be helpful, after all, this *is* their story—"

Now *he* was going to get into the act?

"*You* wait a minute," commanded Harry. "Screw this *cinéma verité* jazz—we are doing a shoot-'em-up B, get me? *Strictly!* Twenty years ago we'd've been lucky to sell this junk to Republic, okay, so nowadays we got all these smart-ass kids at the networks who don't know their ass from their elbow who figure this is how you get an audience in prime time and sell 'em a product, they're the ones putting up the money, so goddamnit, we're not out to make our letter with Pauline Kael, we give 'em their shoot-'em-up B, no more arguments about whether LeRoy ever had a girl, he has a girl now, no more arguments about anything but *this script!*"

His heart pounding, Harry tilted back his chair and waited until the beat subsided . . . if he was going to have a heart attack, he'd be damned if it was going to be over this picture—not when he had bigger problems facing him, the insurance-company payment, the screenings in New York, then the promotion campaign on *Cimarron,* and running the gauntlet of those damn New York critics. Enough already!

Then he returned to the notes.

"Okay," he said. "Next note. We seem to have a problem on the locale of the heist. The network feels the Middle West has had it, and they want to know why we couldn't move that sequence to Arizona? What do you think, Perce?"

Perce glanced at Al, as if waiting for him to reply.

"I didn't ask him, I asked *you,*" said Harry. "He'll give me twenty reasons why it shouldn't be in Arizona but that's not the point—"

Al had risen from his seat on the couch, and when he spoke, his voice was very soft. "You know something, Mr. Elbert?" he said. "Me and LeRoy don't have to sit here and listen to this crap. Perce here has done a good script, he's listened to us, and he got it all down right, and we like the way he done it—"

"—That's nice," said Harry. "You don't want to stick around and listen? Fine." He pulled open a desk drawer and pulled out a folder, opened it, consulted the pages. "According to the deal, you got another two days on the payroll, but don't bother waiting, fellas—I'll have the accounting department make out your last check right now—"

"That's fine with us," said Al placidly. "C'mon, LeRoy."

As the taller man rose, so did Perce.

"*Wait* a minute—" he protested.

"What for?" asked Al.

LeRoy was quietly crossing to the office door; he opened it and went out.

"I want to talk to you," said Perce, urgently, his hand on Al's arm.

"Siddown, Perce!" Harry said. "Talk to him on your time!"

"See you around, Mr. Elbert," Al said, impassive. "See you later, pardner," he murmured to Perce. He winked. "It's time."

He disengaged his arm and went out, closing the door.

Perce turned back to Harry. ". . . Let me have a minute with them, Harry," he said. "I need to talk to them—"

"Pair of middle-aged has-been ex-cons?" demanded Harry scornfully. "What do you need them for?"

Perce began to speak, then was silent.

"—You already did the script, it's okay, they're paid off, who needs 'em, let 'em go! We're fighting time, Perce, siddown!" Harry insisted.

Perce went back to his chair.

"Now that we cleared the air around here," said Harry, "we can get this piece of crap whipped into shape."

Then he turned to Miss Lister. "Oh, say," he told her, "I hope my language doesn't bother you, honey."

Miss Lister smiled. "I'm a big girl, Mr. Elbert," she said.

. . . You can say that again, thought Harry, his eyes flickering past her crossed legs.

If he was going to be in New York for more than a few days, and he didn't have anybody handling his calls there, maybe it might not be a bad idea to fly her in?

Mm. It was the first thought he'd had all day that made him feel halfway decent.

"Okay, Perce, where were we?" he asked.

". . . I don't remember," said Perce.

"Whether or not the heist should be in Arizona," prompted Miss Lister.

"Oh, yeah. Good. Perce, what do you think about Arizona?"

Perce did not answer.

"Hey, Perce, wake up!" said Harry. *"You're* still on salary!"

By the time Perce got back to his office, it was past five—there'd been several calls interrupting the conference, important ones from somebody named Carew which Harry had taken privately. It must have been good news; when he emerged from the last one, he was smiling for the first time all day. "Get to work, baby," he'd instructed Perce. "I'll see you when I get back from New York, and I want it all done by then."

The office was empty. No sign of his two partners.

He called Harry's office to check. Had they left?

. . . Audrey came on to report that they had. They'd picked up their final check from accounting half an hour ago, said good-by, and turned in their office keys. Why, did he need them for anything?

. . . If you only knew how I need them, thought Perce. ''No, I'll find them at home, thanks,'' he said.

''That was quite a conference,'' she remarked. ''Noisy.''

''Well, old Mr. Goldwyn used to say, 'From quiet conferences come quiet pictures,' '' said Perce.

''. . . Are you working late tonight?'' she asked.

''If I am, you'll be the first to know,'' he said.

. . . Any other night, he'd be interested. Not tonight.

He called the number of their apartment, but it did not answer.

. . . Okay, so they'd left the studio half an hour ago, they were caught in rush-hour traffic, he'd try again later.

What was he worried about? Al had winked, hadn't he? The sonofabitch had obviously been out to pick a fight with Harry . . . *why?*

He put his notes together and pulled open the top drawer of his desk. There, on a small piece of paper, he found a note.

''Don't worry about our feelings, pardner,'' it read in simple, childlike printing. *''We'll be in touch.''*

He tried the apartment number again. No answer.

By the time he got home to his own place, it was after seven. This time, when he dialed their number, there was a strange click, a recorded voice came on the line. ''The number you have reached is temporarily disconnected,'' it said. ''Please check your directory to make sure you have the right number, and redial.''

Temporarily disconnected?

What was up?

. . . Oh, hell, what was he worried about? If he and LeRoy were up to something, they'd certainly let him in on it—

—Unless—

Come on, Perce, stop it, you're getting as paranoid as Harry Elbert.

He pulled the Caddy up and parked on the quiet side street

across from the dingy apartment complex where they lived. There didn't seem to be any light in their window.

But maybe they'd gone out?

He took the steps two at a time, rang their bell.

No answer.

He went back down the stairs to the manager's office on the first floor. He rang the bell. Inside, there was a furious barking. The door was opened slightly, it was on a chain. Through the opening peered the manager, a small Chicano lady with gray hair, who was holding back a large Doberman who strained against its leash and barked.

". . . The people in Two-A?" he asked above the barking. "Chester?"

"Who, please?"

"Chester!" he said.

"Ah, si," she said. "Señor and Señor *Chester*. Two-A. They are not here."

"Did they go out?" he asked.

She shook her head. *"No,"* she said. "They go. Leave. They give me their keys, is end of the month tomorrow—they no stay."

". . . But don't they have a lease?" he asked.

"Oh, no lease, señor," she said. "Here is month to month. You need place? Is nice place, rent very good—you give first month and last month, you can move in Monday, first I get the place cleaned for you—"

"No thanks," he said angrily.

She shrugged, and closed her door.

The damned dog finally stopped his barking.

Perce went back across the street to his car.

. . . They'd gone, and so had a million dollars in fives, tens, and twenties. Stuffed away in the trunk of their Vega, they'd taken off, into the night, just like pair of ex-cons in a cheap Republic shoot-'em-up, damn Harry Elbert, he was right about them!

Now what, Perce?

. . . Want to go to the police, tell them to put out an APB for two missing persons? Two ex-cons in a used '72 Vega, one tall, one medium-sized, unarmed but with a million in cash in the trunk—complainant is one-third owner of the said million—which is the proceeds from a recent heist here in L.A.?

He got into his Caddy and started the engine.

Bastards—to pull this on him!

. . . But damnit, *Al had winked*.

It had to have been his signal.

And what about the note? "*. . . We'll be in touch.*"

Okay, Perce, you got a wink and a note.

For your scrapbook of memories.

They'd been playing monkey-in-the-middle, and *you* were the monkey, pardner:

. . . Or was it like those three-card monte games they set up on the sidewalks to catch suckers, the dealer flips the three cards back and forth, shows you the ace, throws it down, flip, flip, flip, you bet on which one you think it is, okay, turn it up—what's wrong, you didn't get the ace, you got the two of spades?

Too bad. You lose.

. . . Want to try again? *sucker?*

* * *

★ Part Three ★

chapter 27

—Sigmund, is that you? Three o'clock in the morning, and you are still awake?
—I cannot sleep, liebchen. I know I am right—but all Vienna is laughing at me!
—Never mind them, Sigmund.
—There *can* be a science that deals with the mind! Fools—*why* won't they understand?
—Sigmund, *I* know you are right, but for the sake of your body's health, please . . . I beg you—come to bed.

(ENTERTAINMENT SECTION: *L.A. Times*. Jan. 16, 1977)

THE ANATOMY OF A "HEIST"

The members of the creative crew responsible for the forthcoming film *Heist* are lounging around their small production offices.

A lean, well-preserved survivor of long years at his trade, writer Perce Barnes is the first to testify to the truth of that old show-business adage, namely, if you hang in there long enough, something has to happen. Barnes had not earned a screen credit for almost half a decade, but now his name is on the script of what promises to be one of the most interesting films being completed in town.

". . . So figure it?" he shrugs over a diet soda. "It never rains but it pours, or maybe it's just that my number came up on the wheel. I ran into the two Chester brothers, they'd come out of prison with their story all written down, I had a feeling it would work today, that even though there's all this outcry against violence, what they had gone through had a lot to say about the quality of American small-town life, how young midwestern kids drift into crime, and all that. I started writing a *cinéma vérité*-type thing about the Chesters, and its original title was *Three Down, Two Left Standing,* and while I'm at it, I have to tip my hat in the direction of Harry Elbert, an old pal, our executive producer. He was the first person who saw its possibilities, from the beginning, when I couldn't get arrested anywhere else."

''Harry gave me enough help to get it going, he hired me and the two Chesters, and we turned out a first draft. By that time it was headed for one of the major TV networks as a two-hour film. But when I finished the final draft, and it went over to them, something happened; they dragged their feet on giving us a go-ahead.''

Which network?

None of the people involved in *Heist* is willing to reveal its name, but the guessing around town centers around NBC.

''Okay, so it sits there, gathering dust on somebody's desk, and then Billy Elbert, our producer, whom Harry had assigned to the project as producer—he'd been in a bad automobile accident but, thank heaven, he finally came out in one piece, got impatient and decided it was time to move the project off the dime. Don't ask me how he did it,'' grins Barnes, ''but he sure did. Want to tell us your secret, Billy?''

This is the cue for Billy Elbert, the second member of the combine, to pick up the story. Still walking with a cane, Elbert is modest about his machinations. ''I went to a party one night, lots of my old buddies, more my generation than Perce's,'' he allows. ''Ran into Doug Pemberton, he's a classmate of mine from Beverly Hills High, would you believe? Of course, he's come a long way since the days when we were both on the baseball team.''

Which brings a guffaw from his partners. Pemberton, at twenty-eight, is the latest wunderkind of the business, as any film exhibitor will be quick to agree. He first became known around town as a creative force with a fine commercial hand by turning out, on a minuscule budget, *Monster-Lover,* a ''cheapie'' with a cast of unknowns, which became the surprise grosser of 1974, and then went on to direct last year's hit, *Sodbuster,* which starred Gene Hackman and Liv Ullmann.

''I got to talking to Doug about Perce's script that night,'' recalls young Elbert. ''Maybe I talked too much. But I have to tell you, I was so darned frustrated that nothing was happening at the network. It was those guys there, see, they were all running scared because of this violence thing, and to tell you the truth, the story of Al and LeRoy Chester isn't that, it's social comment, I mean, it's an honest piece of Americana! Well, I must've hyped Doug pretty good, next day he got the script, he read it, and called me back after lunch and wanted to make a meeting up at his lawyer's. See, he'd been on a project that had come apart that very morning, and he decided to go with this one instead. Would you believe it?'' chuckles Billy Elbert. ''It's too much like a plot twist out of an old movie!''

"Except that no producer would have bought it, even in 1937," interjects Barnes, who ought to know. He was there.

What was Pemberton's reaction to Barnes's script?

"I liked everything about it but his title," concedes Pemberton, bearded and soft-spoken, a young man who's joined the ranks of top-grossing filmmakers in far less time than most. "The writing was sharp and had a fine feeling to it. I sparked to it right away, it reminded me of one of the best of those nineteen forties crime pictures, but it gave me a chance to tackle the material in my own way."

Once *Heist* had been retrieved from the network, a production was set up in short order. "We were lucky as hell," says Billy Elbert. "We put together a cast that is exactly the right mix, Doug brought in his own crew, and a month later, we started principal photography on location, in Ohio."

On the cast list of *Heist* are such well-known actors as Karl Malden, who essays the role of Al Chester, Anthony Quinn, as his brother LeRoy, Arthur Kennedy, as a midwestern upholder of law and order, and Bert Freed, who portrays a small-town banker. "They're all terrific," remarks Pemberton. "Solid pros, who know their business, who don't waste time, who give you back extra dividends in every shot. We were also very lucky to get a girl named Abby Hunter in to play a young farm girl, she's a real find, along with Frank Daugherty, he's done a lot of TV, and another discovery named Wally Condon, keep an eye on him. The marvelous thing was to watch the give and take between the older hands and these young kids. If it shows up in the final cut as well as it does in the rushes, well, all I can say is, I think we've got a shot at something special."

In a larger office down the hall sits Elbert Senior. Basking in the warm glow of good box-office returns on his own latest film, the mammoth *Cimarron,* which stars Vin DeLuca, he puffs on a good cigar and is properly modest about his own contribution to the project. "I'm just an old-time picture maker, what do I know?" he says. "I don't care where a good story comes from, if I read it and something inside my gut responds to it, then all that matters to me is to get it up on the screen. If this one works, it'll make me feel good, hell, at my age, that's the name of the game, right?"

If *Heist,* when edited and scored, proves to be the success with audiences that its creators expect it to be, then television's loss will be film exhibitors' definite gain.

And finally, what of Al and LeRoy Chester, the two reformed criminals who paid their debt to society and who will now be immortalized on film?

How do they feel about the end result of a small saga that began when they brought their story to writer Perce Barnes, over a year ago?

"They haven't seen it yet," remarks Perce Barnes. ". . . But when they do, it should be damned interesting to know how they react to *Heist*—at least, it will be to me, I can promise you that."

Strangely enough, the writer from the *Times* hadn't asked the $333,333 question.

Where *were* the Chesters?

For that one, he had no answer.

Perce hadn't thought about them much, these past few months, who had time to brood about where they and his share of the loot had gotten to? What with script revisions for Billy and Pemberton, and sitting in on the casting, doing the changes each actor had demanded (every damn one of them had ideas, and you had to listen to them), then he'd made a couple of trips to the location, when problems had arisen and Pemberton had insisted that he come out, ("I'm not like these auteur shits," said Pemberton, "man, I respect the *words*.")

. . . So Perce hadn't had much spare time, not for tennis, nor even for Vera.

". . . You know, I liked it better when you were flat on your ass," she confessed ruefully one night when he'd finally arrived for dinner at nine, after a dubbing session Pemberton insisted he sit in on.

Sometimes so did he. These days he always seemed tired.

". . . Whatever happened to our trip to Paris?" Vera asked. "Paris? I don't know about Paris," he sighed.

"Ever since you got hot, you don't even know about anything involving you and me," she said.

Hot?

"At my age, you don't get hot," he said. "You maybe warm up a little, but this is still a young man's business."

"Nonsense," said Vera, setting his dinner in front of him. "The day after *Heist* previews, you're going to be getting offers from all over. That's why I want us to go away *now*."

. . . She was possibly right.

Just this afternoon, Harry Elbert had called into his office to discuss something confidential, behind a closed door. ". . . Something right up your alley," Harry had promised. "If I can get it. Ever hear of the Purple Gang?"

. . . Those mobsters from the thirties who had owned Detroit? Sure, Perce had heard of them. Way back in earlier days, he'd even known some of them, during the war, when they'd all headed out here and started to move into Vegas.

He nodded.

"Now keep this strictly between you and me," Harry instructed, "but I got a line on a story, something absolutely authentic, from one of the boys who's still around. It's Detroit in the twenties, see, and my radar tells me we may be on the edge of a new cycle." He pointed his long cigar at Perce, holding it like a pistol. "Bang-bangs again. Get it?"

"Interesting," said Perce.

"Don't get too enthusiastic," said Harry dryly. "It's absolutely right for you, pal. You *and* me."

"Okay, we'll talk about it sometime," said Perce.

Harry's eyes narrowed. "What'sa matter, you already got a better offer?"

"Ah, come on, Harry," he protested. "I'm *tired* . . ."

. . . He didn't have a better offer, but he had already had calls from three agents, offering to represent him, one of them, by God, had been Miss Judith Hastings, that English bitch who'd tried to screw him out of the story way back in the beginning, now without the slightest qualms, she was on the phone explaining how fascinated she'd been with the material from the start, how she expected *Heist* might be a commercial success, and could they have a chat someday soon?

So obviously there would be offers, and Harry was hustling to nail him down before somebody else did. Okay, fair enough.

"Tired my ass!" Harry had said. "After all I did for you, now you're playing hard to get. Forget it—I'll get somebody else—I don't need scripts out of tired writers!"

Bluff.

Harry would be calling him soon, he knew him well enough to know the symptoms.

". . . All right," he told Vera, finishing his dinner. "Maybe I am the new middle-aged genius. But I'll tell you what I need right now. A nice clean beach, where I can lie down and bake, play a little tennis . . . and no telephones."

"Not Malibu," said Vera. "Rio.'

Rio?

He could handle the expense, after all these weeks on salary . . . but he wasn't supposed to spend, was he? That's what Al had warned him, all those months ago. *low profile*.

Well, damnit, if anybody had won the low-profile award, it was Al and LeRoy.

. . . So if he went to Rio, and somebody got suspicious, it wouldn't be loot he'd be spending, it was his *own* hard-earned cash!

"Okay, I'll think about Rio," he told Vera.

"You do that," she said, and poured him coffee. "Now let's go to bed. That's your dessert."

". . . The best offer I've had all week," he said, and pulled her down on his lap.

He received another one two days later, one that was much tougher to handle.

Sitting in the steam room at the club, where he'd finally managed to steal a morning for tennis, a familiar voice brayed in his ear, ". . . Hey, baby, just the man I'm looking for—how're you fixed for spendable dollars?"

Ziggy Harling, his bulk draped in a towel, lowered himself down onto the seat beside him.

"I'm solvent," he said.

"C'mon, you're flush," said Ziggy. "You got a hot picture and you're loaded, but I'm gonna help you provide for your old age!"

He sat and sweated and explained. Ziggy and a small exclusive syndicate of investors, all of them reliable, solid citizens, members of the club (most of whom, thought Perce, wouldn't have given him the right time of day until lately), had acquired a prime tract of land on a beach in Costa Rica. A gorgeous country, no taxes, little government interference, local businessmen as their partners, a terrific setup. Bank financing already arranged, the plans were already drawn up for a small, very exclusive resort. Vacation condominiums with beach frontage, a restaurant, and first-class tennis courts. "That's where you come in, bubby," confided Ziggy. "We've got one share left open, it's yours. You're in on the ground floor. You'll be our resident tennis pro, with your own condo, you come and go as you please, we're bringing you in on the ground floor—"

"Sounds terrific," admitted Perce. "But I'm not planning to retire. Not yet."

"You crazy?" asked Ziggy. "You show up when you want to, the rest of the time your condo is rented out. We got it hooked up so your initial investment makes you a partner, buys the condo, you live free and you share in the profits—which, believe me, is a tax shelter. You know how much that's worth in your bracket?" he demanded, and proceeded to explain in great detail about 22-percent return on invested capital, and how the profits would be absorbed by expenses in such a way that even the IRS couldn't lay a glove on them.

"And how much does it cost to chip in to this swindle?" Perce asked.

"Forty lousy grand," said Ziggy. "And you get tax credits in the first year, bubby. It's for spit—the price of that Rolls you're planning to buy when your picture goes into profit, *fershtay?*"

Jovially, Ziggy continued to outline all the advantages that had been dreamed up by his crew, with their lawyers and high-priced accountants.

. . . Forty thousand dollars. Spit.

Sure. How was he supposed to explain to Ziggy that even if he wanted to invest, his capital was not, to put it delicately, available?

"I'll get the prospectus over to you this week," promised Ziggy. "Go over it with your tax man, then sign the papers—you won't need to make the down payment for a couple weeks . . .''

''How did I get so lucky?'' he asked. ''I mean—what do you want me for?''

''Bubby,'' said Ziggy. You're one of *us*. Why would we go to a stranger?''

A week later, he had no answer.

He hadn't signed the papers Ziggy had sent over. Not that the deal wasn't a good one; he'd turned it all over to Sy, his lawyer, who'd read the prospectus and pronounced it a very cute setup. ''Not only that,'' Sy commented, ''but you'll get to be buddy-buddy with Bob Vesco, and maybe get another true crime picture out of it!''

Hilarious.

. . . So where was he supposed to come across forty thousand?

Not from a bank, banks needed more collateral than this deal offered. He sure as hell wasn't going to go to one of the Vegas shylocks.

And meanwhile, Vera was pressing him for a specific date, so that they could book a trip to Rio.

What do you do now, Perce? *Mr. Successful!*

That night he came home from the studio, picked up his mail.

The usual collection of junk, sales flyers, appeals, magazine-subscription offers, bills. He started to pitch most of it into the wastebasket.

An odd post card.

One he'd almost missed, it was lying on the floor by the wastebasket.

A picture post card, a photograph of a small, nondescript motel building.

''THE FISHERMANS REST—BEACH VIEW—28 UNITS—HEALTH CLUB—HOUSEKEEPING''—''The Ideal Place To Rest Or Catch That Big One.'' Naples, Michigan. Your Hosts, Al and LeRoy Chester.''

The note on the back, in printed letters, read ''Hi, there, pardner. Come see us some time if you're not too busy. Yrs. A. and L.''

Naples, Michigan?

. . . So that was where his bank was!

Or was this some kind of a gag?

He called Information. Waited anxiously while she checked through to locate Naples, Michigan, and then finally came back with the number, apologizing for the delay, it was a new listing.

So it wasn't a gag.

Instinctively, he began to dial the number—then he checked himself. Was it a good idea to call from his home? Wouldn't a phone booth be better, the old, reliable, anonymous phone booth?

. . . On the other hand, if there were any taps going, wouldn't there be one on the Chester phone, too?

The number rang three times, and then it was picked up. ''Fishermans Rest Mo-tel,'' said Al. ''Can I help you?''

''You sure can, Al,'' he said. ''This is your old friend Perce—''

''Perce who?'' asked Al guardedly.

''I'm calling from a *booth,*'' said Perce.

''How's the big movie writer?'' asked Al.

''Still fooling the people,'' he said. ''How're things in Michigan?''

''Pretty darn fine,'' said Al. ''Say, this is a real pleasure, talkin' to you, Perce. Get our card?''

''Sure did,'' said Perce. ''But I haven't heard from *you* in quite a while . . .''

''That's right,'' said Al. ''Was you worried?''

''Well, I kinda hoped nothing had happened,'' said Perce.

''. . . Nope,'' said Al. ''See, we been right busy gettin' this place into shape. My, my, it was a mess when we took it over . . . real rundown, that's how we got it so cheap, y'know?''

''So now you're a businessman, eh?''

''Yep,'' said Al. ''It's real nice now, Perce, why don't you come pay us a visit? Bring your lady friend, Vera, too—she'd love it.''

''I'll bet she would,'' said Perce. ''How's LeRoy?''

''Oh, fine as wine,'' said Al. ''He's got himself busier'n a flea in a hot bottle, runs around all day. Say, how's our picture coming?''

''Gonna be a real winner,'' Perce said. ''I think you boys are gonna be right pleased,''—and thought, damnit, I'm beginning to do the rube bit like Al—''Listen, Al, I've got a few things I would like to discuss with you—details on the story—you know we changed the title, it's called *Heist* now, and I'd like to talk to you about a few things.''

''Well, we're here,'' said Al. ''We can talk any time.''

''How do you get there from here?'' asked Perce.

''You get to Grand Rapids, then I guess you'd want a car to drive over. About ninety miles or so. Any particular time you want to come?''

''Not sure yet,'' said Perce. ''Why don't I surprise you?''

''Good idea,'' said Al. ''You're always welcome, mind you, Perce, we're a very small place, not too much room, so don't talk us up too much. We're not set up to handle *strangers,* y'see.''

''I get the message, Al,'' said Perce.

''I'll tell LeRoy you called, he'll be right sorry he missed you, but right now he's running some errands,'' said Al. ''You keep in touch, now.''

''You bet I will,'' said Perce.

How long should it take to get to Grand Rapids, rent a car, and drive up to his bank?

The sooner he got to Michigan, the better. At least he could find out if the bank was still open, if his account was still active—

—And whether or not they allow him to make a withdrawal.

The next morning, when he got to the office, he started to call Audrey Lister. She handled all the travel arrangements for Harry's projects, he might as well let her get him booked—

—Then he hung up.

Wrong. He didn't want Harry, or anyone else in the office, knowing where he planned to go.

. . . Vera had a girl who did all sorts of travel stuff, Alice Baker, an efficient kid. Vera wouldn't be in the office yet, let Alice handle it.

Within a few minutes, she called back with all the information. If he left L.A. at 7:50 A.M., United Flight 100 would get him to Chicago at 1:35 P.M.—then he'd wait there for Flight 188, it left Chicago at 3:30, arriving at Grand Rapids, Michigan, at 5:11. Could a car be rented there? Certainly. Should she go ahead and book flights for him? When was he planning to leave? Alice could have it charged to his credit card.—

Oh, no. Charges could be traced. This would be a cash deal.

He thanked her for the information and said he'd handle the tickets himself—

—Would he like to speak to Mrs. George, who'd just arrived in the office? No, he didn't, but how could he now avoid it?

Better to improvise a cover story now.

He told Vera he'd probably have to go out of town for a day or so, this weekend, he had an uncle who was sick in Michigan; he'd probably be back Sunday at the latest.

". . . Is she anyone I know?" asked Vera.

"Ah, come on, honey," he said. "I'm too old and tired for that."

"Old, yes—tired, I'm not so sure," she said. "Call me when you get back—by the way, where will you be if anybody needs you?"

"Nobody will need me," he said. "I'll call you."

"Sure you will," she said, ". . . if you get into trouble."

That afternoon, on the way home, he stopped by the United office and picked up the tickets, plus a confirmed reservation for a rental car out of Grand Rapids.

Friday morning, he'd go.

After lunch on Thurday, he called Audrey Lister, to tell her not to expect him in his office the following day.

"All right," she said. "But what do I tell Mr. E if he suddenly decides he wants you?"

''Make up a story,'' he told her.

''You're the writer,'' she said.

''. . . Tell him to wait until Monday,'' he said.

''Not terribly original, Mr. Barnes,'' she remarked.

''I'm going to visit a sick relative out of town,'' he confided.

''. . . That's even worse,'' she said.

''You've covered for him—you can cover for me,'' he said.

''. . . I only hope he doesn't need you,'' she sighed.

Alice Baker was on her coffee break, leafing through the Friday morning trades, when her phone rang. A male voice on the other end said, ''This is Mr. Duffy, over at Rose Management. We're handling Mr. Barnes' account, Mr. Perce Barnes, I believe you know the gentleman?''

''Yes, I do,'' said Alice, stirring Cremora into her coffee. ''He's a friend of Mrs. George's.''

''Of course,'' said Mr. Duffy. ''I'm trying to locate him, he left his office yesterday and they don't seem to expect him today, now would you have any idea where he might have gone?''

''Me?'' asked Alice. ''No, I wouldn't—wait a minute, he was talking about going out of town the other day—''

''Ah,'' said Mr. Duffy. ''You wouldn't have any idea where he went, would you? I've got some financial questions that need answers, and if I could merely get in touch with him—''

''. . . He was asking about a flight to Grand Rapids,'' said Alice. ''But I don't know if he went.''

''Grand Rapids?'' mused Mr. Duffy. ''That's funny, he never told us he'd be going anywhere near there—''

''It'd have to be there, I guess,'' said Alice, sipping coffee. ''Or maybe near there, because he was asking about car rentals, but that's all I know. Sorry I can't help you.''

''Oh, no,'' said Mr. Duffy. ''You've been an enormous help.''

''I don't know how,'' said Alice, and as she hung up, Vera came into the office.

''Who was that?'' she asked.

''It was a man from Mr. Barnes's business management office, wanted to know how to get in touch with him today.''

". . . Oh, well we're really successful now, aren't we?" commented Vera. "Now we've got a business manager."

"You mean he didn't have one before?" asked Alice.

"No, but he's obviously gotten rich and famous," said Vera. "Do you mind if we get to work on our affairs now?"

* * *

chapter 28

—All right, you men, attention! My name is Major Quinn. In all my years in this man's army, I've never seen a more miserable bunch of riffraff. You're a disgrace . . . but I need you. I'm here to make you scum an offer. There's a job to be done—an ugly job but a vital one. Chances are, most of you who volunteer will never come back. But for those who do, I can promise you this—I will recommend a commutation of your sentences. Mind you, I said *recommend* . . . Now. Which of you scum is ready to join me?

IT was late in the day when he headed north in his rented car through the Michigan farm lands, past the soft rolling fields with their rows of corn stalks that had been harvested, the landscape broken here and there by long stands of trees outlined against the sky. To Perce's eyes, accustomed to the hot and dry smog-enshrouded canyons of southern California, the startling deep green everywhere was a treat.

As were the towns he could see from the main highway. Modest and unspoiled, much as they might have been years back before urban sprawl had taken over.

Naples was a tiny village obviously on the lake, the road signs promised boating and fishing, and there were other billboards extolling various eating places where fresh-caught seafood was the speciality.

"ENTERING NAPLES, A FRIENDLY PLACE" read the sign as he drove in from the main highway. Its streets were lined with simple, white frame houses, often with wide verandas, then small blocks of downtown stores. In the gathering night, the street lights were on, shining through the trees. The whole place looked like a street on the Metro back lot, the one where years back they'd made the Judge Hardy pictures. A Norman Rockwell vision come to life, Republican, safe, solid, unruffled middle America.

Except that when he stopped at a gas station for directions to the Fishermans Rest, there was a cool breeze, one with a sharp edge to it, coming in off the lake. Shivering in his California sports clothes, he knew the night would be even colder. Why hadn't he remembered that it was already fall up here?

". . . Fishermans Rest?" said the kid at the gas station. "They're about closed up for the season, ain't they?"

Great. That's all he needed; to find that the boys had folded up the place and headed south to Florida, maybe.

. . . But when his car bumped down the side road that wound through thick ridges of pine down below near what seemed to be dunes, he saw lights, twinkling in the darkness.

He stopped the car. The high humming of tree toads filled the night. It wasn't a pretentious place, a series of small cabins, set in a wide half circle behind a longish frame building which looked as if it was a restaurant. There seemed to be a few people inside the dining room, a couple of cars parked in the small lot.

He headed toward a door over which was a neon sign that said "OFFICE."

Howard Johnson's it wasn't.

He pushed the door open and went inside. A small, nicely furnished living-room area, soft chairs and a table or two. A radio was playing country-and-western music. From behind the front desk a man looked up, he wore a sweater that did not hide the fact that he'd put on weight. It was Al Chester.

"Why, looky here," he said cordially. "If it ain't old Perce himself. You got a reservation?"

"A friend told me I was always welcome around here," said Perce.

"And he told you right!" said Al, and came forward to shake Perce's hand. ". . . Say, you had any supper? I'll tell the cook to save you some."

". . . I'm on L.A. time but I could use a bourbon," said Perce.

"Well, we don't have us a liquor license," said Al, "but there's no law says I can't offer you a friendly shot in my office."

They sat in the small rear office. The walls were decorated with ancient stuffed fish, and the leather chairs were cracked and well worn. Perce sipped his bourbon and tap water while Al explained that LeRoy wasn't around just now, he was over at the health club, that was the last cabin down at the end. Would Perce like a nice sauna after his long trip?

". . . Maybe after a while," said Perce.

". . . So what brings a big picture maker like you all the way out here to Michigan?" asked Al.

"I guess I could ask you the same question," said Perce. "For a while there, I figured you two had done a disappearing act on me."

". . . And you were sure we'd screwed you, right?" grinned Al.

Perce nodded.

"Don't blame you," said Al. "We had to do it that way so as to get out of town quiet-like, without a fuss. Clean and quick, he told us get lost, and we did. And we headed for here."

"Just like that?" asked Perce.

"Hell, no," said Al. "We had this place lined up for a long time, see? It belonged to one of our relatives, our old uncle Ty Grimes. He was failing, and we heard from his wife they wanted to go south and wanted to sell. So we sort of kept it in the family, and bought it."

"Must've cost you a lot."

"Uh uh," said Al. "Ty had a big mortgage. We took that over, and we used the cash we got working for old Harry for the down payment."

Sounded plausible enough, and yet . . .

". . . Since when did you and LeRoy decide you wanted to go into the motel business?" he asked.

"Didn't I ever tell you?" asked Al amiably. "Why, pardner, that's the whole name of the game."

"Meaning what?" he said, confused.

"You better have your dinner before the cook goes home," said Al, which temporarily closed the discussion.

The walls of the small dining room were also decorated with stuffed fish. There did not seem to be too many other guests, just a couple or so seated at the plain wooden tables. A cheerful waitress, obviously a town girl picking up extra money, brought in Perce's dinner, and it proved surprisingly good. Some sort of a fresh vegetable soup, then a heaping platter of fried chicken, fresh string beans and a side order of cole slaw. The dessert was a deep-dish blueberry pie, topped with vanilla ice cream.

Al returned as Perce finished his pie. "How do we stack up against Hamburger Hamlet?" he asked.

"No wonder you're putting on weight," said Perce.

"Shoot, LeRoy keeps trying to get me to exercise," said Al, "but I keep busy enough hopping around here running our place. You're in Cabin Eight—the best one we got. I put your bag in there."

". . . When can we talk?" asked Perce.

Al patted him gently on the shoulder.

"Soon enough," he said. "When it's quiet."

"Look who's here, LeRoy," said Al, as the big man came into the office.

LeRoy wore a dark blue sweat suit; his face was tanned. Across it came the faintest ghost of a smile as he grabbed Perce's hand and enfolded it into his own. "Say, how about that," he said. "Long time no see."

"You're looking good, LeRoy," said Perce, extricating his hand before it went numb. He flexed his fingers to induce circulation.

"It's the air," said LeRoy, and dropped down into one of the old leather chairs. "Up here you can breathe."

"Cities stink," said Perce.

"People smell," corrected LeRoy. "But not around here."

"Know what LeRoy is into?" asked Al. "Boy Scouts. The kids love him."

. . . What does he give Merit Badges for? thought Perce. Driving getaway cars?

"Ah, I like the kids," said LeRoy. "Al's in Rotary. The Elks wanted him too. He's popular."

There must be something miraculous in the air around here, thought Perce. It's turned these two into solid citizens—and it's also gotten LeRoy to talk.

". . . So what brings you up here?" Al asked.

Okay, thought Perce. Here we go.

He told them about the Ziggy Harling proposition, outlined the Costa Rican venture in detail.

"Sounds great," said Al. He grinned. "Means you'll have the motel business covered north *and* south."

"How's that?" asked Perce.

"Why, you're partners *here,"* said LeRoy.

He was?

"Since when?" he asked.

"From the start," said Al. "I thought you understood that. One third of this is yours."

"Sure thing," said LeRoy.

"Why hell," said Al, "you was the one made it possible."

Disconcerted, Perce murmured his thanks. This was something he'd never figured on . . . that all the while they'd figured him in as their continuing partner—

"Don't thank us," said Al. "Everything's going along fine. Next year we're probably goin' to show a profit, then you'll see some money."

". . . I need some money now," said Perce. Might as well get down to basics, partner or not. "In order to go into this Costa Rican deal, I have to come up with a hunk of cash *now*. The fifty."

"Figures," said Al, slowly. "But if it's as good a deal as you say it is, you shouldn't have too much trouble raisin' it."

". . . Well," said Perce, "I figured I might find some cash *here."*

LeRoy had produced string and was quietly constructing cats cradles between his two hands. "Here?" he asked, not looking up. "We don't have any cash here, friend."

Perce turned to Al.

. . . Who nodded his head in agreement. "All our cash is buried in this place," he said.

The room was silent, but outside the window, there was still that steady thrumming of the tree toads, on and on, like an orchestra tuning up but never playing.

"All of it?" asked Perce.

"Every last dime," said Al. "Like we told you, we used all we had for the down payment, and now we're working on the income we take in at the register each day."

"Business is a little slow now," remarked LeRoy.

"But she ought to pick up in the spring," said Al.

"I sure hope so," said LeRoy.

"Trust us," said Al. "You'll see."

Partners or not, this vaudeville routine had to stop.

". . . Come on, boys," Perce said softly. "Never shit a shitter. Where the hell is the rest of it?"

". . . Oh, you mean that," said Al. "Okay, Perce," he said. He glanced at his watch. Went to the office window and peered out at the quiet parking lot. Then he reached up to a wall switch, snapped it. Outside, the MOTEL sign went off. "Looks quiet enough," he said, opening his desk drawer and removing a flashlight. "Want to take a little walk before we sack out?"

"You take him," said LeRoy, yawning. "I'm goin' to bed."

"Cold out there," said Al cordially. "You'll need a sweater."

"I don't have a sweater," said Perce.

"I'll lend you one," said Al. "Don't want you catching cold."

Barely visible by the faint gleam of Al's flash, the path wound through a grove of trees away from the rear of the motel and then up a small rise. Tripping occasionally on unseen roots and pebbles, he followed the beam. "Lake's over there," said Al. "You can see it tomorrow."

They went a few yards farther, and then Al stopped. Bent down and tugged at what seemed to be a handle. In the darkness, he could make out a large metal lid.

Hinges squeaked as the lid came up.

Al reached down to find a switch, snapped it on. From below, there appeared the faint glow of light.

Looking down, Perce's eyes adjusted to the sight of an iron

staircase which went down into some sort of a room below the ground. Snapping off his flash, Al went down the stairs. "Careful going down," he instructed.

Perce lowered himself down carefully. The iron was damp to his hands, and there were patches of rust here and there.

An overpowering odor of mildew, musty and foul, attacked his nostrils. Now they were in a small room, lit by several dim bulbs in tin fixtures. Moisture dotted the concrete walls. Nearby were a couple of wooden chairs and a small table. In the far corner was what appeared to be a generator, its exhaust running upward in a pipe that went through the ceiling. Against the opposite wall was a small electric stove, and next to it, shelves on which were stacked four small steel cases. He could make out the lettering, faded stencils which read, "EMERGENCY RATIONS CD US GOV'T."

When Perce spoke, his voice echoed eerily against the walls. "What the hell is this, solitary confinement?"

"Looks like it," said Al. "I ought to know. Nah, it's an old civilian defense bunker. My uncle put her in when there was all that stuff about nuclear attack. Cost him a bundle, but I guess it was worth it. Helped him sleep nights—not worrying if the Commies was goin' to bomb Michigan."

He had pulled down one of the steel cases, brought it over to the table and unlatched it. "Here you go," he said, opening the case.

Inside, in shiny plastic bags, Perce could make out neatly piled packages of cash.

"Say hello to your retirement fund," said Al. "You're welcome to count up. Most of it's here."

Perce took out a plastic bag, hefted it; twenties, all safe in their covers. Cash money, how much did he have in his hand? Five thousand, ten? All that loot, Harry Elbert's pay-off, sitting here, thousands of miles away from Costa Rica, underground in this damp hole, not doing anybody any good, unspent, my God, almost a million in cash—

". . . Most of it?" he asked Al.

Al winked. He took back the plastic bag, opened it, and removed four twenty-dollar bills. Then he closed it, took it back to the case, fumbled in another bag and produced five tens. Then he counted out ten fives, and put the money in his pocket. "One hundred eighty dollars," he said. "Tonight's withdrawal."

The lid went down on the case, he snapped the latch, and lugged the case back to the shelf.

The dank air was beginning to give Perce a sinus headache.

"What's with the one hundred eighty dollars?" he asked.

"Goes into the cash register tonight," said Al. "That's how we're going to declare a nice little dividend next year."

Perce sneezed.

"Come on, let's get out of here," said Al. "It ain't healthy. I'll explain the whole setup later."

He waited for Perce to climb back up the steps.

As he did so, Perce turned to glance at the shelves with their cases, all sitting neatly in this improvised vault.

"Pretty neat, eh?" asked Al proudly.

". . . Beautiful," said Perce.

Back in the office, Perce took another drink of bourbon to warm himself. Al went to the front desk, and picked up the guest register. As Perce watched, he began to make a series of notations. "Cabin Six," he said. "Mr. and Mrs., let's see, Harry Williams, they're from Canton, Ohio, okay? Twenty-two dollars a night." He made an entry. ". . . Then there's Cabin Four, who's in there? Mr. and Mrs. Fred . . . Buckley. From Indianapolis, Indiana. The rate's twenty-four dollars there . . ."

When he was done, there were six entries in the register, all in different signatures, and the rentals added up to $192. Reaching into his own pocket, he pulled out the bills from the bunker, added two singles from his own wallet, then went over to the cash register and rang up $192. "Not a bad night," he commented, and replaced the guest book onto the desk.

. . . What kind of a game was this?

"Well, now," explained Al, "the cash goes to the bank in the morning, into our corporate account, see?"

"You do this every night?" asked Perce.

Al nodded. " 'Course, some nights we ain't so busy. Weekends are better. Figure an average of about eight hundred a week coming in from all these out-of-towners. That adds up to about forty thou a year, plus what we take in from other guests, and the restaurant—that all goes down on our tax return, see? Now, take away our expenses, local taxes, payments on the mortgage, food, light, heat, and such—the accountant figures we ought to show a profit of maybe twenty-five thousand this year. That makes your end eight thousand and change. How does that feel, partner?''

''. . . Eight thousand?'' repeated Perce.

''All nice and clean. What they call washed,'' said Al proudly. ''Each year, from now on, you're going to be getting that check—''

. . . Down in that bunker was nearly a million in cash, eight hundred a week being taken out for Al's scheme, that meant forty thousand a year to be washed—at this rate, Christ, it would take almost a quarter of a century to finish the deal!

''You could be doing this for twenty-five years!'' he protested. ''Who can live that—''

''*—Shh!*'' said Al. ''Simmer down. The statute of limitations in California runs out in five years. After that, we figure it ought to be safe to declare a couple of . . . *extra* dividends, see?''

He beamed.

Wily bastard—he'd really done his homework. All the way back from those days when he was in the cell block, sitting and figuring the whole plan out.

. . . And now he was obviously waiting for Perce's approval.

''Beautiful,'' he said. ''Al, you're a genius.''

Al shrugged modestly. ''Wouldn't have worked without you, Perce. We needed you, all the way, and you never chickened out on us—not once.''

''You thought I would?'' he demanded.

''Not me,'' said Al. ''And now, we're coming out of this smelling like roses, right?'' He yawned and stretched.

Perce got up and found the bourbon bottle, poured himself another drink, his mind turning this proposition upside down and shaking it, searching for flaws.

And found one.

''What happens if one of us conks out?'' he demanded.

Al grinned.

"It ain't like an insurance policy, is it? Let's say, it bumps up the share for the other two. Fair?" he asked.

"Okay, sure," said Perce. "But . . . supposing—and I'm just spitballing now, mind you—you and LeRoy go out next week, and some crazy kid who's zonked out comes out of a side road and wipes the both of you out—"

"You sure got an active imagination, Perce," conceded Al. "Guess that's what makes you such a damn good writer."

"Yeah, but supposing—" insisted Perce.

"Then you come and collect what's left in that vault, that's what," said Al. "What the hell, we ain't about to write wills and direct our lawyers to distribute our hidden stash, now, are we?"

Perce nodded.

But he was far from satisfied.

. . . How was he to explain to Al that he did not want to wait five years for a decent hunk of that cash?

Which he'd earned, damn it.

Which, by rights, was *his!*

He finished his drink.

"Al, baby," he began, ". . . suppose I knew how to get real money washed in Mexico—so it would end up in Costa Rica—nobody would ever know where it came from. Out of the country, strictly tax-shelter money. Suppose I asked you to advance me a big hunk of that stash out there. What would you say?"

Al's face hardened. He shook his head.

"I'd say no, and I'd tell you not to ask me again," he said.

"Fifty lousy thousand," insisted Perce. "I absolutely guarantee—it will never surface!"

"Not fifty, not twenty—not a goddamn dollar!" said Al, and there was an ugly note in his voice now. "That's not part of the setup and you know it. You knew it from the go. We got screwed once that way, and we ended up staring at the wall in the slammer for a long, long time. So don't ask me any more, Perce. It could make me lose my temper."

"It could make me lose mine too!" said Perce.

Al stared at him.

"And what would that prove?" he asked finally. "It wouldn't

get me or LeRoy to change our minds, that's for damn sure. No. That money stays right where it is.''

Suddenly, he grinned, reached out and patted Perce's shoulder. ''What the hell's bugging you, Perce? You can make big dough writing your movies, can't you? You need some extra—go borrow it, nice and legal, from a bank.''

Sleepless, Perce lay in his bed in Cabin 8, the blankets pulled over him to keep out the unexpectedly cold Michigan night air.

Nearly a million in cash, stored beneath that damn dune, only a few yards away, in a mini–Fort Knox.

This was certainly the high-rent area of Naples, Michigan.

. . . *His* cash.

Okay. So Al had worked out a marvelous story line, a plot that was perfect for himself and brother LeRoy, they were blissfully happy here in their backwater joint, they could enjoy their old age, each year they'd be sending him a check for eight grand—

Eight lousy grand.

Hell, that hardly covered his rent.

You can make big dough writing your movies, can't you?

Oh, sure. Right now Perce Barnes was hot. His red light was glowing, Harry Elbert loved him madly—

—But supposing *Heist* bombed?

A couple of bad reviews in New York, low grosses in the first-runs, they'd pull the picture, sell it off to TV fast, get rid of it, bury it—that's the way the business operated these days—

. . . And then what happens to Perce Barnes?

He cools off. Fast.

Maybe he gets a couple of TV assignments. He works his ass off for some young hot-shot producer. Maybe he doesn't cut the mustard for him—the word goes out again. Barnes is slow, he's old-fashioned, he's nowhere, he's a has-been.

. . . At the club, Ziggy Harling and all the rest of them will get the message. Fast.

And if they don't, the sight of me giving tennis lessons again will sure do it. Because that's where I'll be. Back on the court, trying to scrape together a few bucks each hour.

With all this money locked away in Michigan?

No.

He wasn't going to settle for that. Nor was he going to settle for eight thousand a year. Not when there was all of his cash here, ready for the taking.

There wasn't any risk, damnit—Al was paranoid! He had to be—he'd been in that slammer too long to be anything else!

By next week the fifty Gs would be gone, down to Mexico, nicely washed for a fee, then it would be back, to Costa Rica—and who the hell would ever know it had come out of a bomb shelter in Michigan?

. . . And if he helped himself, now, it would be months before Al or LeRoy would ever notice that any of the cash was missing. What the hell, did they do a weekly audit down in that hole? Of course not!

. . . Okay, then, if he was to take it, how?

This wasn't like writing a script, where you could sit in your office and figure out all the possibilities, lay it out carefully to make certain that your plotting worked.

No. He was here, he wanted some of that money now . . . and tomorrow morning, he'd have to improvise.

Finally, he slept.

It was past nine when he came into the dining room. The cheerful young waitress poured him coffee and suggested fresh fish, caught this morning? Mr. Al had told her to tell him that he'd gone into town to the bank and some other errands, he'd be back by eleven.

Where was Mr. LeRoy?

"He's out jogging," she said. "He runs an hour every morning, isn't that great for a man his age?"

"Who's minding the store?"

"I guess you could say I was," she grinned. "How about some fish?"

. . . They were both gone?

"Just some toast," he told her. Glanced at his watch. "I'm kind of rushed—got to go back to California this afternoon—"

"No fish?" she said, disappointed. "You won't get those in California."

"I'll have to come back," he told her.

Outside, it was quiet. A bright sun shone down, and there was a fresh breeze from the lake rustling through the pine trees.

He packed his overnight bag, came out of Cabin 8, and looked around. No one in sight. From the next cabin came the sound of a vacuum cleaner; it was the waitress, now busy at her chambermaid chores.

Last night's guests—the legitimate ones, if there'd been any—seemed to have checked out.

Now. It had to be now—before Al returned from town, and LeRoy came jogging up the road.

Hurry up, Perce.

He trudged around to the rear of the motel.

Found the path through the trees.

His heart beating rapidly, he hurried up the rise.

Then, in the path, his eye picked up the rusted bunker lid, with last night's footsteps still plain in the soil beside it.

He knelt down and pulled at the handle. As it came open, it squeaked.

Inside the shaft he found the switch that turned on the lights below, snapped it.

The lights went on; then his nostrils were filled with that same dank odor that rose from the room at the bottom of the stairs.

Bag in hand, he lowered himself down the steps, which squeaked beneath his weight.

There against the wall were the four metal cases, with the cash inside.

Hands trembling, he brought one across the room to the table, unlatched it, pulled out the plastic bag of cash.

—How do you want your fifty thousand, Mr. Barnes? Two pounds of twenties, or would you like some nice fresh tens?

The twenties were bound with paper strips on which was written *$5,000*.

Ten of those would do.

A couple from each case, so that they wouldn't notice they were gone. He took two from the first case. Replaced the plastic bag, closed the case, replaced it on the shelf, opened the second case, took three. The third case, two more packs of twenties—and now he only needed three more and he was home free, with fifty thousand tucked into his overnight bag, back to Grand Rapids, take the plane, change at Chicago, get a plane for L.A.—

—there was a slight squeak behind him.

"Well, now," said a voice, echoing in the room. "Isn't that a pretty sight?"

Shaken, Perce turned.

A man stood at the foot of the stairs, a smallish man in a nondescript suit, he wore glasses and a cheap fedora, he might have been a salesman, except that in his hand was a shiny, nickel-plated revolver which was pointed directly at Perce's stomach.

"Just don't do anything rash, Mr. Barnes," said the man softly. "I'm awful close and at this range I can't miss."

Shit.

. . . Who was he?

"Fuller," said the man, as if reading his mind. "Sid Fuller, of the Peerless Insurance Corp." He came a step closer and his eyes flashed quickly over the cash spread out near Perce's open overnight bag. "Uh *huh,*" he remarked. "That's what I'm looking for. I never could figure where it had gone, but you led me to it. Thanks, Mr. Barnes."

An insurance investigator.

Who could have figured this? It wasn't in the script—no, goddamnit—

"How'd you get here?" he asked.

"Plane, same as you," said Fuller. "Followed you from L.A. Hoped you hadn't left here. You hadn't. Watched you this morning. Guess I got lucky, eh? Saw you head out of the motel and come back here, so now, let's get it all packed up and we'll take it back to L.A. where it came from."

Furious with himself, Perce did not move. Despite the dankness, he was sweating.

''Move now,'' ordered Fuller. ''Before anybody comes back to the motel. I'm no hero, I want to get the hell out of here.''

Reluctantly, Perce began to stuff the cash back into the open metal case. You fucking dumb idiot, he cursed himself. You blew it—you blew it good—Al was right—why in hell didn't you *listen—* *Deal*. Maybe he could make a deal—

''Can we talk?'' he asked.

''Not here,'' said Fuller. ''I'm going up those steps and I'm going to stay up here, and you're going to hand up the cases to me.''

Holding the gun on Perce, he backed toward the stairs, went up with surprising agility, and then leaned down from above. ''Up they come,'' he instructed. ''Nice and easy now.''

One by one, Perce handed up the metal cases.

''Now *you,''* said Fuller.

Holding his overnight case, Perce clambered up the stairs.

Fuller picked up the fourth case and waved his gun at the others.

''You carry those,'' he said.

With effort, Perce stacked them and picked them up. Stumbling beneath their weight, Perce started down the path toward the motel.

''Here we go,'' said Fuller, behind him. ''My car's past the parking lot, we'll load 'em in there.''

. . . And then what? Back to L.A. Tomorrow, in the *Times,* the headlines—''SCREEN WRITER, TWO EX-CONS NABBED FOR EXTORTION—Stole Negative of Harry Elbert's *Cimarron,* Held It For $1,000,000.''

—Sure, they'd use Harry's name. His they'd leave out—why give a lousy writer billing?

Down below, the rear of the motel buildings came in sight.

Quiet, peaceful.

Where was LeRoy? Couldn't the bastard be finished jogging? Or maybe on this morning he'd decided to go another five miles—

Stall, Perce. One of the two Chesters has to show up.

. . . Stall *how?*

Come on, you're a bright boy, sharp, a hustler—improvise. *Contrive—*

He had an idea.

. . . He knocked his foot, as if tripping on a root, reeled beneath the weight of the cases, went off balance, sprawled backward onto the earth, the cases clattering against each other. Cursed.

"Get up," commanded Fuller, his gun pointed steadily at him.

". . . I think . . . I hurt my ankle," he complained.

"Tough," said Fuller. "You can rest when we get to the car. *Up.*"

"You're some kind of a prick," Perce told him, feigning pain, rubbing his ankle.

Keep stalling . . .

"I can be," said Fuller. "I could cuff your hand to that tree, and load the cases myself, and leave you to explain it to your partners, how's that?"

Cute bastard.

Fuller poked him with the gun barrel. *"Up."* he instructed.

Perce clambered to his feet. Began to stack the cases.

". . . Mind telling me how you ever found me up here?" he asked.

"I never stopped looking," said Fuller. *"Move."*

They came to the edge of the parking lot.

. . . Where was anyone? Damn waitress, probably in the back, swilling coffee—

"Keep walking," instructed Fuller.

Some yards down the road, beneath a tree, was parked a rental Plymouth. Fuller opened the rear door. "Put them in here," he said.

When Perce had finished, panting from the exertion, Fuller opened the front door. "You get in there, you're driving," he said.

Perce got in. Fuller carefully circled the car, the pistol never wavering, opened the other door and got in beside Perce. Fumbled in his coat pocket and found a car key, with his left hand he reached over and put it into the starter, turned it. The engine purred into life. "Let's get out of here," he said.

"Listen—" said Perce, "—can we talk?"

"We can talk all the way back to L.A." said Fuller. "Matter of fact, I'm expecting you to do a lot of talking. That way you might help yourself, sonny.''

He jabbed Perce in the rigs with the muzzle of the pistol. *''Go.''*

The metal hurt. Cheap $150-a-week sonofabitch of a snooper—obviously getting his jollies from all of this—

''You feel just great, don't you?'' rasped Perce. ''Big deal—you tracked down some insurance company gelt and now you'll be a big hero in the home office, what do they give you, a ten-dollar raise—a watch? A fucking citation?''

''You'll get a hole in your side if you don't start driving,'' said Fuller, his voice shrill. Sure, thought Perce, he's not happy with this—he knows either Al or LeRoy can show up any minute—then the odds are slightly different—

—But they weren't in sight, were they?

He took off the brake.

''Back her around and head toward town,'' commanded Fuller.

Perce obeyed, backing the car slowly around until there was enough clearance to make a turn. Damn, there wasn't even a ditch here that he could steer into, no sand he could fake as a road hazard—

Now they were headed down the road that led through the pines back toward Naples.

Was that something moving, way down there?

Coming toward them, on the side of the road.

. . . A man, bright blue suit, face contorted. Jogging.

LeRoy. The U.S. Cavalry—in a sweat suit.

. . . Fuller had seen him, too.

The gun was hard against his ribs. ''Don't try to stop,'' said Fuller. ''Keep driving, you hear?''

As they came up to LeRoy, the big man turned his head to stare.

Perce tapped the horn button.

''What was that for?'' yelled Fuller.

''. . . Saying good-by,'' said Perce.

''Do it on your own time,'' snapped Fuller. ''Any more crap like that and I'll forget I'm a peaceful person.''

"You don't go around shooting people, do you?" asked Perce. "Bad for the company's image."

"Never mind about their image," said Fuller. "All they like is results—"

". . . Those two brothers aren't going to let you get out of here alive," said Perce.

Or me either, he told himself.

". . . I can handle this, don't you worry," said Fuller.

But the guy was as nervous as a cat.

"Yeah, but why do you have to?" asked Perce. "Risking your balls for a pile of cash they gouged out of schmucks all over the country—where's the percentage for you?"

"Keep your philosophy to yourself!" said Fuller. *"Drive."*

They were nearing the turnoff that led to the main road into Naples.

What was that up there? A small pick-up truck, it was moving in a strange way, turning, pulling up, broadside to the road.

As they came closer, it was plain that he would be unable to get past.

—It was a roadblock!

Out of the front seat came a figure, a man, who was waving.

Al. Good old Al, on his way back from town—how did he know enough to stop them—

"Hold it!" commanded Fuller.

Perce braked.

"Back up!" said Fuller.

"Back up where?"

Al was trotting toward them, something in his hand glittering in the sunlight? A gun?

"Back up!" rasped Fuller, poking him sharply with the pistol.

Perce went into reverse, the tires slewing gravel. "Where do you want me to go?"

"Move it!" said Fuller, glancing backward.

Some yards back there was a turn-off, a road that went where?

"Take that one," said Fuller.

"I don't know where it goes!" warned Perce.

"Take it!" insisted Fuller. *"—Get out of here!"*

Man was uptight, he had a gun in his hand, you listened.

. . . Perce stopped the car, wheeled it around, headed down the side road, it was not much more than a track, it seemed to be heading toward white dunes up ahead, low branches snapped angrily against the windshield, a sign that said "KEEP OFF" flashed by, this had to be a road used by kids at night, there were broken bottles and junk scattered on its tracks—

—And then there was a patch of white sand ahead, gleaming white to one side—

—That would do it.

Recklessly, he steered the car directly across the white. The front wheels hit it, passed across, but the rear wheels caught, sank—began to spin with an angry, high-pitched whine—

"Damn you!" said Fuller.

"You want a chase, get yourself a stunt driver," said Perce, taking his foot off the accelerator.

. . . Behind them came the steady hum of an engine.

The pick-up truck came slowly, carefully into view, Al at the wheel. He stopped, some feet away.

Then there came the sound of an engine roaring at them from another direction.

It rose up from the dunes ahead, a fat, black-tired dune buggy, with LeRoy steering it toward them. At the sight of the stalled car, he stopped. Climbed out.

Reached into the buggy and took out a rifle.

". . . Checkmate, pal," said Perce.

A brisk wind came off the lake.

Fuller, pistol in hand, opened the car door and got out.

He waved the pistol at Perce. "Out," he ordered.

Perce obeyed.

Fuller jammed the pistol in his back, pushed him to the side of the car, away from the sand.

"Don't come any closer!" he yelled to Al. "I got your pal here—and I can knock him off very easy—"

He turned to face LeRoy, who stood, rifle in hand, beside the dune buggy, yards away. "You drop that," he ordered. *"Now."*

LeRoy slowly put down the rifle.

"He's got the money, too!" called Perce.

"Does he, now?" called Al pleasantly. "I figured there was something wrong when LeRoy called me on the CB—but I didn't figure it was this wrong. Who's your friend, Perce?"

"He's not my friend!" called Perce.

"You're right, he don't look a bit friendly," said LeRoy, coming closer.

"He's from the insurance company, and he's taking me and the money back to L.A.!" said Perce.

"Is that a fact, now?" said Al, strolling casually forward. "You wouldn't be hustling us, now, would you, Perce?"

"Me, hustle you?" asked Perce. "You crazy?"

". . . I dunno," said Al. "Seems kind of funny, you and him driving off without even saying good-by, don't it, LeRoy?"

"Yeah," said LeRoy.

Fuller waved at LeRoy. "You come over here and unload this heap," he commanded, keeping Perce between him and the brothers. "Put the cases in the dune buggy—then we can all go back to town."

LeRoy did not move.

". . . I just do not understand this," said Al. "If you are an insurance dick, then you sure are acting peculiar. Why would you want to bring all that cash back to L.A.? What the hell's in it for you?"

"It's my goddamn job, that's what," said Fuller.

"We already went through this," said Perce. "He's a dedicated man—when he gets back, he'll get a nice raise, and a pat on the back from his boss—

"—And you're all going to the can!" said Fuller.

"You do seem kinda nervous, though," said Al. "For a fella who's done such a good job . . ."

"*You* start loading!" Fuller told LeRoy. Who did not move.

". . . I'll admit it does look as though you got us by the left hind tit," continued Al. "On the other hand, friend, maybe I ought to point something out to you. There's only three of us, but there's less of you. Now maybe you could shoot all of us—but chances are, you probably could only get the one before the two others was on you—''

''Yeah,'' said LeRoy, ''and if it's me that's left standing, I'm in better shape than you are.''

''. . . And when LeRoy got through with you,'' said Al, ''there are places around here where he could hide your body so's nobody could ever locate it, not even your home office.''

Fuller's gun still bored into Perce's back.

If the boys started something, *he*'d be Number One on the hit list!

''. . . Now, on the other hand,'' Al remarked, ''if this smart old insurance boy was to tote all that cash back to our place, and stick it where it belongs—and we was all to forget what happened here this morning—we'd probably be able to see our way clear to arrange some sort of a deal.''

The wind was blowing harder now, a patch of clouds was obscuring the sun. It was suddenly cold.

''. . . What sort of a deal?'' Fuller asked finally.

''Well, there's enough here for everybody, isn't there?'' asked Al. ''Say, a hundred?''

Fuller snorted. ''You have to be kidding,'' he said. ''Ten percent? That's for small stuff. Medical frauds, or phony car accidents. This is big time. *Half.''*

Startled, Perce turned.

''Half of what?''

''Half of what's here,'' said Fuller. The sweat was running down from beneath his hat.

''Jesus, he's a goddamned thief!'' cried Perce.

''. . . Now, Perce,'' said Al softly, ''like the Bible says, he who is without guilt, let him cast the first stone.'' He chuckled.

Perce did not answer.

''Let me take him, Al,'' said LeRoy, his fists clenched.

''. . . You cool down, LeRoy,'' called Al. ''As our old uncle Ty used to say, ten per cent of something is better than a hundred per cent of nothing. Mister Whatever Your name is—would you take two hundred and a half?''

. . . Two hundred and fifty thousand hard-earned dollars? It was a stiff inflated price to pay, to buy off this nervous creep just because he had a gun in his hand—

—And a finger on the trigger, pointed at Perce's spine.

". . . No," insisted Fuller. "I said five."

The wind sighed around the four men.

"Sure you did," said Al. "But just think how little you have to do to pick up a quarter million. Whereas, if you're gonna be stubborn, you'll be rolling dice with us for five hundred . . ." he grinned, ". . . and you just might crap out."

"Yeah," said Fuller slowly. "It's only money. Deal."

But the end of his gun stayed firmly planted in Perce's back.

"Good," said Al.

"Wait a minute—" protested Perce. "How do we know we can trust this creep?"

"Shoot, Perce," said Al sadly. "How do we know we can trust anybody?" He turned and called to LeRoy. "Okay, LeRoy, unload the car. We can take all those boxes back to where they'll be safe." He turned back to Perce. "I guess the two hundred fifty will have to come out of *your* third, wouldn't you say, pardner?"

"Hold it," said Fuller. "My piece goes with *me*."

". . . that's kind of a hefty hunk of cash to leave around loose," cautioned Al. He might have been a burglar-alarm salesman . . . "L.A.—that's a real high-crime area. You could be robbed, friend."

"Thanks for your thoughtfulness," said Fuller. "I know a lot about security. That'll be my problem."

"Suit yourself," said Al. "You're the boss, I guess."

"I'll take it in twenties and tens," instructed Fuller. "And no fast count, either, get me?"

. . . And for the first time, he took the gun out of Perce's back.

"Count it yourself," said Al. "I'll be glad to hold your gun while you do."

". . . The art of screen adaptation is a highly complex craft," said Alan Arkin. "The play, the novel, the short story, the true story, all are unique to their own form, and so is the screenplay. The writer who is charged with the task of reshaping the material for the screen must be a craftsman who understands it all."

"This year," said Shirley Jones, "the nominations for Best Screenplay from Material from Another Medium are *California Suite,* screenplay by Neil Simon, based on his own play, *See No Evil,* screenplay by Reginald Rose, based on a novel by Evan Hunter . . ."

"*Fedora,* screenplay by Billy Wilder and I. A. L. Diamond, based on a novel by Tom Tryon," read Arkin from the Teleprompter. "*Heist,* screenplay by Perce Barnes, based on a true story by Al and LeRoy Chester, and *Caroline, the Queen,* screenplay by Terence Tolkin, from a novel by Richard Condon. And the winner is—"

Shirley Jones ripped open the envelope, pulled out the card.

"*Heist,* by Perce Barnes!" she announced.

Amid the applause, Perce reached over and kissed Vera, then jumped from his seat and went up the aisle.

Onstage, Shirley Jones handed him the Oscar, and kissed him on the cheek. "I loved it!" she said.

"Thanks," said Perce, and hefted the golden statue in his hands. "Long time no see," he said. He turned to the audience. "I guess it's a traditional speech," he said. "It couldn't have ever happened without a lot of other people. Vera George, Harry Elbert, the first one to believe in it, Billy Elbert, who stuck with it all the way, Doug Pemberton, who did a beautiful job, a cast who did right by the words, a terrific crew, and last, but by far not least—two men who really ought to be here instead of me. They earned a big piece of this statue. Al and LeRoy Chester. Thanks, partners!"

There was snow outside the Fishermans Rest, but inside the office the heat was on and the room was comfortably snug. In one corner, the TV was on, and Al and LeRoy sat watching the Academy Awards telecast.

''How about that!'' said Al, and took a large swig of his beer. ''It's a big night for our old buddy.''

''Yessir,'' said LeRoy. ''The chicken really came through.''

''That ought to help the grosses,'' said Al. ''They say an Oscar gets you a whole new set of bookings.''

LeRoy yawned. ''Now I can get to bed,'' he said and rose.

''. . . You know something?'' asked Al. ''I been thinking about our friend Sid Fuller.''

''. . . Mr. Postcard?'' said LeRoy. ''What's he want now? I already sent him some from that tag sale last week in town.''

''He's been working for that Peerless outfit for a long time, wouldn't you guess?'' said Al.

LeRoy nodded.

''. . . And all that time, he's been hustling,'' continued Al. ''Now I figure, he must have a lot stashed away by now.''

''Including ours,'' said LeRoy.

''. . . In some place where nobody would ever know he has it, I guess,'' said Al.

''That's for damn sure,'' said LeRoy.

''Well, then, I want to ask you something,'' said Al. ''Things are a little dull around here right now. Before the spring comes, why don't you and me take us a little vacation out to L.A. maybe—get us a little sun, visit our old buddy Perce—''

''. . . I hate that town,'' said LeRoy.

''Yeah, but while we're there,'' said Al, ''maybe we might get a line on where old Mr. Postcard is keeping his money. And then if we got lucky, we might get a hunk of it back. *Our* hunk.''

''. . . You just bullshitting—or have you got some sort of a plan?'' asked LeRoy.

Al finished his beer, and then belched.

''What do *you* think?'' he asked.